THE ANYWHERE HOTEL

GISELE STEIN

www.giselestein.com

Stein Books & Publishing

1101 Hay Street, Suite #1031

West Perth, WA 6005, Australia

Book Cover Design by ebooklaunch.com

ISBN

Paperback: 978-0-6458929-1-8

EBook: 978-0-6458929-0-1

For my family.

If I had only one place left to go
I'd go anywhere,
as long as it's with you.

1

THE DAY AVA MARLEY DISAPPEARED

Ava's phone buzzed against a cup of coffee long gone cold.

She'd become the type of customer she loathed to serve, back at the deli in Shepherd's Bush. The type that ordered the cheapest beverage on the menu and then sipped on it forever, waiting for a bus, a date, or maybe for the rain to stop.

Only Ava wasn't waiting. She was already half an hour late.

Hence, the phone call.

"Are you going to answer that?" The businessman beside her raised an eyebrow in annoyance. Wordlessly, Ava pressed the power button to reject the call. Downing what was left of her coffee in one last gulp, she savoured the cup's complex character – vibrant and fruity, but with a mild body. A peaberry, her favourite bean. She stood and grabbed her bag. "Thanks," she called toward the counter and strode out the door, glaring at the businessman now taking a call himself. As if his stock market shouts weren't *more* annoying. He didn't even fit in at a place like this.

She'd arrived at Canary Wharf earlier than planned, and it had taken her a while to find a decent coffee shop to bide her time in. London's financial district was littered with franchises: Pret A Mangers, McDonald's, and, of course, Marley's Cafés. There were three on South Colonnade alone – absurdly, within view of one another. Way to mark your territory, Ethan...

But Ava never stepped inside a Marley's, not since her mother's passing.

She had felt a rush of gratitude when she'd stumbled upon the quaint little Portuguese café tucked away on a street corner. The owner, who had a thick white moustache and a kind, weathered face, ran a one-man show, offering nothing more than bottomless, freshly brewed filter coffee and flaky, warm pastéis de nata. Ava had found herself lingering, contemplating whether or not she should miss the meeting Ethan had arranged on short notice. She could already guess what it was about, anyway.

Now she shouldered her bag – an heirloom from her mother, the strap soft as a lamb's ear – and merged with the pavement crowds. Her phone buzzed again, and this time Ava took the call.

"Yep," she said as she crossed the street, stepping into the shadow cast by the tallest building at Canary Wharf.

"Sweetheart, are you on your way? He's got another meeting at eleven, but he really wants to see you." Laura, Ethan's first assistant, spoke in a cloying, maternal tone despite being less than a decade older than Ava. She also had a habit of calling Ava nicknames her own mother hadn't even used. Sweetheart. Darling. Honey. It was painfully obvious Laura was sleeping with Ava's father, but that didn't make her whatever Laura seemed to think she was.

"Entering the lobby now," Ava replied, casting her gaze

upward at the giant company logo emblazoned above her. Marley's Coffee Corporation, her mother's face with her endearing smile immortalised as the brand's emblem. Looking at it would never *not* twist Ava's heart.

Approaching the receptionist, a polished woman with a tight bun and a practised smile, Ava introduced herself by first name only. "I have a meeting with the big boss," she added. The receptionist appeared sceptical. Her demeanour transformed, however, when she found Ava's name in the system. "Of course, Miss Marley, your father is expecting you," she replied, her voice now saccharine. "You've grown up since I last saw you. How old are you now?" She handed Ava a company badge.

"Twenty-six," Ava answered, forcing a polite smile.

Exiting the elevator onto the executive floor a few minutes later, Ava found Laura waiting for her, a tablet clasped in her slender hands. Laura was the epitome of poise and professionalism, her hair flawlessly coiffed, and her tailored outfit crisp and pristine. In comparison, Ava felt out of place in this corporate environment: the combination of her dark brown, frizzy hair and her button nose, covered with a smattering of freckles, always reminded her of a woodland creature. A squirrel, maybe. Or a raccoon.

"Hey, sweetie, how are you?"

"M'all right. You?"

"Oh, just splendid, darling." Laura took Ava's coat and bag, stroking her back. "*He* is a bit on edge today, though," she said, nodding at the double doors across the room. "Odd, considering the share price rose overnight. Usually, that lifts his spirits. I don't know what's bothering him."

"I do," Ava muttered, but Laura didn't hear. Pressing a button on the intercom, she breathed, "Ethan? Ava's here," then she winked at Ava, encouraging her to proceed.

Ava nodded curtly and made her way to the polished wooden doors. She paused before she entered, taking a breath, her fingers tapping the handle. This wasn't going to be pretty. She shook off the feeling and stepped inside.

"You're late," Ethan said, his voice a mixture of irritation and authority.

He sat behind his desk, an impressive view of central London behind him. His salt-and-pepper hair was immaculate. His tailored suit screamed supremacy.

"Ava, darling, so good to see you. I haven't seen you in what? Two months? What have you been up to?" Ava mocked his voice, slumping into a seat across from him.

Ethan glanced up from his paperwork, anger flickering in his eyes. "Oh, I know what you've been up to. Dean Hawthorne called me the moment you left his office yesterday. Are you trying to embarrass me? Is that your grand plan?"

Ava rolled her eyes. "Absolutely, Ethan. My entire existence revolves around you. I'm like a tick, living solely to suck on your blood."

"Drop the sarcasm, Ava. This is serious. It's the third time you've flunked out of university. First, it was marketing, then politics, and now economics."

"Thanks for the recap, boss." Ava considered her fingernails.

"I'm running out of favours to call in, you know?"

"I never asked you for any favours."

"You think you got into Oxford on your own with those grades?"

Ava scratched her temple, shaking her head. "Why am I even surprised?"

"Be that as it may, I won't continue to support this aimless path you're on any longer."

"I never took a cent from you, and you know it."

It was true; she had never accepted any financial help from Ethan, not once. She'd gotten by solely with her mother's inheritance and an impressive accumulation of odd jobs. And she didn't know what bothered him more: His own daughter's refusal to ask him for help or his consequent lack of control over her.

Ethan leaned forward, elbows on the desk as he studied her. "You think Luciana would have wanted this for you? Floating around like a leaf on the wind?"

"I know she would have wanted me to find what makes me happy."

"And have you found what makes you happy?" He enunciated each word deliberately as if mocking her.

"Working on it."

"Well, as long as you're still busy chasing a feeling, I see no other choice but to intervene and ensure you have a job that pays your bills at the end of the road."

"I have a job."

"You're a part-time waitress at the Mousehole Deli."

Ava bit the inside of her lip, caught off guard that he knew where she worked.

"You have zero qualifications," Ethan went on, "and your CV reads like a stack of sticky notes."

"And what are you going to do about it? Chain me down in Hawthorne's lecture room? Bribe an A student to write the exams for me? Your wealth can't fix everything, you know? It can't fix..."

She had wanted to say "me," but she stopped herself. Admitting she needed fixing would have implied that she was broken.

"I'm not giving you an easy way out if that's what you're expecting. You'll have to work for it. Here, at MCC."

"I'm never going to work for you, Ethan. You know that."

"*For* me, no. But *with* me?"

Ava looked up, startled by the offer.

Ethan stood and approached the floor-to-ceiling window, looking out at the bustling city below. "Your mother and I built this company together. She divorced me, and I bought her out before it turned a profit. So, when she passed, you didn't inherit what I always believed to be rightfully yours."

"Is there a point coming up soon?"

"The MCC trainee program starts again at the end of next month, on the 25th of April. I'm offering you a spot, with the prospect of becoming my chief operating officer if you excel."

"What on earth makes you think I'd want that?"

Ethan leaned against the window, his profile edgy before the grey clouds. "Because I know how much you loved her. And I know how much she taught you. You would do well here, Ava. It's what Luciana and I always wanted for you. It's the one thing we agreed on despite our issues: that we did all of this for you." He turned to look at her, his eyes locking with hers. "Besides," he added in a casual tone, "it might be good for your old man to have someone to spar with again."

With his smirk, Ava's instincts kicked in, and she recognised the situation for what it was. It brought to mind a newspaper article she had read about her father once, likening him to a cunning fox with an uncanny ability to turn on the charm whenever it suited him. Pity his performance of the caring father had long ceased to convince her.

"I'm not interested," Ava said but remained seated.

Ethan cleared his throat. "I figured you might say that. Which is why I am upping the ante, so to speak."

Another thing about Ethan: he always had something else up his sleeve.

"If you perform well throughout the program, I'm willing to transfer portions of my shares over to you: 3.5 percent per year over the next seven years. By the time you turn thirty-three, you'll have earned the same number of shares as I have, thus giving you equal voting power to me. All you have to do is sign... right here." He took a Montblanc pen from his breast pocket, clicked it, and placed it on what appeared to be a contract.

"Well, you just thought of everything, haven't you?" Ava fluttered her eyelashes and crossed her arms in front of her chest.

"It's one hell of an opportunity," Ethan said, mirroring her posture. "You'll do the right thing." He nodded as if the matter was settled and turned away from her, signalling that the conversation was over.

Ava shifted in her seat, her gaze fixed on the contract in front of her. "But there's one thing you failed to consider," she said, her voice low and measured. "Mum despised what you did with Marley's after she stepped away from it. Always said the expansion ruined everything you guys built together. In the end, she was ashamed she ever agreed to this." Ava tapped a finger on the contract's letterhead, where her mother's face was frozen in a forever-smile.

Ethan buttoned up his suit, his expression guarded. "Well, this is your chance, then, to make it right."

Ava huffed and stood abruptly, her hands balling into fists at her sides. She crossed the room, angry at herself that she'd ever entered it.

"I know you care about this company, Ava," Ethan said. "Much more than you'd have us both believe. Your anger gives you away."

Ava paused at the door, her fingers tapping the door handle, lingering, hesitating. At last, she pressed it down and slipped out, swift as a cat spooked by a sudden noise.

Maybe he was right. Maybe on some level, she did still care.

But she sure as hell knew better than to act on it.

~

"HEY, MISHA – SORRY, AM I LATE?" Ava called out as she approached the Mousehole Deli, her anger still simmering beneath the surface. From the MCC headquarters, she had taken the tube back to Shepherd's Bush, her mind consumed by her emotions, oblivious to her surroundings all along the way.

Misha, the deli owner, was seated outside at one of the tables, meticulously rolling a cigarette between his fingers. He was in his late thirties but looked much younger. His dark hair was neatly trimmed, and he had a youthful glow about him.

"No, not at all. Early, actually." He flashed a warm smile and gestured to the empty seat across from him. "Why don't you sit for a minute."

"What's up?" she asked, settling into the chair. It was unusual for him to occupy a whole table by himself; the deli was tiny, and he always advised his staff to reserve the limited seating for customers.

Misha hesitated, clearly uncomfortable. "I'm not quite sure how to put this, actually, so I'm just going to come right out with it." He paused again, looking at her as he struggled to find the right words. "Your, um, your father came to see me, early this morning."

Ava's heart sank, a cold dread settling in her stomach. She clenched her jaw, maintaining her composure. "Go on."

"He..." Misha cleared his throat, and his unease seemed to grow. "So odd, but he basically asked me to... fire you. Told me not to tell you, of course. But I mean, of course, I would."

Ava's heart stuttered, but she managed to keep her voice steady. "What exactly did he say?"

"It was weird, really. He said you have this great opportunity to work for him, but that you wouldn't do it as long as you worked here. Asked me if I had kids of my own. It felt like he knew about Tammy, to be honest. So bizarre. Anyway, just thought I should tell you."

"Yeah, no, you did the right thing. Thanks for the heads up," Ava said quietly.

Misha lit his cigarette, considering her through the smoke. His posture was tense, and he couldn't quite meet her eyes.

"You know I wouldn't want to hold you back, right?" He asked, wiping the perfectly clean table. "I mean, this... this is just a part-time gig, anyway. Nothing to bet your future on."

"What else did he say, Misha?"

"What? No, nothing. I just think that maybe he's right. You know, it sounds like one hell of an opportunity you got there."

Ava's stomach churned as she realised Misha had used her father's exact words.

"So, you want me to quit?"

"I want you to do what's best for you. You know, for everybody." Misha's body language was guarded, but his fingers gave him away, fidgeting with the cigarette.

"Seriously, Misha, what else did he say?" Ava demanded, her patience wearing thin.

Misha sighed, blowing out a puff of smoke. "Oh man, I really didn't want to tell you." He looked up at Ava with genuine regret. "He... he kind of... threatened me."

"*Threatened* you?"

Misha scratched his temple. "I told him he should talk to you about this and that I thought it best if he left. But he didn't. He sort of walked around the shop and pointed out things that might be concerning from a health and safety point of view. You know, I'm still working out a system for the rubbish, and the main fridge broke down last week. Anyway, before he left, he said, 'We wouldn't want a customer complaining about these things, now would we? Especially one with connections in high places.'" Misha mimicked Ethan's voice with surprising accuracy. He looked at Ava, pain etched on his face. "I'm so sorry, Ava. I feel terrible."

"Why would *you* feel terrible? You're not the one whose father is a prick." Ava clenched her fists beneath the table.

"I just can't afford a fine right now or any other disruption to the business. You know, Judy is doing that nursing course, and Tammy wants to take riding lessons."

"I get it, Misha. Like, *totally* get it. You still want me to work the shift today, or should I...?" Ava gestured vaguely at the pavement.

Misha's brow furrowed. "I don't know. I mean, I don't know if I can risk – you know – having you around. He wasn't exactly specific on the timeframe."

"Right. Not a problem." Ava tried to keep her voice steady.

"I'm so sorry." Misha's eyes were filled with discomfort. "You're such a good worker, and the customers love you... I'm really, really sorry."

Ava rose from the table, her composure firmly in place.

"Don't be," she reassured him and forced a small smile. "You're doing the right thing, Misha. I'm not angry."

"I'M FUCKING FURIOUS."

"Yeah, nah, I'd be *fuming*, girl. What an absolute jerk. Your dad, I mean. Not Misha. Misha's good people," said Melanie, Ava's flatmate.

After getting fired without having done anything wrong, Ava had left a seething message for Ethan with Laura, as *he* had been, predictably, unreachable. But if Ava was being honest, she'd preferred it that way.

She'd made her way back home, and now she sat in the cramped kitchen with Mel, stewing over her father's latest appalling deed. Their flat, while small, was nestled on the upper floor of a renovated factory building and boasted charm, with just the right amount of clutter and chaos.

"I mean, who actually *does* that? Like, I always knew he could be controlling and manipulative, but to actually go through the effort of finding out where I work, because – mind you – he never cared to ask me, did he? He never once stopped by to see what I was up to, did he? He's never been here in this flat, has he?"

"Not that I know of," Mel replied as she mashed avocados for a fresh batch of guacamole. Mel hailed from Perth in Western Australia, her golden curls a testament to her sun-kissed roots. A chef by trade, she had travelled the world, immersing herself in various culinary styles and all sorts of alternative spiritual practices. She had spent a year in Mexico, which she fondly referred to as her "enchilada year." These days, she worked in a trendy restaurant in the City, her culinary talents on full display.

"But to go behind my back and bully my boss into firing me, what kind of person does that?" Ava retrieved her laptop from the corner bench, typing in her password.

"Trump. Trump would do it, mate. For sure," said Mel with a smirk, licking guac off her fingers. "So, what are you going to do?"

"I'm getting the hell out of here, that's what I'm doing." Almost frantically, Ava called up a flight booking platform, scrolling aimlessly.

"O...kay?" Mel set the guac aside. "Just like that, huh? Don't you wanna face him, though? Tell him straight up what he did was out of line?"

"I mean, I will. Of course, I will. At some point. But I think it's best to clear the air first," Ava said. However, deep down, she knew she had no intention of resolving the issue. Like always, it felt easier to distance herself from the turmoil than to face the messy tangle of feelings head-on. Dealing with Ethan, especially, seemed like an insurmountable task, a wall she couldn't scale or break through. Whenever conflict arose in the past, she hadn't fled the country, exactly. But there were other ways to disappear. Phone in flight mode and binging all seasons of Downton Abbey (including both movies) in bed, for instance. But this time, going incommunicado didn't seem enough. No, she had to go someplace out of Ethan's reach entirely — not an easy task, seeing as the man practically had tentacles. Her father had the Prime Minister on speed dial, for crying out loud.

"That's cool, too, actually," Mel said. "Yeah, simmer down a bit first, mate. Much more of a Zen approach. So, where you going?" Mel, forever a backpacker at heart, was quick to get on board with any plan that involved travelling.

"I've got no idea," Ava sighed. "Where would you go?"

"What, like, *anywhere*?" Mel scooted closer on the bench, peering at the laptop screen.

"Yeah. Where would you go if you could go anywhere in the world right now?"

"Probably home to Oz, to be honest. Haven't seen my folks in, like, forever. But I mean, if I were you, I'd go somewhere super exotic. Like a tropical island or something. Sri Lanka, maybe, or Bali. Somewhere with lots of palm trees and cheap cocktails."

"Palm trees and cheap cocktails. Right. That is exactly what I need now."

Ava continued browsing, her eyes scanning the screen for potential destinations. "Hey, check this out: Zanzibar. It leaves this evening from Heathrow. What are we thinking, Mel?"

"How much is it?" Mel asked, leaning in to get a better look. She whistled when she saw the price. "Cheap as chips, mate!"

"Right. Nothing to it, I guess," Ava said, clicking past the return flight options and punching in her credit card details.

"One-way ticket, huh? Feeling adventurous."

"Adventurous? More like desperate..."

Mel pulled Ava's hand away from the laptop. "Hey, hey. Stop for a moment, all right? You know you don't *have* to do this," she said softly. "We could just stay in, order from the greasy Vietnamese place on the corner, and hide from the world forever. Or at least until we run out of money."

Ava let out a sigh, and her gaze drifted off, the screen becoming a blur. "No. I'm going," she said with resolve. "Fuck it, I'm going. I need to disappear for a while."

Mel gave a supportive nod. "Your call, babe."

And with that, Ava booked the flight.

"March *is* the perfect time to visit Zanzibar – the beaches are amazing, and it's just before the rainy season."

"To be honest, anywhere is better than here right now," Ava sighed. "All right, I better get packing then."

"Don't forget to pack a few cute outfits as well. You never know who you might meet over there. I, for one, can't even remember the last time you—"

"Yeah, yeah. Cut it out now." Ava rolled her eyes but smiled nonetheless.

A SHORT WHILE LATER, Mel came to see Ava in her bedroom, where she was busily stuffing clothes and essentials into her backpack.

"So, when do you think you'll be back?"

"I don't know. Couple of weeks, maybe. I just need to cut out the bullshit for a while, you know? Clear my head."

"Totally," Mel agreed, slumping down on Ava's bed. "I'm all for cutting out bullshit and clearing heads. Cleanse your aura. Clear your chakras. I told you, your heart chakra has been blocked for a while, haven't I?"

"Totally." Ava zipped her backpack.

Mel grabbed it and headed out into the hallway, calling over her shoulder, "Before you go, you've got to try my latest michelada though. I think I finally cracked the code."

In the kitchen, Mel handed Ava a tall, salt-rimmed glass. Ever since her time in Mexico, she had been trying to perfect her version of the drink, which she dubbed "Mel's Mean Micheladas."

Ava took a sip. "It's your best one yet," she said.

"Nah, something's still not right," replied Mel, tasting it

herself. She furrowed her brow, contemplating the elusive missing ingredient. "Maybe more chilli sauce?"

Ava swirled the ice in the glass. "How did you know, Mel? How did you know cooking is what you want to do in life?"

"Tell you how," Mel said, licking her lips. "Through a fuck ton of fucking around. I always wished I'd been one of those overachieving kids who knew what they wanted to be at, like, age eleven or something. But that was never me. I had to get out there and explore first. If anything, I always thought that was you."

"*Me?* What? I'm as lost as one can be at twenty-six."

"You do struggle to stick with... well, *anything*, it's true. At least since I've known you. But I also don't know anybody who knows more about coffee than you. I mean, look around us!" Mel gestured toward a shelf cluttered with an espresso machine, various coffee beans from around the world, a Marley's Press, a grinder, and an array of mugs and coffee cups. "I'm not even allowed to drink my favourite instant cappuccino anymore! I still do, though, by the way, whenever you're not around."

Ava clicked her tongue, ruffling Mel's curls as she contemplated her words.

"You're sure you don't want to take the Marley's gig?" Mel asked.

Ava finished her drink and put the glass down. "Even if I did – which I don't – how could I possibly work with someone who does something like that?"

"Right. I hear you. Well..." Mel opened her arms, ready to be hugged goodbye. "Safe travels then. Let me know when you get there."

"Of course. Hey, rent's paid up for next month, all right?

And don't worry, I have some savings in the bank that'll get me by until I find a new job."

"Literally zero worries. We're cool," Mel replied, following Ava to the front door. "Hey, mind if Parker comes to stay while you're gone?"

"Still on a last-name basis, are you?"

"What can I say?" Mel opened the door for Ava. "I will never acknowledge his name's actually Rupert."

"I mean, you know I'm not a fan of him. Think he's quite the jerk, actually. But yeah, fine, whatever. *Rupert* can come to stay. Just promise you won't do it on my bed."

"Massive pinkie swear."

They embraced each other in another heartfelt hug, saying their goodbyes. As Ava finally descended the stair-well, passing a couple of neighbours, Mel shouted after her, "I put some condoms in your bag, just in case!"

Ava brushed a strand of hair from her face, blushing. "Yep. Thanks for that, Mel."

And then she was out the door, ready to disappear.

2

PEOPLE YOU MEET AT A HOTEL BAR

Zanzibar's Old Town was a cacophony of colours and sounds, a maze of alleys with crumbled walls, mouldering from centuries of monsoon rains. Ava had landed at the island's tiny airport earlier that afternoon. Now she sat on her narrow balcony at the Kasa Bed and Breakfast, a charming guesthouse Mel had recommended next to the freight port. Her room boasted high ceilings, ornate wooden furniture, and a canopy bed with mosquito netting. The air conditioning unit rattled like a washing machine in spinning mode but provided a welcome respite from the stifling humidity.

As Ava watched the bustle below her feet, the muezzin's call to prayer blared from an ancient speaker on a nearby rooftop. The air smelled of the ocean and jasmine, of tropical fruit and old frying fat. Power cables snaked in knotted bundles across an alley so narrow a car wouldn't fit through yet teeming with activity: Street vendors touting their goods, kids chasing one another, motorcycles rattling past a pair of elderly gentlemen engaged in a game of Bao, sipping tea as they contemplated their next moves. The traditional

Tanzanian board game was a local favourite, as Ava had learned from the receptionist earlier.

This place was everything she needed now – a bustling city where she could be just another stranger. So chaotic and vibrant and noisy, it drowned out any thoughts about her future as soon as they arose. She could have spent hours sitting here, observing life without being a part of it. Her peace, however, was disrupted when she spotted a figure lurking in the shadows – a Zanzibari woman who had fixed her gaze directly on her, sending an unsettling chill down her spine. Ava withdrew back into the room, feeling uneasy to have become the watched instead of the watcher.

Deciding to head to the rooftop bar, she wrapped herself in a kikoi – the traditional scarf she'd bought at the airport to blend in better. Mel's advice to "pack some cute outfits" had proven to be slightly misguided, as the island's Islamic influence called for more modest attire, something Ava hadn't exactly packed.

She grabbed her bag and slipped out the door, passing through the dimly lit hall adorned with intricately carved wooden doors and vibrant paintings.

Up on the roof, she was greeted by a gentle ocean breeze and the hum of languages from around the world. The bar was a relaxing space, with tasselled cushions scattered about, low tables surrounded by flickering lanterns, and views of the Old Town silhouetted against a setting sun.

Ava climbed onto a bar stool, ordering a gin and tonic. She gazed around, feeling a bit self-conscious about being alone, so resorted to her phone. She had avoided switching it on until now, knowing Laura must have bombarded her with messages, but she had promised to update Mel. With a reluctant sigh, she turned on international roaming, and the messages started trickling in.

LAURA: *Please return my call asap.*

MEL: *Hey babe, you there yet?*

LAURA: *He is truly sorry about the Misha thing. Please call.*

LAURA: *Are you getting my messages?*

Ava huffed and deleted Laura's messages, focusing on replying to Mel's. As she sipped her G&T and typed, a blonde-bearded man dressed head-to-toe in khaki sat down next to her at the bar.

"Hi," he said to her with a self-assured grin. He ordered a drink, conversing with the bartender in fluent Swahili. Ava pretended to be engrossed in her phone, hoping to avoid the interaction she sensed was imminent.

"I'm Tom," the khaki man said, extending his hand. "And you are?"

Ava looked up. "Ava," she replied, giving what she hoped was a dismissive smile.

"Nice to meet you, Ava. What brings you to the island?"

"Just, you know, holiday."

"All by your lonesome, a beautiful woman such as yourself?"

Ava widened her eyes affirmatively, her fingers pretend-tapping away on her phone.

"So, what do you do, Ava?" Tom asked, clearly oblivious to her disinterest.

"Nothing much," she said. "Just studying. You?" Ava mentally slapped herself. Why was she engaging in this man's small talk?

Tom's eyes lit up as if he'd been waiting for her to ask. "I'm a safari guide on the mainland. Here with some clients to go diving with whale sharks over on Mafia tomorrow," he boasted, his enthusiasm mounting. "Mafia Island, that is."

"Fascinating," lied Ava.

"It is. It is, yeah." Tom took a sip of his whisky and Coke.

"Nothing compares to the endless African savannah. I'm grateful I get to call her my office." He looked at Ava, anticipating a reaction which never came. "Need to have your wits about you, of course. It's a jungle out there, you know?" Tom puffed up his chest. "For example, I bet you didn't know a lion's tongue is so rough it can literally lick its prey to death. Pretty cool, huh?"

"That is... that is pretty cool, Tom," Ava said, her lips thinning.

"Hey, if you've got a couple of days to spare, I could show you around. Take you on a real adventure, if you know what I mean..." He leaned in closer, his breath reeking of alcohol.

As he reached out to touch Ava's arm, she recoiled and was just about to reprimand him, when a female voice called her name, and she swivelled around.

"Hey, Ava! I didn't see you there. You wanna..." The woman gestured toward the other end of the rooftop. "I found us a table."

"Yes! Coming," Ava replied without hesitation. She stood, raising her glass to Safari Tom in a silent farewell.

"Sorry, you looked like you might need rescuing," the woman said as she settled into one of the cushioned seats far from Tom's reach. She appeared to be in her early forties, speaking with an American accent that was nearly flawless, save for a subtle Zanzibari undertone. Her hair was cropped short, framing a pair of arresting eyes, dark as heartwood.

"Yeah, no, thanks for that. You're a lifesaver." Ava joined her at the table. "How did you know my name, though?"

"I saw you at reception when you checked in. I work for the guesthouse."

"Right. Sorry, I don't remember that. What's your name?" Ava asked.

"My friends call me Sunny," the woman replied. "So, are

you enjoying your holiday so far, Ava? When you're not being hit on by sleazy tour guides, that is..."

Ava forced a smile. "I mean, I just got here, of course. But it's been... interesting. Yeah, I'm having a great time so far."

Sunny studied Ava intently. "You don't seem like it, if you don't mind me saying so."

"I don't?" Ava, taken aback, sipped her drink.

"Not really. You appear a little tense, as if you're trying to get away from something, maybe."

Ava set her drink down on the table. "That's quite the assessment for someone you've just met."

"My apologies. I work at the massage parlour; it's part of my job to read people, figure out where it pinches the most, you know?" Sunny replied with a smile, her gaze still unwavering.

"Right. Occupational hazard, is it?"

"Occupational hazard, indeed." Sunny poured herself a glass from the complimentary water jug.

Ava looked out over the rooftops where a sickle moon, thin as a toenail, had risen in the sky. "Truth is, I *am* here to get a break from reality," she said. "Got a lot going on at home at the moment."

"Like what?"

"Like a controlling father who wants to pressure me into a future when, really, all I want is not to leave a mark at all?" Ava answered impulsively, regretting her honesty straight away. "Sorry. That was more than you wanted to know, I'm sure," she mumbled and picked up her drink again, taking another big sip.

God, she'd become one of *those* people. Oversharers who mistook the kindness of a stranger for an invitation to spill the most tragic aspects of their lives within the first minute of conversation. *Shut up, Ava. Just shut up.*

Sunny stroked the rim of her glass, which produced a whistle. "Impossible, don't you think?" she said, lifting her brows. "Trying not to leave a mark on the world? Might as well try not to leave footprints in the sand. We're here to touch other people's lives; that's the whole point. Or at least, that's what this place has taught me lately."

Ava nodded, tracing circles on the table with the condensation from her glass. "So, you live here in Stone Town, then?" she asked, not hiding that she was eager to change the topic.

"Born and bred just around the corner," replied Sunny. "And I assume you're from the UK?"

"London." Ava nodded.

"There's something about your accent that's a little off, though, isn't it? You lived there all your life?"

Ava cleared her throat. "I spent my teenage years in Costa Rica," she said. The observation struck her as a little odd; hardly anyone picked up on those tiny fragments of Spanish she didn't even notice herself anymore.

"Pura Vida!" Sunny raised her glass. "Tell me, what brought you there?"

"My parents' divorce," Ava said. "My mum was from there. After they split, the two of us moved back." She fidgeted in her seat, her eyes scanning the bar. Maybe she had been too trusting with her saviour.

"How old were you when your parents split?" Sunny asked.

"I was nine. Sorry, but do we know each other from somewhere?" Was this going to be the second conversation that evening she needed saving from?

"I... don't think so." Sunny leaned back in her seat. "Why?"

"It's just... you talk like maybe you've met me before or something."

"Don't you think you'd remember that?" Sunny's gaze held an almost knowing air, making Ava feel exposed.

"I guess," she said, leaning back as well. A moment of silence settled between them, the sounds of laughter and clinking glasses drifting over from the other tables.

"So, what's your plan for tomorrow?" Sunny asked, trying for a casual tone. "Snorkel tour? Hit the beaches, or maybe a shopping spree at Darajani Bazaar?"

"I'll be leaving the city tomorrow, actually," Ava lied. "Might head up north, or maybe to Mafia for the whale sharks. I haven't decided yet."

"Hey, you should come with me!" Sunny suggested. "I'm catching a dala dala up the east coast tonight."

"Tonight?" Ava jerked her head back. "I already paid for this place."

Their encounter had officially turned sour.

Sunny leaned in, murmuring. "Don't worry, I know a cheap little hotel by the sea, much better than this one. It's one of the few places still off the beaten track, a real adventure. I grew up there; that's how I know about it."

Ava's eyes narrowed. "I thought you said you grew up here in town, just around the corner."

Sunny's expression faltered as if she'd been caught stealing. "I did say that, didn't I..."

An awkward silence settled over them. Who *was* this woman? Some kind of a con artist, here to lure tourists over to her family's place up the coast? Mel had warned Ava about the beach boys, aggressively trying to palm off their merchandise at horrendous prices. Maybe Sunny was in that game, too?

Before Ava could make sense of it, her phone rang. It

was Laura – the last person on Earth she wanted to talk to. Still, she took the call, grateful for an excuse to get away from Sunny, if that was even her real name.

"Sorry, I should take this," Ava said, rising from her seat. "Thanks again for your help earlier. Have a good night."

"Course," Sunny said, her tone defeated. "Enjoy your escape, Ava. I'll see you around."

"What does he want now?" Ava hissed as soon as she picked up, serpentining past the tables and away from Sunny. She retreated down the staircase and back to her room, the phone pressed against her ear, checking over her shoulder to make sure no one followed her. Laura's voice filtered through in fragments, delivering apologies on Ethan's behalf.

"Hey Ava – I'm so glad I reached you. Listen, Ethan feels really bad about what he said to Misha. I told him it was out of line, too. But you know what he's like, honey. He just... he really wants you to join the company, that's why. You have no idea how much. He talks about nothing else. I mean, you know, when he finds the time to talk."

"Well, you can tell Ethan that if he wants to apologise, he can find the time to call me himself," Ava retorted.

"What?... Ava? I can barely hear you... The connection's awful. Where are you?"

Ava stepped out onto the balcony, but it didn't do much to improve the signal. "Hey, Laura, did you know that a lion's tongue is so rough it can literally lick its prey to death?" As if on cue, the muezzin's song resounded again, adding to the effect she hoped to achieve.

"What?" Laura's confusion was palpable. "Ava, where on earth are you?"

With a sly grin, Ava hung up. She leaned on the

balustrade, and her spirits lifted as she pictured Laura relaying to Ethan that his daughter had gone haywire.

The smile, however, faded quicker than it had appeared.

That was the problem with running: It provided only fleeting relief, and somehow, life always found a way to catch up.

Ava wrapped her kikoi around her shoulders like a blanket, gazing past the freight port and out to sea. Trailing the lights of a cargo ship as it left port. Wishing she was on it.

Not noticing someone was watching her from the street corner down below.

3

THE INNKEEPER

Ava woke on her stomach, cheek in the sand, head heavy as a coconut. Gentle waves resounded from a distance. Wetting her lips, she tasted salt.

"What the..." she mumbled, feeling a tickling at her feet. Drugged with fatigue, she flutter-opened her eyes. "*What the hell?*" A fully grown *cow* was licking her toes! She crab-crawled backwards, and the cow moved off, utterly unimpressed.

Ava frantically scanned her surroundings, her hands checking her body for any signs of injury, her eyes darting around in search of something – anything – familiar to lock onto. Before her, a beach of glinting white sand stretched out as far as the horizon, where giant clouds billowed in the vibrant colours of early morning. The air was thick with humidity. Cicadas buzzed. Seagulls chit-chatted as they glided overhead. Palm trees snaked along the shoreline, where thatched umbrellas sprouted like mushrooms from the sand. In their shade, dilapidated steamer chairs gave the impression that this beach didn't see many tourists.

How the hell did she get here? And where even *was*

here? Had she been kidnapped? Worse, had someone spiked her drink and taken advantage of her? Her panic surged when the realisation hit: She had absolutely no idea.

Ava picked herself up.

She had a splitting headache, and her mouth felt dry like the caked sand on her cheek. The remains of a campfire smouldered beneath a nearby palm. Next to it: her bag. She crept toward it, grasping the worn leather strap like a lifeline. A wave of relief poured over her when she found everything inside was still there – wallet, passport, phone.

She hugged the bag to her chest, and her panic faded to confusion. Her mind was like a closet in the lead-up to a first date; nothing was where it belonged anymore.

The last thing she remembered was Safari Tom chatting her up on the rooftop, followed by the phone call from Laura. Everything after that had become a blur. She didn't even remember going to bed last night. There had been a reason for her going to the beach, though – she still remembered that – but she couldn't for the life of her remember what it was.

Ava fished out her phone. No signal. The display, however, flashed green with old messages from Laura, desperately trying to get a hold of her after last night's call.

But, hang on... that had been on *Wednesday* night.

According to her phone, it was Friday morning now. What happened to Thursday?

Someone *must* have drugged her.

As unsettling as it was – that was the only logical explanation. But *why*, if not to take advantage of her or steal her things?

That's when Ava realised: Her backpack wasn't with her.

Had she left it in the guesthouse at the freight port? No, she hadn't, had she? She had packed it and taken it with...

Well, great. So she *had* been robbed.

And yet, the pack carried nothing but shirts, pants, and old socks. Why not take her valuables?

Confused beyond measure, Ava got up and staggered through a minefield of ripe coconuts, thanking her lucky stars that none had knocked her out.

Although, on second thought...

She frisked the back of her head, almost disappointed when she couldn't find a bump. At least that would have explained her sudden onset of amnesia.

Shielding her eyes from the sun with her kikoi, she stumbled on in search of someone to talk to, her desperation growing with each step. But at this early hour, the seashore was devoid of any beachgoers. Only a few fishermen cast their nets from a sailboat far out at sea, where the moon conjured up the next high tide.

At last, her eyes latched onto something at the far end of the beach, something bright red – *her pack!*

Ava rushed toward it like one of those poor fighting bulls in Spain, swirling up hot sand. As she approached, her mind swirled with a jumble of thoughts, each one as confusing and disorienting as the next.

The pack sat below a dingy sign mounted on a paddle. A shabby white wall towered behind it, a round garden gate in its centre, yellow paint flaking off the wood like snakeskin. She paused for a moment, taking in the oddness of the scene before her.

But as she lifted the pack, she was relieved to find it was still as heavy as she remembered. However, the whole thing made even less sense to her now.

As she heaved it onto her shoulders, at last, she read the words written in bold capital letters on the sign:

Welcome to the Atlas – your anywhere hotel.
Please note:

By entering these premises, you agree to adhere to the below house rules.

1. Guests must not bring visitors to the premises.
2. Guests must never talk about the Atlas.
3. Guests must always return before curfew.
4. Guests must not engage in any criminalities.
5. Guests must never exit through the garden gate.

Any transgression will result in expulsion.
We trust you will enjoy your stay.

The Atlas Management

Ava chortled. She scanned the coastline, almost expecting to spot someone sitting there laughing, reaping the fruits of the prank they'd played on her – only to wince when she actually noticed a woman hiding in the shade of a nearby palm, watching her. Ava locked eyes with the stranger, and fear overcame her like a cold gust. She stumbled backwards – almost fell – when from behind her, a voice washed up the beach like driftwood.

"Were you looking for me?"

A man walked up the shore, cradling a basket filled with seashells. He was close. Strangely close. It was almost as if he'd appeared out of thin air. But that was silly, of course. He must have been there the entire time; Ava had just been too occupied to notice.

Wearing a dark blue polo shirt and old jeans, torn in places, he was maybe in his mid-fifties and a little out of breath, as if he'd been running. Lean as a palm tree and with a thick shock of black but greying hair, he wore wire-framed glasses, a pair of knowing eyes lurking behind them.

"I can never stop collecting these. They are all so different," he said with an Italian accent as washy as his jeans, stroking over the shells and abalones in his basket. His eyes, however, busily scanned the shoreline, as if searching for something.

"They are beautiful." Ava nodded. She followed the man's gaze, but whoever had been crouching beneath the palms just a moment ago was now gone. "I'm sorry, is this your place?"

"Well, I wouldn't say it's *mine*," said the man with the shells. "I look after it for the time being. I'm the innkeeper." He shifted the basket to free up a hand. "Bruno di Mare, at your service."

"Ava," she said, noticing the awkwardness that came from withholding her last name. "Marley," she added a bit too late, then shook his hand. She loathed telling people who she was. Too often, someone would recognise the name and then make a snide comment. Ethan wasn't exactly popular with the crowds. Another reason why Tanzania had been so perfect for her escape: Few people here would have heard of Marley's Coffee. It was ironic, really: MCC opened at least two new cafés a day, somewhere in the world. Yet, in countries actually producing the coffee beans, you'd search for a very, *very* long time to find one.

"A pleasure to meet you, Ava Marley. Are you... are you alone?"

Once again, Bruno di Mare's eyes darted in every direction, making him appear a little mad.

"Yes. Yes, I am," Ava responded, striving to anchor his focus with her assertive tone.

"Oh, that is a relief... I mean, that is good to know." The innkeeper fumbled in his pocket and produced a key chain, which he clattered nervously. "You see, because I only have a single room left. I take it you have come to stay with us?"

Just then, Ava's phone rang; she must have hit a sliver of signal. She glanced down at it. Ethan. Who'd have thought?

"Actually, no," she replied, rejecting the call and switching to silent mode. "That's not why I'm here."

Bruno di Mare paused his fiddling for the right key. "I'm intrigued. Why are you here, then, signorina?"

"I... I just had to get my pack." She gestured over her shoulder. "It ended up here somehow."

The innkeeper tilted his head slightly, examining the backpack. "How mysterious," he said. "And you are certain you don't want to come in?" There was a hint of something else in his accent beside the Italian, but Ava couldn't put her finger on it.

"I... don't think so," she replied.

"Why is that?"

The phone buzzed again. Again, Ava ignored it.

"I..." She cleared her throat. "To be honest, I don't think I can afford a room."

That wasn't true, but it seemed easier to lie than to tell the man he seemed a little suspect.

Bruno di Mare put a tarnished silver key in the gate's lock, but Ava noticed it was already open. "Well, you are in luck then, Fräulein Marley," he said.

German! That's what he sounded like, a fusion of Italian and German.

"Here at the Atlas, you don't pay for a room if you can't afford to," Bruno continued. "We pride ourselves on having established a very successful volunteer program. Guests assist in the hotel's upkeep in exchange for free lodging."

Ava cocked her head. "Not exactly a promising business model, is it?"

Bruno pushed down the gate's handle as if to check for any squeaking. "I guess we are more of a non-profit."

Another buzz from Ava's phone, this time for a voice message.

"Someone really wants to talk to you, it seems." The innkeeper inclined his head at the phone.

"Yes. Sorry about that." She pressed the power button, savouring the small victory of making Ethan wait.

"Boyfriend?"

"Father."

"Well, maybe he has good news."

"Doubtful." Ava weighed the phone in her hand like the words on her tongue. "We're... not exactly on good terms."

"Oh, das tut mir aber leid," replied Bruno di Mare. "I'm so sorry to hear that. Allora, how about it? I could use some help with the breakfast shift." Bruno di Mare looked at her like a dog hoping for a treat.

"If you must know..." Ava shifted her gaze to her feet, piling up sand. "It's not just the money stuff – it's this." She gestured at the sign.

"Ach ja, natürlich." Bruno di Mare sounded familiar with the problem. And how could he not? Surely, that sign worked more as a deterrent than an invitation.

"Yeah, what's up with all the rules? Sounds more like a prison than a hotel."

"Well, I should think our rules are self-explanatory, are they not? Let's see..." The innkeeper turned to the sign, trailing the words with a finger as he read.

"You must not bring visitors to this establishment –

pretty standard for most hotels around the world, I should think. We'd like to keep off the beaten path, so don't tell people about us, please, especially not on TripAdvisor. The curfew is for your own safety, of course. No criminalities – that's for the *other* guests' safety. As for the exit through the garden gate" – Bruno tilted his head – "I must admit that one would strike me as odd, too."

"How *do* your guests leave if it's not through here?"

"There are ways." Bruno examined one of the snail shells in his basket. "Many, *many* ways." He peeked into the shell's aperture with one eye pinched. "It makes a lot more sense from the inside, I suppose."

"I see." Ava took a step back. She would have been lying if she'd said the strange front – of the hotel *and* the innkeeper – hadn't aroused her curiosity. But frankly, she'd be mad to take this man up on his offer, what with the unsettling way she'd ended up here in the first place. For all she knew, *he* could have spiked her drink.

"Well, I really must get on. Is there anything else I can help you with for the time being?" Bruno smiled, fluttering his eyelashes.

"Actually, there is," Ava said, relieved he'd cleared the runway for her departure. "This might sound strange, but would you mind telling me where we are right now? My... taxi driver must have dropped me off on the wrong beach."

"Hm. If I am not mistaken, these grains of sand accumulate to what the locals call Pomboo Beach on the east coast of Zanzibar. I could be terribly wrong, though."

"Thank you." Ava nodded, retreating a few steps. "Also, for your kind offer. But I best be on my way now."

Bruno bowed. "Piacere." He swung open the gate and scanned the beach one last time before he crossed the doorstep quick as a mouse caught stealing cheese. Ava tried to peek inside, but she could only see a winding pathway framed by freshly trimmed hedges.

"If you could be a darling and close the gate when you've come in?" Bruno said over his shoulder. "I don't want the dog to run off."

"But I'm not going to..." Ava called out, but the innkeeper had disappeared behind a bend.

Ava shook her head, feet shuffling through the sand as she walked away from the Atlas Hotel. However, she stopped when it occurred to her that she could at least do the man the courtesy of closing the gate as he'd asked.

She backtracked. She set one foot on the doorstep. She reached for the handle. As soon as she touched it, she felt a subtle pull, like the current tugging at a piece of driftwood, carrying it out to sea. And despite better judgement, all the doubts she'd had about the hotel and how she'd ended up here washed away like tracks in the sand. After all, what did she have to lose? *My old life and the whole mess that comes with it,* she thought. But wasn't that the whole plan?

Ava sat down on the doorstep, resting her pack against the gate's frame. She ran a finger along the edge of her phone, scraping out grains of sand from the speaker's groove, Ethan's voice message still lurking. Filling her lungs with a deep breath of sultry ocean air, she tapped the screen and listened. Her father sounded distant as usual, cold like London rain.

"Well, you wanted me to call, so here I am. But don't expect an apology, Ava. Because you are acting like a *child*, and running off to wherever the hell you are right now is all the more proof that what you need is a firm hand..."

Ava drew another breath – this one sharper – and her stomach tensed as if bracing for a punch.

"...I have issued a press release, announcing you're

joining the company. The trainee program starts on April twenty-fifth. Sow your wild oats or whatever it is you need to do until then. But I expect you to be there for my inaugural. Don't ruin this for yourself, Ava. You will never forgive yourself if—"

Ava cocked her head as if to dodge a blow, deleting the message then and there. Why did he always have to do this? Why couldn't he – for once – let go of what *he* wanted and put himself in her shoes? Couldn't he see how this sort of pressure only pushed her further away?

Ava huffed and considered the shaded path beyond the garden gate. Around the bend, birds twittered teasingly. A cool breeze swished past, playing with her hair.

"Fuck it," she muttered and rose to her feet. She knew it was a little reckless – given how she'd ended up here – but hell, maybe she wanted to be reckless. She switched off her phone, and then she stepped inside.

Past the threshold, Ava turned around once more and gazed back out, the open gate now a perfect picture frame for the turquoise waters and white sands. She was about to close it when, out of nowhere, a figure rushed into the peaceful scene, causing her to stumble backwards. Tripping over a rock, Ava fell onto the gravel and kicked the gate closed, just as a woman with a shorn head dashed toward it, grimacing in a panic when it snapped shut inches in front her nose.

4

A NEW TENANT FOR ROOM FIVE

Ava scrambled to her feet, struggling with the heavy pack on her shoulders. Her heart pounded in her ears, her gaze fixated on the gate. What had she seen out there that had made her react so swiftly and slam it shut? She did a double take, attempting to conjure up an image of the previous moment, but her mind had gone completely blank – *again*.

What on earth was going on lately? It was like trying to grasp a dream upon waking up in the morning; the more she tried, the quicker it slipped away.

But, just like a dream, the scare was also forgotten just as quickly. One moment she had wanted nothing more than to peek out the gate and see what had frightened her so much. The next, whatever – or whoever – was out there didn't seem to matter anymore. In fact, as Ava gave a small hop to readjust the backpack on her hips, she had all but forgotten about the incident.

Dusting herself off, she advanced further down the pathway, tunnelled by perfectly cut hedges. The air was thick with floral shop scent, an intoxicating, humid mash-up of lilies and jasmine, orchids and hibiscus. Birds chased each other somewhere behind the hedge, and there was something utterly soothing about the sound of gravel crunching beneath the soles of her sandals.

The pathway curved, leading to a courtyard centred around a fountain. The gentle sounds of the dabbling water provided a pleasant background noise. Behind it, the Atlas Hotel lay sheltered beneath the bows of an ancient fig tree with a crown so thick it created its own cooling climate. The rundown exterior outside the gate was truly an understatement. With its lustrous white facades and forest green shutters, the hotel was a charming double-storied beach house in immaculate condition, framed by a veranda reaching all around the building. A sweeping staircase led to the main entrance, where double doors unfolded like an invitation card. Tropical flowers craned their necks to greet Ava as she walked up the stairs, and the mellow voice of a woman singing to an acoustic guitar resounded from inside, carried over on an ocean breeze sweeping through the hall.

Ava took off her backpack, resting it against the doorframe. When she stepped inside, the white-painted floorboards creaked with history beneath her feet. The hall opened to a foyer draped with Moroccan rugs; in the centre of the room was a round table made from polished, dark wood, holding an antique globe and a phoenix palm in a delicate vase. Spread across the table lay a selection of books in all kinds of languages, including a few that Ava recognised as the latest *Sunday Times* bestsellers, as well as a stack of fresh newspapers and magazines from around the world. Behind the table, a carpeted staircase led to a mezzanine, along which Ava could see a handful of gold-numbered doors, each of a different colour.

As she advanced through the foyer, one thing immediately struck her, as it certainly would anyone upon first arrival: the room was filled to the brim with what appeared to be souvenirs from around the world, all pocket-sized. Thousands upon thousands of trinkets spread across shelves and tables and hung from nails or doorknobs. Arabian oil lamps, snow globes, Buddha figurines, and miniature versions of every famous architectural marvel in the world – the Eiffel Tower, the pyramids of Egypt, the Statue of Liberty, the Tower of Pisa, the Sydney Opera House.

She entered the living room through a sliding door to her right, where the collection of trinkets continued. Teacups in glass vitrines, wooden shoes dangling from the chandelier, chess pawns sitting next to scarab beetles, a collection of palm-sized bottles filled with sand and labelled with hand-written locations. Russian dolls, boomerangs, hand fans, marionettes, spoons, necklaces and rings, post-cards and photographs, magnets, keys and key chains, seashells, and rocks and crystals in every shape, hue and form. But despite the curiosities scattered across the house, the Atlas didn't appear cramped. On the contrary: Everything seemed to have its designated place. The hotel was tastefully decorated and had an airy, homely feel. Each table was decorated with fresh flowers. Well-stocked bookshelves lined one wall, selected artworks the other.

Crossing the living room, Ava realised the singing and guitar playing came from an old television. Next to a fireplace and amid plush sofas, a doe-eyed Audrey Hepburn sang "Moon River" from the fire escape of a furniture-less Manhattan apartment.

"Don't you just love that?"

Ava swivelled around at the sound of the innkeeper's

distinct accent. But there was something else in his voice, something heavy she'd felt drawn to since first meeting him. His words were tinged with buried sadness as if a clump of pain had clogged his throat.

Bruno leaned against the staircase balustrade in the hall, his chin resting in his hand as he gazed into the living room. "I'm obsessed with old movies. I have all the classics on tape."

"On tape?" Ava asked and approached him.

"We are old school around here, Signorina Marley." The innkeeper quirked a brow. "The Atlas doesn't like modern technology much. Allora, ti troveremo una stanza, sì? We shall find you a room, yes?" Were the Italian and German phrases to show off his language skills? Or maybe to preempt any speculation about where he might be from?

"So, where exactly are you from, Bruno? Italy, I take it?" Ava asked, rising to the bait. She retrieved her backpack from the entrance and followed the innkeeper.

"I grew up in Germany, actually," he said. "But my family stems from Umbria originally. My nonno was a truffle hunter. Had his own pigs and everything." Bruno grunted, which made Ava recoil, then chuckle over her shoulder. Who *was* this guy?

"And what about you, Miss Marley?"

"I'm a barista at a London deli," she replied to keep things simple.

"Oh, wie wunderbar. Just the right fit for our breakfast shift, then."

As they climbed the staircase, the steps creaked and groaned, but otherwise, the hotel lay quiet.

"So, am I the only guest?" she asked and considered the gold-numbered doors, five in total.

"No," replied Bruno, "as a matter of fact, with your arrival, we are fully booked, at last."

"You seem pleased about that."

"Well, it had occurred to me lately that she might not like to welcome a new guest," Bruno said, stroking the handrail as if it were a horse's back. "Room five has been empty for months. Allora, sì: Sono contento del tuo arrivo. I am very content with your arrival, Signorina Marley."

"And where is everyone else?" Ava asked. She had to admit, she would have felt more at ease seeing another guest. Because the innkeeper – however "contento" – was also a little "bizarro".

"Atlas guests usually spend the day exploring," replied Bruno. "There is just so much to see, isn't there?"

"Mm." Ava nodded. But as alluring as a tropical island was, she could already see herself going absolutely nowhere and exploring absolutely nothing during her stay. The Atlas had charmed her with its cosy corners and its atmosphere of times gone by. The only thing she wanted to do was sit on the porch, stick her nose between the pages of a ridiculously thick book, and forget about the world. In fact, with all the memory lapses happening to her recently, she wouldn't have minded if Ethan's deadline had slipped her mind as well. But no such luck. The date was firmly lodged in her brain. Twenty-five days from now, counting down.

"This is you, dear."

They had arrived at the end of the hall, where the innkeeper pushed down the handle of a green door marked with a golden five.

He stepped aside so Ava could enter the room, where she was met by excited barking. A dog with fluffy, speckled fur jumped from an armchair by a French window, greeting Ava with a wagging tail.

"My sincere apologies. I should have known he was in here. It is Captain's favourite room. Vieni qui, Capitano," he said to the dog and then to Ava, "I hope you are not allergic?"

"Not at all – I love dogs." Ava came down on her knees, fondling Captain's fur as she gazed around.

A queen-sized bed, white-framed and draped with a patchy quilt and fluffy pillows, took centre stage; a round window above the headrest, rimmed with green and red shards of glass, cast colourful reflections on the floor. Neatly arranged seashells studded the shelves on the walls, which were also decked with seafaring paintings and a large mirror framed with driftwood. In the corner by the armchair sat a small study desk, cluttered with what appeared to be scientific papers and uni textbooks – Harvard, if Ava read the insignia correctly.

"I'm sorry, I should have cleared these long ago," Bruno said, grabbing a pile of study notes from the desk. "They belonged to a former guest." He cleared his throat, tugging the papers under his arm. "Allora, will this work for you?" He sounded genuinely concerned.

Ava nodded, smiling as she stroked the bedframe. "I wouldn't have picked any other room."

"You haven't seen the other rooms," the innkeeper said with a smirk.

Ava chuckled and dropped her pack on the bed, fresh laundry scent soaring upon impact. A copy of Adam Smith's *The Wealth of Nations* rested on the bedside table next to a bouquet of sunflowers.

"Do these grow on the island?" Ava touched one of the flower petals.

"I'd be surprised if they did," the innkeeper said mysteriously. "Now, let's get some fresh air in here."

Grabbing more papers as he walked past the desk, he opened the flaking white doors with a screech, which revealed a small balcony with a yellow-striped hammock and the feel of a ukulele song. Although Ava could hear and smell the ocean, she could not see it; the thick tree canopy shielded the view, giving the space perfect privacy.

"Your room isn't ensuite, I'm afraid. The bathroom is down the hall. Let me show you." Bruno gestured for Ava to follow him, Captain on his heels. "You share with two other guests, but both are usually out all day." He opened a cabinet in the hall, and with an embarrassed smile, dumped the papers inside.

"Are there other guests who, you know..." Ava tapped her chest.

"Who volunteer? Yes, everybody helps to keep the Atlas up and running." He placed a hand on door number four. "Molly from Australia. She does the cooking Mondays and Wednesdays. Best Lamington sponge cake you will ever eat in your life." He patted his belly, then worked his way down the hall door by door. "Helene from France is in number three. Interior design student. She helps me with housekeeping. You have to thank her for the gorgeous flowers in your room. You're sharing the bathroom with her and Yash from India in number two. He's an incredibly talented photographer. Cooks Tuesdays and Thursdays – *very* spicy. You have been warned.

"And number one is Joao from Florida. He's our gardener. Barely fifteen years old, can you believe it?"

"A kid all on his own," Ava noted as they reached the bathroom, where Bruno drew back the shower curtain in the bathtub.

"Everybody is on their own," he said, and Ava wasn't sure if he was referring to his guests or humans in general.

"And how long is everybody staying?"

"Oh, this particular assemblage of guests has been here for quite a while now," replied Bruno. "We've got a good dynamic going at the moment. Everyone's happy to stick around and contribute to our little community. No one's missing their old lives much."

"I should fit right in then." Ava adjusted a towel on the rack that didn't need adjusting.

"I had a feeling you might." The innkeeper considered her but broke the silence before it bordered on awkwardness. He cleared his throat, tapping the shower lever. "Be patient with the hot water. Sometimes I swear it comes all the way from Panama, but trust me; it *will* come. Just open the faucet, then wait a minute – or *ten*. Collect the cold water in the bucket, please. You can use it to water the gardens... *if* Joao lets you anywhere near his hibiscus."

He opened a dresser beneath the sink, withdrawing a set of towels he handed her. Egyptian cotton; the good stuff. "These are for you. Now, you take your time to freshen up. Have a pisolino, a little nap, if you like. There's absolutely no rush. Whenever you're ready, come find me downstairs, and we'll get you started on your Atlas journey."

"Thanks so much, Bruno, really. This is" – she pressed the towels against her chest – "so much more than I expected."

"We are glad to have you, Miss Marley." Bruno bowed his head like a Buddhist monk. "Come on now, Capitano, time to get to work." He tapped on his thigh as he walked down the stairs. The dog scurried past Ava, collecting another cuddle on the fly, which made her smile. However strange the circumstances that had led her here, there was no denying the Atlas Hotel was, uncannily, exactly what she needed, exactly when she needed it: the perfect escape.

Leaning against the doorframe, Ava cradled her towels and gazed back at the innkeeper and his dog. She knew she couldn't run from her life forever. Of course, she knew that.

But – for a while...?

5

THE BOOK OF DOORS

Captain's tail wagged like a flag in a storm. The dog waited for Ava at the bottom of the stairs, and she ruffled his fur as she scanned the hall for any sign of the innkeeper. Passing cloud shadows swept across the wooden floors. Charles Trenet's "La Mer" played on a turntable in the living room, the needle crackling on the old vinyl like wood in a campfire. After Ava had unpacked her things in room five, she had taken a hot shower and watered the flowers on her balcony with the excess water, as instructed. Now water dripped from her hair onto a clean shirt, and although she must have had a rough night, she felt surprisingly rested and refreshed.

She whirled around when the kitchen door at the end of the hall swung open. The innkeeper appeared, carrying with him the smell of freshly baked bread. "Ready to get started?" he asked, flashing his eyebrows.

"Absolutely. Let's tackle that breakfast shift." Ava rubbed her hands but felt silly at the gesture.

"Oh, don't you worry about that today. All the guests have already gone out, and I took the liberty to make you a little stuzzichino, as the Italians say. Or a Häppchen, if you prefer ze German expression." He put on a heavy German accent and handed her a sandwich wrapped in wax paper. "Most of ze guests, zey forget to eat on zer first day."

"Thank you. That's very kind."

Ava took the sandwich and unwrapped it. Instantly, her mouth watered, and she realised she had no idea when she'd had her last meal.

"Do you mind?" she asked, finding Bruno's eyes.

"No, no. Go ahead. You must be starving."

Ava took a bite as the innkeeper led her toward reception.

Tucked away below the staircase, it was a converted broom closet with dark-blue walls and a liftable counter. Crammed bookshelves framed the sides, lit by elegant sconces. Twenty-four palm-sized clocks labelled with the time zones ticked on the back wall: a concert of time.

"This is delicious," Ava said between bites, lifting the top slice of her sandwich to see what was on it.

"Home-made sourdough, roasted portobello mushrooms, balsamic vinegar, fresh basil, San Marzano tomatoes, and my favourite dairy-free mozzarella from Brandenburg," listed Bruno, not without a hint of pride.

"How do you get all this fresh produce delivered to the island?" Ava felt a splinter of guilt, what with the long transport ways. This was a major point of criticism for Marley's Coffee Corporation, one the press regularly targeted. Where did the coffee plants grow? Were the farmers sufficiently compensated? And how did the beans get halfway across the globe from plantation to cup? Like no other commodity, coffee was accompanied by the expectation of fair trade, not that the end-consumer knew what precisely the label should entail. Ava's mum and dad had often argued about the topic, back in the day when they had still been on speaking terms, and Luciana had still been alive.

"An excellent question that transitions perfectly into my little introductory speech." Bruno lifted the counter and stepped inside his little nook. Now he looked like a puppet; only the strings were missing. "Here at the Atlas, we pride ourselves on relying on 100 percent carbon-neutral shipping," he said, smirking as if he had told an inside joke. "Now, tell me, Fräulein Marley," he said, thrumming his fingertips on a world map attached to the counter, his underlying sadness yielding to childlike excitement. "If you could go anywhere you wanted today – *right now* – where would you go?"

"Um. I was just going to stay in today if that's all right?" Ava said, covering her full mouth with her forearm.

"But this is your first day at the Atlas!" Bruno called out, spreading his arms. "Your Anywhere Hotel! You must go somewhere exciting, even if it's just for an hour or two."

Ava turned her head away from him as if he had just sneezed. "You – you mean on the island or... what do you mean?"

"Va bene, cara. It's all right, dear. Everyone is confused on day one. Here, let me explain." The innkeeper pulled a thick accounting book from the shelf to his right. "This is what I call the Book of Doors," he said solemnly, flipping to a random page. "In here, you find a list of every item you can use to travel. I have organised them by continent, country, region, and town. You see?" He turned the book so Ava could read his expansive inventory of figurines and snow globes, crystals and key chains.

"I'm afraid I still don't understand." She scratched her temple. Was this some test? An initiation for new guests, maybe?

Bruno leaned over the counter, signalling Ava to move in closer, too. When he spoke again, his voice was a murmur of mystery. "The Atlas is no ordinary hotel, Miss Marley. The Atlas" – he let a dramatic pause linger in the air – "is a portal to the world."

"C- come again?" Ava's gaze swung between Bruno's eyes as if watching a pendulum.

The innkeeper took to his inventory log. "Every item in this book represents a souvenir on the premises. I refer to them as doorways, or doors, each taking you to the location where it was collected."

"I see." Now Ava did that thing you do when you realise (too little, too late) that you're in the company of a lunatic. She began to humour the innkeeper whilst secretly plotting a getaway. "And how does one travel with these... these *doors*, you say?"

If only I could travel back in time, she thought. *Rewind the last two hours and run from this place as fast as I can.*

Bruno smiled so broadly it only seemed to underline his madness. "It's as easy as clicking your heels," he said. "All you have to do is pick an object from the book, retrieve it from the shelves, and then toss it in the air. When you catch it, you will find yourself at the destination of your choice."

Straight back to room five, fetch my stuff, then over the balcony and down the tree, Ava planned her escape route.

"Einen Augenblick, bitte." Bruno tapped a finger on his lip, flicking through the pages while Ava took a careful step back. "I think a fun door to start with this time of year would be... this one." His finger landed at the bottom of the page. He bent down behind the counter, conjuring up a colourful elephant figurine carved from wood, which he balanced on an open palm.

"You're serious."

At this point, Ava was convinced Bruno di Mare had a screw loose.

The innkeeper hunched his shoulders, a gesture of encouragement. "Indulge me," he said. "If you don't believe in it, it's nothing but a game of catch."

"Fine," Ava sighed. Anything to buy some time now. But just when she was about to toss the elephant, Bruno cupped her hand with both of his – which felt way too intimate for Ava, but she allowed it. If anything, so that he wouldn't get irritated. One had to tread gently with this kind of crazy.

"Remember," Bruno said with urgency, "if you want to come back, all you have to do is throw the elephant back up and catch it. *Beh*," he said and squeezed her hand before letting go, "now, give it a toss!"

Ava rubbed an eyelid, clinging to a last sliver of hope that the innkeeper might just have a twisted sense of humour that took some getting used to. She tossed the elephant in the air, trailing its flight path as it soared toward the ceiling. Any second now, Bruno would burst out laughing, delighting in the joke he'd played on her. Either that, or he'd unleash his madness, pretending she'd been beamed inside a zoo enclosure or something.

The miniature animal landed in Ava's palm, and she closed her fist around it. The instant she did, she felt an unbridled force grabbing hold of her hand, wrenching her down like an anchor. It happened as quickly as batting an eyelash. One heartbeat, she was standing at the reception; the next, she'd turned up in a brimming market square, penned in by a cheering party crowd.

Vibrant music roared over a sea of bouncing heads, classical sitar sounds mixed with blaring hip-hop beats. A potent blend of sweat and incense travelled up her airways. Bursts of powder soared through the air – green and yellow and blue and red – an explosion of colour right before Ava's flabbergasted eyes.

A bull of a man wobbled toward her, rows of fat jigging beneath his T-shirt as his pot belly bumped into her. Losing her balance, Ava toppled over, and the elephant slipped from her hand. Now she was down on her hands and knees, a forest of legs dancing around her as she searched the dust for the tiny figurine. At last, her fingers clutched around it, and Ava jumped up. In a primal reflex, she tossed the elephant back up into the mottled sky and, as soon as it was within reach, clasped both hands around it like a baseball catcher desperate to steal a sure home run.

Instantly, the noise cut off, and Ava reappeared in the hotel's hallway.

"*Holy* shit!" She flinched, colour dust snowing from her shoulders. Hurling the elephant away from her, she dodged backwards to avoid any body contact with the bedevilled object and banged into the wall behind her, where she tore down a picture frame, glass splintering as it shattered on the floor.

Captain barked as if he'd seen a ghost. Bruno, however, burst out laughing so much he had to hold his thighs. "Yes, it was indeed Holi – the Indian festival of colour," he called out, fetching a feather duster to brush her off. "I'm sorry, I couldn't resist."

Ava's knees buckled. She collapsed onto the floor, the echo of Indian hip-hop beats still thrumming inside her ears. "Wha... what just happened?"

Bruno came down on his haunches, eyeing Ava. "You, my dear, just experienced your first Atlas trip. To New Delhi, in case you were wondering." He picked up the broken picture frame and, with his feather duster, swept away the shards of glass, careful Captain didn't step on them.

"Trip? What kind of trip? What was *on* that sandwich?" Ava asked, and Bruno chortled at the question. She, however, was deadly serious. "What the *hell* did you do to me?" It must have been the innkeeper, after all, who had drugged her to lure her in, and now she was hallucinating from whatever *mushrooms* he'd been feeding her.

"I'm sorry," Bruno said, spreading his arms as if to calm a cornered animal. "I'm so sorry if that scared you. I should have eased you into our ways. Please. Let me... let me show you properly."

Captain came to rest his head on Ava's thigh as if to back his owner's good intentions.

"Here, take my hand. We'll do the next one together." Bruno extended one hand out to her, drawing a smooth, black rock from his pocket with the other. "I assure you it's perfectly safe. And Captain can come, too."

Ava hesitated, considering the innkeeper with suspicion. It had looked and smelled and felt so real. The colours, the sweat, the music – all of it. She picked a clump of red powder from her hair, tangible as a pinch of salt between her fingers. And then, with a shaking hand, she reached out to the innkeeper. As they touched, Bruno nodded reassuringly.

"Hold on to Captain," he said, casting up the rock with a flick of his thumb. When he caught it, all three disappeared as if the earth had swallowed them whole.

THE EXPERIENCE WAS MORE pleasant this time, almost like waking from sleep. Slowly. Gradually. Ava didn't dare open her eyes after she felt the pull from Bruno's hand wane, but that didn't mean she could keep out her surroundings.

First, she noticed the ground beneath her feet, soft and cushioned and most definitely not the old floorboards of the hotel. Next came the sounds. A stream trickled close by. Bird song travelled on the air, twittering high above, trilling far away, chirruping nearby. A woodpecker's drill echoed through the trees, which groaned and creaked as the wind whooshed through the canopy. Last came the smells. Clean and crisp but also damp and earthy. It smelled of old trunks and fresh rain, of mushrooms and pinecones, and something tangy and herby she could not quite place.

Ava didn't need to open her eyes to believe this place was real. When she finally did, she found herself standing in a forest meadow. Tussocks of plump moss covered the ground, sprinkled with tiny white flowers gleaming like stars against the greens. Captain bustled around fallen tree trunks and lichen-covered rocks, sniffing out all the new scents around him, tail wagging as he gave excited barks.

"We better put this one on a leash," said Bruno. He came down on his haunches to stop the dog as he scuttled past. "The Förster... the – how do you say in English? – the... *ranger* won't be happy if he catches a rabbit." He glanced up at Ava, who took in her surroundings as if admiring the ceiling of the Sistine Chapel.

"I guess this would have been the better choice for your first trip," he said with a smidge of guilt. "Please let me apologise again for my misguided attempt at an April Fool's joke."

Ava gazed around, hardly listening to what the innkeeper had said. "Where are we?"

"Just south of the town of Münster," he replied. "Wild garlic season is slowly starting in the German forests. My favourite time to be here."

"Is this... is this really... *real*?" Ava stroked the bark of a tree as if it were the first one she'd ever seen.

Bruno nodded, his lips thinning into a genuine smile. It was clear that he was making an effort now to calm her nerves and ensure that she was all right. More than anything, it was this changed demeanour of his that helped her believe that maybe the whole thing wasn't just a figment of her imagination or some drug-induced hallucination. Maybe this *was* for real.

"But how is it possible?" she asked, slowly warming up to her innkeeper.

"Well" – Bruno came to walk beside her, keeping Captain on a long leash – "if I were to guess, I would say the hotel appears for those who have a desperate wish to escape their lives. Of course, this applies to most people on the planet right about now, but I believe you also need to be in the right place at the right time."

Ava turned to look at him. "But how does it *work*?"

Bruno fluttered his lips. "You might as well ask me how the universe works."

"But there must be an explanation."

"Would it suffice if I told you it was magic?"

"No. No, it would not." Ava considered the innkeeper. "Don't you want to know?"

"I used to," Bruno said, turning the pebble in his hand. "Naturally, it is the one question nagging every guest upon first arrival. But sooner or later, we all come to find that one doesn't need to understand electricity to appreciate a glowing lightbulb. Some things are best kept under the veil of mystery, Signorina Marley."

"Call me Ava, please," she said, balancing on a rock in the stream. "And for the record, I bet Thomas Edison would disagree with you."

She hopped from rock to rock further down the stream. "Is that why the other guests are never there?" she asked, picking at random from the countless questions floating like free radicals through her head. "Have they all started new lives somewhere awesome around the world?"

"I'm afraid that's not possible. Whenever you leave the hotel, you have twenty-four hours in any given location; then you must return."

Ava stopped jumping. "What happens if you don't make it on time?"

"If you don't return before curfew, you won't be able to come back at all." Bruno sat down on a fallen tree trunk.

"What do you mean?"

"I mean, the portal will be closed. For good."

Ava remembered the sign at the gate. *All guests must return before curfew*. Suddenly, that made a lot more sense. Expulsion, then, was not at management's discretion. It was an inevitable consequence.

"But why would the hotel do that?"

Bruno shrugged. "I guess a line had to be drawn somewhere."

"Can't I just take several objects with me and then move from place to place?"

"The doors only work from within the hotel, I'm afraid."

"But couldn't I just keep coming back for a second, then use the same door again?"

"Guests have done that in the past, yes."

Ava sat down next to him, and they went quiet for a while, watching Captain dig for something.

"Can you make new doors?" Ava considered the innkeeper, who seemed to retreat to a different place – a *darker* place – whenever he wasn't spoken to. Only he didn't need a trinket for it.

"Sì, claro. You certainly can," he said, now back in the forest. "In fact, I made this one." He handed Ava the pebble. "Purely for nostalgic reasons. I used to play in this forest as a child."

Ava examined the pebble. "Is it difficult to make one?"

"On the contrary: It's too easy. Hence, the sheer overload of doors back at the hotel. All you have to do is collect an item and bring it back to the Atlas. Next time you cast it up, it will take you back to the exact location you last tossed the old object from."

"That is so cool," Ava said, overwhelmed by the possibilities this opened up.

"It is one of the perks of being an Atlas guest, yes. A word of advice, though," Bruno cautioned her. "Make sure the object is pocket-sized. Rumour has it your bed in number five is a door to Greenland, but it would take an entire basketball team to lift that one in the air and catch it. Not very practical, as I'm sure you'd agree." He smirked. "Oh, and do add any new doors to the inventory, please? It is so very hard to keep track of everything."

"So, why Zanzibar?" Ava returned the pebble to the innkeeper. "Of all the places in the world – why was the Atlas built on the island?"

Bruno nodded. "There is something you need to understand," he said as if he'd been meaning to get to that point for a while. "The Atlas is not located in Zanzibar."

"But—"

"I know, I know," Bruno said, pushing down his hands as if to calm a racehorse. "For *you*, the hotel appeared in Zanzibar, as it has for other guests in the past. But the truth is, the Atlas may present itself on all kinds of beaches all across the globe. Molly crossed that front step on a remote shore in Far North Queensland. Yash joined us while on assignment in the Philippines to photograph some influencer, and I'm pretty sure Helene was on honeymoon in the Caribbean when the yellow garden gate appeared for her. Don't ask me what happened to her husband, by the way."

"So, you're saying..."

"I'm saying the Atlas can be *anywhere*. It may appear on any given beach in the world, to any given soul craving to get away."

Ava pondered on that for a moment, picking some wild garlic, which released a pungent smell. "Why only beaches, though? Why can't it appear in downtown Manhattan or on a ski slope?"

"I can only give you my own two cents," said Bruno.

"That's all I'm asking for."

"Well, if you were to ask my folks – devoted Catholics who came to Germany as migrant workers during the Wirtschaftswunder – they would probably tell you all about the biblical significance of the ocean, how it symbolises the formless, the chaotic, the unfathomable. The beach is a stepping stone to the sea, which is boundless, a place of temptation where one can easily get lost. The perfect hotbed for a place like the Atlas, which is all about getting lost, is it not?"

"And that's what you think, too?"

Bruno di Mare moved his head from side to side like an owl. "I don't think it's all doom and gloom. I'd like to believe the ocean is where all life on Earth came from, and the beach is where we humans made our first clumsy steps. What better place to start a journey of discovery?" A smile unfurled on his face. "Anyway, the origins of the Atlas are just that: they are whatever you choose to believe. Sadly, there are no records anywhere. But, safe to say it has been around for a long time. The exterior would have changed, of course. As did the name, I assume."

Ava felt curiosity leaping within her. "So, do you think the hotel is standing in the world somewhere, or is it entirely out of space?"

"If I were to take a guess," replied Bruno, "I would say there is an original beach, and it is most likely located somewhere in the Americas. But that is the closest I can narrow it down to."

"Why the Americas?"

"Because of the hotel's time zone. It's roughly on American Eastern Standard Time. Besides, I've walked through many doors. If not all of them. It was the only way to compile a comprehensive list, you see? The old doors have always interested me the most, and those relics all seem to originate somewhere in the Americas."

"How old, you think?"

Bruno leaned back, gazing at the treetops. *"Old,"* he said, stretching the word to the length of a tree. "Think, Maya Empire old. And those would just be the doors that withstood the test of time."

"So, the whole world is covered in this invisible, ancient network of doors?"

"Well, nowadays it is," the innkeeper said, "but back in the day, there would have been hardly any connections. I like to use this story from a newspaper article I once read about rescue helicopters in Antarctica." Bruno scratched his head and came down on his haunches. "From its base camp, a helicopter can fly only so far until it runs out of fuel, yes?" He placed his river rock in the soil, suggesting it symbolised base camp. "For the sake of simplicity, let's say it can fly a hundred kilometres before it needs to turn around and refuel. So, what the chopper pilot does to prepare for emergencies is to go on fuel runs, dropping full drums at depots within the hundred-kilometre radius from her base camp."

Bruno drew a circle around the base camp with a stick, placing more rocks on the periphery.

"Now each of these fuel depots becomes its own base, from where the pilot gains another one hundred kilometres, you see? So, by the time she needs to embark on a rescue flight to – I don't know, maybe save a climate scientist stranded on a remote ice shelf – the pilot won't run the risk of fuel shortages during evacuation."

"You lost me somewhere on the ice," admitted Ava.

Bruno pushed his glasses up the ridge of his nose, locking eyes with her. "I believe that the Atlas would have started in the same way. From the location of the first door," he said, pointing at the pebble in the centre, "a person would have had twenty-four hours of travel time. Which, by the way, I assume they would have found out the hard way back then by throwing an object in the air long after that deadline and getting nowhere."

A strange image appeared in Ava's mind's eye, of a Mayan priest somewhere in the jungle, throwing a rock in the air again and again.

"The older doors are all centred in one rather small area. I imagine because, without cars or aeroplanes, twenty-four hours could only get you so far. Back then, they would have made doors within this original radius, slowly expanding the circle by taking new objects back to the original location, where they turned into doors. Next time, a traveller could throw the new one in the air and start from where this one was created. And so on and so forth, until today's vast web of connections was established."

Ava ran a hand through her hair, trying to fathom all she

had learned within the last half hour. "And you promise *this* isn't an April Fool's joke?" she asked.

Bruno curled his lips. "This is not a joke."

He picked up the pebble and rose. "What do you say, shall we go back? You must be itching to try out more doors."

Excitement prickled on Ava's skin. She absolutely was.

Bruno reached out a hand, and when Ava took it, he looked at her from the corner of his eye. "Where will Miss Marley go first, I wonder," he mused.

Ava smiled, raising her eyebrows. Instantly, an image of the lush, rolling hills below Costa Rica's Arenal Volcano came to her mind, but she pushed it aside.

Unlike the innkeeper, she was nowhere near prepared to revisit childhood memories.

6

BUCKET LIST

"So, this isn't Zanzibar right now?" Ava asked as she sipped a mimosa from a champagne flute, looking out the window at the Atlas's tropical garden, where Captain snoozed in the shade of the fig tree.

Bruno crossed his legs over, bouncing his foot. "Nope," he said and took a sip of his own drink.

After returning to the hotel, he had fetched the Book of Doors from reception, suggesting they take a seat in the living room for more instructions. He'd also insisted on serving 'something a little stronger' to calm the nerves.

"Couldn't we use this whole travel network for good?" Ava asked as they sat on the cushioned bench of a sweeping bay window, Bruno's favourite place in the house. "Just think of the possibilities if everyone travelled like this!"

She also couldn't help but imagine shipping coffee beans through the hotel. The possibilities were mind-boggling.

Bruno refilled his flute from a carafe. "The Atlas doesn't operate on a grand scale like that," he said. "Remember the house rules? You can't tell anyone about the hotel, let alone bring guests to the premises. The gate simply wouldn't appear for them. And think of all the evil out there, too. Wars have been started over much less."

"But then what's the purpose of it? If we can't use this place to do good, what's the point?"

"I didn't say you can't do good using the doors. On the contrary, there are lots of ways in which Atlas guests make a difference, you'll see.

"Now, I strongly suggest you stick to the book." Bruno tapped the Book of Doors in his lap. "Don't just pick any object and toss it. Because some of them can be tricky." The innkeeper reached for a delicate object on a coffee table. "This one, for example, is a south-pointing spoon and one of the older doors I could date. It stems back to the Han dynasty and the first Chinese seafarers. But unfortunately, walking through this door will drop you somewhere in the middle of the Pacific Ocean. When I tossed it, I plunged right into a shiver of sharks. Couldn't get out of there fast enough. To think if I hadn't caught that spoon, and it had sunk to the bottom of the ocean... Guter Gott." Bruno shuddered like a goose ruffling its feathers.

"Who would make a door like that?" Ava took the spoon with two fingers.

"I assume it was an accident," Bruno said, biting off the tip of a strawberry. "Maybe they tried to make a new door from a sailboat, thinking it would take them back to their deck the next time, only it didn't. Doors seem to ignore your mode of transport. They only take your geographical location into account. Something to keep in mind when you make your own."

"What other dangerous ones should I be aware of?"

"This one here is another good example." Bruno reached for what looked like a mini version of the *Venus de*

Milo. "Takes you straight past the queue of the Louvre, right in front of the *Mona Lisa*. A favourite for every culture buff. But you can't use it after closing hours – I mean, you could, of course. But if you did, you'd set off the alarms and probably end up in a Parisian jail if you don't catch that souvenir quick enough. So be careful with that one."

He put the statue back with care. "You'll find a list of all the dangerous doors at the back of the book. When in doubt – always refer to the book." He touched his wristwatch, an elegant gold piece with a thin leather band, reading the time as if performing an eye test.

"Mein lieber Herr Gesangsverein, is that the time?" he said, finishing his drink. "I'm afraid you'll have to excuse me. I have a prior commitment I must attend to." He stood, suddenly in a bit of a rush, and Ava followed him back to reception.

"It would be great if you could do breakfast tomorrow morning, by seven a.m. hotel time. I will be up to show you the ropes. But other than that, I expect you to be gone for most of the weekend," he said over his shoulder. "Just for your info, though: every Saturday is movie night if you care to join us. It would be a great opportunity to meet everyone. I make original Napolitano pizza, there will be bottomless Chianti, and it was Molly's turn to choose the movie. We'll be watching *Casablanca*."

He grabbed two bum bags from behind the reception counter, strapping one around his waist and handing Ava the other, which she took, albeit with confusion.

"I insist every guest wear one of these," the innkeeper explained, unzipping the bag resting in Ava's open palms. "Not very fashionable, but I don't want to risk losing any of you to curfew. In here, you'll find a stopwatch. Please always remember to start it as soon as you leave the hotel."

"Can't I just use my phone to keep track of time?" Ava asked, not exactly thrilled to look like a tourist everywhere she went.

"Never trust smartphones with something as important as this," said Bruno. "Batteries die, things get dropped in the loo. Believe me, these stopwatches are the way to go. They are indestructible." He popped the watch back into Ava's bag. "Now, there's enough space in here to store your door's object. Please also keep your passport on you at all times, just in case. And finally: some pocket money." He unzipped the back pocket, revealing a few bills. "It's US dollars, which you'll get by with in most places. If not, just go through this door." Bruno pointed out a holed coin on a string next to the counter. "It will bring you to an exchange bureau in New York City. They've got decent rates."

Ava jerked her head back. "I can't take your money," she said, handing the bum bag back.

"Oh, but it's not my money. The Atlas provides for its guests," Bruno said, cupping her hands in his.

"But where does it come from?"

Bruno turned to the counter and gestured at a box on the shelf. "Each day, that box fills up with a certain amount of money. It's not riches, but it's enough to get all guests through the day with ease."

"That's impossible."

Bruno furrowed a brow. "You can believe tossing a fridge magnet allows you to travel halfway across the world in a second, but you think it's impossible that box fills up with money every day?" He drew said magnet from his pocket, holding it between his index finger and thumb. It was well-worn and shaped like an ice cream cone, the scoops' paint fading from what appeared to be excessive use.

"Well... *yes*," said Ava, still repelled by the idea of taking someone else's money and still unconvinced this type of magic existed, Atlas or not.

Bruno rechecked his watch. "You surprise me, Miss Marley... I mean, Ava," he said, then zipped up her bum bag as if prepping his kid for school. "Now I really must go." He folded his hands in prayer to apologise, the fridge magnet still between his fingers.

"Anything else I should know before you go?" Ava asked and watched Bruno fix his hair in a mirror on the wall.

He sighed, considering a thought. "Not for now, my dear. You've taken in a lot today. Go enjoy yourself. The rest will come to you soon enough."

"So, where are you off to?"

But the innkeeper had already tossed the fridge magnet, and before he could say another word, he caught it and was gone.

Ava pounced on the Book of Doors as soon as he had vanished, flicking through the pages like a kid locked up in a candy store. Where should she go first? What had she always wanted to see? Where would be the most fun? It was as easy as clicking her heels, yet as hard as picking a single star in the sky. Overwhelmed by her choices, Ava closed her eyes, flicked to a random page and tapped her finger on the paper. Opening her eyes again, her heart thrummed inside her chest. But when she looked down at the page, the excitement escaped like air from an old, floppy balloon.

"Sheffield?" Ava blurted out, a sour taste on her tongue as if she'd bitten into a foul strawberry. "I don't think so."

She closed her eyes once more, turning over a chunk of pages to get as far away from Sheffield as she could. Her finger landed on the new page with a decisive thud, but as she squinted to see the destination next to her fingernail, her anticipation yielded an onset of old familiar sadness.

Costa Rica.

"You've got to be kidding me," Ava sighed. Out of all the destinations stacked in Bruno's book, her finger just *had* to land on this one. She couldn't help but curse the odds, bristling at the lifetime of memories those two words evoked. It was almost as if the Atlas knew.

Ava had come to live in Costa Rica, her mother's home country, at nine years old, right after her parent's divorce. Ethan had been a no-show throughout her teenage years, but it had been the happiest time of her life, growing up on her aunt's coffee farm deep in the Monteverde cloud forest.

No other place held so much for her. So much joy, yet so much pain. It was here where she had, at last, fallen in love with the wonderfully vibrant world of coffee, far removed from the business that broke her family. It was here where she had laid her mother to rest when cancer claimed her so long before her time.

Ava shuddered and turned a page in the Book of Doors, shaking off memories like flies. She didn't want to go there, not now. This was supposed to be an escape from reality, not a deep dive into it. And yet, as she turned the page, she could practically hear the song of the clay-coloured robin, smell the plumerias, and taste the freshly roasted coffee. Indeed, trying not to think of Costa Rica was as futile as being told not to imagine a bright yellow lemon. The country had left an indelible mark on her.

She gave a deep sigh and closed her eyes a third time, giving the Atlas one more chance to sweep her elsewhere as she planted her finger on yet another page.

"Now, that's better," she said to Captain as she opened her eyes. The dog had come back inside, begging for cuddles. She gave him plenty, comforting him as much as herself. He followed her into the living room, where she searched for the right souvenir. Bruno had done a thorough job; even the exact whereabouts of the objects inside the hotel were documented in his inventory.

Ava opened the top drawer of an antique dresser, revealing an expansive collection of explorer tools: a pith helmet, a compass, a pocketknife, spent rifle cartridges, a leather-bound diary, and lastly, the thing she'd been looking for. A pair of green binoculars, just small enough to fit into her open palm. Ava turned them over in her hand, and her heartbeat picked up again, spurred by the thrill of the unknown.

She exhaled loudly. This was even more nerve-wracking than her first solo drive after getting her license at eighteen. It was strange not having the innkeeper here to guide her.

"All right, Captain. Nothing to it," she said. But the dog better stay behind for this next adventure. He might not be safe. Ava tossed the binoculars just high enough to be aloft. When she caught them with both hands, they swept her away with that forceful pull she had almost gotten used to by now.

The moment she arrived at her destination, her feet struggled to grip the ground, slipping on what appeared to be slimy rocks. Roaring thunder droned inside her ears, and within a split second, Ava was soaking wet. She maintained her balance on the slippery rock just long enough to fling her head around and see the place. Standing on the edge of the mighty Niagara Falls, she was enshrouded in clouds of water spray, a field of rainbows surrounding her as sunlight scattered in the droplets. It was a beautiful sight. Or at least it would have been, had Ava not tumbled to her death as the violent current swept her off her feet!

Flailing about, she tried to fight gravity, but it won. Ava tilted backwards in slow motion, her "whoa, whoa, whoa" like the undertone to her windmilling arms. Clasping her fingers around the binoculars, her gaze turned upwards, and she spotted a bird in the sky, getting smaller dangerously quickly the further she fell. In a last-ditch attempt, Ava passed the binoculars from one hand to the other, barely letting go of them as she soared into the abyss, hoping – praying – it would be enough to take her back.

The familiar pull on her arm triggered a wave of relief so big it flooded her eyes with tears. As soon as she reappeared in the hotel living room, Captain came running, howling like a wolf.

Ava collapsed onto the floor, water dripping from her clothes, forming a puddle around her. "Okay, I nearly died just then," she gasped, pushing the binoculars away and holding the dog for comfort instead. "I need to give this some more thought."

Captain gave a sharp bark as if he agreed.

A SHORT WHILE LATER, Ava stood in the Atlas hallway in dry clothes, Bruno's bum bag strapped around her waist, a half-circle of souvenirs around her feet – her own personal train, only each wagon would drop her off at a new destination. It had taken her the better part of the midday, but eventually, she had curated the perfect itinerary to a tee. The whole thing was much more complicated than she'd thought because she had to consider the time zones. She also couldn't turn to the internet for her research; within the Atlas, her phone picked up neither Wi-Fi nor phone signal.

"Time to work off the good, old bucket list," she told Captain, but the dog was snoozing in a patch of sunlight on the veranda, not even looking up at the mention of his name.

Starting her stopwatch, Ava tossed up the first object with ease. There was little chance this one would put her life in danger, but it might just take her back in time.

The instant she caught the miniature Eiffel Tower, the ground began to tremble from a subway train rattling past. Metro-scent wafted up to her nose, warm and rubbery. Mopeds honked as they trundled over cobbles, their engines humming through the streets like bumblebees.

With a fresh but pleasant breeze in the air and a puffy clouded sky above, Montmartre in spring had to be the most cliché place she could have chosen. But who cared? The heart wanted what the heart wanted. And sometimes, clichés existed for a reason. She had come to Paris with her parents as a child once, pre-divorce, and images of the winding streets and the iconic Sacré-Cœur Basilica, be it on social media or in movies, would forever remind her of a time when she had been young enough to still believe that her parents were headed for a happy ending.

She'd wondered what would happen if she popped up out of nowhere in a crowded place such as this one, worried she might land in someone's lap or scare a dog-walker to death. But tourists and Parisians alike didn't even seem to notice the woman who had appeared amongst them out of thin air.

Ava sauntered down the pavement (as one did in Paris). On the balconies above, the first geraniums were budding. Crates of fruit and vegetables were piled up outside a cute magasin, where a morose truck driver loaded off even more fresh apricots, asparagus, and green beans, his grumpy mood but another vibrant colour to Ava's French palette. The smell of newspapers, fresh off the press, wafted over from one of the last historic newsstands not yet replaced, its ornate, dark-green roof sitting like a crown atop neatly stacked magazines and postcards, cigarettes and souvenirs.

Gradually, she made her way uphill, getting lost in the crowds. No matter which megacity, locals seemed to avoid the tourist hotspots for the most part. The inflated prices and overall slowness of foreigners kept them at bay. But Ava had never subscribed to that. Back in London, she loved getting lost around Piccadilly Circus or Covent Garden on the weekends, dropping her pavement-weaving skills as she melted in with the slow folk, listening to all the different languages swooshing past, seeking a break from reality as she pretended to be one of them.

Entering Le Place du Tertre, a tree-shaded market square where artists drew caricatures of tourists beneath umbrellaed stalls, the rich boulangerie scent of bread and pastries made Ava's mouth water.

She had decided not to use the money in her bum bag unless it was an emergency, so when she saw the fresh croissants piled up in the glass case, with their perfectly crescent shape and their baked-to-perfection golden colour, she headed for the next best exchange bureau to swap some of her own pounds for euros.

Stepping inside the boulangerie with a handful of bills a short while later, she ordered "Un croissant, s'il vous plait." She also stopped off at another newsstand, purchasing a disposable camera and a copy of *Numéro* magazine – acts of defiance against modernity she figured the Atlas would appreciate.

As she strolled past old city walls and half-timbered houses clad in ivy, the magazine folded under her arm, she indulged in her croissant, crumbs sticking to her cheeks as she took in all the little things that made Paris *Paris* (always pronounced the French way in her head). The tangy smell of cheese wafting from a fromagerie. The hidden windows nestled in house corners, each holding secrets to be mused about. The laced-up shoes hanging from the powerlines – was it art or a cruel joke? The corner cafés filled with people, all but extras of Ava's vie-en-rose fantasy – hard to imagine they had real lives with jobs, and bills, and worries.

At last, the white domes of Sacre-Coeur came into view, gleaming above worn-out stairs, which made Ava wonder how many feet it would have taken for them to wear down like a river smoothing stones over centuries. She joined the tourists resting their tired explorer legs, the city's rooftops sprawling at their feet, the Eiffel Tower appearing no bigger than the mini-version in her bum bag.

Sitting cross-legged on a patch of grass, she listened to an accordionist and flicked through her magazine, looking at the pictures rather than reading the articles. Her high school French left much to be desired, and soon she found herself gazing around instead, soaking up the warmth of the sun on her face until something caught her eye.

A nearby tourist, Scandinavian by the looks of him, was sipping Marley's Coffee, but to her surprise, from one of the original, edible cups, the old familiar logo burnt into the side. Ava hadn't seen these in years. Ethan had stopped using them long ago, prioritizing profit over sustainability – or so she had thought. She was tempted to track down the café and investigate but dismissed the idea. Her father had probably brought them back in another cunning move to silence some environmental organisation. Or, on a less accusing note, maybe France simply had different regulations. With a global empire like MCC, regional alterations from the "brand bible" were common. Marley's Cafés in

Japan had interiors heavily influenced by Shintoism, the country's religion, while in India, they primarily served tea.

Ava's Mum and Dad had designed the first one together, the now world-famous flagship store in London's Soho. With her Costa-Rican roots and his engineering genius, Luciana and Ethan had complemented each other like coffee and cake during those first blissful years of marriage, or so the sugar-coated brand story went. Sharing a passion for a good quality brew, they had invented the perfect coffee maker, 'Marley's Press', which Ethan had designed, and Luciana had tried and tested until it was perfected. That part, at least, was true. Ava still remembered how freshly ground coffee was the signature scent of their tiny family apartment in Kensington, how the kitchen table was always cluttered with coffee bags and her dad's tools, and how, from her bedroom, she could hear her parents discussing ideas until long after midnight, pumped from all the coffee they'd sampled throughout the day.

When they'd finally gotten a loan to open their own café, Marley's had occupied a niche in the market, sourcing only the best Arabica beans from hand-selected plantations, and serving only the highest-quality black coffee, paired with a selection of Costa Rican sweet pastries, traditionally served during the country's afternoon cafico hour. Stemming from Luciana's family recipes, fruit-filled empanadas, arroz con leche rice pudding, and coconut flan were only some of the treats the Soho shop used to serve.

However, when a couple shared not only their private life but also a business, friction can abound. As long as Ava had been around, she could hardly remember a time when her parents had not been quarrelling. Their divorce had terminated not only their marriage but also their business partnership. With the signing of the papers, Ethan had bought Luciana out.

She had henceforth dedicated all her energy to her family's coffee farm in Costa Rica; he had begun upscaling. Although started as a contra-movement to fast-food coffee shops, under Ethan's solo leadership, Marley's had rapidly become popular in the UK, soon expanding into European countries, and from there, into the entire world, falling into the jaws of capitalism quicker than you could brew a cuppa.

The edible cups had become only one of the many ideas Ethan had ditched since taking the company public, amongst them the original slogan 'No froth, just coffee.' Nowadays, Marley's served cappuccinos and lattes just like any other joint, and the beans had long ceased to be sourced from the small, owner-run plantations Luciana had first made introductions to (although Marley's PR team did a fabulous job at hiding the fact). Ava had loved the old Marley's and still remembered it well. She had never understood how Ethan could turn it into a generic fast-food chain that had lost all its character.

Frustrated that the issue had found a way to creep into her mind again, she got up, dusting off the grass, intent to visit *Le mur des je t'aime*. But when a sudden rain shower forced the people indoors or below the trees, she took it as her exit sign. She tossed the accordionist a coin with one hand and the mini-Eiffel Tower into the air with the other, ending her French mini-holiday in a rush. There was, however, something delightful about coming and going as she pleased. Now she could literally turn her back on any given storm.

Back at the Atlas, Ava wasted no time before she set off again, swapping one souvenir for the next like a juggler tossing oranges. After all, a whole world was out there waiting to be explored, and now she really craved the distraction. For the remainder of the day, she burnt through places like wildfire through a hay field. She watched the sunrise at Machu Picchu and the sunset at the Lost City of Petra within the span of an hour, was chased from the Taj Mahal by indignant guards, as it was closed on Fridays and reserved for prayer, and mixed up a.m. with p.m. in China, arriving at the Great Wall way past midnight, which was strange but delightful as she had it all to herself. She headed to Acapulco for an early dinner (which was lunchtime in Mexico) at the cantina where Mel used to work, and after devouring her tacos and a michelada every bit as lethal as Mel's mean ones, she watched cliff-divers at La Quebrada plunging into the Pacific. To finish off her day, she joined a baby turtle liberation ceremony at the beach.

It was only long after midnight, hotel time, that Ava reappeared at the Atlas and found the darkened hallway eery and quiet. She felt exhausted but, at last, fulfilled, like she'd just finished hiking up a steep mountain. Cicadas buzzed outside, and a subtle snoring resounded from behind room two as she tip-toed up the stairs and down the hall to her own room. Someone had come in to close the shutters and let down a mosquito net, which made the bed look like something straight out of a fairy tale. A bedtime candy rested on the pillow. Ava unwrapped it and popped it into her mouth. Chewing on salted caramel fudge, she collapsed into bed with her clothes still on. A whole lifetime of memories flashed before her eyes. Yet she had collected them in barely even a day.

A pretty *good* day. Probably the best one she'd had in a long time. And as Ava dozed off into exhausted sleep, she wondered if she should ever pick up the threads of her old life. Or if she even wanted to.

7

RUNNING ON EMPTY

The box sat on the shelf as inconspicuously as any other box. It was a plain box made from pinewood, and when you opened the lid, it gave a squeak, as if to ward off any pickpockets trying their luck. Ava had spent the last fifteen minutes staring at the box, leaning over the reception counter ever so often to check the insides. But every time she did, it had remained as empty as a brand-new piggy bank.

Gentle sunbeams broke in from the windows just as the garden birds began their morning song. She had woken up early without setting the alarm; her body seemed confused from all the time zone hopping.

Giving up on the box when it refused to work its magic, she consulted the Book of Doors, selecting a hand-woven jewellery basket, which she retrieved from the living room. She tossed it in the air for a quick trip to Ethiopia – the alleged birthplace of coffee. The Atlas travel network in the country was still rudimentary, so she took a stroll through the highlands, passing villagers herding goats and school-children on the way home until she found a coffee plantation, where she purchased a bag of Gesha beans – the most sought-after coffee on the market, known to score exorbitant bidding prices at auction. For a coffee enthusiast, the Atlas was a dream come true. After all, the fresher the roast, the better a cup would turn out. With the coffee beans, she also purchased an enamel cup to take back to the hotel, thus turning it into a door for future purchases. Back at the Atlas, she couldn't resist a test and threw the cup in the air. Sure enough, it dropped her right where she'd just been, at the entrance of the coffee plantation. She added the cup to Bruno's inventory, pleased with her newfound magical powers, then headed for the kitchen to sort out breakfast.

In the kitchen, a massive wooden table decorated with a fruit bowl took centre stage, the surface scarred and speckled from decades of knife edges and spilt drinks, the chairs a patchwork of styles and colours. Apothecary cabinets with brass handles lined the far wall, shelves with blue-and-white crockery another. A traditional cast iron stove rested in the corner, so impressive that it seemed to have a soul, and a say. Copper pots and cast-iron skillets sat on the shelf above, surrounded by all kinds of jars, filled and labelled with spices and herbs. On the countertop, remnants of what must have been last night's cocktail hour: orange peels and ginger ale cans, bottles of spiced rum and Cointreau.

Tiptoeing over the mosaic floors, Ava opened a window to let in the morning breeze. She cleaned up the counter, replacing the booze with the fresh coffee beans and a French press she found on a shelf.

It took some tries to get the stove to work, but eventually, she managed to put water to a boil in a crimson kettle, which looked more like a steam locomotive.

Before it began to bubble, Ava tossed up a castanet for a

quick fruit haul in Spain, where she picked some strawberries to make a fruit salad with the apples, bananas, and mangos from the bowl on the kitchen table. Opening drawers, each creaking with age as she slid them open, she found a knife, spoons, and cereal bowls, and arranged them on the table, together with some cheeses and a loaf of Bruno's home-baked sourdough. She ground the coffee beans in a handheld grinder and poured them into the French press, just when the boiling water provoked a whistle. Ava rushed to the stove, removing the kettle to stop the noise just as the kitchen door swung open.

"I thought I heard someone in here. Guten Morgen." The innkeeper leaned against the doorframe, a tired smile on his face and dark shadows under his eyes. "Did you have a good time yesterday?" He walked inside, putting the rum and Cointreau bottles back into a well-stocked liquor cabinet.

"The best time," said Ava as she poured hot water into the press.

"And did you... did you notice any strange occurrences while you were out there?"

Ava looked up, wrinkling her nose. "What, you mean besides the obvious?" She chuckled as she stirred the brew. "I'm sorry about the noise, by the way. I didn't know where anything was. Did I wake you?"

"Don't worry. I dozed off in an armchair by the TV last night – a *Godfather* marathon. My neck thanks you for it." He rolled his shoulders back and stretched. "Besides, I'm one of those people who don't need much sleep." The innkeeper sat down at the table. He took off his glasses and wiped his eyes. "Not since I came to this place, anyway. My inner clock has all but given up on me."

"How did you end up at the Atlas?" Ava asked, searching

for coffee cups. "I guess there was no ad in the papers for the innkeeper gig?"

"On the top shelf to your right," he said, pointing at a selection of handmade pottery mugs. "Well, I used to work down in the mines in the German Ruhr valley. My wife's brother got me the job at an early age. But I never liked it. So, I quit and went back to school. Lehrer-Ausbildung. I became a language teacher and found work with the Goethe-Institut. They sent me all across the world to teach German and Italian, and later English.

"Anyway, it happened during a stint in Thailand that the yellow gate appeared for me. One rainy Monday morning on a beach in Koh Chang... Now, when was that?" Bruno considered the ceiling as if it were a calendar. "Maybe eight or nine months ago?"

Ava retrieved two coffee mugs and poured the fresh brew into them, passing one to the innkeeper. "Do you take it black?"

"As black as my soul," he said, taking the mug by the handle with a wink. "Thank you. Oh, and how about some biscotti? I baked some yesterday." He put the mug down and rose, fetching a cookie jar from the counter.

Ava considered the innkeeper as he unscrewed the lid, handed her a biscotti, then dipped another one in his coffee. "And what did you make of all this when you first arrived?" she asked. "Did you handle it as badly as me?"

"Ach, you were *fine,* Liebling." Bruno wiped her words from the air. "As for me, when I got here, only one other guest had already checked in. I believe her name was Dawn. She used to occupy room five. But I only called her il fantasma – the ghost. I rarely saw her. Maybe once or twice, but only for a split second whenever she swapped doors."

"What happened to her?" Ava remembered the study

notes Bruno had so swiftly removed from room five. She also couldn't help but worry what might happen to her if the ghost returned. Would the hotel kick Ava out?

Bruno clicked his tongue. "Non sicuro. I'm not sure. I hope she's still out there, doing her thing. But truth be told, it has been months since I got a glimpse of her."

"You don't think she missed curfew, do you?" Ava sipped on her coffee, noticing sweet hints of florals and honey.

"Heavens, I hope not. I really hope not." Bruno nodded absentmindedly. "I do feel bad because I never saw her long enough to give her a stopwatch, you know? I don't know *how* she kept track of time." The innkeeper wetted a finger and picked a few biscotti crumbs from the table. "Anyway," he sighed, "I never *accepted* the position, you see? But with il fantasma always gone, there was simply no one here to manage the place. By the time new guests arrived, I was the only one with a vague idea of what was going on." Bruno took a sip of coffee, and steam soared up inside his mug. "This is good stuff," he remarked, admiring the brew through fogged-up glasses.

"Oh. Yeah. I'm a bit of a coffee snob, I'm afraid. This one's from Ethiopia."

"Molto bello," the innkeeper said. "I could get used to this."

"So, but you like it here, you say?" Ava asked, if anything, to direct the conversation away from her.

"*Love* it. This is my home now. I will never leave," replied Bruno and put his cup down. "But what about you, cara? Could you see yourself sticking around for a while?"

"I mean, who wouldn't, right? This is the best thing ever." Ava looked around the kitchen but noticed she didn't sound as enthusiastic as she'd wanted to. She stroked the cup's rim and said, "But you know... if I do, Bruno, I should probably go back to London and take care of a few things first." The mere thought of confronting Ethan instantly made her chest tighten. She didn't even know why she wanted to. Given how he'd behaved, she should feel more than justified in letting his deadline slip by without a second thought.

"Sì, claro. I understand." The innkeeper folded one leg over the other, tapping his foot restlessly. There was a silence then, filled with biscotti crunching and coffee slurping. "Why don't you leave that for a couple more days, though?" Bruno suggested with an impish grin. "Just go out there. Have some fun this weekend. When was the last time you got to travel the world in a day, huh? Surely, Monday morning will be soon enough to face reality."

Ava glanced at him, noticing an eagerness in his eyes that struck her as peculiar. Why did he care whether she went to London or not? She considered asking him but decided against it. His words were like the voice of mischief, tempting her to abandon her worries and just have fun. And she liked it. Besides, he had a point, didn't he? Why not let Ethan sweat a bit?

"You're right," she said, finishing her coffee. "I should go out there and enjoy myself." She rinsed her cup in the sink, then headed for the door.

"That's the spirit," said Bruno, folding his arms. "Have a lovely day, Liebling. And remember, movie night is tonight!"

Out in the hall, Ava couldn't resist another peek inside the box at reception. She squinted when she found a neat stack of twenty-dollar notes. Biting the insides of her cheeks, she gazed back at the kitchen door, behind which Bruno was now cheerfully whistling a tune.

The deep laugh-like call of a hippopotamus echoed across the azure water channels of the Okavango Delta, their banks overgrown with rich green reeds, where antelopes stalked through swampy soil and kingfishers clung to the culms, their tiny heads tilted as they scanned the water for a snack. A fish eagle throned on the tallest branch of a sprawling tree, its white chest swollen with might as it gazed across a dapple-shaded lagoon strewn with water lilies.

It was almost midday in Botswana, but the hot and humid air was made bearable by a cool breeze. Ava sat high up in a treehouse that served as a viewing platform for a nearby safari lodge. She was giddy with joy. Twenty metres from her, a herd of at least a dozen elephants were about to cross one of the channels. Striding into the water in a single line, they kept the little ones safe in the middle. Not far away, crocodiles lurked below the surface, their yellow, slitted eyes sticking out as they waited for an opportunity to strike. Colourful wading birds with feet as long as spider legs trotted across lily pads, pushed aside by mighty trunks and legs.

Soon, the water reached up to the mother elephants' shoulders while the babies had all but disappeared, save for their tiny trunks, which they raised like submarine periscopes. Emerging from the water on the other side, right below Ava's dangling feet, the grown-ups flung their heads around nervously to assess the danger. Maybe they'd sniffed out a lion pride or possibly even Ava atop the treehouse. The youngsters, however, couldn't care less. Trumpeting uncontrollably, they chased one another, flopping their fluffy trunks about, splaying their fuzzy ears to appear bigger to their cousins.

Ava snapped photos with her disposable camera, her heart at breaking point as it struggled to cope with the cuteness. A deep rumble resounded from the largest adult, which seemed to gather the entire herd, and they trotted off into the undergrowth, their pathways meandering through the reeds like the palm lines of a hand.

It was a tough act to follow, but somehow the serene rice terraces of Bali pulled it off. As Ava walked at twilight along a rural trail speckled with ducks, the lush green fields around her rustled under a pleasant drizzle of rain. She took off her sandals, grounding her body as she felt the wet earth beneath her feet and filled her lungs full of the peace and calm the Indonesian island was renowned for.

Behind a bend, the tangerine shingle rooftops of Ubud emerged from steep jungle ravines, illuminated by the moon now pushing through the clouds. Travellers throughout the decades had been lured in by this laid-back creative hub at the foothills of the Balinese mountains – many of them settling here for good. Ava had always wanted to uncover what all the fuss was about.

As she entered the fabled town, ancient trees towered over the sidewalks, their roots like curtains dangling from the branches. An ocean of scooters lined the narrow streets. Laundrettes were shoved in next to massage parlours. World-renowned clothing stores rubbed shoulders with ancient temples, their doorsteps guarded by moss-covered stone dragons and adorned with palm-leaf baskets filled with flowers and incense sticks, which Ava knew were offerings to the Hindu gods.

Her skin prickled with the old familiar mixture of annoyance and longing when she caught sight of the rainbow parasols of yet another Marley's Café. Watching a couple leave the store, she did a double take. They, too, drank from the original cups. Once again, she was tempted to step inside and suss it out, but she pushed on, determined to ensure Bali wouldn't turn into yet another place laden with her own nostalgia.

She strolled past restaurants bustling with digital nomads eating gado-gado for dinner as they hovered behind their laptops, their faces illuminated by the screens, their vision statements so ardent, their faces seemed to glow even brighter from them. Although maybe that was just a result of their latest juice cleanse. Mocking these people would have been too easy. Ava, however, envied them. She liked to imagine they all worked on some passion project to make the world a better place. They seemed so free, so purpose-ful, so driven. So not like Ava. The only thing that drove her was the gales of a monstrous legacy breathing down her neck, pushing her yonder like a leaf on the wind, aimlessly floating about.

She entered a warung and secured the last free seat on a bar stool at an open window, trying to blend in, picturing herself living here. There was much to love about this lively, trendy town. Ubud practically oozed mindfulness. A flyer on the table advertised a "Green School" in the nearby jungle, and many shops and restaurants in the area priori-tised sustainability. It made sense, really, that Marley's would use the old, eco-friendly cups here, Ava caught herself thinking. But there was so much else that could be done, so many ideas Luciana had always spoken about. She could practically hear her mum's voice inside her head, preaching about reducing waste, making plant-based milk the default choice, and pushing agroforestry. Boy, how Ava would love to drive this kind of development if given the chance one day. Only... she had been given the chance, hadn't she?

"Hi, what can I get you?" A waiter squeezed through the crowd and approached Ava, ready to take her order on a tablet. "Um..." She scanned the menu. "A dragon fruit chia smoothie, please?"

"Coming right up," said the waiter and disappeared into the kitchen, leaving Ava to ponder. She was about to get her phone out to arm herself against the loneliness but decided not to. Everybody else seemed way too busy to pay her much attention anyway, and perhaps it was the electrifying energy of the place, or the passion that seemed to pulse through every person here, but now a flood of innovative thoughts coursed through Ava's mind. She borrowed a pen from the girl next to her and began to eagerly scribble ideas on the Green School flyer:

- *Use biodegradable straws and utensils*
- *Reduce water waste*
- *Change to renewable energy*
- *Implement a recycling program*
- *Reduce food waste*
- *Sustainable shipping?*
- *Take company private again?*

"Hi, what can I get you?"

Ava looked up. The same waiter had appeared beside her, smiling and fluttering his eyelashes, clearly stressed but trying to gloss over it.

"A dragon fruit chia smoothie, please." Ava repeated her order patiently, knowing all too well that rush hour sucked when working in the service sector. However, even she lost patience when he appeared on her other side thirty seconds later, asking what he could get her a third time around.

"A dragon fruit chia smoothie," she said extra slowly. "It's there, on your tablet." She nodded at his tablet, to which the waiter rolled his eyes and buggered off.

Ava huffed and shook her head, turning back to her notes. But when her order still hadn't arrived fifteen minutes later, she began to wonder if the waiter needed to pick the dragon fruit in the jungle to make her damn smoothie. She looked around to find him when her gaze landed on the girl next to her. Bubbly and excited, she was speaking in Dutch to two people whose images appeared on her laptop screen – her parents, by the looks of them. Ava stole side glances at the screen. The father wore one of those hideous but kind of adorable call-centre headsets; the mother stood behind him, arms twined around his neck, listening in as best she could, both smiling proudly as their daughter shared her recent tales of life on the road.

But Ava couldn't watch for long. The scene stirred an unexpected ache in her chest, leaving her hollow, and she felt the urge to keep moving. She shot up when the waiter approached her.

"Can I get you anything?"

"Are you *kidding* me?" Ava burst out and left in a huff. "Bloody idiot," she murmured.

She cast up a dragon figurine and returned to the Atlas, walking straight through another door, seeking distraction in yet another place. But the aching feeling kept haunting her long after she had appeared in Tokyo, where she had takeaway sushi for lunch and tried to appreciate the cherry blossoms, illuminated by street lanterns as it was almost midnight in Japan. She walked around for hours, not just in Tokyo but in a succession of cities across the world she hadn't even planned to visit this weekend. She roamed Central Park in New York City and went on a street art tour in Berlin, watched deer in Sweden's far north and penguins in Cape Town's south, landed briefly on Mount Everest as well as on top of the Jesus statue in Rio de Janeiro. One minute she was freezing cold; the next, beads of sweat pearled on her forehead. In one place, it was dark as night; in another, the sun stood at its peak.

By late afternoon hotel time, she disappeared into a crowd at Santa Monica Pier. Excited screams resounded from the rollercoasters, seagulls stole French fries from unwary tourists, and kids ran barefoot over the planks, hair wet with salt water, hands sticky with candy floss.

Ava didn't pay much attention to any of it. The ache had now grown into a fully formed longing, and she was literally running on empty. What was wrong with her that she had grown tired of this so quickly? Why couldn't she enjoy herself? It was such a gift, wasn't it? Skipping the ordeal to get to all these places under normal circumstances. The airport security checks, the queues at immigration, the traffic-clogged streets, the weeklong jetlag.

But maybe that was just it. Maybe the ordeal was necessary, a rite of passage that was required to make a trip worthwhile.

Or maybe, she thought, *just maybe, running isn't the answer.*

Ava sank onto a bench, allowing for the emptiness to catch up at last, to consume her so fully, she felt like she had disappeared, like no one around her even knew she was there.

She scanned the pier for the rainbow parasols before she'd even made a conscious choice.

It was time to step inside.

8

SPIDER MONKEY

Ava didn't know if Marley's had a café at the pier, but she would have taken any bet on it. In every major tourist hotspot across the globe, you could count on finding one, and nine times out of ten in prime real estate. Not to her surprise, she spotted the iconic parasols only a short while later, slap bang in the middle of the Ocean Front Walk.

Walking up to the café was like walking up to the front door of her own home. However, not in the happy sense of the word. For Ava, home had never been just a place of happiness. It was one of history, of fights around the dinner table and pillows soaked in tears. Of hurt feelings and of thoughts unspoken, of regrets and hopes, traditions and memories. The coffee shops, sprinkled across the globe like breadcrumbs, bearing her last name and her mother's face, were constant reminders of all that she'd lost, the good and the bad.

As Ava approached the entrance, her heart began to race with anticipation. It had been almost a decade since she last stepped foot in one. She had heard rumours of a complete overhaul, a modernization Ethan had undertaken to keep up with the times, and – despite herself – she was curious to see it for herself. Would she recognise anything, or would she feel like a stranger in the place that had once been so familiar to her?

Her breath caught in her throat when she stepped through the doors and looked around. It was like stepping back in time to her childhood. Nothing, absolutely nothing, had changed. As if she'd never left this earth, Luciana was literally everywhere.

She was in the bossa nova music and the ornate silver trays. She was in the comfy hammocks and the hanging basket chairs, piled with colourful pillows. She was in the sweeping mahogany counter and the dark wooden tables. She was in the lush ferns spreading their fingers from the ceiling.

Ava's heart skipped a beat as she looked around, her eyes darting from one familiar object to another. She could feel the memories flooding back, and a lump formed in her throat. It was as if her mother's spirit still lingered in the air, enveloping her in a warm embrace.

For a moment, she stood frozen in the doorway, trying to process what was happening. But when someone came in behind her, she approached the counter and joined the queue, taking in every detail as if seeing it for the first time. When it was her turn to order, she hadn't given a single thought to what she even wanted.

"How can I help you today?" A young man – Mike, according to his name tag – was busy preparing five of the cylindric Marley Presses simultaneously, brows pushed together in concentration. He barely looked up as he poured hot water into the presses (hot, not boiling), but he did pull off an amiable service voice.

"Um... Can I get a pot of black coffee, please?"

"Sure. What would you like? We've got a mild Mocha Java with lovely notes of cocoa, a nice and strong Black and Tan from Colombia, or maybe my personal favourite: The Santa Monica Blend with Caturra and Bourbon varietals – it tastes rich and full, with hints of caramel, hazelnut, and berries." Mike gave each tray the usual finishing touches (arranging teaspoons and saucers in perfect symmetry, decorating each with some coffee beans), then sent a waitress on her way with the orders.

"I'll have the Black and Tan, please, and a coconut flan," Ava said and paid with her credit card. Even the food menu was back to the original.

"Thank you very much. You're our spider monkey today," Mike said and handed Ava a replica of the animal on a stick. "Please pop this into the hole of your table, and we'll bring your order as soon as it's ready."

Robotically, she reached for the token. It was another one of Luciana's ideas, to assign each order a miniature version of a Costa Rican animal or flower. As Ava crossed the café in search of a table, she spotted jaguars, toucans, blue morpho butterflies, scarlet macaws, tapirs, leatherback sea turtles, caimans, mariposa flowers, hibiscus, and of course, the country's national flower, a purple orchid named Guaria Morada. Deeming the tokens impractical, Ethan had replaced them with numbers immediately after Luciana had left the company, or so Ava had thought.

She found a table in the far corner by the window, where she cosied up in an armchair, still deeply puzzled. Did this mean her father had reverted everything back to the way it was before? Why? And how could he not tell her? She felt a mix of emotions – surprise, confusion, and even a hint of anger. But above all, there was a sense of nostalgia that tugged at her heartstrings. She had prepared herself for the worst, for a complete departure from the Marley's she had known and loved, but here it was, unchanged and welcoming her back with open arms.

Mike came over with her order, gently placing the coffee and flan on the table. "Sorry that took so long. Busy day – I almost forgot about you, spider monkey. Is this everything, or are you waiting for anything else?"

"I just have a question, actually," Ava said. "Do you know when they changed the concept of the café back to the original?"

Mike pulled his earlobe. "Um, I'm not quite sure what you mean. The café has been around for over ten years. To my knowledge, it hasn't changed much since. Slight alterations to the menu, yes. But other than that, it's still pretty much the same as it was."

"I see... thanks."

"Enjoy," Mike said with a wink. "The flan is extra-good today."

Ava sat at the table, sipping her coffee and enjoying spoonfuls of the coconut flan. Mike had been right, it *was* delicious. And yet, it made her feel sour. She couldn't help but wonder: Was this Santa Monica branch a one-off occurrence, or had Ethan really done the impossible – reverting his entire empire back to how it had been before going global?

Despite her love of a good cuppa, Ava left her Tan and Black unfinished – though not the flan. Stuffing her mouth with it, she tossed up the tiny Ferris wheel she'd used to get to the pier and returned to the hotel. There, she gathered a random selection of souvenirs from the cabinet in the front hall and was on the move again before she'd even swallowed the last spoonful of flan.

Within the span of an hour, she popped up in tourist hotspots around the globe – Barcelona, Moscow, Bangkok, Vancouver, Cape Town, Stockholm, Washington, DC. Everywhere she went, she scanned for the rainbow parasols, hastening inside the cafés to confirm: Luciana had never left the building. Exiting Marley's at the Dubai Mall, Ava wearily collapsed onto the pavement, feeling the heat from the sun-bleached concrete through her clothes, the chaotic symphony of car horns and foreign languages filling her ears. She couldn't believe Ethan had kept something as significant as this from her. Or did he assume she knew? And if she *had* known, would that have changed anything? Would she have taken him up on his offer? Ava felt torn. Betrayed, even. She pulled out her phone, connected to the mall's Wi-Fi, and called him before she could think better of it. Naturally, he didn't pick up, so she left him a text message: *I want to talk. When can I reach you?*

Ava returned to the hotel, her body weary from all the travelling and her mind in overdrive, trying to process all that she'd learnt. She headed straight to the bathroom, the anticipation of the warm water running down her body filling her with relief. However, as she stepped into the tub, she realised the bucket for excess water wasn't there. Frustration crept up her spine as she scanned the room for the missing item. Just as she was about to give up, her gaze caught a glimpse of yellow through the window. The bucket was in the hands of a curly-haired boy, shuffling between the flower beds outside. This had to be...

"Joao?" Ava asked minutes later when she approached the boy, who was busy repotting a banana plant.

The boy looked up, squinting as he tried to see her face against the evening sun.

"Are you the new one from room five?"

He spoke with an American accent and had a thatch of brown hair with blonde tips. A pink scar on his left eyebrow made him look particularly cheeky.

"I am indeed. My name is Ava."

"Wow, everyone's dying to meet you! We've all been wondering for a while who you'd be."

"Well, here I am. I am me." Ava showed her palms.

Joao drew a pair of hedge clippers from his belt, cutting off a bright-red flower with yellow tips.

"Welcome to the Atlas, Ava," he said and handed her the flower.

"Thank you." Ava nodded gratefully, turning the flower in her hand. "A false bird of paradise, isn't it?" She knew the flower well; it grew abundantly in Costa Rica and was another one of the tokens used for orders at Marley's. "You know, because it pretends to be a bird but isn't?"

"Heliconia rostrata, also commonly known as lobster claw. Pollinated by hummingbirds, not insects. Which is unusual," listed Joao.

"So, you know your botany, then," Ava mused. She touched the petals as if caressing a loved one's cheek. "Sadly, we don't get these kinds of flowers in London."

"Is that where you're from?"

Ava nodded. "I am indeed."

"The UK gets some unusual flowers, though, especially down south, did you know that? That's because of the Gulf Stream. Even palm trees grow in some places."

"We do indeed. Not these ones though." Ava twirled the false bird between her fingers. "They're too tropical for our climate, like coffee. Coffee only grows in the bean belt."

"What's that? The bean belt?"

"It's an interesting concept, actually, if you're into plants," Ava began, her eyes lighting up with the excitement of sharing knowledge. "You see, there are different growth zones for all kinds of plants across the world. The bean belt is one of these zones. It wraps around the earth's middle, between the Tropics of Cancer and Capricorn. This region has the perfect climate for growing coffee beans."

Joao knitted his eyebrows. "I should have known that."

"Well, now you do."

"Can you help me with this one?" Joao pointed at the banana pot, and Ava helped him carry it to a sunnier spot.

"You wanna meet my girls?" He gestured to the path that meandered through his precious gardens. As they walked, he pointed out a hibiscus here and an aloe plant there, specimens he seemed to have grown himself and was particularly proud of. Joao's eyes sparkled with excitement as he pointed towards a peculiar-looking plant. "Oh, you've got to see this one!" he exclaimed.

Ava leaned closer, trying to understand his enthusiasm. All she could see was a mess of tangled green roots sprouting just above a swampy part of the garden, clinging to the lichen-covered trunk of a rotting tree. "What's so special about it?"

With a swift motion, Joao pulled out a pocket flower guide, flipping it open to a well-worn page. "Take a look at this," he said, holding the book out to her. "I believe this is a white frog orchid. It's hard to tell without it flowering, though."

Ava took the guide, her eyes landing on the image of a snow-white orchid, its petals shaped like the jumping legs of a frog. "They are extremely rare in Florida," Joao added, his voice trailing off in reverence.

"Is that where you're from, Florida?" Ava asked, looking up from the guide. Joao nodded, his focus still on the tangled roots.

He continued, an absentminded tone in his voice, "This one could be worth a lot of money, you know."

Ava knew, albeit vaguely, that orchid enthusiasts across the globe would pay a fortune for rare specimens. Many orchids were notoriously difficult to keep alive, let alone coax into bloom. This humble cluster of roots and fungus could be the beginnings, or perhaps the remnants, of such a coveted orchid.

"I see you two are getting along." The innkeeper's voice came from the house. Ava looked up and found Bruno on the veranda, one hand on his hip, the other one swirling a glass of red. "Ava, mein Schatz, the Chianti is uncorked! Joao, the pizza is in the oven, and the movie is ready to play on the rooftop as soon as everyone has returned."

"Great, I'll have a quick shower, then I'll come help you," Ava called out to Bruno.

"No need. Helene and I have things under control... Well, Helene does, anyway." The innkeeper took a sip, then trundled off around the house corner.

Ava headed back inside, where Italian mandolin music resounded from the turntable, and a campfire smell wafted in from an open window, probably from the pizza oven. Upstairs, she checked her phone again, but there was still no reply from Ethan – which was unsurprising, seeing as she hadn't been able to pick up any signal inside the hotel. She did another quick trip to get a Wi-Fi connection – selecting a Manchester United button from the UK drawer in the living room – but Ethan still hadn't replied, not even Laura had. Irritation cursed through Ava's veins. It was one thing to want to escape, but quite another when the person you tried to escape *from* did the same to you.

Frustrated, she sent a follow-up, then returned to the hotel, where she stepped into the bathroom, yellow bucket in hand. She slipped out of her clothes and turned the faucet. Standing naked in the tub, she kept testing the water, which seemed to take even longer to heat up today. At last, it became warm, and she was about to pull the shower curtain closed when out of nowhere, a man popped up in the tiny bathroom, his nose only a hairsbreadth from her own!

Ava shrieked like a spooked owl, and the intruder jumped back and crashed into the wall behind him. A canvas rucksack slipped off his shoulder and landed on the tiles with a heavy thud. Ava grabbed the curtain to cover herself but slipped and tumbled over, tearing the curtain from the rail.

"WHAT THE HELL?" she blurted out, shivering as the cold-water bucket spilt over.

"Oh my God, I'm so sorry!" The man spun around and buried his face in his hands. "I... I used a door from in here, so that's where I returned to!"

He was about the same height and age as her, brown-skinned and black-haired, wearing olive green pants with lots of pockets and a khaki T-shirt.

"Do you mind?" Ava exclaimed when – instead of leaving – he unzipped his rucksack to check on an expensive-looking camera with a lens the size of a tank gun.

"Sorry – I'm sorry... I'm out! I'm out!" He grabbed the rucksack and headed for the door, which he slammed into before slipping out.

Ava picked herself up, one foot stuck in the bucket, bruises throbbing on her arms, shame flushing her cheeks.

She had just met Yash from India.

9

CASABLANCA

Yash sat on the bottom step of a pull-out ladder, shooting up when Ava emerged from the bathroom – this time in clothes, a maxi summer skirt with florals and a black long-sleeve T-shirt. For the first time in days, she'd also put on some make-up despite the humidity.

"I am so sorry about before." Yash clasped his hands behind his head with a show of teeth. "I cannot even tell you how much."

"Don't worry about it," Ava said, scratching an eyebrow. "I guess these things happen around here. Let's just make it a rule never to use a door in the bathroom again, agreed?"

"Agreed." He reached out a hand to her. "I'm Yash, by the way. Room two?"

"Ava," she replied and shook it. "Room five." He was actually a little shorter than her.

"I figured. We've been wondering for a while who'd fill the last spot." He stepped aside and gestured at the ladder. "Well, room five, can I buy you a free glass of wine?"

"After you," she said, pointing to her skirt.

"Course, my bad." He clapped a hand on his forehead, but a cheeky smile escaped him as he climbed ahead.

Taking his hand, Ava clambered through the hatch onto the rooftop, where fairy lights hung from a wisteria-clad pergola. A stone pizza oven rested at the far end. A bedsheet was put up on the wall opposite an ancient-looking projector. The other hotel guests sprawled across white linen couches.

"Ah, now we are complete!" Bruno exclaimed. "Alle zusammen!" He clapped his hands, then gestured at Ava. "This is Ava from London."

Bruno stepped behind the couch, touching the shoulders of the woman closest to him. "Ava, this is Molly from Queensland, Australia."

"A pleasure to meet you, dear. God bless. And how are you getting on?" Molly reached out a hand, her short-cut silver hair contrasting with her tanned, leathery skin.

"Well, it's... it's a lot to take in, but I'm managing," Ava replied.

"Do let me know if you need anything. We all help each other out around here. Makes the transition easier," Molly added with a wink. She had a grandmother's face, which instantly made you feel at home, every wrinkle a story waiting to be told. But there was also a tiredness there. Molly's shoulders seemed slumped, her handshake weak.

"And I'm Helene. From Nantes in France," the woman next to Molly introduced herself. She was maybe in her late twenties, and her French accent was just as endearing as her hazel-brown eyes, which sparked with curiosity. Her long brown hair was tied back in a ponytail. "This must be tough for you. I still remember my first day."

"Thanks," said Ava, "I don't quite know about 'tough', but I certainly feel like my head won't stop spinning." She appreciated the concern from everyone, although it struck her as slightly over the top.

"It'll get easier, I promise."

"And, of course, you've already met this rascal here." Bruno ruffled Joao's hair. The boy was leaning on Helene's shoulder, his eyes focused on an old-school Game Boy. "I'm only here for the pizza," he said.

"Joao has a problem with my movie selection," said Bruno with a smirk.

"The new *Spiderman* is out in cinemas, you know?" Joao said over his shoulder, quirking his scarred eyebrow at Bruno.

"I'm sure I have the original *Superman and the Mole People* somewhere...." Bruno stroked his chin.

"Is it in colour?"

"No, but—"

"I'm out! How long until pizza?"

"All right! Let's get this party started," Helene exclaimed with a clap of her hands. She reached for a baker's peel, which she shoved in the oven, then balanced a pizza the size of a tractor wheel over to the table, where Joao began to slice it with a pizza cutter.

Bruno fiddled with the projector but struggled to get it going, and Yash came to his aid.

By the time the opening credits of *Casablanca* appeared on the make-do screen, the innkeeper had circled back around to Ava. Her eyes were still on Joao, now busy pulling the cheese on his pizza slice with his teeth.

"When he first arrived, I was incredibly worried," Bruno said under his breath. "I mean, can you imagine? A teenager with the keys to the world?" He whistled, pouring Ava a glass of Chianti. "Luckily, he's only interested in soccer. Goes to every game all over the world. Watches his favourite players train."

"Why would the hotel even appear for a kid?" Ava took a sip of wine and grabbed a slice of pizza.

"Abusive parent. He doesn't talk about it much, but Helene manages to get through to him sometimes. I think he has a crush on her." Bruno winked. "But I was surprised, too, that the hotel appeared for children. Might have to add a whole childproof section to the Book of Doors."

"Speaking of which," said Ava, struck by a thought, "those Niagara Falls binoculars better be added to the dangerous list. I nearly drowned yesterday!"

Bruno's eyes widened with panic. He flashed his teeth, tinged purple from the wine. "That one was completely fine when I tried it. I suppose the water level fluctuates."

"Guys, do you mind? We're watching a movie here," teased Joao in a grown-up voice, likely meant to impress Helene. But as soon as Ingrid Bergman had set foot in Rick's Café, he had slumped over his Game Boy again.

And as time went by on the screen, the Chianti flowed from the bottles like a running faucet and pizza after pizza emerged from the oven. Yash borrowed Ava's disposable camera and documented the whole evening from start to the dramatic finish, when Rick Blaine once again delivered the most quotable line in cinema history, which Bruno lip-synced, his eyes swimming in tears.

"Bogart had to stand on a box for that scene to be eye to eye with Bergman! Did you know?" said Yash to everybody around.

"You would know all about that, wouldn't you?" Helene teased, and Yash winked at her with that cheeky smile of his. Ava sipped on her wine, a burst of jealousy quickening her heartbeat. But that was silly, of course. Just because he'd seen her naked didn't mean she could lay claim to the man. After all, Helene and Yash had been here for weeks. Who knew how close they'd become?

Ava shook her head, a slight movement meant to fling away the feeling. She thought she had grown cautious of the 'Yashs' of this world – the handsome, aloof type she had always fallen for in the past, the kind who always broke her heart in the end. She had never been interested in one-night stands, but it was a pattern of hers to enter these impossible semi-relationships with people she knew would not stay – probably a twisted version of her running from problems.

There was Katie, a fellow student at Oxford who left her for a woman the spitting image of Megan Fox. Terry Hays, a married man with two kids she'd met at Borough Market. Adao, the exchange student from Portugal, entangled in more love affairs than he had curls on his head...

But a year or so ago, Ava had had enough of dating, and as a result, became perpetually single. A lifestyle choice Mel had since teased her for – *her* bedroom saw so many visitors, it was hard to keep track.

"Did you know," said Molly, bringing Ava back to the present, "there actually is a Rick's Café in Casablanca." The old lady suppressed a yawn. She had dozed off during the movie.

"I might be misinformed, Molly, but I'm pretty sure the entire movie was filmed in a studio," said Bruno in a polite but assertive tone as he emptied another bottle of red.

"That is true, but a dedicated fan recreated the café," yawned Molly. "I went years ago with my daughter."

"Is it any good?" asked Ava.

"It certainly was back then." Molly sat up on the couch, grimacing slightly. "Damn old bones," she muttered, rubbing her hip.

“There’s only one way to find out, then,” Bruno said with a mischievous smile. “Meine Damen und Herren, do we fancy a nightcap in Morocco?”

“But what about the vote? I got a good one this week!” Joao called out.

“Of course, how could I forget? Achtung, everyone! Before we hop over to Morocco, and before this one is off to bed,” Bruno announced, nudging Joao in the side, “it is time for our weekly vote on a random, or should I say, *not* so random act of kindness. You all had seven days to come up with great ideas. Let’s hear them, folks!” Bruno directed his guests like a marching band.

“What’s this about?” Ava whispered to Yash.

“It’s just this fun little group activity,” Yash leaned in and whispered back. “Every Saturday, we come up with a challenge to use the Atlas for a random act of kindness somewhere in the world. Like, last week, we went to a refugee camp in Syria to drop off some much-needed supplies. The week before we made Helene’s sister quit her horrible job at this insurance company—”

“How did you do that?”

“Was brilliant, actually. We each kept crossing paths with her and staged all kinds of synchronicities to make her remember her childhood dream of starting her own fashion label. By the end of the week, she’d handed in her notice.”

“Ha!” exclaimed Ava. She loved the idea.

“Let’s hear it then, buddy,” said Helene and took the Game Boy from Joao’s hands, switching it off.

“Okay, listen up, everyone.” Joao straightened his chest. “You know how all boys – and maybe some girls – love to play soccer, right?”

“And especially this boy here.” Bruno placed a hand on Joao’s head.

"But in poor places, kids don't even have a real ball to play with, did you know? I saw this on TV once. They make their own balls from, like, trash and rags and stuff. So, I thought we could buy a whole bunch of soccer balls and deliver them to all the kids who don't have one." He looked up from underneath a pair of bushy brown eyebrows. "Obviously, we would need to deliver pumps as well," he continued, fiddling with his shoelace, "and maybe some repair kits, too. But yeah. That's... that's my idea." He hunched his shoulders and looked at his feet when everybody else remained quiet.

At last, Yash broke the silence. "Mate, no one here's even going to come forth with their own ideas after *that* pitch," he exclaimed. "Got my vote. Let's do it!" He raised a hand, and Joao broke into a relieved smile.

"It's a beautiful idea," Helene said, giving the boy a hug, which made him blush. She, too, raised her hand in favour, followed by Bruno, Molly and Ava.

"I love it," said the innkeeper. He clapped his knees as he rose. "I will provide the soccer balls, and you can all come up with a few locations each where they shall be dropped off – sounds good?"

Everybody agreed and grabbed plates, glasses, and empty bottles, carrying them to the kitchen. Bruno insisted on leaving it all in the sink to clean in the morning.

"Molly, mia cara?" He placed a hand on the old lady's shoulder. "Since it was your idea, would you like to choose the Casablanca door? I think one of the oil lamps might be best."

Molly supported her hip with both hands, squinting in pain. "You know what, friends? I think I might retire. It's getting late, and I've been to the café already, so..."

"Of course, dear. We understand." Bruno nodded. He

opened the kitchen door, leading everyone back into the hall.

"Besides, someone has to make sure this one stays in bed." Molly placed an arm over Joao's shoulder, who insisted on keeping it there as he helped her up the stairs.

"Good night, everyone," Joao said over his shoulder, and Molly gave a half-hearted wave.

"Bisous," said Helene, and Yash whispered, "Damn, what a nice kid. I was nowhere near that nice when I was his age."

"Why does that not surprise me?" mocked Helene, and Yash tickled her.

"She's pretty pale, isn't she?" Ava whispered to Bruno as they both looked after Molly. "You think she's okay?"

The innkeeper sighed. "I hope so," he said, "I hope so. But she really does not look well, does she?" He scratched his temple and adjusted his glasses, and Ava turned her head toward him. Bruno truly had embraced his innkeeper role, always concerned with his guests' wellbeing.

A SHORT WHILE LATER, Ava and the innkeeper leaned against a balustrade overlooking the indoor courtyard of Rick's Café, each holding a double whisky that lingered like a bonfire of peat on the tongue and crackled with notes of black pepper. The place was slowly emptying, as it was long past midnight in Morocco. Nevertheless, the music was still playing. A jazz musician had just finished another piece on the grand piano tucked away below an archway. Bruno joined in the applause resounding from the ornate walls like falling leaves. Ava checked her phone, trying to pick up a signal but not finding one. Frustrated, her eyes wandered across the restaurant, searching for Yash against her better judgement. The traditional, two-storied riad in the Ancienne Medina was lovingly restored and pulled off that same oasis feeling from the movie, with its international crowd enjoying the amuse-gueules, its potted palms in every corner, and its white-clothed tables lit by lamps with beaded shades. The film looped on a draped screen next to the bar, where Ava spotted Yash – fighting with Helene over the last bite of a piece of cheesecake. She averted her gaze, walling off another flush of jealousy, when she noticed Bruno looking asquint at her.

"What?" she asked, stroking her nose.

"Please stop me at any time if I'm being too intrusive," the innkeeper said to the sound of ice cubes tinkling in his glass. "But I couldn't help noticing your last name, and paired with your passion for coffee..."

"Yes?" Ava hid behind a big sip, her body stiffening.

"Any..." Bruno cleared his throat. "Any relationship to a certain coffee magnate?"

"He's my father," Ava confirmed, a burning in her throat she couldn't blame on the whisky alone.

"I thought so." Bruno leaned back, taking a long sip. "So, what's the famous Ethan Marley like? Is he truly as cunning as the British press portrays him to be?"

"He's probably worse," Ava replied, putting down the glass. "Controlling, hot-tempered, difficult to talk to." She scratched her neck, retracting. "Well... to give him some credit, though, I remember him being more fun when I was a kid. It was like having a child gave him permission to be carefree, too. But after my parents' divorce, when the business really took off, that despotic side of him took over, probably only fostered by his position in such a high-profile company. He has to be tough these days, I get that. Just wish he'd swap the CEO hat for the dad cap every once in a while."

"I see," the innkeeper said. "And when you mentioned at the garden gate the two of you weren't on good terms, was that referring to the general terms and conditions or a particular quarrel?"

"Well, let's just say he really has become the manipulative bastard everybody always assumed he was." The words came out much harsher than she had intended, and she added more softly, "He offered me a job, and now he's doing everything in his power to pressure me into accepting it."

Bruno lifted his glass, half-melted ice cubes sticking to the bottom. "Must be a terrible job," he said, tapping the bottom to make the cubes slide toward his lips.

Ava swirled her own whisky. "It's... complicated." A space opened up between them, and it was filled with questions. To her own surprise, Ava decided to fill it.

"My parents divorced when I was nine," she said as she watched couples dancing in the courtyard. "I still remember it like it was yesterday. Like, I couldn't tell you what happened last Wednesday, or if it snowed the last Christmas we all spent together, but the day they told me? I remember everything about that day. The soft pitter-patter of the rain against the kitchen window, and how dark it was in our flat despite the early morning. The sandpaper sound of my dad's fingers, stroking his chin when he broke the news. The olive-green dress my mum was wearing, and how it had a stain of coconut oil on the chest that I could smell when she hugged me... Do you know days like that, Bruno? Days you wish you could forget?"

"One," the innkeeper said. He considered a brass lantern dangling from the ceiling, returning, it seemed, to that dark place in his mind. "What did you do after your parents told you?" he asked eventually.

"I ran," Ava replied as the pianist struck up "The Girl from Ipanema." "I ran away as fast as I could. My father only caught up with me at the next tube station because I couldn't get past the barrier. A week later, I left England with my mum for Costa Rica to live with my aunt and uncle, and my dad became what you'd call the 'provider.'" She air-quoted the word. "Transferred money, had his assistant send the birthday gifts. But when I was seventeen, my mum passed away, and I went back to the UK, back to him. I think neither of us knew how to live together anymore at that point. We were like two strangers under the same roof."

"Couldn't you have stayed with your aunt and uncle?"

"I didn't want to. I don't know, after the funeral, I just wanted to get out of there. I just had to—"

"You just had to run away," the innkeeper finished her sentence. "And I would imagine you still remember everything about that terrible day, too." He put his now empty glass down and stole another side glance at her.

Ava retreated into silence, and to her relief, Bruno followed her there. It was as if he knew he had exhausted his allowance of questions for one evening. As if he knew everyone's song had a verse not meant for other ears.

"And look at me now," Ava said after a while, exhaling sharply. "Spoiled Fräulein Marley, occupying a room at the Atlas because Daddy dared to offer her half of his empire on a silver platter. How pathetic am I?" She drank a toast to herself.

The innkeeper shrugged. "Pain is pain, no matter what caused it."

"Doesn't mean I deserve to be here," Ava replied, arching her back like a cat.

"For what it's worth?" Bruno leaned in closer, his eyebrows curving into half-moons. "I'd like to believe the Atlas has a plan. It somehow pairs the right people at the right time. You might just find your place among us, you'll see."

Ava scoffed. "I can't hide at the hotel forever, Bruno."

The innkeeper turned to her in response. "Listen, there's something I've been meaning to..."

Yash appeared beside Ava, pulling her away. "Helene refuses to dance with me," he exclaimed. "Will you please do me the honour?"

"Oh, so I'm second choice—"

"First, second – who cares? Come on! We're young, we're in Morocco, we owe it to ourselves to have a dance! Rick would have wanted us to."

Yash pulled her towards him and down the stairs into the lounge. Placing a hand on her hip, he began flinging her about.

"You're a terrible dancer," Ava said when he stepped on her toes for the third time around.

"What do you mean? It's my thing," Yash replied, guiding her under his arm, which made her forehead bump his elbow, and they both laughed.

They danced until the song's end and made it all through the next one without calamities. When the pianist announced a short break, Yash suggested getting some fresh air, and Ava agreed. Not because she was in much need of air but because of the way he kept holding her hand long after they'd stopped dancing.

Stepping through the entrance curtain was like clambering back up the rabbit hole. Outside, two royal palm trees flanked the café, as did two bouncers who appeared just as tall, although much bulkier. Taxis clogged the street, waiting to pick up one of the many tourists who had flocked to Rick's that night. The café was situated right across from the city's oceanfront. The sound of crashing waves travelled through the air, which was salty and cold.

As they sat down on the sidewalk, a shiver escaped Ava.

"You cold?" Yash asked, wasting no time putting his arm around her. She allowed it, albeit with a cynical snort. She hadn't experienced this kind of forthright attention since high school. Maybe not even then. Yash was straightforward in his pursuit. No mixed messages. No vague comments. No fuss.

Despite herself, Ava let the old pattern resurface and leaned into his arm.

"So, what's your plan for tomorrow?" Yash asked, taking her hand with the casualness of a long-term boyfriend.

"I might go to London tomorrow," she replied, arranging the folds of her skirt with her free hand. "Got some unfinished business I need to take care of. Besides, these constant travels... after a while, they get a bit..."

"Boring? Yeah, I know what you mean." Yash hugged her closer. So close she could smell his shampoo. Eucalyptus, maybe, or tea tree, with a hint of sandalwood. "Happened to me after the first month or so. When the whole world is your oyster, there comes the point when the oyster starts to taste a little bland."

Ava stuck her head into the breeze as shame rose within her. It had taken her less than a weekend to reach that point.

"But listen," said Yash, "why don't you come with me tomorrow? Maybe all you need is someone to share it all with."

Ava raised her brows. "And what about Helene?"

"Frenchy?" Yash made a face that suggested he was about as attracted to Helene as he was to the palm tree they were

leaning against. “Nah, she’s like a sister to me. Besides, I’d get into trouble with my mate Joao if I made a pass at her... not that I’d want to. Really, she’s... just a friend.”

The way he said it kind of implied his interest in Ava was about more than just friendship.

“I don’t know.” Ava looked down at their interlaced fingers. “Where did you want to go, anyway?”

“I *could* tell you,” Yash said, and his lips twitched into an irresistible smirk. “But I think I’d rather keep it a surprise.”

“I don’t like surprises,” said Ava, attempting a cheeky smile.

“You’ll like this one.” He looked down at her lips, then switched to a whisper. “I promise.” He leaned in.

“Sorry to interrupt, guys, but I could use some help in there...”

At the sound of a French accent, Ava and Yash flung around like school kids caught making out in the broom closet. Helene had appeared in the doorway, annoyance on her face.

“What’s the matter, Hel?” asked Yash.

It did sound quite brotherly.

Helene rolled her eyes. “Bruno,” she said.

“Oh man, not again...” Yash rose promptly and followed her back inside.

“What’s going on?” Ava asked, bewildered by this sudden resentment towards the innkeeper.

But as soon as she pulled back the curtain on the drama playing out at Rick’s tonight, she understood why. Bruno was hard to miss, spilling whisky as he leaned over the grand piano, badgering the musician to “Play it again, Sam.”

“My name is Ishmael. Not Sam,” the pianist corrected. He probably heard that line at least thrice a day.

“Come on, play it! Play ‘As Time Goes By,’ Sammy!”

Bruno pressed down on the piano keys, which made Ishmael shut the fallboard over the keys.

"How many has he had?" asked Yash, putting his hands on his hips.

Bruno yelled *Casablanca* quotes, attempting an American accent, much to the growing disgust of the other guests.

"I don't know," said Helene. "But the bartender has cut him off. Look, I bet he's getting the bouncers as we speak!"

As the bartender stomped toward the door, Bruno began encouraging the crowd to sing. "Alle zusammen!" He grabbed Ishmael's face with both hands to plant a kiss on his cheek, which made the musician push him hard in the chest.

"Okay, this is our exit." Yash dashed forward, snaking past the tables toward the piano.

"Does this happen often?" asked Ava, rushing after him.

"Well, normally, he doesn't accost strangers. But yeah, it happens," Yash said over his shoulder. "Come, let's get him out of here before he ends up in a Moroccan drunk tank." He retrieved the oil lamp from his pocket, which they'd used to get here, then reached for Ava's right hand while Helene grabbed her left. Ignoring the other guests casting angry looks, Yash threw the souvenir in the air. "Go get him, girl," he instructed Helene, who grabbed Bruno by the arm just before the lamp landed in Yash's open palm.

Back at the Atlas, Helene and Yash linked arms with Bruno, swiftly escorting him to a bedroom off the kitchen. Ava followed but felt quite useless. There was a routine in place here, but she didn't know the steps.

"He just needs to sleep it off now," said Helene a short while later as she made her way through the kitchen, shaking her head. Both she and Yash seemed rather keen to get upstairs. They were almost out the door when a thud came from inside the innkeeper's room. It sounded an awful lot as if he had tumbled and fallen.

"I'll go," Ava announced.

"I'll help you," said Yash, touching her shoulder.

"No, don't worry. It's… it's my turn. You guys go to bed."

"You sure?" Yash hesitated, but it was clear that it had been *his* turn on too many occasions.

"Absolutely." Ava nodded.

"Okay. But we're still on for tomorrow, right?"

"Of course," she said, smiling, then shooed him out the door.

"Thanks," he whispered. Helene, too, put her palms together in gratitude.

After they'd left, Ava fetched a glass and filled it with tap water. Entering the innkeeper's room, she found Bruno sitting on the floor, battling to take off his shoes.

"Of all the hotels in all the world…" he grumbled when he saw her.

Ava scanned the innkeeper's chamber. Whereas all the guests' rooms were warm and homey, this one bore more resemblance to a prison cell. There was next to no furniture, just a narrow single bed and a fitted wardrobe. No pictures decorated the walls; no flowers rested on the nightstand. In fact, there *wasn't* even a nightstand. Just a stool with a harshly glaring bedside light and a tattered, old guestbook.

Ava placed the glass on top of it, then reached under Bruno's arms to help him up. "Come on, let's get you to bed."

"You know what I always wondered about that movie?" Bruno asked, stumbling over his shoes, then collapsing onto the bed.

"What's that?"

Bruno floundered to sit up but managed to rest his back against the wall, elbows on his knees to hold up his head.

"Why didn't Ilsa stay in Casablanca with Rick? She didn't *have* to get on that plane with Lazlo, did she?"

"No idea," Ava replied, arranging his shoes. "Why did Jack have to freeze to death in *Titanic*?"

"Ganz genau, Fräulein Marley." Bruno removed his glasses to rub his eyes. "There was room for two on that floating thingy! Why didn't they make Rose scoot over? Just a... just a little..."

"Why didn't they?" Ava handed him the water in exchange for his glasses.

"I tell you why," continued Bruno, "because humans are *twisted*. We... we thrive on tragedy. We crave the... the... misery and the drama." He took a sip but spilt most of it. "Happy endings are bullshit. Fairy tales created by Hollywood..."

"Here, let me." Ava took the glass from him as he crawled forward to place it on the stool.

"But the *sad* endings... the sad endings stick. Because they turn Rick and, and Jack... and all those other poveretti into these larger-than-life heroes, selflessly stepping aside to leave a legacy much grander than themselves. And the rest of us... well, we all aspire to be like them."

"Whisky goes in, wisdom comes out, huh?" Ava reached for the blanket, tucking him in.

"That's right, Miss Marley. As I always say: the problem with the world is everyone else is a few drinks behind," he mumbled into his pillow. "Don't quote me on that one, though. I might have stolen it from Bogart..."

"All right then, good night. I'll see you in the morning." Ava switched off the light, about to leave when Bruno reached for her hand again.

"Would you sacrifice yourself for something grander?" he asked, his face pale in the moonlight coming through the window. "Would you step aside if you believed your loved one might live a better life without you?"

"I don't know, Bruno. Would you?"

She expected another profound reply, but the innkeeper had dozed off.

"Yeah. I bet you would," she whispered and squeezed his hand. That's when she noticed the object clasped in his palm.

It was the old fridge magnet shaped like an ice cream cone.

Ava carefully removed it from his hand, her gaze instinctively flitting over to his face to check if he was really asleep. He was.

She flipped the magnet over in her hand, stroking the scuffed surface. She could just give it a quick toss. It would only take a second. No one ever needed to know. But the moment the thought arose, it was pushed aside by clouds of guilt. After all, the innkeeper had respected her own boundaries tonight. Had refrained from shining a light into a corner of her own home she preferred to keep in the dark. The least she could do was extend him the same courtesy.

Ava slipped out the door, silent as a teardrop.

The fridge magnet remained on the stool not far from Bruno's careworn face on the pillow.

10

CLICK, CLICK... BANG!

The motorboat glided down a serene channel of the Brazilian swamps, the silky waters a perfect mirror for the pink clouds, the shoreline a tangled silhouette against the morning sky. A million birds sang their wild chorus. The air was dotted black with mosquitoes, struggling to latch onto Ava's skin in the fair wind. Yash sat next to her on the bench, still good-looking despite the giant, puffy life vests they both wore.

Ava had also strapped one of Bruno's bum bags around her waist. Naturally, Yash had teased her for it; he kept his own deeply buried inside his rucksack. Still, her fashion faux pas didn't seem to deter him. Camera in his lap, he rested one hand casually on the small of her neck as if she were his girl.

They'd appeared on a rickety jetty at the edge of the Pantanal wetlands at the crack of dawn, Ava still flabbergasted that no one ever seemed to mind them appearing out of thin air. Benjamim, their boatman, had been no exception. Gaunt and grey-haired and rugged like his boat, he'd given zero indication that he was in any way troubled by their supernatural mode of transport. On the contrary, he seemed perfectly content this morning, driving around a newlywed couple on their honeymoon, which was what Yash had told him they were, leaving Ava no choice but to play along.

"So, where's my diamond, then?" she exclaimed over the engine noise.

"What's that?" Yash leaned in closer.

"My ring," Ava replied, splaying her fingers on her thighs. "If we're newlyweds, shouldn't we be wearing rings?"

"Maybe we are one of those modern couples who don't need rings to prove how much we love each other." He took her hand, threading his fingers through hers.

"À frente! À frente, agora!" shouted the boatman in Portuguese as he steered them into a smaller tributary. "Watch out now!"

"All right, keep your eyes peeled." Yash straightened, adjusting a few settings on his camera. "We're looking for a jaguar this morning."

"Remind me again, when exactly did I sign off on this honeymoon?" Ava rested her head against his shoulder. "Seems to me, this is more of a work trip for you."

Scanning the shoreline, Yash smiled. "You caught me, darling. I spent all our wedding money on my selfish dreams. In my defence, though, the Pantanal is every wildlife photographer's fantasy. It's the biggest wetland in the world, the size of the whole UK!" he exclaimed, water spraying in both their faces as the boat turned a sharp corner.

"Yeah, yeah, tell that to the wedding china we can't afford." Ava wiped the water from her face in an exaggerated gesture. But really, she was having a marvellous time. Until Benjamim halved the pace, that was. As soon as the boat slowed, the tropical heat caught up to Ava. As did the mosquitoes, which seemed to love her dearly, but left the two men in peace. She could barely sit still, eliminating one bloodsucker after the other with targeted slaps of her hand, until Yash pulled out a spray bottle. "Ain't nobody gonna take a sharp photo with the boat rocking like that," he teased, handing it to her.

After she had enshrouded herself in a cloud of insect spray, Ava could finally appreciate where he had taken her. Like a garden of Eden, the pristine wetlands unfolded in front of them. Birds stalked through the shallows, storks and spoonbills, egrets and herons, all attracted by an abundance of fish bustling below the surface. The heady scent of the jungle lay thick on the air, a pungent mix of flowers and fruits, soil and decay. A family of overly large rodents grazed on the shore – capybaras, according to Benjamim. Looking like giant hamsters, they always kept at least one nervous eye on the water surface, where caimans lurked beneath the lily pads.

Ava snapped a few pics with her disposable camera, choosing her subjects carefully. She had only twelve photos left on the film, after all. Yash's shutter, on the other hand, went off like a machine gun, shooting picture after picture as if his finger had cramped on the button.

Ava watched him out of the corner of her eye. Although he appeared in his element, snapping away as he did, he was also an oddity. Something that didn't quite belong, maybe no matter where he went.

"So, do you miss your real life?" Ava asked, eyes still on him.

"Nope," replied Yash, capturing a marsh deer nibbling on some leaves. "I'm in a much better place now."

"But what about your family? Your friends? When did

you last visit them?"

"I don't know. I pop by sometimes, I suppose. Watch them from afar. Make sure my mum's all right."

"You don't talk to them?"

Yash made a motorboat sound with his lips. "What's the point?"

Ava sensed resentment brewing inside him and decided not to pry. She knew all too well how complicated families could be. Ethan still hadn't replied, as she had discovered during a quick morning trip to signal-land before setting off on her adventure with Yash.

"Where did you grow up, anyway?" she asked, reverting to more neutral ground.

"Mumbai."

"And did you always know you wanted to take photos of animals?"

"I didn't, actually. Photography, yes. Animals, no. I used to do high-end fashion."

"What made you switch?"

Yash put down the camera. "You really want to know things, don't you?"

Ava shrugged. "It's what wives do."

"All right, here it comes. My sad little story." Yash resumed his seat, gesturing at Benjamim to pick up the pace again. "We can keep going, mate! Let's not waste the good light!"

Eyes on the camera display, he flicked through the pictures he had just taken. "When I was a kid, I could never sit still," he said, showing Ava a particularly nice shot of a caiman. "For the longest time, my parents tried to engage me in all sorts of activities – soccer, books, music – but it was only when I held my first camera in hand that my interest was sparked."

"What is it that you like about it?"

Yash didn't hesitate to reply. "A camera is a license to see the world," he said. "It allows you to keep moving, keep growing, you know? I guess that's what I always wanted: to escape mediocrity and find something greater for myself."

He zoomed in on a photo to check for sharpness. Ava watched him. "Is that why the hotel appeared for you, you think? Because you wanted to escape?"

"You could say that." He nodded at the display. "After art school, I ran completely off the rails. Got successful real quick – *too* quick, probably. Constantly moved around on the job. Parties, drugs... every day a different city, a different hotel, a different girl..."

Ava shuffled in her seat but chose to ignore that last comment.

"But it was never enough," Yash continued. "I always wanted more. *Needed* more. Only the faster I moved and the more successful I became, the less gratified I felt." He picked up his camera to capture the fly-by of a toucan, the rapid click-click-click of the shutter a fitting soundtrack to his story. "Anyway, I think that's why the Atlas appeared for me. The hotel is the epitome of instant gratification. Only when I had the whole world at my feet did I finally slow down."

"And have you? Slowed down?" Ava nodded at his thumb, frantically turning the dial to flick through the toucan pictures.

"Should have seen me a few months ago, girl." He turned the camera off. "Animals are very different to photograph. They don't sit still like models do. I've developed a lot more patience doing this kind of work. Check out the monkeys." He gestured at the treetops of a fig, a subtle hint that he wanted to cut off the conversation.

"Well, I'm glad things worked out for you," Ava said,

stroking his shoulder. But she didn't quite buy it, this new version of himself he claimed to have become. Yash seemed to like talking about how much he had changed. But whether his words were backed by actions remained to be seen.

"There's one! There's one, mate," Yash called out. He jumped up, snapping his fingers as he pointed at a thicket.

There, creeping through the vines, was a jaguar!

Ava's heart drummed with primal excitement when she spotted the massive cat. She had thought them to be more slender, even elegant. But jaguars, as it turned out, were extremely bulky predators, with thick muscle around their necks and a quartet of sturdy, powerful legs made for pouncing on large prey.

"A nice, male jag that is," mumbled Yash, busy adjusting his camera settings before he fired her up again.

Ava, too, whipped out her disposable. But it was near impossible to keep track of the jaguar, let alone take a decent photo of it. The black, rosette markings on his golden fur gave him perfect camouflage against the jungle. He kept slipping out of sight.

"Slow down, mate. Slow down, please," Yash instructed Benjamim.

"Pare por favor, señor," Ava translated instinctively.

"Impressive," noted Yash, switching to a more compact lens. "Where did you learn Portuguese?"

"Spanish, actually. My mum was Costa Rican."

Benjamim steered the boat further upstream, positioning them downwind from the jaguar, now busy stalking a capybara on the far end of a sandbank.

As soon as the bow had trenched the sand, Yash took off his life vest and dismounted, his gaze still trained on the giant cat. "What did you do, anyway? You know – *before*?" He asked, lending Ava a hand.

"Is this… safe?" She, too, slipped out of the vest and took Yash's hand but looked back at Benjamim for reassurance. "Es seguro?"

The boatman shrugged, picking his teeth.

"I'm a barista in London," Ava said, scrambling after Yash.

"Dangerous," he teased.

It was the first time he'd asked her something personal, but the conversation immediately stagnated like swamp water. And as Ava marched up the beach in Yash's wake, that bothered her a little.

Yash was into her; that much couldn't be denied. However, he didn't seem particularly interested in who she actually was. This sounded some alarm bells. Did she really want to go down this same old road again? Then again, they were about to approach a wild jaguar on foot. Maybe now was not the time to chat.

"All right, hold onto me now and don't let go, no matter what," Yash whispered over his shoulder as he snuck up the sandbank, hiding from the jaguar behind the giant roots of a fallen tree.

"Não muito perto!" The boatman yelled out.

"He says we shouldn't get too close."

"Don't worry, London. We'll be out of here before things get hairy."

They crouched down behind the tree, now less than thirty meters from the predator, still immersed in the stalk.

With a scarred face and piercing, honey-coloured eyes, the jaguar kept his head low to the ground, his scratched-up nose sniffling. His tattered ears twitched in all directions, picking up even the faintest whispers of the jungle. Yash snatched a few photographs through the tree roots. "I need him to look at me," he whispered. As if on cue, the jaguar jerked his head around.

"That's it, my boy. Keep those eyes on me." Yash's breath fogged up the display as he pressed a cheek against it.

"Let's see if he gives us a charge." Yash was about to step out into the open when Ava pulled him back.

"A *charge*? Are you mad?" she hissed.

"Don't worry. Big cats always mock charge first," Yash said, his eyes still on the jaguar as he dragged Ava after him. "They'll come bolting straight for you to see if you'll run. If you don't – they stop."

"And exactly how scientific is this observation, *Darwin*?"

"Ugh – come on, girl, you only live once."

"Which is why I was hoping to make it past fifty, at the least."

"Hush now," Yash cautioned her, then dared a few more steps. The jaguar was less than two boat lengths away.

Ava considered her options. The last thing she wanted was to get any closer to the beast. But Yash had the souvenir back to the hotel. She'd better stay close to him. Reluctantly, she followed in his footsteps. As soon as they entered his line of sight, the jaguar crouched down and snarled, showing his fangs.

"*Yash*, come on, that's close enough." Ava tried to reason with her fake husband, but it was the jaguar answering. Twitching his tail like a whip and swirling up sand, he gave a sinister growl. But Yash kept on pushing, further and further into the cat's comfort zone.

"I want that charge on camera. Just hold onto me. I got this."

At his words, the jaguar retreated a few steps down the bank.

Still snarling, though.

"No. No, don't leave, boy! Don't leave..." Yash came down on his haunches, and Ava copied him.

"I don't like this," she whispered, clasping the hem of his shirt for dear life. "I don't like this at all."

Yash lay flat on his stomach, elbows in the sand to support his camera. And maybe it was this kind of stalking behaviour or the fact that the jaguar couldn't see them anymore –whatever it was, something made the beast charge!

What happened next happened so quickly, Ava thought she'd died and saw her life flash before her eyes.

With a ferocious snarl, the jaguar pounced, coming straight at them as if on wheels, jaws gaping wide, sand flying in all directions. Yash jumped up, camera at the ready, shutter going off at staccato speed while he yelled, "HEY! HEY! HEY! STOP, BOY! STOP!"

"He's not going to, Yash... HE'S NOT GONNA STOP!" Ava screeched. She staggered to her feet, pulling so hard on Yash's shirt she almost choked him. But only when the jaguar had already leapt – all fours in the air – did Yash finally lower the camera, dive into his pocket, and conjure up the mini toucan he'd used to get them here.

"Toss it! Toss it! Toss it already!" Now Ava shook Yash, and at last, he did as told.

"A fucking mock charge?" Ava yelled, hitting him in the chest as soon as they'd appeared back in the Atlas living room.

"Well, come to think of it, *that* one might have been a real charge..." Yash grinned, flicking through his pictures.

"You have a death wish or something?" She pushed him again.

"*Relax*, girl. I had it under control."

"You didn't have *shit*!"

"Come on," he said, taking her by the hips, "when was the last time you felt this alive, huh?"

"Pr-probably when I came out of the womb, naked and afraid," she stammered, trying to remove his hands, but he wouldn't let her. "I don't need this kind of thrill, Yash," she sighed. "I'm an incredibly boring person. The only rush I ever got was from a double shot of espresso on an empty stomach. I've never had a one-night stand, and on Friday nights I usually do my laundry."

Yash put a finger on her mouth. "I don't think you're boring." And then his lips curled into that smirk she felt entirely ill-equipped to handle.

"And now what?" she said, hitting him in the chest one last time.

Yash took her chin and turned her face to look into her eyes. "Now I show you the world."

Ava scoffed and furrowed a brow. "On a magic carpet ride?"

Yash snorted out a laugh. "You're tough, London," he said, sliding his hand down her arm, interlacing fingers with her. "Let's go." And with the other hand, he tossed the next souvenir in the air.

~

TRAVELLING with Yash was like falling into the pages of a *Nat Geo* magazine. Within a few hours, he took Ava to see the mountain gorillas of Rwanda and the grizzly bears of Alaska. He taught her how to photograph the night sky in the Atacama Desert and compose perfect symmetry amid the rice terraces of China. They visited the famous white horses of Camargue and their traditional guardians, both deeply rooted in a rugged stretch of coastline in southern France. Back at the hotel, Yash fetched a blanket, which turned out to be a doorway to the Lofoten archipelago, where Ava snuggled up to him beneath the Northern Lights. To top it all off, he'd arranged a candlelight dinner on the rooftop of a cosy boutique hotel – somewhere in the Middle East, judging by the spread on the short-legged table, which was surrounded by colourful pillows and rugs.

"So, you *are* Aladdin, after all. I knew it," Ava joked as Yash handed her a glass of champagne.

"Enough with the sarcasm. Admit it," he said, pointing a finger, "*you,* Ava Marley, are impressed!"

"Fine." Ava took a sip, then a seat on a round ottoman. "My name is Ava Marley, and I'm a sucker for romantic rooftop dinners and expensive bubbly."

"That's better." Yash grinned and joined her at the table. "Now, you absolutely must try the baba ghanoush here. It's the best you'll ever have." He tore off a piece of flatbread, rolled and dipped it in a bowl, then handed it to her.

Ava took a bite and nodded. "Delicious."

"Told ya."

They worked their way through the spread of delicacies, talking about the food and the things they'd seen that day. But when Yash grabbed his camera to set up a long exposure shot of the rooftop, Ava retrieved her phone. She had full signal up here and instantly received a text message from her provider, welcoming her to Turkey and informing her she could use the data from her plan here at no extra cost. Still no message from Ethan, though.

"Am I boring you?" Yash asked, gesturing at the phone in her hand.

"Am I boring *you*?" Ava retorted, nodding at his camera. "Sorry," she added, sliding the phone into her pocket.

"You're not boring me. It's just... I'm still anxious to hear from someone back home in London, that's all."

Yash nodded understandingly. "It'll pass," he said, his voice gentle. "Try not to think about it."

Ava mirrored his nod but was all too aware of the silence coming from her pocket. What was Ethan's game now? Tit for tat? Ignore her the way she had ignored him? Whatever it was, it was working: she was positively on edge.

"So, what's up with Bruno?" she asked, trying to focus on Yash again. "He drinks a bit too much, does he?"

"Nah, we're not going to do that." Yash held his hands up as if to shield himself. "We're not going to talk about the sad, old innkeeper right now. Look where we are!" He shuffled over the pillows until he sat right next to her.

"Yes, where are we, actually?" Ava asked, gazing at the nearby rooftops.

"You'll find out in the morning." Yash winked and reached for a piece of sweet baklava, which he guided to her mouth. Ava had a bite but felt self-conscious when he kept looking at her lips.

"So, I take it we're not going back to the Atlas, then?" she said, wiping her mouth in case she'd made a mess with the pastry. She was eager to get to London and confront Ethan but also realised the UK was nearing midnight. It would have to wait till morning.

"We can go back," Yash murmured. "If you want to." With his thumb, he removed a crumb from her cheek. "*Do* you want to?"

Ava looked up into his eyes and found them wandering over her face, her hair, her neck, taking her in like one of his photographs.

She shook her head no.

"What do you want, Ava?" Yash breathed, and she inhaled deeply, drinking in the same air.

She knew he was probably wrong for her. Knew this couldn't last. But she also knew she wanted him, now. Wanted to stay, on this rooftop, in this moment.

Ava leaned in. A slight movement, but it was all Yash needed to read her.

Like a wave triggered by the faintest quiver, he moved closer. Slowly at first, he sat up on his knees, cupping her jawline with both hands while his lips found hers. But as soon as she kissed him back, hands twining around his neck, he rolled over her with fervour. Pressing her into the pillows, he braced himself on one forearm while the other hand glided down her side in ardent longing. There was a sureness in his every move, a confidence she wasn't even surprised he had. If anything, it was what had first drawn her to him.

A moan escaped Ava, and she gazed up at the stars, grasping his sandalwood hair. Holding on to a moment. Forgetting who she was.

AVA WOKE to the song of swallows on the crisp morning air. With high-pitched chirps, they twisted and turned above her head, soaring in and out of their nests beneath the roof tiles. Her nose sat cold like a river pebble in her face, but the rest of her body had stayed nice and warm throughout the night, buried under a heap of blankets and pillows. She unfurled her arms and sat up, shivering as her back was laid bare and morning dew pearled off the pillow tops onto her skin. She wiped the sleep off her eyes and swivelled round to look for Yash amid the pillows, but he was gone.

Ava wasn't sure if she should be unnerved by that fact but decided not to worry just yet. Wrapping her naked body in a blanket, she rose and walked to the rooftop edge. Below, a cave village ranged along the rock face of honeycombed hills, many roofs decorated just as dreamily as the one she stood on. The sky was tinged in morning light, a cloudless, golden canvas expanding above an ocean of sandstone rocks, rising from the desert like giant chimneys.

Down in the shaded valley, it was still dark, but every once in a while, sparks of warm light went off like fireflies. All sleepy-eyed, Ava needed a moment to fathom what they were. When the realisation sank in, she knew not only what she was looking at but also where she was. Below her, a fleet of at least a hundred hot air balloons fired up to rise on the cold spring air of what must have been the Anatolian plains in central Turkey.

"How's the honeymoon now, darling?"

Ava turned around just as Yash's head appeared up a stony staircase. Dressed only in his jeans, he balanced a silver tray with a steaming teapot and a couple of gold-trimmed glasses.

"Cappadocia?" she asked, taking a glass from the tray. "We're in Cappadocia?"

Cappadocia, the picturesque mountain village in the Turkish backcountry, was deemed one of the most Instagram-able destinations in the world. Occasionally, it had popped up in Ava's feed as well.

"Only the best for my missus." Yash flashed his brows and put the tray down to free up his arms, which he then wrapped around her.

"You're cold," she complained and shivered.

"I can't even tell you how glad I am that you won't forget me," he whispered and kissed her on the cheek.

"Don't flatter yourself." She turned her head, stroking his nose with hers. "You weren't *that* good."

But this morning, Yash refused to engage in the banter. "You know what I mean, though," he said with intensity, tightening his embrace like he was scared she might vanish if he didn't hold onto her.

Ava reached for her bag. She fished out the disposable camera, taking a selfie with him, which he tried his hardest to prevent.

"A-ha! At last, he reveals a crack in his confidence," Ava laughed, taking another photo of Yash alone, and he covered his face. "Point the camera at *him*, and he becomes all shy!"

"Stop it now, or I'll..." he warned, then broke into a tackle, throwing her back onto the pillows. He tickled her until she dropped the camera in her bag.

"All right, all right! I give up! I give up!"

And then, they kissed again. It was a different kiss, gentle and honest.

Ava liked this one – this Yash – much more. Maybe she'd been wrong. Maybe this might be for real, after all.

"We'll better get going," Yash whispered. "Curfew is fast approaching."

Ava pouted, wiping a strand of hair from his temple. "I guess you're right. I should really get to London today," she said, rolling over to fetch her T-shirt. The hot air balloons had now risen high above their heads, dotting the morning sky.

"Who is it that you can't forget over there anyway? Some ex-boyfriend?" Yash said, searching for his own shirt.

"Worse: it's my dad," she replied, slipping into her pants.

"Right, I hear you." Yash put on his socks. "It's tough at first, but after a while, you come to realise it's all for the best.

Now, not speaking to my family has become almost normal."

"But why won't you speak to them anymore, Yash? What happened?" Ava sat down on a pouffe, slipping into her sneakers. He seemed more open this morning, so she attempted another approach to learn about his family.

"I mean, I *would*," Yash replied. "Course I would. But I can't. You know, with the whole being-forgotten mess."

"What mess is that?" Ava asked, paying only half attention as she tied her shoelaces.

"Atlas guests are forgotten by everyone they meet and everyone they used to know?" Yash said, making air quotes.

"What?" Ava rose, suddenly all ears. "What was that?"

"That's why I can't talk to my parents anymore – or at least they won't remember it." Yash shrugged, putting on his shoes. "The deal with the devil we all agreed to when we checked in."

"WHAT?" Now Ava yelled the word, which made Yash look up at last.

"Holy fuck, you don't know." He covered his mouth, mirroring the panic Ava felt rising in her own face. "How can you not know?"

"How do *you* know?"

"*Everyone* knows!"

Ava's heart pounded so loud in her ears it drowned out everything else, like a jackhammer on Oxford Street.

"If this is meant to be a joke, you better stop it, Yash. Because it's… it's not funny." She brushed a strand of hair from her forehead, her palm all clammy.

"I'm so sorry, Ava," Yash sighed. "I'm so sorry you had to find out like this."

It wasn't what he said but how he said it.

Ava sat down again, dizzy as her mind zipped from one

memory to the next, trying to correlate them with what she now feared to be the truth. The waiter in Bali, forgetting her order three times in a row. Ethan not replying to her messages...

"So, when you said earlier, you're glad I won't forget you, what you really meant was..."

"Only Atlas guests remember other Atlas guests. Did... did Bruno not tell you? 'Cause he's supposed to tell you! He's the innkeeper!"

"But, wait a minute..." Ava shook her head, confused. "If that's true, why wouldn't you just leave? Check out of the Atlas and go home? Surely, then everything would be back to normal."

Yash came down on his haunches, touching her knees. "Ava," he said, his voice delicate, as if he feared what he said next might shatter her. "We... we cannot leave. If we did, we would remain forgotten, and the Atlas would be gone, too."

"No..." Ava breathed, her vision turning black. "NO!" She pushed his hands away and stood, pacing up and down the rooftop, fighting off a panic attack, which was now fast approaching the more she hyperventilated. She turned to the table, coming down on her knees to reach for all the objects scattered there – ceramic bowls, teaspoons, candles, salt and pepper pots. She tossed them all in the air and caught them but stayed right where she was.

"Which one is it?" she shouted. "Which one's the doorway, goddammit?"

"It's... it's this one." Yash drew an indigo evil-eye amulet from his pocket.

Reaching for her bag with one hand, Ava snatched the amulet from him with the other, then tossed it in the air.

"*Hey* – you can't just leave me here!" Yash shouted, but Ava had already caught the amulet and was gone.

11

LONDON RAIN

"Bruno!" Ava yelled as soon as she arrived in the dark hotel foyer, bolting for the kitchen. "Where are you? BRUNO!"

She slammed open the door to his chamber, but despite the late hour (it was past midnight at the hotel), he wasn't there.

"Bruno!" she yelled again, pacing out the kitchen and then up the stairs. The door to number three opened a slit, and Helene stuck her head out.

"Ava? What's the matter?" she asked sleepily.

"Where's Bruno?"

"I think he's still out. Are you okay? Where is Yash? I thought the two of you were together."

"He's in Turkey," Ava growled.

"He is – *what*? Did you leave him there? Ava, you cannot do that! How long has he been there?"

Emitting a single breath like dragon fire, Ava tossed the Cappadocia souvenir once more, fetched Yash from the rooftop, and returned with him.

"*Fuck's sake, Ava.* Don't you ever do that to me again,"

Yash blurted out as soon as they landed. "You know how dangerous that is?"

Heat rose to Ava's head. She didn't reply but stomped back down the stairs, Yash on her heels. Somewhere amid her anger, she was terribly embarrassed for the scene she was causing, but that didn't matter now.

"Let's... let's just sit down and talk about whatever it is that's going on with you two," Helene called after them.

"Ava, you need to calm down, seriously," Yash said, probably realising her fury was far bigger than his. "It's... it's not as bad as you think."

"Not as *bad*?" Ava spun around, glaring. That shut him up.

She turned her back on him, heading straight for the entryway cabinet, which housed a souvenir collection of all the famous buildings in the world. She reached straight for a mini version of Big Ben, tossing it in the air without even another look at Yash.

She had to see it for herself. Had to know for sure. Keeping her eyes open this time, she watched as lightning-fast images flashed before her eyes like two passing trains, only much faster. Catching the mini clock tower, she needed a moment to find her bearings. She'd expected to arrive somewhere in the vicinity of Parliament House, but of course, Big Ben statues were scattered across London like Easter eggs.

This one had dropped her in a pub somewhere. Her nose knew before her eyes did; the heady notes of spilt beer and varnished teak were unmistakable.

It was early morning in Britain, and the place was still empty except for a cleaner mopping floors.

"We open in an hour!" he barked at her in a thick Cockney accent.

"Where are we?" Ava barked back.

"Wha?"

"This pub." She tapped on the bar. "What part of town's it in?"

The cleaner leaned on his mop. "Had one too many already, have ya?"

"Ugh, never mind." Ava stormed out the door, only to come right back in.

"We open in an hour!" the cleaner barked again.

"Look at me!"

"Wha?" He lifted his head.

"Have you ever seen me before?"

"Why?"

"*Have* you? Just now, a few seconds ago?"

"You know, come to think of it," he said, scratching his scruff, "your face does look familiar..."

"Does it?" Ava tightened the grip around her bag, hope sparking.

"Nah, just messing with ya." The man grinned, exposing a row of teeth the colour of old frying fat. "Never fuckin' saw ya in me life."

"Dammit." Ava cursed. The cleaner cackled as she bolted for the door.

But – although certainly not encouraging – this didn't prove anything. The man hadn't exactly been the sharpest tool in the shed, and maybe he *had* been messing with her after all. No, this didn't prove a thing. There was still a chance. There was still hope. She just had to get the hell home.

Outside the pub (the Beast & Bull), the city welcomed Ava with a routine downpour of rain. She scanned up and down the pavement but couldn't make out anything familiar, except for a distinct feel of 'Central Londonness' – a street clogged by traffic, a Marley's Café on the corner, a torrent of commuters on the sidewalk, clashing umbrellas and avoiding eye contact like the next pandemic.

Ava spotted a bus stop across the street. She broke into a sprint, only to recoil when a car horn blared up to her ears, paired with the horrid sound of squealing tires on asphalt.

She'd just had a near-hit with a taxi.

"*You bloody mad?*" Despite the deluge, the driver stuck his head out the window to yell at her.

"Sorry... I – I'm sorry!" She reached out a hand but didn't even look back as she kept on running.

The bus stop was Aldgate High Street.

Sopping wet, Ava scanned the map attached to the back of it. Aldgate High was somewhere between Liverpool Street and the Tower of London – at minimum a vexing forty-five minutes from her Shepherd's Bush flat, and that was if the trains ran smoothly.

Head spiralling, she entered the nearest tube station, changed back into her old London self, quick as a magician changing outfits – keeping her Oyster card at the ready, anticipating everyone else's moves like a poker player, seething with anger when she had to wait a whopping *four* minutes for the next train, ranting at strangers in her head ("Yes, *do* stop right in front of the ticket barrier! That is a fucking fantastic idea!").

Riding the tube on a work day was abysmal at the best of times, but when in a desperate rush to get home and confirm your flatmate still remembered who you were – it was torment.

She took the Circle Line via Liverpool Street, counting down the stops. Moorgate, Barbican, Farringdon... Outside King's Cross St Pancras, the train came to an abrupt halt, probably waiting for another one in front to move out of the station. The same thing happened again at Wood Lane – one bloody stop from where Ava had to get off! As she waited in agony, her foot tapped so hard against the seat the man next to her actually took out his AirPods to make conversation, asking her to please stop before she kicked a hole in the plastic.

At last, she got out at Shepherd's Bush Market, flying through the neighbourhood on old familiar paths from there.

The downstairs door was open – it was *always* open.

Every other day, Ava would have complained about that one neighbour hooking up the door, inviting every Tom, Dick, and Harry to come in for a snoop. Because – *why*?

Today, however, she was relieved as it sped up her way home. Taking two steps at once, she bolted up the stairs, hoping – *praying* – and cursing her and Mel's decision to rent a flat on the fifth floor without a lift.

Huffing and puffing, she arrived at the door plastered with a Fleetwood Mac poster ('You can go your own way', under which Mel had scribbled 'Or you can come in for a drink'). Seeing the poster, Ava's heartbeat tripped. She'd been there the day Mel bought it from Flea at Flat Iron Square! They'd hung it up together – Ava had handed Mel the marker herself, had been watching her add the note!

Yash was wrong. *Had* to be wrong. For here was proof – solid proof – of a shared memory that hadn't been wiped out. Ava still remembered precisely what had been said that afternoon two years ago, remembered even the exact day (an incredibly hot early May Bank Holiday).

Relieved yet still out of breath, she fished for her key, safely tucked away in a side pocket of her bag. It had all been a bad dream. Any moment, it would be over. Any moment, she'd be home. As soon as the door squeaked open, Mel would stick her head out in the hall, her genuine smile and blonde hair like the sun breaking through the clouds. "How was your day, babe?" she'd ask like she always did. And then they'd sit down at the corner table in the kitchen and talk forever about deep stuff. Maybe order take-away from the Vietnamese on the corner. Maybe she would even let Mel do a palm-reading. Although that'd be a stretch.

Ava put the key in the lock, her hand shaking so much she needed to steady it with the other one. She closed her eyes and drew a breath, sharp like the draught whistling up the stairwell. And then, she turned the key.

It wouldn't move.

Ava pulled it out. Inserted it again.

Still, nothing.

She rattled the handle. "Come on. Don't do this. Don't do this..."

That's when her gaze flitted over to the nameplate. 'HOLBORN + MARLEY', it should read in her own handwriting.

It didn't.

Sure enough, Mel's last name was there, in printed Arial and sharing the space with – not 'Marley' but 'Parker.'

It was like a punch in the stomach. Ava held onto the doorframe, forcing her breath to steady. With the desperation of someone pressing the fire alarm, she rang the doorbell. Like the sound of her favourite sad song, it echoed down the hall behind the door, familiar yet dolorous. When no one opened, she rang again, twice this time, then began knocking – *pounding.*

"Mel, it's me! Come on, open the door! My... my key won't—"

At last, the door sprung open, and Mel poked her head out.

"The fuck?" she grunted, her voice raspy like it always was in the morning. As a chef, Mel worked late nights on weekends, so Monday mornings marked her undisturbed me-time.

"So sorry to wake you, Mel. My key doesn't seem to fit anymore," Ava sighed, relief spreading through her body when she was faced with her flatmate's favourite unicorn shirt.

Her hair a tousled mess, Mel considered Ava head to toe, eyes squinting as if she needed glasses.

"Who are you?"

And just like that, Ava's knees buckled, and her heart fell down all of five floors, shattering into a thousand wretched pieces before the gaping front door.

"Mel, it's... it's me – Ava. My... my key doesn't work anymore." Her mouth felt dry, the words like gravel on her tongue.

Mel puffed up her curls and yawned. "Yeah, we... we changed the lock 'cause I lost mine. You used to live here or something?"

Ava stared into her friend's eyes, swallowing down a breath as she searched for any sign of recognition there. But Mel still looked at her as if she were a Jehovah's Witness, ruining her Monday morning slumber with God's gracious gifts.

"But the... the poster..." Ava gestured at Stevie Nicks's face on the door. "How did you get the poster?"

Mel cocked a brow. "Got it from Flea at Flat Iron Square with my boyfriend." Now she took a closer look at Ava. "You from body corporate or something? 'Cause this" – she ran her hand over the poster – "this is just taped on here. I can easily remove it if you want."

"No, I..." Ava cleared her throat, retreating a few steps.

"I'm not from the body corporate, I... just... I used to live here, like you said."

"Huh." Mel nodded, knitting her brows.

"Sorry, I... I guess I better go." Ava turned away, holding the handrail for support.

"Thanks for bloody waking me," Mel grumbled and stepped back inside.

"Who was it, babe?" Parker yelled from what sounded like the bathroom.

"Some nutcase," Mel replied. And then the door clicked shut.

Clutching the handrail, Ava descended to the ground floor then sank onto the steps, Mel's face looping before her mind's eye like a GIF.

Who are you? Who are you? Who are you?

She huddled on the stairs for what felt like an eternity, arms wrapped around her knees, shivering, maybe from the cold, but more likely from the shock. Only when she heard voices from the top floor and then footsteps clattering down did she pick herself up, flushing back onto the pavement like sewage – or whatever else was discarded from a house, a home.

By now, the rain had begun to pour down in long streaks. Regardless, Ava began to walk. She made her way south until she reached the banks of the Thames, the river becoming her point of reference as she ventured on.

There was a conversation she still yearned to have, forgotten or not.

~

HOURS LATER, a soaking-wet Ava entered the lobby of the tallest building at Canary Wharf, her shoes squelching with every step, leaving a trail of puddles behind. Approaching the reception, she wiped her face and pushed some sodden strands of hair away from her eyes.

"I'd like to speak to Ethan Marley, please," she said to the receptionist, whose indifferent gaze was fixed on her.

"Do you have an appointment?"

"He's my father," Ava said, her voice barely audible above the rain drumming against the windows.

The receptionist snorted. "Nice try," she said, looking past Ava to address the man queuing behind her. "Yes, how can I help you, sir?"

"No, really." Ava leaned over the desk. "My name is Ava Marley. I'm Ethan's daughter."

"And I am his fairy godmother. Please step aside, miss. You're wasting everyone's time."

Exasperated, Ava stepped away from the reception desk, joining the queue again. And again, and then some. Each time she approached the counter, she weaved a different story and a different name for herself, seeing as no one remembered her. But the receptionist wouldn't budge an inch, no matter what Ava said or did. At last, she gave up her futile attempts and walked away. Spiralling thoughts of sneaking past security ran through her mind before being quickly extinguished – without a company badge, getting anywhere near Ethan was impossible.

Ava trudged out of the building, her shoulders slumped in defeat. She dragged her feet across the street until she passed the little Portuguese café on the corner. When she glanced in the window, she could hardly believe her eyes. There, he was: Ethan Marley, perched on a bar stool, sipping coffee.

She watched him for a moment as he gazed at passers-by, eating pastry, lost in thought. When his eyes met hers, she pressed down the door handle with shaking fingers and entered. Inside, it was warm and cosy; coffee gurgled in the filter machine behind the counter, and the owner greeted her kindly as she ordered and paid. He filled a cup and handed it to her. She took it and sat next to her father by the window.

"Really coming down out there, isn't it?" Ethan said.

Ava nodded silently, rain dropping from her forehead into her cup. It was wild, not being recognised by her own father, not having him look at her with the old familiar blend of expectation and disappointment.

"Don't I know you from somewhere?" she asked him, not sure where she was even going with this.

"You might." Ethan took a sip, gesturing at Marley's across the road. "I'm that guy."

"Thought that was you. How come you are here, then – and not there?" Ava nodded towards the rainbow parasols.

"Best coffee in town," Ethan said, raising his cup. "Trust me, I should know."

Ava took a sip, silently agreeing with him. "Mind if I ask you something else?"

Ethan swivelled around on his bar stool, looking bemused. "Why not?"

"Why did you change back to the original concept?"

"The original concept of what?"

"The cafés. The interior, the menu, the music – everything. The entire brand is back to how it was when – correct me if I'm wrong – when your wife was still involved in the business."

Ethan tilted his head slightly. "Are you a journalist?"

"No. God, no. I used to live around the corner from your first café in Soho, that's all. Came for a coconut flan every weekend with my parents." It was the truth, a long-lost

Sunday tradition Ava missed to this day. "So, why did you? Change it back, I mean?"

Ethan crossed his arms in front of his chest, looking sceptical. "I hardly veered from it. The company went public, yes, and as a result, we had to start with the frothy drinks to compete with Starbucks, but apart from that, I made it my life's purpose to honour what my wife and I built together."

Ava nodded absentmindedly as the truth finally sank in. It appeared, in this reality – the one that had forgotten her – things had turned out differently. Mel was in a serious relationship with Parker, Marley's had never changed course, and her parents...

"I didn't know you were still so fond of her," Ava said. "I mean... the press always made it sound like the two of you weren't on good terms after the divorce."

Ethan briefly stroked his nose. "I think you mistake me for someone else," he said. "My wife and I never divorced. We stayed married until she died of cancer nine years ago."

Ava swallowed, struggling to keep her composure. "No, of course. I knew that. I did. And I'm sorry for your loss. I didn't mean to tap into it like that."

She drank her coffee, thinking she might have said too much. For a while, they both watched the raindrops cascading down the glass, some uniting to create a stream, others going off on their own.

To Ava's surprise, her father wasn't done talking.

"We did fight a lot, though," he admitted. "My wife and me. Maybe that's what you read in the papers. But in the end, she'd always win – that's how stubborn she was. And that's what made the company: Her winning." He sighed into his cup. "After she passed, I figured the best thing to do was to imagine what *she* would do. Whenever an opportunity came my way, I tried to look at it through her eyes. I'm the brains of the company, but the heart – that was all her. I will always be grateful I realised that. If I'd had my way, things might have turned out a lot differently. You see, a company needs a heart much more than it needs brains."

"Wow," Ava said. She couldn't believe what she was hearing. "Will you charge me for these trade secrets, or are they free for the taking?" she teased, a smile curling her lips.

"Ha!" Ethan burst out. "I suppose this one's on the house. Thank you for listening to my TED Talk," he said and bowed his head, chuckling.

It felt good to have a laugh with him again like when she'd been a kid – a moment, however fleeting, that was unburdened by their past.

Ava looked at her father's reflection in the window, another question burning in her throat. "So, no kids, then?" she said, her voice now thin and brittle.

Ethan shook his head. "Probably for the best," he said. "Knowing me, I would have been all terrible at it."

The café owner came by to refill their cups, allowing for a moment of silence.

"But if I'm being honest," Ethan said as soon as they were alone again, "lately, I do catch myself thinking how nice it would be to share all of that" – he nodded at Marley's – "with a daughter or a son, have someone to spar with again, you know?" He smirked, and it was the same smirk he'd shown in his office when he offered Ava the job with those exact same words. "Can't help but wonder what the point is now. What's it all for if no one will continue the legacy?"

Ava turned towards him, her face pale. For a moment, she simply stared, then she pressed her lips tightly together, her knuckles turning white as she gripped the edge of the table. "Is that why you wanted me to..." She stopped herself, remembering that *she* was no longer remembered.

"Why I wanted what?"

"Never mind."

Ethan put his cup down, finding her eyes. "Who are you, seriously?"

"Just a fellow coffee lover," Ava said with a small smile and stood. "I should be going."

"Hey, now, wait a minute."

Ava went to grab the door handle, but she hesitated and looked back again. "You weren't all terrible at it, Dad," she said, tears welling up in her eyes. "You made mistakes sometimes. Big ones, too. But you always tried to do your best. I get that now. And I wish I had given us another chance while I still could."

She stepped outside, and the tears began to fall as she fought the childlike hope that he would come after her. But he didn't. Of course, he didn't. He had forgotten all about her as soon as she'd stepped out of sight. Ava reached inside her pocket, retrieving the Big Ben replica. She looked up at the clouds, and her tears mixed with the London rain as she tossed the souvenir, caught it, and was gone.

Ethan sat at the window of the tiny corner café unfazed, sipping coffee, a half-empty cup next to him, slowly going cold.

12

THE PLACES WE WOULD GO

"She's back – everyone! Come quick, Ava is back!"

The moment Ava reappeared at the Atlas, Helene jumped up from the stairs in the hall, where apparently, she'd been awaiting Ava's return. While it was lunchtime in London, at the Atlas, the pastel colours of a new day crept through the windows, casting mellow shadows on the floor.

"Hey, how're you doing, girl?" Helene stroked Ava's shoulder, concern flaring in her eyes.

Molly came and wrapped a blanket around Ava. She did her best to rub her dry and guided her toward the staircase, where Ava collapsed onto a step.

"There, there," Molly whispered, still rubbing.

Joao and Captain bustled down the stairs, the dog sliding his head straight into the gap between Ava's arm and ribcage, the boy sitting down two steps above her.

"Yash went looking for you in London," Joao said. "I told him it was a silly idea, 'cause it's a massive place, but—"

"But he couldn't sit around and do nothing," Helene took over. "You gave us all quite the fright. We were scared you might do something reckless."

"Well, I think we should all sit down and talk," Molly said, supporting her frail body on the handrail. "How about you take a hot shower, dear, and I'll go make us a pot of tea?"

But then a noise hit them, and like a deer in the woods, Ava flinched, then froze.

The kitchen door had swung open with the old familiar squeak. Now the onerous creak-creak-creaking of the floorboards made her body stiffen as she listened to a pair of feet passing through the hall.

Slow as the tide, the innkeeper's face appeared behind the staircase. All eyes on him, he kept his own gaze lowered.

Ava glared at him. "Look at me," she said, not even trying to suppress the tremble in her voice.

At last, Bruno lifted his head. His eyes swam with emotion (was it guilt or something else?), and she could tell he'd been drinking again. But he held her stare, and for the longest time, the only sound was his shallow, nasal breaths, wheezing like a kettle.

"I want you to say it," Ava gritted through her teeth.

The innkeeper's expression tightened. He parted his lips, then closed them again. When no words came out, he passed a hand over his five o'clock shadow, a sandpaper sound that would always make Ava cringe.

"Say it," she demanded – now louder, which made Bruno flinch into a reply.

"Everyone you meet will forget you as soon as you slip from their sight," he said. "Everyone you used to know won't recognise you anymore."

Ava smouldered with resentment. "And why – may I ask – did you decide to keep this from me, when you told *everyone* else?"

"Trust me," he said, "it wouldn't have mattered if I had told you upfront."

That was the last answer Ava had expected. Hell, she thought she even detected a hint of smugness creeping into his voice.

"*Of course*, it would have mattered!" She stood in anger, dropping her blanket, and Captain gave a flustered bark. "Had you told me outside that garden gate everyone I know would forget me if I entered – I never would have!"

"Wouldn't you?"

There it was again, that smugness. It made Ava fume with rage.

"How dare you?" She clenched her fists, her whole body quivering.

"I- I know it's a tough thing to admit, but what you must realise is that your thoughts and words have a lot of power, Ava. So do your actions, maybe more than you might like." Bruno took a step toward her, his voice somewhat softer now. "Deep down, you know you asked for this – *prayed* for this. You just never expected your prayers would be answered. But, well" – he shrugged – "they have." He turned to the other guests for support, and to Ava's amazement – they all nodded.

"What are you saying?" She took further steps away from the group. "That I asked for *this*? That I… that I *wanted* to be forgotten?"

Bruno's lips thinned into a fine line. "You've been running from your life since the day your parents divorced, mia cara."

Ava scoffed and folded her arms in front of her chest, shielding herself from whatever it was the innkeeper dared to suggest.

Sure, she'd had no problem subscribing to the idea that the Atlas had appeared for her because she wanted to escape – she did, for a while. But – *forever*?

Forever was a hard pill Ava was not prepared to swallow.

"Why wouldn't I just leave?" she said, pointing at the door. "Why wouldn't I walk out that gate *right* now?"

"DON'T!" The innkeeper reached out a hand in warning. Just then, Yash appeared between them as if he'd dropped from the ceiling.

"Thank God, you're back." He came towards Ava, dripping London rain all over the floorboards.

"Don't do that, Ava. Don't leave," Bruno continued as if the photographer hadn't just popped up out of thin air.

"What's going on?" Yash stepped aside when he seemed to realise that whatever conversation he'd been rehearsing in his head was already underway.

"Believe me, Ava," urged Bruno, "if you walk through that garden gate, you will regret it. I promise you that."

"Why?" Ava threw a hand up in the air.

The innkeeper rubbed his hands as if drying them on an invisible towel. He closed his eyes, then nodded with resolve. "Because once you step through that gate, not only will you be forgotten, but you won't be able to come back in, either. The hotel will disappear for you, and you will become a castaway, stranded in the world forever – *and* without the Atlas's network at your disposal."

"I don't believe you." Ava shook her head, her cheeks burning. "You've been lying to me from the start."

"Ava," Molly chimed in, putting her palms together as if praying, "if you don't believe Bruno, maybe you believe me when I tell you, you always would have entered. The Atlas would not have presented itself to you if you hadn't really wanted to get away forever. You see, dear? Your fate was already decided when you showed up at that doorstep.

Nothing Bruno said or didn't say could have undone that. It's all in God's hands."

"It's true," Yash cut in. "That's what I wanted to tell you all day. Bruno wasn't even there when any of us came in. We all made the decision alone. And I'm sure I speak for everyone here when I say, if it hadn't been for him easing us into the whole thing, I don't know how we would have coped."

A mumble of agreement followed his words.

"Please, I… I did nothing." Bruno waved them off.

"You might have your flaws, mate, but you did an awful lot for me. Don't you ever doubt that." Yash touched him on the shoulder. "And as for the Atlas, I am living proof that this place can turn someone's life around. I was a mess before I came here. I would not go back, even if I could. I wouldn't have it any other way."

"We're better off this way, Ava," whispered Helene, and both Joao and Molly nodded.

Ava grimaced in disgust. "Well, I think you're all cowards," she said, then stormed past them up the stairs.

"Ava – wait." It was Bruno coming after her. "Please, Ava. Don't leave it like that."

She spun around. "Why did you appear on the beach the morning I arrived?" she snapped, and he looked at her like she'd slapped him. "Why did you come to talk to me? What the *hell* were you thinking, Bruno?"

"I… I don't know," the innkeeper stammered. "I was in the gardens, raking the pathway, when I looked out and saw you standing there, hesitating. I still remembered my own doubts upon entering. So, I ran to grab a souvenir from inside and tossed it in the air to get to your beach. I- I thought I could make it easier for you if I just talked to you."

"Well, you didn't," Ava retorted. "Not one bit."

She walked off, but then swivelled around once more. "You know what you've done, Bruno?" she said, clenching her fists. "You have robbed me of the assurance that this was all meant to be. That I always would have entered on my own accord! The others all made their own choice." She gestured down the stairs. "They have *no one* to blame but themselves. But me? I will never know for certain. And I'm sorry, Bruno, but for that, I have only you to blame."

"Ava, I..."

"Don't." She closed her eyes, the corners of her mouth drawn down in loathing. "Don't you dare explain yourself to me right now."

Opening her eyes again, they flooded with tears, and she glared at the innkeeper. She could tell by his shell-shocked expression that he hadn't thought of it this way. Hadn't realised until now what he had done.

But what of it?

The one thing neither the innkeeper nor the Atlas could do was turn back time.

"Now, if you'll excuse me," Ava said, her voice trembling. "I'd like to go to my room and try to forget *you* ever existed, too."

She turned her back on the innkeeper and went to her room, slamming the door shut, then turning the key.

~

"Go. Away."

Ava coiled up on her bed like a snake in hibernation. No one had come to check on her for a couple of hours now, and she thought they'd gotten the hint at last. But apparently not – judging by yet another knock on the door.

After the clash in the hallway, she had dug herself in for

the remainder of the morning, sending away everyone who dared to come even in the vicinity of room five.

What troubled her most was not the innkeeper withholding the truth from her – although it certainly hadn't helped. It was whatever emotions his words had stirred and which still raged through her body like a storm trapped in a bottle.

Was it true? Had she wanted to be forgotten? Had she – whether consciously or unconsciously – *asked* for this to happen?

If the other Atlas guests were to be believed, she would have entered the hotel no matter what. Which meant she'd always been destined to give up. A non-starter. A misfit, not supposed to leave a mark on the world but to be swallowed up by it instead, as if she'd never existed in the first place.

It bothered her – this blind acceptance from the group. It was as if they were relieved they had escaped their lives, contented they could finally stop trying and hide forever in the Atlas's fold, with the innkeeper fanatically leading the way. And she didn't know what upset her more – their complete surrender or what it reflected about her own life.

Granted, she had developed a habit of running from her problems. Whenever she encountered an obstacle, she took off, leaving the unresolved issues behind. And she could see how she was scared to make a choice about her life, about what she wanted it to mean.

But – who wasn't scared and lost at twenty-six? And in Ava's case, could you even blame her?

Her father, maybe in an effort to get over a painful divorce, had spent the last decade expanding MCC like a man possessed, fighting tooth and nail to claim every inch of market share he could get his hands on, plastering the entire world with her deceased mother's face – not to mention, the company bore Ava's own last name! Was it really any wonder she was petrified to leave a mark of her own?

But to believe it had doomed her to a life forgotten – that was a leap of faith she struggled to make.

The knocking subsided, and Ava sighed with relief – only to flinch when she heard a key clattering in the lock. Before she could thwart it, the door opened a slit.

"I *said*" – she rolled over and locked eyes with the innkeeper, which made her voice darken even more – "Go. Away."

But Bruno wouldn't leave. He just stood there in the door crack like a valet waiting for a tip. "I need to show you something," he said calmly, clipping his key chain onto his belt.

Ava scoffed. "What makes you think I'd be interested in anything *you* have to show me? How do you not get this, Bruno? You're the last person I want to see right now – or ever."

But – instead of taking the not-so-subtle hint – the innkeeper walked across the room, gazing out the window, where ocean gales jolted the fig tree branches, a furious display.

"Can you guess what most people will say when asked where they would go if they could go anywhere in the world?" he said to the glass.

"Ugh..." Ava rolled back over, covering her ears with the blanket. Still, she listened.

"Paris, they'll say... the Serengeti... Hawaii. All those glamorous destinations we've been force-fed by the travel industry ever since planes were invented."

A dash of shame mixed into Ava's resentment. Those were exactly the kinds of places she'd visited.

"That's the catch with going anywhere you want: It's as shallow as a puddle. In fact, anywhere might as well be nowhere. But what if you had only *one* place left to go?" The innkeeper said, turning around to face her. "Now *that*, would be a deep dive."

Ava sat up on the bed. For a moment, she thought he expected to hear *her* answer – which, although she already knew it was Costa Rica, she was most certainly not willing to share with the innkeeper, not after what he'd done.

But then Bruno reached out a hand for her to take, and Ava understood: This one wasn't about what *she* had to share. This one was about his own sad little story.

"Why the hell would I go anywhere with you?" She crossed her arms, looking at his hand as if it were verminous.

With his other hand, Bruno reached for something in his pocket. "Because it might be the only way I can give you back the assurance you seek," he said, then gave her a half-smile, turning his wrist over to reveal the object nestled in his palm.

Ava considered his hand, this time not in disgust but in astonishment when she saw what it was holding.

It was the fridge magnet.

13

THE FRIDGE MAGNET

Ancient oaks and chestnuts bowed their heads under the afternoon sun. Their crowns carried the first spring leaves, their knobbly trunks lined the pathways of what appeared to be a public park. Mausoleums towered as high as the rows of narrow cypress trees, which gave the place that distinct Italian look.

"Where are we?" Ava asked, watching a father and son rowing a paddle boat across an algae-greened lake. Clusters of terrapins stuck their noses out for air. Ducks burrowed their heads in their feathers on the waterside.

"These are the gardens of Villa Borghese – the third largest green space in Rome," Bruno said as they walked past marble fountains and weathered sculptures, crested with a sparrow here and a blackbird there. "I used to come here during my lunch breaks. The Goethe Institut is not far." He gestured in a direction from where car horns blared and engines clattered.

Suddenly, he seemed a lot more Italian. It came through in his tone of voice, yes – but even more so in his gestures.

Maybe it was the proximity to the mothership. Maybe Ava just hadn't noticed before.

"How long were you deployed in Rome for?" she asked, keeping in step with him.

"Oh, the Institut used to send me here for regular work stints over many years."

Bruno considered his watch. "Quasi al volo. Almost on cue," he said and inclined his head at a man sitting down on a park bench beneath a giant umbrella pine. Slender, tall, and dark-haired but with a few greys curling at his temples, he looked like a businessman. Maybe the CEO of a bank or something. Wearing an immaculate indigo suit, he unfolded a newspaper and crossed one leg over the other.

"Come, sit with me." The innkeeper gestured at another bench across from the one the stranger had occupied.

Ava's gaze wandered from Bruno to the other bench.

"Who is that man, Bruno?"

"Matteo Capparelli," Bruno sighed. A smile played around the corners of his mouth. "This was our place. He doesn't remember why he comes here every day, of course. But this is where we first met."

Ava gaped at Bruno. This... she had not expected.

"It was a particularly cold and windy Tuesday in April 1998," Bruno said as if reciting the prologue to a romance novel, his gaze lingering on the man he seemed to know. "Not many people were sitting or strolling through the park. We were the only ones holding out against the cold. I guess we both had nowhere else to go for our lunch break. At one point, the wind got so strong his... his newspaper blew off and landed right in my face. I spilt coffee all over my shirt." Bruno chuckled. "He came over and apologised. Offered to pay for the dry cleaning.

"I said to him, 'L'unico rimborso che accetto è un altro

caffè' – the only repayment I accept is another coffee, and that he'd have to drink it with me." Bruno cupped his jaw. "I don't know how I mustered the courage." A flabbergasted laugh escaped him. He blinked twice and nodded then. "I was very taken with him right from the start," he said as if to remind himself.

"What did he reply?" Ava watched Matteo turn a page.

"He..." Bruno cleared his throat. "He smiled at me and said he would love to, but his mama had forbidden him to talk to strangers. So, I introduced myself, and we went to a cafeteria around the corner for a caffè. We talked for so long I showed up half an hour late for my next class!

"From that day on, we met in these gardens every day. Same time, same bench. Even on the weekends. He was from Napoli originally, but he worked for an investment firm here in Rome. Sent most of the money back home to his family. We went to all the museums together, all the restaurants, visited the countryside... eventually, he even started coming to my classes." The innkeeper snickered. "His German was pretty good, actually."

Bruno smiled at Matteo, who shifted uncomfortably on the bench, looking at them with furrowed brows. Clearly, he was beginning to feel uneasy with these two strangers so obviously talking about him.

"But... didn't you say you had a wife?" Ava remembered Bruno telling her over coffee and biscotti one morning.

"Sì."

"So, you..." She gestured at Matteo, but Bruno interrupted her before she could make sense of it herself.

"Ava Marley, you didn't think this story was headed for a happy ending, did you?"

Ava swallowed her initial question. "What happened?" she asked instead.

"She found out." Bruno took off his glasses, polishing them with a corner of his shirt. "Of course, she found out. When I returned to Germany after my stint in Rome, she noticed. Instantly, she noticed how much I had changed. How... *happy* I suddenly was. We..." He flicked his wrist as if throwing some dice, then put his glasses back on. "We weren't exactly what you'd call a happily married couple, as you can imagine. She was the daughter of my parents' best friends. I had known her all my life. And in those days, well, the Italo-German community stuck together like struffoli. Ours was as close to an arranged marriage as you could get."

"Children?"

"No children. Thank God. Martina – my wife – she had always wanted some. It was only one of the many areas in which I fell short as a husband."

"But how did she find out about you and Matteo?"

"I told her." Bruno brushed his nose, nodding. "I told her. Call me crazy, but I believed after all these years we'd become much more friends than... Well, we were never *lovers* to begin with. I thought – or maybe I hoped – she'd understand. That deep down, she must have wanted more from life, too. Most certainly, I thought she deserved better than me."

"But she didn't understand." Ava looked at Bruno, who seemed to fight off a shiver.

"She did not," he sighed. "Not at all. She threatened to tell everyone if I didn't break it off with Matteo – my parents, my friends, my colleagues..." He cast a glance at Ava. "You must understand, those were still very different times back then. Plus, Martina and I came from this toxic, tight-knit circle of orthodox Catholics. It took me half of my life to admit to *myself* that I was gay, let alone tell anyone else."

Ava nodded, feeling his struggle. Her own experience of

being bi had not been an issue for her family and friends growing up, but she, too, had had to deal with her fair share of bigotry. Thankfully, at home, she had always felt safe.

"But there was no way." Bruno shook his head with fervour, biting the inside of his lower lip. "No way I was going to let Matteo go. I loved him. Still do." He shrugged, and the movement made tears well up in his eyes.

"How did you… you know, manage it?" Ava whispered.

"I lied."

The innkeeper pointed his nose toward the sky, holding back the tears. "I got a second cell phone, which I used to keep in touch with Matteo over the coming months. By the time the next stint for the Goethe Institut approached, I told Martina I had asked to be transferred to Florence. I told her our marriage was more important to me."

"And she believed you?"

A shadow passed over his face then. "I can be a convincing liar when I need to be." He crossed his arms. "Still, as time passed, she grew more suspicious. She also developed this, this – panic disorder." The innkeeper fluttered his eyelashes. "Whenever I wasn't around, she'd have these… attacks. Which was strange because it wasn't like she ever loved me, either. She just wanted to force me into staying home with her. 'If I can't find happiness, neither can you…' Something like that.

"Anyway, it was bound to happen: I became sloppy. And one autumn day, she found the phone. Three and a half years after I first met Matteo." He passed a hand over his mouth. "She was so furious," he said through his fingers. "Absolutely furious. It was then that I discovered a viciousness in her personality I didn't know she was capable of."

"Maybe you shouldn't have lied to her…" The words escaped Ava before she could filter them.

Bruno flared his nostrils in anger. He glared at her as if to say, 'You *think*?'

"So did she… did she tell everyone then?" Ava asked quickly.

"She didn't." Bruno snuffled. "She never told anyone, actually. I suppose she would have been too embarrassed herself. Martina was all about upholding appearances. A gay husband wouldn't have looked good on her part, either."

"So, she just let it go?" Ava asked but sensed the darkest part of the story was yet to come. She was unsure if she should push Bruno further into the pain, but then again, why else – if not for this part – had he wanted to take her here in the first place?

"No, she would not let it go. She, um…" Bruno swallowed, his voice leaving him. "She threatened to k… to kill herself if I ever saw Matteo again."

Ava winced and covered her mouth with both hands.

Matteo folded up his newspaper, rose from his bench, and walked away.

Bruno trembled as he watched him go. He finally gave up the fight against his tears, which quickly began to collect in the corners of his mouth. He pushed his glasses up the ridge of his nose, pressing a thumb and index finger onto his eyes.

Ava put a hand on his shoulder. Liar or not – the man was in agony and needed comforting. "Did you ever see him again? Before the Atlas, I mean?"

"I didn't." Bruno drew a handkerchief from his pocket, blowing his nose. "Martina had gone completely off the rails. The way she acted… I had to assume she was capable of the worst." He shook as he suppressed another wave of sobs, watching Matteo disappear in the distance. "No, I never saw him again. But Martina did."

Ava's eyes widened. If she'd thought the story was at an end, she had been mistaken.

"When I ended things with Matteo out of the blue, he came to Germany to find me. He'd always wanted to run away together." Bruno laughed, a sad laugh. "He never thought things through."

The innkeeper went quiet then, staring at the row of cypresses Matteo had vanished behind.

"That was the first and only time they met..." he whispered, and his whole being seemed to drown in the past. "I wasn't home when he came knocking on our door. Martina must have opened. To this day, I don't know what they said to each other. But that was when she finally snapped." His eyes widened in terror; his voice sounded like a recording. "And when I came home that evening... I parked my car in the garage... like I always did... and there, um... there she was."

Bruno's face froze in a blank stare, directed slightly upward at what might have been a memory of the garage ceiling. Suddenly, he sucked in air through his teeth, holding his ribs as if he had been stabbed. "It was like she wanted to make sure I was the one to find her, you know? She even left me a letter," he said, grimacing with pain. "And I deserved it. I deserved every word of blame she had scribbled on that paper. *I* did that to her! I do bad things to good people..."

It was a line from yet another movie, but Ava couldn't put her finger on it. She looked down at Bruno's shaking hands, her own now gently stroking his shoulder as he trembled and sobbed. And for a while, they both remained quiet.

"That is my one day, you see? The one day I will always remember with all its grisliness like it was yesterday," Bruno said at last. He straightened mechanically and wiped away the tears. "Anyway, that was also when the... you know, the" – he lifted an invisible bottle to his mouth – "started. I asked the Institut for a position as far away from home as possible, and they sent me to Thailand, amongst other places. Naturally, I never saw Matteo again. I couldn't. Not until the Atlas."

He rubbed his thighs, then stood, walking in the direction Matteo had taken, and Ava followed.

They found him again, queuing at a small cafeteria selling everything from espresso to sunglasses to ice cream – and fridge magnets, shaped like ice cream cones.

Bruno considered Matteo from afar, his head slightly cocked. "Sometimes, I walk up to him. Ask him for the time or for directions. And then he always engages me in a conversation." Bruno's face brightened slightly. "One day, we even sat down together. Had a caffè, thought up lives for the people passing by. And I remember looking him in the eyes and saying – out loud, you know, to his face – I said, 'If I could spend every day of my life sitting here with you, it would be a life well lived.'" Bruno exhaled, laughing at himself. "We become so brave, don't we? When our actions don't have consequences. When we know our voices don't carry."

Ava bit the inside of her lip, remembering her encounter with Ethan.

"Well, clearly, he still loves you – he comes back here every day," she said, nodding at Matteo.

"He has forgotten we ever met, remember?" Bruno raised an eyebrow. "Andiamo?" he asked and drew out the fridge magnet, his gaze forever fixed on the man who used to know him.

At the Atlas, silence lay thick like a blanket over the house, except for an eerie wind howling through the hall. All guests had gone out for the day. Only Molly had stayed behind, asleep in an armchair by the fireplace, cradling a book, Captain at her feet.

"Why did you tell me all that, Bruno?" Ava asked as she spooned leftovers from a baking dish in the kitchen. The innkeeper had lured her down here, insisting she eat something. She hadn't wanted to, but her rumbling stomach had betrayed her. And thank God for that – Molly had made a mushroom lasagne and her famous sponge cake, both of which Ava would not have wanted to miss out on.

"I've never told anyone about Matteo." Bruno took a seat across from her. "I told *you* because I needed to restore faith within you. I must. You were right, I should never have come and talked to you that morning at the gate. I should never have interfered. But my wrongdoing cannot be the reason you refuse the Atlas's call. I couldn't live with myself if you did."

Ava poked around in the leftovers. "You sound like you believe there was some higher plan to all of this."

Bruno leaned forward. "That is just the thing," he said with urgency. "There *is*. And you would see it, too, if I hadn't interfered that morning."

When Ava didn't object, the innkeeper went on.

"It might be hard for you to believe now, but some people deserve to be forgotten – not as a punishment, but as a relief. Ask any Atlas guest, and they will tell you they're better off this way."

Now Ava put her spoon down with a snap, upset boiling in her stomach. "I'm sorry, Bruno, but you guys just suffer from a bad case of confirmation bias, that's all. And I don't blame you. Of course, you'd want to make sense of this mess we're in. It's only human."

"You're wrong." Bruno smiled, a sureness in his voice that vexed Ava even more. "Think about it. What is the Atlas, if not proof of some higher power?" He considered the air around him as if he could see something Ava could not.

"I didn't take you for the religious kind," Ava said.

"This isn't about religion." Bruno leaned back in his chair. "This is about letting go. There is a great amount of peace to be found when you are given permission to stop fighting, stop trying to fix and mend your life over and over again. I would have thought you'd embrace that idea."

There it was again, this... this *notion* that she was broken beyond repair, that she had somehow asked for this to happen. It stung Ava like a wasp.

To her surprise, Bruno slipped off his wristwatch and offered it to her.

"Another door?" She sighed, only half-willing to find out where this one would take them. If he carried it around all day, it had to mean quite a lot.

"Remember your first day when you asked me about the purpose behind the Atlas's existence?" Bruno inclined his head at the watch.

Yep, it did mean an awful lot.

Ava placed her elbow on the kitchen table with a thud, bracing her forehead in her palm. But she put her other hand on Bruno's shoulder, a silent assent to take yet another trip inside the innkeeper's world.

The next place arrived in a blur of bright lights and hollow sounds. The wristwatch had dropped them inside a museum, that much was apparent as soon as they'd landed in an arched hallway lined with statues staring down from their pedestals.

Bruno invited Ava to walk down the checked marble floors. "This is the Museo Archeologico in Napoli," his voice echoed from the walls. He sounded more Italian than ever now. "Matteo took me here once on a weekend trip."

They entered a vast gallery where the quiet lilt of voices floated on the air, distorting in the vast space like ghosts. The room was empty except for a collection of oil paintings on the walls and a hulking statue, backlit by the evening sun flooding through a floor-to-ceiling window. A couple of visitors silently gazed upon it.

"I've taken everyone else here, too. Think of it as an initiation if you like." Bruno walked up to the statue, hands interlaced behind his back.

Positioning herself between the sun and the statue, Ava could make out who had been carved in marble here. A muscular, full-bearded man, naked except for a giant cloak draped over one arm, buckling under the weight of a massive globe he carried on his shoulders.

FARNESE ATLAS read the sign next to his foot.

"As you well know," Bruno said solemnly, "the hotel is named the Atlas. But do you actually know who Atlas was?"

Ava cocked her head back. Until now, she'd thought the hotel was named 'Atlas' for the apparent reason that it could take you all across the globe. She had never considered the origin of the word. "Wasn't he a Greek god or something?" she asked, looking up into the statue's eyes.

"Quasi. Almost." Bruno nodded as the other visitors moved on. Now they were alone in the room. "Atlas was one of the titans who declared war on Zeus and the other gods. But the titans lost the war, and Zeus punished them all. Our friend Atlas here was made an example of, condemned to carry the—"

"The weight of the world on his shoulders?"

"Well, that is what most people get wrong." Bruno braced one arm with the other in front of his chest, resting a finger on his lip. "Atlas didn't carry the weight of the *world* on his shoulders, but that of... *il globo celeste*... the... the celestial globe, or in short – the sky."

Ava took a closer look at the globe Atlas carried. Indeed, it depicted not continents and oceans but constellations.

"You see, after Atlas screwed up going to war with the gods, he was given a chance to repent. Zeus bestowed upon him the responsibility to literally keep the sky from crashing down on us. In the olden days, farmers even began to worship the titan for sending fair weather their way so they could bring in a rich harvest."

"So, what you're saying is..." Ava couldn't help but scratch her head.

"When I took a closer look at all the Atlas guests I've met, it occurred to me that we all have one thing in common: We are all damaged goods. We all come from flawed backgrounds." The innkeeper's voice rose with excitement. "But what if – just like the titans – we were given a second chance? What if we could go out there and use the hotel's gifts to do good? And what if that's the reason the Atlas appeared for us in the first place?"

Ava looked below the statue's arm at the innkeeper. "Is that why you started the whole random acts of kindness thing? Because you think that's what we're meant to do?"

She felt thrown back to her first day at the hotel when she'd thought the innkeeper was a lunatic.

"I mean, why not?" Bruno flashed his brows. "Why can't Atlas guests become these unsung heroes to humanity, making sure that other people's lives improve, even if their own do not?"

Ava exhaled through her mouth, her lips fluttering. She turned away from him and walked toward the window. Behind the glass, a pigeon perched on the sill. She watched it for a while, lost in thought, but when the innkeeper approached, the bird startled and took flight.

"You reckon there's more than one hotel?" Ava asked.

"Definitivamente," said Bruno. "I believe there are all sorts of miracles in this world we have turned not one, but two blind eyes to. Besides, with all the suffering going on out there, I simply must believe the Atlas is not the only escape of its sort. If it were, I could never live with myself for taking up a spot."

"I don't know, Bruno." Ava shook her head. "I get why you need to add meaning to this... this *prison* we're in. You've been an inmate for so long. But, quite frankly, I think it will take a lot more to fix this world than some weekly act of kindness from a bunch of misfits."

"Maybe that is why the Atlas picked you!" Bruno walked past Ava to lean against the window frame. He looked at her intently. "Maybe you can elevate our mission to a whole new level! Find your purpose with us. Leave a mark on this world far removed from your father's oppressive legacy!"

Ava met his gaze then and, for a split second, saw herself reflected in his glasses. Maybe it was all the movies he'd watched, but Bruno truly seemed to believe his little band of misfits was destined for greater things. And to be fair, how could he not? The Atlas was undeniable proof of the supernatural. Was it so far-fetched, then, that he would start to feel predestined? Called to use these powers to do good?

"I'd like to go back now, please," Ava said and looked down at his wristwatch.

Bruno's posture deflated like a burst tyre when she refused to reciprocate his excitement. He nodded in defeat and slipped off his watch.

"Why didn't you tell me, Bruno?" Ava asked.

Slowly, as if lifting a heavy load, the innkeeper pulled his shoulders all the way up to his ears. "I was waiting for the right moment. It's never an easy thing to drop on someone, I'm sure you'll agree. Besides, life will never be as carefree again as it was during those first blissful days of Atlas travels. I guess I wanted you to enjoy that."

Ava nodded, then took his hand – not in amity but because it was the only way to get back.

"It will get easier." Bruno squeezed her hand. "Maybe you can at least believe that. It will get so much easier. If anyone knows that to be true, it's me."

He tossed the watch in the air with his usual flick, then caught it, and they left Atlas the titan to labour under the weight of his own mistakes as he'd done for centuries.

All alone, in an empty room.

14

DEVIL'S ISLAND

The coming days passed by in a fog of sameness and denial. Ava didn't walk through any more doors – not even the one to her own room – save for two she'd made herself: A paper cup which dropped her right in front of the Mousehole Deli. That was her sorted for food, at least until her money ran out. The other one was a key wrist strap from the London Aquatics Centre. That was her sorted for showers and toilet breaks, as she didn't want to risk bumping into anyone on the way to the Atlas bathroom.

On Wednesday morning, Joao invited her to join the crew for the soccer ball delivery in fulfilment of his kind act, but Ava wasn't up for it. To participate would have meant buying into Bruno's whole narrative of titans and unsung heroes, and she was nowhere near willing to do that. Thanks, but no thanks. She'd rather spend her days in bed.

For the first time since her arrival, she noticed the Atlas struggled with regular power cuts, often leaving her for hours with nothing to do but stare out the window or flick through the copy of *The Wealth Of Nations* on her night-stand. Not that she had much else to do when the power *did* come on. By Saturday, she was bored out of her mind and decided to leave her room.

Much to her displeasure, she bumped into Yash on the stairwell.

"Hey, I've been..." He cleared his throat, fiddling with the strap of his rucksack. "I've been meaning to talk to you."

Ava could tell from his expression that he had meant to do no such thing. She covered herself with the kikoi from Zanzibar. Her tank top was stained with food spills, and she hadn't shaved her armpits in days.

"You all right?" Yash placed a hand on her arm, his skin chilling hers.

"Yeah. M'fine," Ava said and took another step down.

"Hey, hey. Don't do that, girl. Don't just walk away from this."

"Away from *what*?" Ava gave a tired shrug. "You don't actually fancy me, Yash, and we both know it. You were just excited to be with someone who won't forget you."

Yash didn't even object. He just sort of flinched, then breathed out heavily through his nostrils.

"I don't blame you," Ava said. "Really, I don't. It would have been nice to have someone here, someone to – you know – *be with*." She swallowed, realising only now that by entering the hotel, she had not only forsaken a career but, much more importantly, the possibility of a relationship, of starting a family – of love. It saddened her deeply. "But we can't force those feelings, Yash," she whispered. "So, let's not pretend, okay? I don't think I could handle any more make-believe at this point."

Yash walked down to meet her on the same step. "Okay, but... we're good, yeah?"

"We're good." Ava nodded.

"You sure?" He cocked a brow.

"I'm sure," she said, and her stomach growled. Right on point, for once. "Sorry, I'm just really hungry. You mind if I..." She gestured down the stairs.

"Yeah, no, of course. I'll... I'll leave you be."

Yash ruffled his hair. He turned away, then back toward her. His mouth opened as if he wanted to say something else but thought better of it. And then, with a flick of his thumb, he tossed an object in the air and was gone.

And that was that.

Ava nodded once at the empty space, then made her way to the kitchen.

Like a squirrel hoarding for winter, she gathered all sorts of foods she could take up to her room – a box of cereal, half a loaf of sourdough, a jar of peanut butter, a can of ravioli she didn't know how to open, let alone heat up. Each time a drawer squeaked, or a cupboard slammed shut, she cast nervous glances at the innkeeper's chamber, but to her relief, the door remained closed. Bruno must have gone to Rome; it was lunchtime in Italy after all.

Just when Ava was about to sneak back upstairs – arms filled with provisions – the double doors swung open, and Joao stuck his head inside. As soon as he saw her, he yelled up the stairs, "I found her!"

"What's this about, Joao?" Ava said, but Joao didn't reply. A couple of feet came down the stairwell. "In here," he said to someone in the hall.

Moments later, Helene entered the kitchen, followed by a slightly out-of-breath Molly.

"You look awful," said Helene, assessing Ava like she was judging a beauty contest.

"Don't sugar-coat it, Helene. Thanks."

"Sorry, I—"

"It's all right," Ava interrupted, cradling her provisions.

She dropped the ravioli, and the can clunked to the floor, then rolled away despite her trying to stop it with her foot. "I'm... I'm going back to bed anyway."

"Oh no. No, you're not," said Molly. The three barred Ava's way, arms folded like a police squad. "This is an intervention."

"Guys, I'm tired." Ava shook her head, avoiding eye contact.

"You've in bed for the last four days – you're not tired; you just need some fresh air, that's all," insisted Helene. "So, why don't you run back upstairs, put on a clean shirt, brush your hair and your teeth, and then we go."

"Go *where*?" Ava pulled a face like a cat sprayed with the garden hose.

"The three of us have decided to take you on a trip down memory lane, so you can see with your own eyes why the Atlas was a blessing for each of us." Molly placed an arm around Joao's shoulder, and he nodded bravely.

"You don't need to do that." Ava bent over to pick up the ravioli but dropped the peanut butter jar instead. "Really, I feel... I feel fine."

Helene cocked a brow. "You don't look fine."

"All right, I feel dreadful. So what?"

"Come on, what do you have to lose?" said Joao. He picked up the jar and handed it to Ava. "Besides, I've been meaning to go back for a while. Would make it easier for me if you came along."

He looked at her in anticipation. There was a pain in his eyes, a dread no fifteen-year-old should carry with him. If there was even the slightest thing she could do to help – who was she to refuse?

"Arrrgh!" Ava dropped her hoard on the kitchen table.

"*Fine*. I'm coming. I'm coming. Just let me eat something first."

~

AVA WALKED beside Joao down a palm-lined street, awash with puddles from what appeared to be recent rains. Storm clouds still mushroomed on the horizon, and the humidity seemed to melt the skin. The place had a strange Middle Eastern feel, with street names like Sultan, Ali Baba, or Sesame. Some abandoned buildings in the neighbourhood looked straight out of the Arabian Nights, with their horseshoe arches, minarets, and decorative tile works. Yet, the town was unmistakably American if you looked at the traffic signs and lights and the cars passing by.

"So, where did you carry me off to?" Ava asked, considering Joao from the corner of her eye.

"Opa-locka," he said. "I grew up here. Miami's not far."

He took a corner, and Ava followed him down a street littered with discarded furniture, where sad-looking houses slouched behind security fences and barbed wire.

"You know, I've been meaning to apologise to you," said Ava as she followed Joao's lead. "I should never have called you a coward – none of you. I was... upset. Really, really upset. But that's no excuse for what I said to you guys."

"S'all right." Joao shrugged. "Been called worse."

They walked in silence until Joao stopped in front of a red-plastered house behind a rusty garden fence. Paint peeled off the facade like scabs from an old wound, and the concrete courtyard was scarred with deep cracks.

Joao sat down on the sidewalk opposite the house, and Ava did the same.

"That's my old home." He inclined his head across the

street. "My dad still lives there."

"What does he do?" Ava said, not knowing what other safe question to ask.

Joao cleared his throat. "He used to be a bricklayer, but he had an accident when I was like... six maybe?" He looked up at the clouds to remember. "Fell off a scaffolding and injured his back. At least that's what he told the insurance. They ended up paying him good money for watching TV on the couch and pretending to be in pain for two years. He never went back to his old job after that. Now he makes money on the internet."

"How so?"

Joao pouted his lips. "Fills out online surveys, plays poker... that kind of stuff. He bets on horse races, too. Loses most of the time though. But whenever he does win, he invests the money in all kinds of counterfeit from China, then sells it on eBay as the original. He's got like... I don't know, probably sixty different email addresses by now 'cause his shops get banned all the time."

"You and your dad close?" Ava knew the answer already. Still, it felt right to ask.

"Not really." Joao hugged his knees. "He gets, like... pretty angry over pretty much everything. Mum always used to say he's like an attack dog – doesn't know any better than to lash out when he's triggered."

"Where's she now – your mum?"

Joao gave a sigh as big as the storm on the horizon. He needn't say any more.

"I'm so sorry, Joao." Ava stroked his back. "My mum's gone too, you know?"

"How old were you when it – you know – *happened*?" asked Joao. He rested his head on his arms and looked at Ava.

"Seventeen."

She didn't dare ask him the same question, but Joao replied on his own.

"I was eight," he said, his fingers playing with a weed pushing through a crack in the pavement. "She was a good person, my mom. A florist," he smiled, picking a tiny flower which he handed to Ava, and she gave him a friendly nudge as a thank you. "Never got how she ended up with someone like him. Before she died, she told me an angel would come and take me away from here one day." Joao sniffled and looked down the street. "She was right."

Ava placed her arm around his shoulders. She looked in the opposite direction, giving him a moment in case he wanted to wipe away his tears.

"When did you find the Atlas?" she asked.

"Two months ago. After I got this." He gestured at the scar on his eyebrow, which was still a little pink. "Dad threw a bottle at me. Needed thirteen stitches. Course, he was only pissed about the costs for the ER visit."

"Didn't they ask you what happened at the hospital?"

Joao shrugged. "Told them I ran down the stairs with a glass in my hand."

Ava wanted to say something about the incompetence of whatever nurse had been treating him, but she bit back her indignation. Judging by the neighbourhood, she could only imagine what the hospital was like. They probably dealt with more pressing issues than a cut on the eyebrow.

"When they released me from the ER, I never went home. Just kept on walking until I ended up on the beach. And there it was, the yellow gate. I didn't even think twice when I read the sign. Figured, anything had to be better than this." Joao nodded at his old home. "First person I came across was Helene."

"Your angel." Ava nudged him again, and he smiled a little.

At that moment, a man in a tank top and joggers stepped out of the red house, a baseball bat in hand. "Hey – you two! The fuck you're watching my house for?"

Ginger-haired and pale-skinned, he looked nothing like Joao. Still, Ava didn't have to ask to know who this fine gentleman was.

Joao trembled. He stood and walked toward his father, but stopped in the middle of the street, probably afraid to get too close.

"The fuck you want, you little shit?" His dad slammed open the fence gate, swinging his baseball bat.

"Come on, Joao. Let's get out of here. He's not worth it." Ava took Joao by the arm, but he jerked his elbow free.

"What did you just call me?" He glowered, his eyes filling with tears.

"A little shit, I called you. Fucking go back to where you came from!"

Joao clenched his fists. "Why don't you step aside then and let me in?"

His dad puffed up his chest. "The fuck you saying? You high or something?" Now he looked beyond Joao at Ava. "Hey, take your filthy little roach and get the hell away from my property!"

"I *said*" – Joao gritted his teeth, fuming now – "why don't you step aside and let me in?"

"You come any closer, and I beat the shit out of you!"

"Would be a proper homecoming, then." Joao folded his arms. "Yeah, that's right: I'm your son, Liam Reed!"

His father flinched at the mention of his name.

Now tears streamed down Joao's cheeks. "I'm your *son*! And *you*—"

A school bus came around the bend, honking at Joao, who was still in the road. Ava yanked him back just in time before the bus swooshed past.

As soon as it had rumbled by, and Liam Reed came back into view, Ava could tell he'd forgotten all about them. He looked lost, standing there on the pavement with his baseball bat.

"The fuck you looking at?" he barked at Joao. Then he turned around and went back inside, slamming the door shut.

"Come on, let's go," Ava said, gently pulling Joao away. "Nothing left here for you."

~

"ARE you ready for some Australia time, dear?" Molly asked Ava as they made their way up the hotel staircase, the old lady taking each step with both feet. They had left Joao with Helene in the kitchen, where she'd made him crepes to lift his spirits.

"Listen Molly, we really don't need to do this," Ava said. "I have no right poking around your lives like this."

Molly opened the door to number four, ignoring what Ava had said. "Look, Robert Darling, I brought a visitor today," she said to an urn resting on a coffee table by the door. "Don't worry, dear, I'm not crazy," she reassured Ava. "I've just made it a habit to talk to my husband's ashes. I find it comforts me."

"When did he pass?" Ava asked. She did think it was a little crazy, to be honest.

"Two years, five months, and twenty-one days ago. We agreed to wait to spread the ashes of the first to go until the other was ready to leave."

"I'm so sorry for your loss."

Molly nodded and stroked the urn. "He was a good man, my Robert."

Her room was bigger than Ava's, with a king-sized canopy bed and yellow-striped walls – of which you could see rather little because the space was overgrown with plants. It was so green, in fact, entering felt like stepping into a jungle.

"I love my plants," Molly said, stroking a leaf. "All Australian natives. Helps me not to get homesick too much."

"So, you miss it, then – your home?"

"Well, I go back every day, but it's not quite the same anymore. When the postman you've known all your life doesn't remember your face and your own daughter thinks you've left this earth – can you still call a place home?" Molly walked toward what looked like a little shrine next to her bed. About a dozen items were neatly arranged next to a pill box on the little bedside table.

"All my favourite doors," she said, gently touching a few, then picking up a tiny porcelain sea turtle.

"A green loggerhead. They abound on the reef in Far North Queensland, where I'm from." She took Ava by the hand. "Shall we, dear?"

Ava smiled encouragingly. "We shall," she said and gave Molly's hand a squeeze, which she regretted instantly – it felt like Molly's bones might crumble as easily as Melba toast.

On the other side of the world, the sun had just risen, topping a rich green mountain range and bathing the sky in luscious colours. Molly had taken her to a pearly-white beach, framed by a tangle of mangroves on one side and an ocean flat as a millpond on the other.

Molly took off her shoes, and Ava followed her example,

strolling barefoot next to the old lady down the beach. There was no other soul in sight except for a couple of seabirds flying overhead.

"I've been taking walks on this beach for over forty years, but it never gets old," Molly said with a smile. She interlaced her hands behind her back, her shoes dangling from a finger. "My husband and I were from New South Wales originally, but shortly after we got married, we moved up here. Took over an old ice cream shop in Port Douglas and never looked back." She inclined her head at a raised peninsula in the distance, where a flock of houses nestled on the slopes. "We were always happy there. Bought a small house right off Flagstaff Hill. Had a handful of good friends. Raised our daughter with a great love for the outdoors but a healthy fear of the salties." She looked at Ava. "Saltwater crocodiles. They love the calm backwaters here where the Daintree River spills into the Coral Sea."

Almost imperceptibly, Ava veered away from the shore.

"Don't worry, they are most active at night." Molly winked.

She guided Ava up a pathway in between the mangroves, bare feet scrambling over gravel.

The path spilt onto a circular parking lot, shaded by giant fig trees and deserted, save for a station wagon parked at the far end.

Molly walked towards the car and reached for the back left tyre.

Ava followed at a distance.

Upon closer inspection, the car appeared rather rundown. A layer of dust and dried bird scat tinted the once-white metal in a muddy brown. Twigs and seeds had piled up on the windscreen. Rust covered the frame rails, the exhaust, and the wheel screws. The inside appeared even worse. Clothing, bedsheets, and towels pressed against the back windows, folders upon folders of documents piled up on the dashboard, photos and letters choked the glove compartment. Only the passenger seat was clutter-free, save for a blanket and a pillow.

"Molly, did you…" Ava swallowed. "Did you live here?"

She was going to say 'like this'. Did you live *like this*? But she thought better of it. She didn't want to insult her friend.

Molly showed what she'd retrieved from the back tyre. It was the car key. She unlocked the driver's side, then stepped back for Ava to see. A toiletry bag rested on the seat, a stockpile of water bottles, packet soups and cans on the floor by the pedals, next to a camping cooker. But it was the photograph that brought tears to Ava's eyes. Taped to the gear lever was a picture of what must have been Molly's daughter with her two children.

"Now you see why the Atlas was a blessing for me." Molly wiped some dust off the window seal with her finger.

"What happened?" Ava shook her head, brows furrowed in shock. How could someone go from such a beautiful, happy life to… to – *this*? It frightened her.

Molly shut the car door and leaned against the bonnet. "I wasn't prepared." She wrapped her arms around her torso as if cold. "I absolutely was not prepared to handle life without Robert."

Ava came to stand beside Molly, pressing her hand again, only this time much more gently.

Molly snuffled. "He was a good man. He really was. But he was never good with money. I knew that. And, of course, I knew an ice cream shop was not where riches came from.

"But only after he passed away did I learn the full extent of our debt. He had taken out our superannuation as a lump sum – that's the Aussie pension. When that was all gone, he must have taken out a mortgage on the house next. You see, we never discussed the money stuff. I felt I didn't need to know about these things. Women my age rarely do. Shameful, I know. So shameful." Molly's shoulders trembled, and her cheeks – usually pale, almost translucent – had taken on a blush.

"Seven months after Robert's death, I couldn't pay the bank anymore. And then, one morning, two men came knocking on my door and took possession of the house. 'But where am I supposed to go?' I asked them. 'Where must I live now?' They did feel bad, I could tell. Gave me the address of a home for the elderly. But how on earth was I going to pay for that, when I couldn't even pay my electricity bill?"

"But what about your daughter? Why didn't you go stay with her?"

Molly brushed the sole of her foot against her leg, and a couple of rocks trickled to the ground. "Thought about it," she mumbled. "Course I did. But I was so ashamed. And I didn't want to be a burden to Annie. I couldn't. She... she raises my grandkids alone, you see? She's got enough trouble as it is."

"But how did she not *know*?"

"She lives far enough away." Molly shrugged. "And she works so very hard. I'd only been living like this for a few months. It was still easy enough to hide it from her. I was usually the one to visit her, not the other way around. Whenever she called, I pretended I was out driving somewhere or in the garden. Besides, she knew I was old school and had always preferred letters. So, for the most part, that's how we kept in touch."

"But you didn't even have an address anymore!"

"I caught the mail at the post office before it was delivered. The postman knew me. That wasn't the problem." Molly looked down the road. "But I just couldn't make the money work, no matter how much I turned over every dime. So, when I ran dangerously low, I spent the last bit on a bus ticket down to Mission Beach, where Annie lives. I wanted to tell her. Really, I did. But that weekend, she had a terrible fight with her ex-husband. I couldn't bring myself to add more weight for her to carry. It was like a sign from God, you know? 'You must not tell her,' He seemed to say. 'Can't you see how much she's got on her plate right now?' The hotel appeared for me the morning I left Annie's house. Naturally, I found it strange at first, with the sign and all. But I was curious. Thought I'd have a quick peek, you know? A quick look inside. And thank the heavens I did.

"Of course, it was a shock when Bruno told me I am now forgotten. But far greater was this sense of relief... this sheer gratefulness to know that God had heard my prayers, had blessed me with one of his greatest secrets."

"Don't you wonder what would have happened had you told Annie?"

"I don't have to. I know this is what He intended for me." Molly reached for a necklace with Jesus on the cross.

Ava stroked Molly's back. She thought it concerning, this talk of God's greater plan. Yet, she couldn't deny that anything was better than spending your retirement broke and alone, living in a rusty old car.

"Now, whenever I want to see my family, all I have to do is throw my cross in the air – and it's free, too." Molly rubbed the pendant in her palm. Like Bruno, she kept her most precious souvenir close.

"But what does Annie believe has happened to you? I mean, she literally *cannot* forget about your existence – we all know we had a mother once. It's biology!"

"It's not always as simple as being wiped off the earth entirely. For Helene and Joao, it happened that way, but in my case, it's different. I suppose because I am a parent. My own child cannot forget me. Annie still has her memories of me. She still looks back on her childhood in my care. I overheard her talking about me to a friend once. In her reality, I passed away shortly after Robert did. She likes to tell people I followed him because we always came in a set." Molly smiled. "I like the sound of that."

"But doesn't it make you sad that she believes in a lie?"

"On the contrary. Now I can watch my grandkids grow up without being a burden. I've been saved, you see? If anything, that makes me happy, not sad."

Ava gave a deep sigh. "As long as you're happy."

"I am," said Molly. "And you can be, too, dear. You're just trying so terribly hard not to be."

~

THE IBIZA BEACH club pulsed with energy, the music's bass vibrating through the floor and deep into the bones, the party crowds dancing like there was no tomorrow. Helene and Ava sat at a dimly lit table, their vibrant cocktails almost glowing in the darkness.

"All right, what are we doing here, Helene? Spit it out," Ava shouted over the music.

Helene took a deep breath, sipping her drink nervously. "That's him," she said, her voice barely audible over the pounding music as she pointed out a man in the crowd. With dark hair slicked back and an arrogant smirk, he danced provocatively with a group of women, his hands lingering on their hips a little too long.

Ava leaned in, her eyes following Helene's gaze. "Who is he?"

Helene hesitated. She took another sip of her drink and finally spoke. "He's my husband, or he was for a short time."

Ava's breath hitched when she remembered Bruno mentioning the Atlas had appeared for Helene during her honeymoon.

"Tell me everything," she urged gently, sensing her friend's vulnerability. Helene nodded her head toward the outside. She stood, and Ava followed her onto the beach. Here, the music was quieter, and Helene sat in the sand, looking out onto the starlit ocean.

"His name is Andre, or at least that's how he introduced himself to me. We met on a dating app," she began, her voice trembling slightly. "He claimed to be a successful businessman from Spain. Renewable energies, whatever that means." Helene rolled her eyes. "Our first in-person meeting happened on one of his business trips to France. Our relationship took off from there. Long conversations, romantic getaways, surprise gifts – the whole, how do you say? The whole shebang." Helene smiled sadly. "He was very charming and attentive – and he always paid for everything!" She added this in a defensive tone. "And he made me feel special in ways I'd never experienced before. He was like a true knight in shining armour." Her French accent lent an air of enchantment to the fairy tale romance she had once lived.

Ava listened intently, pressing a fist against her lips as Helene continued.

"One day, he mentioned a unique business opportunity, something to do with desalination or something, and he wanted to encourage me to invest in it."

Ava looked over at Helene, alarm bells going off.

"We could do it together, he said." Helene shrugged. "He really made it sound like he wanted the best for me. *For us.* He wasn't pushy at all, trust me. You see, I had told him early on in the relationship that my grandmother had left me quite a substantial inheritance. She was a self-made woman who wrote children's books. But I didn't want to give him the money; it was meant for my own future, after all."

"How did he react?"

"That's the thing: he was very understanding. He didn't pressure me any further, said it was okay if I didn't want to, and that he would look after us financially." Helene smiled, remembering the tender moments they shared.

"He only brought it up that once. Over the coming weeks, our romance intensified, and one weekend, he surprised me with a trip to Paris. And in a hidden rose garden in the Latin Quarter, illuminated by fairy lights, he got down on one knee, and he proposed. I said yes without hesitation."

Helene looked down, her eyes brimming with tears. "We got married on a whim in Vegas and afterwards went on honeymoon in the Caribbean. It all seemed so romantic at the time."

Ava's eyes narrowed. "What did your family say? And don't you have girlfriends to talk some sense into you?"

"I didn't tell anyone," Helene said, her voice tiny. She hugged her knees to her chest and avoided looking Ava's way. "It was on our honeymoon that he started pushing the investment idea again. He said we could triple my inheritance, and then I would never have to work again. And this time, I gave in. He was my husband, I trusted him completely. So, I granted him access to all my bank accounts." Helene buried her face in her hands. When she looked up again, she wiped tears from her cheeks. "The next morning, he was gone," she said, her voice detached. "Along with all my money."

"What did you do?" Ava whispered.

"Nothing." Helene pouted, shaking her head. "I did nothing. I stayed at the resort, too ashamed to go home and tell everyone what had happened. I think I still hoped he'd come back, or maybe that he'd drowned on a morning swim. That would have been easier than facing the shame."

Ava nodded, thinking she might have done the same.

"But then, one morning after another sleepless night, I found it – the yellow garden gate." Helene brushed the sand off her hands and stood, and the two of them began to walk down the beach.

"I have used the Atlas since to confirm what I had already feared, that everything he told me about himself was a lie. Last week, I finally managed to track him down." Just when she said this, Andre came back into view, seated at a table where he popped a champagne bottle, the golden bubbly overflowing and cascading down the ample curves of a woman's décolleté. "His name is actually Pascal. He's currently dating three women at the same time, one in Frankfurt, one in Helsinki, and another one in Vienna. At least, those are the ones I know of."

Ava's felt disgust twisting her insides, and she reached for Helene's hand to comfort her. "I'm so sorry, Helene. That's horrible."

Helene wiped away a tear, taking a deep breath to steady herself. "Yeah, well, it's my own damn fault."

"Have you ever, you know, talked to him?" Ava asked. As they continued to walk closer, she glanced over at Andre again. He was now leaning in, whispering something into the ear of the woman, who let out a boisterous laugh that rang out over the music.

"*Talk*? No." Helene slowly approached the table, her eyes fixed on Andre. "Talking doesn't do much for me at this point. But I usually do something like this..." With a nonchalant shrug, she picked up her pace, snagging a piña colada from a nearby table. Just as she reached Andre, he turned, and she splashed the milky drink in his face.

"*What the fuck?*" shouted Andre, as Helene turned to Ava, grinning. "And then, I do this." She doubled back, swung at Andre, and landed a punch right in his colada-covered face.

"Damn, that felt good," she sighed, rubbing her fist. "Now, let's get the hell out of here." She took Ava by the hand, tossed a souvenir, and they both disappeared.

They landed in the hotel's hallway, where Helene invited Ava to her room. It was a similar set-up to her own room, only one wall was dominated by a world map, covered with photographs and newspaper articles. Red strings connected different locations, creating an intricate web reminiscent of a detective's investigation board in a thriller movie.

"It's absolutely horrifying what happened to you, Helene," Ava said as she considered the map. Helene nodded, sitting on the bed.

"But I mean, come on." Ava came to sit beside her. "I know this is tough, but it's not a reason why you should have to give up your entire future. You could have gotten through it – you're tough, girl." She nudged Helene in the side.

"You act like we have a choice in the matter," Helene said.

Ava shook her head. "You know, I've been thinking about this. There must be a way out. If there wasn't, where are all the other hotel guests? All the people who made the doors – what happened to them?"

"Personally, I've begun to assume every homeless person

I see might be a stranded Atlas guest." Helene shrugged. "Your perception changes, you see? From now on, nothing will ever be the same."

"If that's true, you do realise you'd meet the same fate one day, right? Not exactly a thrilling prospect, to end up on a park bench somewhere..." Ava had to think of poor Molly living in her car. Assuming Helene was right, the old lady would end up no better than before the Atlas.

"It's just one of many possibilities, of course," Helene said, her fingers gliding over her pillow without much intention. "Also, just think of the odds, would you?" She stood to face Ava. "There are five rooms at the Atlas – well, six if you include the innkeeper's – and you've been given one of them! Out of eight billion people in the world, you and I are two of six to find that yellow gate! It's got to *mean* something!"

"What does it mean, Helene?" Ava said under her breath, her tone almost pleading.

"I don't know." Helene placed both hands on Ava's shoulders. "*Yet.* But until I do, I'm not going to sit around and whine about the past. I'm going to continue my own random acts of... well, not kindness – but vengeance."

Her eyes glittered with fiery resolve, but Ava sensed the hurt lurking underneath. It seemed the Atlas had turned Helene into a woman possessed, forever haunting – or rather being haunted by – the man who had so callously swindled her.

Ava stared out the window, watching a patch of sky amid the tree canopy change colour. Feeling lost. The remainder of the day had faded away in a spiral of thoughts, one less helpful than the next. With a twinge of panic, she'd rummaged around her bag, searching for her passport, which – to her relief – was still there, still showing her name and picture. Her phone's photo album had also remained unaltered. In it, she and Melanie were still friends. In it, her old, messy life was still untouched.

She could only guess that, within the Atlas, her true self was preserved somehow, and that any object she had taken with her still upheld her old story.

A story now forever lost... Or was it? Clearly, Melanie had forgotten about her, and so had her father. But what about her other relatives? Her aunt and uncle in Costa Rica? There was a sliver of hope they might still remember some version of her, just like Molly's daughter Annie did. After all, they'd been an integral part of half her life. Hacienda Madre Tierra, the family's coffee plantation, had been her home for eight beautiful years. Had at least some of those memories withstood the hotel's spell? Or had she, in the light of this new world, really never cast any shadows?

She wanted to find out, but at the same time, she was dreading it. Joao and Molly – and in a way, even Helene – had used the Atlas to return to their own pasts, to those places and moments that had caused them tremendous pain. Was it time Ava did the same?

She retrieved her phone, flicking through old pictures of her and her mum, out on a morning hike through the lush green hills of Madre Tierra, memories of Luciana's infectious laughter flooding her mind, filling her with a bitter sense of longing. In all those years, she had not once returned. Her aunt and uncle had wanted her to come, but Ava could never bring herself to do it. Grey and rainy London was a mood, and her sadness fed on it like a parasite. For as long as she held on to the past, her mother wasn't truly gone. As long as she didn't go back to the place where she'd lost her, she could pretend Luciana was still out there, weaving through the coffee fields, picking ripe red cherries, humming a tune.

The shuffling of feet past her door interrupted Ava's thoughts, and only now did she realise her room lay in complete darkness. It was Saturday evening. Movie night was about to commence.

Upon their return from Ibiza, Helene had tried to convince Ava to join, but she had declined, alleging the day had given her a lot to contemplate.

Now Ava sat coiled up in her armchair, resisting the pizza scent wafting through the door slit. Luckily, Helene came down a short while later, dropping off a big slice on a plate outside the door, covered with a cloche so Captain wouldn't steal any. Ava bolted for the door as soon as Helene was gone and grabbed the plate. She ate it all in her room and would have stayed there had it not been for Captain whining in the hall.

Licking her fingers clean, she went to check on him.

The dog sat at the bottom of the pull-out ladder, begging to be helped up. His complaints, however, went unnoticed by the people on the roof – the movie was already in motion, and the hatch closed.

"What's the matter, buddy? They forgot about you?" Ava petted him. She took heart, lifted him off the ground, and carried him up the stairs. Carefully opening the hatch, she sat on the top step, and Captain stayed in hiding with her.

Tonight's movie was *Papillon*, the prison escape epic from the seventies starring Steve McQueen as safecracker Papillon and Dustin Hoffman as his unlikely friend and infamous forger Louis Dega.

As Ava watched what was left of the film from her hideout, her eyes kept wandering back to Bruno. He appeared to be at ease tonight. The usual shadow across his face had lifted, his expressions softened. For once, he didn't seem to lose himself in his thoughts but stayed present throughout the movie, engaging with the other guests, baking pizza after pizza with a passion. Ava was also pleased to notice he refused the wine when Yash offered him a glass.

At last, the movie came to its dramatic finish, with Papillon counting the waves on the high cliffs of Devil's Island, then jumping into his freedom, leaving Dega imprisoned of his own volition.

"I don't get it," Joao said as Steve McQueen floated out into the endless blue ocean on a self-made raft, and a piece of weighty harp music set in. "Why did Dega stay on Devil's Island? Why didn't he jump?"

"That is an excellent point, and one I believe many people get wrong," Bruno paused the projector. "You see, at first glance, it may appear as if Papillon were the brave one and Dega the chicken too afraid to jump. But I never thought of it that way. This is actually one of the few movies I watched the remake of." The innkeeper gestured at a frozen frame of Dustin Hoffman's tearful face. "And the remake dares to give the viewer a bit more insight at the end."

Joao turned around to look at Bruno. "How so?"

"By suggesting there was no hope left for Papillon on Devil's Island – that's why he needed to escape, even at the risk of his own life." As he spoke, Bruno threaded his fingers through the air like an orchestra director. "For Dega, on the other hand, there was no hope to be found in the real world – that's why he chose to stay. Does that answer your question?"

"I think so..." Joao turned back to look at the screen.

"One more thing, though."

"Vai avanti. Shoot."

"If there's a remake, why did we have to sit through three hours of this ancient one?"

At that, everybody broke out in laughter. Even Ava, on her step, couldn't suppress a snort.

"All right, all right, duly noted," said Bruno. "Next Saturday, you get to choose the movie, and I will sit through it without complaint, even if it's starring Shia LaBeouf or whomever you kids worship these days." He offered Joao his hand. "Deal?"

"Deal!" Joao gave him a high five.

"And now, signore e signori, before I release you into the night," Bruno announced, and Ava knew what was coming. "It is time to agree on next week's random act of kindness. Joao set the bar high this week, and we're not even going to attempt to top that. But any good deed will always be appreciated. Let's hear your ideas, folks!"

At that moment, Captain wriggled out of Ava's embrace and, with a hearty bark, ran over to the others, giving away her hideout.

"Ava, darling! Come over here," said Molly.

Ava stood and straightened, and before she could stop them, words cropped up in her throat, formed on her tongue, and then slipped from her mouth. "I've got one," she said and stepped into the shimmer of the fairy lights. "I've got an idea for next week."

The innkeeper gazed at her, eyes beaming with what could only be described as deep relief, and maybe a faint glimmer of triumph. He had won her over. Or so he seemed to think. "Where would you like to take us?" he asked.

"Costa Rica," Ava said and sounded much braver than she felt.

15

PEABERRY

The instant Ava took her first breath of Costa Rican air in over nine years, it swept her away with all the force of the Papagayo winds. At this time of year, the lightly sweet scent of Guaria Morada – a shimmery, purple orchid and the country's national flower – floated through the highlands, reminding her of all the weekend hikes she'd taken with her mum. The end of the dry season bore a perpetual campfire scent as farmers burned fallen leaves and branches in preparation for the rains. Ava and her cousins had always loved to pile up the foliage and fight passionate leaf battles. And maybe she imagined it, but Ava could have sworn she detected the scent of pancakes drowning in maple syrup. As the dry Papagayo winds swept across from Nicaragua, coasters poured sticky sweet molasses over the dirt roads to settle the dust. How many of Ava's sandals had gotten stuck on the way back from the beach, she could only guess.

And then there were all the other smells she had gathered here as a child, only to shut them away in the darkest corners of her grown-up mind. The earthy, verdant notes of the cloud forest. The salty ocean breezes. That distinct scent right before it rained. The crisp mountain air, getting cooler the higher she climbed. And – maybe most important of all – the bittersweet aroma of freshly ground coffee.

"The smell is incredible," said Bruno. He took a slightly overstated breath. "Wakes me up without drinking a cup myself!" He was in good spirits this morning, trudging up the winding gravel road. But even though he seemed to think he'd succeeded, the innkeeper hadn't exactly convinced Ava of his grand Atlas mission. Rather, she'd needed a false pretence to trick herself into returning to a place so heavily laden with her own history. That, and she'd preferred not to go alone.

Her act of kindness had been accepted without anyone even wanting to know what it was. They were all just relieved Ava had come back to the living.

Now the Atlas crew took their first steps on Costa Rican soil in her wake, waiting for instructions on what to do with the crates of seedlings they carried. The day before, Ava had picked up coffee plants in a secluded forest village in Sierra Leone, which had reported promising growth results in recent years. Allan, her uncle, would go nuts for them.

As she led the crew up the old familiar mountain path, dawn cracked coral red on the horizon. The occasional yawn resounded from behind her, and morning dew pearled on the grasses and flowers on the wayside. Ava turned the last bend, and the ramshackle but quaint entry gate to her aunt's plantation came into view.

"This is Hacienda Madre Tierra. It belongs to my aunt and uncle," Ava said. She unhooked the gate's chain like she'd done numerous times before, and her heartbeat quickened as her hands recalled the motion from muscle memory. "We're a six-generation family of coffee farmers. It's the end of the harvest season, which is when the number of workers usually declines. I thought we could help them out today." She shrugged, realising only now that her act of kindness might not sound quite as elaborate as Joao's idea with the soccer balls.

"And what about these?" Helene asked and showed the crate she carried.

"Ah, yes." Ava clapped her hands, pointing her fingertips at the crate. "I thought we could bring these along as a gift. They're saplings of a wild coffee variety thought to be extinct until a couple of years ago. They're very resilient to our warming climate – the future of coffee, so to speak."

"Fantastique," said Helene. Although she looked like she'd rather drink a coffee than deliver some.

As they entered the plantation, they were greeted by an orchestra of bird song. However, unlike instruments, there was nothing coordinated about the tweets and chirps resounding from the treetops. The deep, hooting notes of the motmots, the woodpecker's drill, the hummingbird's musical chirps – all chimed into Mother Nature's wild and jumbled rhythm, a vibrant display of the hacienda's name, as Ava's mum had always said.

Past the gate, a shaded avenue led up to Madre Tierra House, flanked by towering pacay and jackfruit trees, old oropendola nests hanging from the branches like baubles. At the end of the lane, the maroon-red hilltop villa stood against lush, primary rainforest like a hibiscus flower in bloom, luring in visitors like bumblebees.

About a dozen people had gathered in its shade, busy strapping baskets around their waists, which they would use to collect the coffee cherries. Once a basket was full, the pickers would empty it into their designated bag, then fill the basket anew. At the end of a shift, the bulk of cherries in each bag was measured, and the worker was paid depending on the total amount.

As Ava and the crew approached, a foreman gave instructions in Spanish. Her heart skipped a beat when she recognised Luis, her youngest cousin.

"Hola! ¿Puedo ayudarte?" Luis shouted when he spotted the strangers approaching. He had grown a lot bulkier – and hairier – since Ava had last seen him, now looking the spitting image of his father with his scraggly beard and broad shoulders. Three years younger than Ava, he'd left Madre Tierra for the city of San José in the hopes of a stable career in accounting. Ava wasn't surprised he had returned. City life had never agreed with his wild spirit.

"Hola, Luis! It's Ava. Do you... remember me?" She decided to speak English, knowing Luis was fluent in both languages, but embarrassment flushed her cheeks when she realised how desperate her question might sound to the Atlas guests. It took only a split second, however, to ascertain that Luis had no clue who she was. Swallowing down her disappointment, she quickly added, "I'm from Volunteers for the Earth? We met a couple of years ago."

"I'm sure I'd remember you," Luis said with a wink. Ava couldn't help but wrinkle her nose when her own cousin attempted to size her up. Wrong, so wrong...

"So, you've come to help for the day? Fantastic!" Luis said, fist-bumping Joao.

"Yes, that's right," Ava said, relieved Luis took the bait so easily. "And the volunteers brought these along as a gift for our hosts." She gestured at Bruno's sapling crate. "They're Coffea stenophylla."

"You're joking! Ah, gracias mis amigos." Luis took the crate off Bruno's hands. He looked upon the saplings as if they were newly born puppies. "My old man will go nuts for these."

"Are Allan and Adriana around?" Ava craned her neck past Luis' shoulder.

"They're still sleeping. Son viejas ahora – they're getting old now!" Luis laughed. "Don't tell them I said that." He touched Ava on the shoulder. "You'll see them later. Now, amigos, let's go pick some coffee!"

A half-hour later, Ava, Bruno, Yash, and Helene were traipsing around the eastern slope of Madre Tierra, each with a basket strapped around the waist, picking coffee cherries. Luis had assigned them a large patch that needed stripping. Toward the end of the season, most of the cherries remaining on the trees were already red and ripe. Stripping was the easiest harvest method and great for beginners, as it required only a simple sweep of an entire branch rather than the more tedious hand-selection of each red fruit amid the yellows at the start of the season. Still, it was hard physical labour, especially in this heat – which is why Ava had suggested Molly engage in more gentle activities.

She had taken over the nursery from a mother assigned to look after the workers' kids that day. Most coffee pickers in Costa Rica came from Nicaragua, travelling across the border with the entire family for the season. By relieving this woman from her child-care duties, Molly made it possible for her to pick coffee and bring home an extra day's worth of wages. Joao had also become a babysitter to help Molly with translations.

Ava and the others spent the morning weaving through lush green rows of coffee trees like a swarm of bees browsing through honeysuckle. To her, there was something meditative about this kind of physical labour immersed in nature.

It felt right to use her eyes and hands the way evolution had intended, scanning for ripe fruits, then picking them.

It felt right to have only one objective: filling the basket strapped around her waist.

It felt right to notice her surroundings and how all was connected.

How the canopy of mature trees provided shade and shelter for the understory. How shrubs and herbs, saplings and mushrooms flourished in the dark soil, covered with tracks left by coyotes and racoons, wild pigs and rhinoceros beetles. How a stream trickled nearby, and lizards sunbathed in the patches of light breaking through the treetops. How an explosion of butterflies fluttered overhead, some occasionally landing on a leaf, or if one was lucky – a hand. How toucans called from the higher branches, their song like the croaking of a frog, mixed with the rhythmic tapping of their bills. And how, underneath it all, the buzz of insects composed the backdrop of abundance, taken for granted unless it faded.

Madre Tierra truly was a wild forest garden, and it was calling Ava home. Every sound was a hymn, every living thing a friend, every smell a memory. And yet, she had never felt so uprooted in her life – defined by a past now forever lost, headed for a future forgotten by the world. How could her body feel so in place, she wondered, when the rest of her was completely out of it?

"I must admit, this is not what I expected a coffee plantation to look like," Bruno said, interrupting Ava's thoughts. Head buried in waxy coffee leaves, he reached for a branch laden with red cherries. "It's like the Garden of Eden!"

"That's because this isn't just a coffee farm," Ava explained. She worked with quick, experienced hands and had easily collected twice as much as the others already.

"Madre Tierra is a permaculture project. Besides coffee, they grow mangoes, oranges, three different varieties of bananas, sixty different kinds of native trees, pineapples, beans, peppers, cashews… and all of it organic."

"Unglaublich." Bruno stopped his work to peek through the branches at Ava. "And do they supply Marley's, too?"

"Not anymore. During the switch-over to organic, the crop yield went down, and they could no longer guarantee the quantity Marley's requires from suppliers."

"So, Marley's coffee isn't organic, then?" Helene asked, deterring flies that weren't there. Being out in nature clearly made her jumpy. The continuous sound of her hands slapping away yet another insect had quickly become the snare drum to the toucans' beat.

"Hardly any coffee from big corporations is organic," Ava said to the leaves. "It's not feasible."

"That's disappointing." Helene scratched her forearm, checking for insect stings.

"It's not that easy, you know? It takes years to go organic. And during the transition period, production goes down so much most farmers wouldn't survive. So, they won't even start in the first place."

"Then how did these guys do it?" Yash joined the conversation with the swirl of a finger.

"Madre Tierra is kind of an exception," Ava said, gazing at the treetops. "My family stayed committed to their goal of becoming fully organic. It paid off in the end, but coffee is only one pillar the farm stands on these days. They run a successful eco-lodge and an education centre for other farmers. And they have their own roastery on site, which keeps every stage of the process within their control. For the most part, they're self-sustaining. They're not about profit;

they basically live off the land. The coffee they do sell, they sell directly to tourists and locals."

"So, they're kind of a unicorn in the industry," Yash concluded.

"At least for now." Ava nodded and kept on picking, remembering her mum's ferocious commitment to educate the neighbours. It was Luciana who had convinced her sister and brother-in-law to make the shift. Allan had long complained about health issues related to the pesticides, and Adriana was growing weary of the industry pressures, so they were quick to get on board. But as Ava grew older, she'd come to understand that, for her mother, the shift had been about more than that.

After the divorce, Luciana had been determined to do *her thing*, unapologetically, to create something on the exact opposite side of the spectrum. Ava had thus been caught in the middle. She still remembered taking all her friends to Marley's on a school trip to San José once – the only place in Costa Rica that had one. Brimming with pride, she'd shown everyone around (naturally, she'd never told her mum about it). But with Luciana's passing, Ava had taken a side, honouring her mother's memory by refusing to visit any Marley's ever again.

"You know, there is this great little coffee company called Aldilà," Bruno said as he weeded out a couple of yellow cherries from his basket. "They run a lovely little café in Sicily, right off the port of Trapani, and they foster a close relationship with a family-run farm very much like this one. I think it's in Honduras, but I'm not sure... Anyway, they ship the roasted coffee over to Italy on a sailboat – 100 percent carbon-neutral – and they split the profits equally with the farmers. Isn't that great?"

"It sure is," Ava said. "It sure is."

She knew only too well about these kinds of small-scale projects. Over the past few years, they had popped up like mushrooms. It was a part of the industry she had always felt passionate about. If you asked her, the whole sector of private label companies like the one in Sicily could become a major player in the future of coffee, making the journey from bean to cup transparent and personal, and totally sustainable.

"It's called Aldilà, you say?" Ava asked casually, trying to hide her spiked interest.

"Aldilà, esattamente. It means 'beyond' in Italian. They're still very small scale, but they're great people."

"Didn't I read somewhere that Italy is the only European country without a single Marley's Café?" Helene sat down on a tree stump, stretching. Coffee picking clearly wasn't her vocation; her basket was still nearly empty.

Ava cleared her throat. "There was one in Rome. But it shut down after only a year."

"What happened there? Bruno, you're Italian. What do you think?" Helene turned to the innkeeper, who had paused his work to fetch a bottle of water.

"I suppose we're people of habit, that's all. And we're not exactly fond of franchises or big corporations." He shrugged and took a sip. "Romans especially are very proud of their caffè. It might have felt presumptuous to them for a foreign business to come in and tell them how to do coffee."

Ava nodded, still stripping cherries. It was precisely what her mum had warned her dad about when discussing an Italian branch over the dinner table all those years ago.

"Why's coffee so huge over there, anyway?" Yash raised a hand, signalling Bruno to toss him a bottle.

"Caffè, in Italy, it is un diritto sociale... an Italian social right – catch!" Bruno chucked him a bottle. "After all, Italy was one of the first European importers of coffee beans. We invented the espresso machine, and, of course, caffè sospeso."

"What's that, caffè sospeso?" Ava cut in, surprised (and a little embarrassed to admit) there was something in the coffee realm she didn't know about.

"Oh, it's this lovely tradition born in Naples," Bruno replied, eyes gleaming. "Caffè sospeso means 'suspended coffee'. In many cafés around the city, a customer can pay not only for his or her own coffee, but one extra for a stranger – mostly the homeless who can't afford a cup."

"That's so cute," said Helene. "Aargh! Bête à merde!" she cursed in the same breath and slapped her calf to kill off yet another insect, just when the clattering of an engine drew nearer.

A moment later, Luis appeared at the crest of the slope on an ancient three-wheeler tractor. He switched off, shouting down into the valley in Spanish. "Who are you guys?"

Naturally, he'd forgotten they had met before.

"Hola, you must be Luis!" Ava shouted back. She took off her basket and made her way up the slope. "Sorry, we haven't met yet. I'm Ava." She reached out a hand to her cousin. "We're the team from Volunteers for the Earth. Allan assigned us to this patch."

"I see. Of course, he didn't think to tell me." Luis rolled his eyes as he shook Ava's hand. "Classic, my old man. Anyway – guys!" He switched to English and back to his shouting voice. "Morning shift is done! After all the coffee picking, it's time we got to drink some, what do you say?"

"Oh. My. God. Yes, please!" Helene yelled, and it sounded like she was drowning. She couldn't strip off her basket fast enough.

Back at the main house, Luis had forgotten who they were, yet again. But it didn't matter anymore. By now, the hacienda had filled with day visitors and guests spending the night at the lodge. A good two dozen people had flocked to Madre Tierra that day, making it easy for the Atlas crew to blend in.

While Luis was busy measuring the cherries picked that morning, his father Allan showed the tourists through each stage of the coffee-making process. Excitement leapt in Ava's chest when she first spotted the old man's floppy chonete hat. He had worn it every day for as long as she could remember. She also knew every word, every joke, and every fact of his lecture by heart; it hadn't changed one bit over the past fifteen years. Neither had his passion for Madre Tierra. Allan was a born performer; each time he gave the tour felt like the first time.

"That's my son Luis over there, if you couldn't tell already by his good looks," he said with a wink. "The box in front of him is called a cajuela. A cajuela is the official unit of measurement established by the Costa Rican government, and it is used exclusively for coffee. Now, how many cajuelas do you think a coffee picker can fill on a good day?"

The visitors considered the box Luis filled with ripe red cherries. It was quite large, roughly the size of half a rubbish bin.

"Five!" shouted a voice from the left.

"Eight?" said a blonde girl at the front.

"Twelve, no, maybe thirteen..."

"Twenty," Ava said from the back row, a sureness in her voice that came from knowing. She couldn't resist initiating a little interaction with her uncle. It came as natural to her as breathing; the two of them had always engaged in plenty of banter.

"Ah, someone did her homework this morning!" Allan applauded, and the crowd parted. "On a good day, a picker will fill twenty cajuelas. That is correct. Now, señorita, if you know this next one, too, you can have my job!"

Ava inclined her head. "Try me," she said, smirking.

"Where does the word 'coffee' originally come from?" Allan flashed his bushy eyebrows at the crowd.

"It comes from the Arabic word for 'wine' – qahwah, which later became kahveh in Turkish, and then koffie in Dutch."

Allan took off his chonete and offered it to her. "Job's yours, señorita. You're the boss now. Great, now I can put my feet up at last!" He laughed, a hearty old man's laugh, and the crowd joined in.

Ava was about to step forward and take her uncle's hat, but then a man pushed in front of her. Tall and bulky, he'd only meant to wave off a bee on his wife's shoulder. Still, he'd caused Allan to lose sight of Ava. It lasted only a second or two, but when her uncle came back into view, he seemed to have lost his train of thought, looking down at his hat as if it were a script.

"Now, where was I? Whew! I'm getting old, folks! Someone wants my job? I'm ready to put my feet up," he said, breaking into the same laugh as ten seconds before. "Come on, amigos," he said and waved at the group to follow him. "Time for my favourite part of the process – coffee tasting. By the way, anyone here know where the word 'coffee' comes from?"

Ava stayed behind, the suddenness of being forgotten hitting her with the weight of twenty full cajuelas.

"It happens so quickly," she said when Helene appeared next to her.

"I know." Helene crossed her arms. "It can be super

random. I've had actual eye-to-eye chats with people before, and they forgot me mid-conversation. And then other times, a fella can doze off next to me and still remember who I am when he wakes up. The worst was when I had to see a doctor for a bladder infection a couple of weeks ago. After I went to the loo to pee in a cup, I came back, and she'd forgotten all about me. You see, I had to put the urine sample in one of those discreet hatches in the bathroom. I went another two times, but eventually, I had to insist on peeing right in front of her. The embarrassment..." Helene fluttered her lips.

"That's a lovely story, Hel," Yash interrupted, dragging the crew's cherry bag with Bruno. They'd collected a decent amount, albeit mainly by Ava's doing.

"Ava, should we give our yield to the farmers now, or would you like to wait?" Yash asked. He'd been overly polite to her since their run-in on the stairwell, an attitude she gladly reciprocated.

"Yes, you guys go ahead. They will be very grateful. And then you can follow Allan for some coffee and treats. I just... I need a minute, if that's all right."

Ava trailed off. She passed through an arched entryway overgrown with creepers. She didn't know where she was going exactly. Yet, she knew every corner of the house by heart. A two-storied building with a sweeping balcony encircling the first floor, Madre Tierra had been constructed in the nineteenth century for some influential minister who happened to father no children of his own. With his death, the estate had passed to his nephew – Ava's great-great-grandfather, who had transformed it into the coffee plantation it was today. Steeped in old-world charm, the U-shaped premises harboured twelve bedrooms and fifteen bathrooms. Nowadays, the west wing served as a guesthouse while the east wing remained the private quarters for the family.

The courtyard harboured an orange and avocado orchard, where seasonal fruit, homemade granola, and pastries were served for breakfast in good weather. The ground floor had no walls. Ornate columns supported the upper storey, allowing for plenty of natural ventilation, which kept the humidity at bay. Throughout the day, a fresh ocean breeze swept through. At night, the cool mountain air shepherded everyone underneath thick quilts. Ava had never slept as well as she had at Madre Tierra, listening to the frogs' concerts as she drifted into dreams and waking up to the howler monkeys come morning.

She crossed the courtyard and veered toward the living room on her right. Out of habit, she took off her shoes, and the terracotta tiles felt cool beneath her feet. A sprawling linen couch took up the centre of the room, big enough to fit the entire family and then some. Ava sat down on a corner, her toes distorting a thin line of ash running around the couch – a natural deterrent for the army ants, which came sweeping through the house about once a month. 'Cleaning squad', Aunt Adriana liked to call them. They attacked and killed all other insects around the house, carrying them off into the jungle. A memory struck Ava of a time one of those squads had invaded the living room. The whole family had huddled up on the couch together as the insects swept through the house. There'd been so many entire walls had blackened.

Ava's gaze wandered around the room. Not much had changed in nine years. A new plant here, a cushion there. She considered the picture frames on the coffee table beside her, lingering on a photo of her parents she was sure had been removed after their divorce. Now, in this reality, it had resurfaced. Ava picked it up. She, too, was in the photo, although still in hiding. It dated back to the opening of the Soho flagship store; Luciana had been three months pregnant at the time. Ava traced her parents' profiles with a fingertip. Both looked so happy here, so full of love – for the business and the family they were about to start.

"Can I help you?" A voice resounded in Spanish from behind her.

Ava put the picture back, swivelling around with the haste of someone caught snooping. "I'm sorry, I didn't mean to snoop," she said and looked up.

There, leaning against a maroon-red column, stood Aunt Adriana.

"Didn't you?" she asked, amused, then strode across the room like the grand landlady she was.

As always, Adriana was superbly dressed, like she was about to attend a fabulous party. Today, she wore a rose-coloured cocktail dress embroidered with a delicate flower pattern and complemented by what Ava knew were her grandmother's pearls. She had the same button nose as Ava and her mum, the same brown curls, naturally bouncy thanks to the humidity. In Adriana's case, however, they were dyed; the narrow crest of greys framing her face gave it away.

"Maybe just a little," Ava confessed, shoving her hands in her pockets. Her aunt was about the gentlest soul ever to come into this world, but she was also the matriarch in the family, thus demanding respect simply by being in a room.

Adriana came to stand beside Ava, picking up the photo she had just put back.

Ava considered her aunt. She would have turned eighty-six last month, but apart from the bits of grey curling around her forehead, nothing gave her age away. She didn't look a day older than sixty.

"My youngest sister and her husband," Adriana sighed, brushing some dust off the picture frame. "I assume you recognise them from the media?"

Ava nodded.

"Quite the couple they were. I always said their relationship was like a dance between fire and wind. They ignited each other's passions and fuelled their creativity. In measured doses, the wind fanned the fire, but when the wind grew too strong" – Adriana whistled – "then the whole thing turned into a raging inferno."

"Why didn't they..." Ava cleared her throat, thinking her voice sounded strange. "Why didn't they have any children?"

"Now that's a tragic story." Aunt Adriana sighed and looked down at the photo. "Luciana was pregnant when this photo was taken. If you look closely, you can make out a tiny bump." She stroked her pinkie over Luciana's belly. "My sister had a miscarriage a short while later."

Ava flinched, her heart tightening.

"They never tried again after that, but the experience brought them closer together. Despite all their fiery arguments, they always came back to one another, and when she passed, he found solace in upholding her memory. You know, sometimes I catch myself thinking that a child might even have tipped that delicate balance between them."

Ava's heart clenched, and she fought to conceal the ache from showing on her expression. But her aunt's gaze lingered on her, and Ava blushed. She had to look away.

"You know what? You remind me of her a little. My sister, I mean. Maybe that's why I find you so easy to talk to," Adriana said. "My, ain't that strange?"

"Not really," Ava said and smiled sadly. "Anyway, I

should head back. My friends must be wondering where I am. But thank you for our little chat, Adriana. You've given me a lot to think about. And again, so sorry for the intrusion." Ava entered the courtyard, where she slipped back into her shoes.

"Did I tell you my name?" Adriana's voice echoed from the walls, but as soon as Ava had disappeared behind a column, her aunt had forgotten she'd ever asked the question.

Through the orange branches, Ava caught one last glimpse of Adriana. She couldn't help but think it was what her mother would have looked like – one day, in another life.

"PENNY FOR YOUR THOUGHTS?"

Ava had walked back through the archway toward the front terrace, where the innkeeper's voice reached her. She hadn't planned on sharing her thoughts with anyone for a while. They were still raw, unfiltered. Still, she said, "I just spoke to my aunt." She touched her earlobe absentmindedly as Bruno closed the gap between them.

"What did you learn?" He sounded neutral to a degree, but Ava suspected he'd probably pay a lot more than a penny for her thoughts if this was what it took. She was like a unique orchid, and he a collector still desperate to add her to his garden.

Ava walked down the front steps. To her right, a winding path lined with palm trees led away from the house and up a slope into the forest. As she took it, the innkeeper fell into step with her. He always walked like a prisoner, shoulders slouched, hands behind his back as if in chains.

"I learnt that, in this reality, my parents were happily married, right until my mum's death," Ava said, kicking a pebble. "They never had me, and that seems to have saved their relationship. And what's more, it compelled my father to hold on to Marley's original values in honour of her memory." Her conversation with Ethan at the corner café came back to mind. It seemed, even MCC was better off without her.

Bruno kicked the pebble back. "Sobering, isn't it? To discover the rest of the world doesn't seem to miss us much. How does that make you feel?"

Ava kicked the pebble one more time, and it landed in a ditch. She stopped and looked ahead, where the palm leaves formed a natural archway. Madre Tierra regularly held weddings during the summer months, and this was always the favourite photo spot for the happy couples.

"I feel better," Ava said. She didn't want to share this with Bruno yet, but for the first time since she'd learnt the truth about the Atlas, she could see that maybe she had been meant to enter the hotel after all. Because if the result was her parents' happiness, then that was a good thing, wasn't it? In fact, wasn't that what most children of divorced parents prayed for? For their parents to get together again? Yes, Ava had struggled to warm up to her father, especially in recent years. But it hadn't always been that way. Without a doubt, Luciana had loved him once. Where had that love gone? And didn't it make sense that it had persisted if a significant variable, such as having a child, had not come into the picture? Besides, the damage was done. Ava could never leave the Atlas now. This made staying easier. Much easier.

"I guess you've figured out by now that this is the one," Ava said and resumed the walk.

"What's that?" Bruno asked. He picked up a dark blue flower in his path, a slightly wilted yet still lovely salvia Costa Rican blue.

"The place I would go if I had only one place left?" Ava said. "This is the one."

"I can see why." Bruno twirled the flower between his fingers. They'd reached a clearing where the jungle parted, revealing a breath-taking view of the Arenal volcano.

"I still remember when we first moved back here," Ava said, "I was terrified to go to a new school." She slid down with her back against a tree trunk and came onto her haunches. The air was cooler this low to the ground. It smelled of wet earth and rotting wood. "So, when my cousins and I left the house in the mornings, I would come up here and hide all day. But after a few days, Luis ratted me out."

"Was your mother angry?" Bruno asked, sitting down on a rock.

"Nah, I think she understood how tough it all was for me. She just sat me down on her lap, right where you're sitting now, and she said, 'Peaberry, I understand you're scared, but now it's time. You can't remain inside the cherry forever. You're meant to blossom out.'"

"Peaberry?" Bruno raised his brows.

"It's what she used to call me." Ava took a deep breath as the memory knifed her heart. "In around five per cent of every coffee harvest, a natural mutation occurs where only one seed – instead of the usual two – develops inside the cherry. Because of the extra space and nutrients for that single seed, a richer bean develops, which is considered rare and quite precious amongst coffee lovers. That is a peaberry. It's… kind of like an oyster's pearl…" She shrugged, a little embarrassed.

"How lucky you are," the innkeeper said to the blue salvia still in his hand. "To have known a mother's love like that."

Ava nodded, fighting back the tears. "Actually," she said, struck by a thought, "it was my dad who first came up with the nickname." She wiped her face dry with the hem of her sleeve. "When I was, I don't know, maybe seven or eight, I asked him why I had no brothers or sisters. He told me they had tried for a second child, but it wasn't meant to be. Hence, the peaberry." She pointed at her chest. "So odd. I'd completely forgotten about that until now."

It was when the innkeeper placed a hand on her shoulder that hot tears welled up. She wiped them away, patting Bruno's hand – if anything, so that he'd remove it. (What was it about human touch that always made the tears pour out as if a pipe had burst?)

The sound of feet running up the hill was a welcome distraction. "We should go," she said and rose.

"Bruno! Ava! Come quick!" It was Joao, hastening toward them.

"You need a moment?" Bruno asked gently, and Ava nodded. He patted her shoulder, then returned to the house. A storm cloud had pushed in front of the afternoon sun, darkening the path ahead.

As soon as the innkeeper was out of earshot, Ava buried her face in her hands and let out a deep sigh. She pressed her fingers on her eyelids as if she could stop the tears she felt pushing through. But the harder she tried not to weep, the stronger her body shook. Soon, her chest quivered until her cheeks were awash with tears, and she was sobbing like a child, crying like she hadn't done in years.

"Ava!" Bruno and Joao cried out urgently then, and she could sense from their voices that something was off-kilter.

She hurriedly wiped away the tears and spun around to face them. “What happened?” she shouted and broke into a sprint when she noticed the alarm on Joao’s face.

He met her halfway, holding his kneecaps as he caught his breath.

“It’s Molly,” he gasped, “she’s collapsed.”

16

LIAR, LIAR...

"Take her to the living room!"

The Atlas crew had reappeared in the hotel hallway, a chain of people holding on to each other's shoulders. Yash carried Molly under her arms, her toes skimming the floorboards. She was barely conscious and pale as paper.

Yash settled her gently on a green velvet couch by the fireplace, and Helene sat down next to her. The rest backed off and gathered by the sliding doors separating the living room from the hall. Only the innkeeper stood apart, staring out the front door as if he considered running.

"Tell us what happened, Joao," Ava said, touching the boy's shoulder. "How did she faint?"

"I- I don't know. She was busy teaching the other kids and me how to make didgeridoos from bamboo, and then she sort of rolled her eyes back and fell off the chair."

"I can't say I'm surprised," Yash spoke under his breath. "She hasn't been looking well for weeks."

"But what's wrong with her?"

Yash shrugged wordlessly, concern flaring in his eyes.

"She has anaemia," Bruno said and turned toward them. He seemed barely present.

"What's that?" asked Joao simultaneously as Ava burst out, *"You knew?"*

The innkeeper's gaze flitted from one to the other. He answered the easier question. "It's a condition where you don't produce enough red blood cells to carry oxygen around the body."

"Is that serious?"

"It can be, depending on the type," said Yash.

"But what type does she have?"

"I don't know," Bruno said, absorbed with his fingernails peeling a paint splinter off the door. "I caught her taking... ferro... how do you say?" He flicked his fingers, trying to think of the word. "*Iron*. I caught her taking iron supplements one morning. Tutto qui. That's all. It didn't seem serious at the time."

"Well, it is now," Ava said. She cast Bruno an irritated glance. His absent-mindedness was galling. "We need to take her to the hospital, guys."

"And then, what?" Yash showed his palms. "Aren't they going to run blood tests and stuff? They'll forget her before we ever get a diagnosis!"

"We must try anyway. We have no choice. Go fetch a wheelchair from somewhere and bring it back here, will you?" she instructed Yash. "And then we take her to a hospital. The Royal London, unless anyone has a better idea?"

Yash shook his head and went to consult the Book of Doors, just as Helene called out from the fireplace. "Guys, she's conscious!"

Ava rushed over to the couch and came down on her knees at Molly's side.

"Molly?" she said, stroking the old lady's icicle fingers.

"We're going to take you to the hospital now, okay?"

But Molly shook her head, surprisingly firm given that she'd fainted only minutes ago. "No. There's no need," she said. "It happens sometimes when I don't get enough air. I'm an old woman, dear. We stumble and fall sometimes. Nothing out of the ordinary, trust me."

"I would still feel better if we brought you to a doctor." Ava looked over her shoulder, seeking backup from the others.

"Yes, Molly," agreed Yash. "We need to take you to hospital."

"No." Molly insisted. "Please, you guys. This is my choice, not yours. Let's see how I'm doing in the morning." Molly patted Ava's hand. "I realise I've given you all a big fright, but, really, I don't expect anything bad to happen. I've been here before. And if I feel worse throughout the night, I promise I will let you know."

Ava glanced over at Helene, who gave her a look that conveyed she was out of her depth.

"Would you like some water, Molly?" Helene offered the glass.

"Oh, that is kind. Thank you, dear. If... if someone could be a darling and fetch my supplements from my nightstand as well? I might just..."

"I'll go!" Joao was up and running before Molly had finished speaking.

"I might just sleep down here tonight," she continued. "I feel fine, I do. But I don't think I could tackle stairs just yet."

"All right. You're the boss. We'll leave you to rest for now." Ava squeezed Molly's hand slightly.

The group reassembled in the hallway. "What you guys think?" Yash asked, scratching his stubble.

"I don't know," Ava sighed. She sat down on the staircase. "She seems well enough for the time being, but who knows if her fainting even was because of the anaemia?"

"Anaemia can also be fatal, you know?" Yash placed a foot on the stairs. "Didn't want to say it in front of the boy, but an uncle of mine died from it."

"Let's not panic just yet," Helene cut in, pushing down air with her hands. "She says she's been here before, and she doesn't seem so bad now, non? Besides, we did save a considerable amount of time thanks to the Atlas."

Ava nodded. "Let's keep an eye on her for now, see how things develop. In the meantime, let's be proactive, though. I'll go check out the hospital and make a door that will put her right in front of the best doctor there is. The less time she spends in some waiting hall, the better."

"Out of the way, please!" Joao blustered down the stairs, Molly's pillbox in hand and her bedsheets under his arms.

Ava stood and brushed his hair as he skidded past.

"I'll go cook dinner for her," Helene said and headed for the kitchen. "Salmon would boost her iron levels, non?"

"I'll fetch some fresh ones at a fish market somewhere," Yash offered and fell into step with her.

Ava was left contemplating. She would have felt better taking Molly to the hospital right away. But she had to admit, this one wasn't as straightforward as a simple click of the heels. She peeked inside the living room, where Joao was busy hand-feeding Molly her pills. Ava was about to walk over, but when a smell wafted in from the front door, she followed it instead.

Outside, Bruno leaned against the balusters, a cigarette tucked between his fingers.

"Didn't know you smoked," Ava said.

"I don't, really." He considered the cigarette. "Matteo does. I bought a pack the other day, so I could offer him one.

Anything to strike up a conversation," he said and puffed out. There was not the slightest breath of wind, and the smoke looked almost liquid as it billowed upward, obscuring the innkeeper's face.

"I know what you must be thinking." He tapped the cigarette, ash sprinkling the flower heads. "But this time, it really wasn't my secret to tell. And she did assure me it was nothing serious."

Ava crossed her arms. "Anything else you've kept from us? Now would be the time to tell." It sounded challenging. She meant it to.

Bruno took another drag, his expression unaltered as if he hadn't heard her. He flicked the cigarette. "Let's just see how she's doing in the morning," he said and walked off – not inside, but down the veranda toward the back of the house.

"So, there *is* something else?" Ava asked, but once again, she was ignored. She followed him.

"Bruno."

No answer.

She threw her hands in the air, vexed.

She turned the corner.

"Bruno, come on. You can't just disap—"

But Bruno had done precisely that: He had disappeared.

Ava placed her hands on her hips, annoyance building in her chest like a scream. It was exhausting, this air of mystery the innkeeper constantly tried to create around his own person. He wasn't Bruce Wayne, for crying out loud. She returned inside, consulting the Book of Doors for a passageway to London Royal Hospital, where she spent the rest of the day contriving an emergency plan she prayed they would not need.

She didn't sleep at all that night, clasping the stethoscope she'd turned into a door, listening for noises from downstairs. Twice, Ava had snuck downstairs to check on Molly. But each time, the scene couldn't have been more peaceful. Embers glowing in the fireplace, they shone a dim light on Molly, whose chest gently rose and lowered like ocean waves rolling into a protected cove.

It was only when distorted morning light spilt through the curtains, and Ava could already make out the contours of her room, that she dozed off into a vestige of sleep.

~

AVA AWOKE WITH A START, like she'd overslept and missed an important exam. Wiping drool off her chin, she got up to look out the window. The sun had long peeked its forehead over the garden wall; she must have slept all throughout the morning. Down in the garden, she spotted Bruno escorting Molly through the flower beds – what a relief to see her out and about! She must be feeling much better.

Ava slipped into a fresh T-shirt but left on her pyjama bottoms for now. About to head down to the kitchen for a coffee, she cast another glance out the window. Bruno had guided Molly down the gravel path and toward the garden gate. The hedges stood so high Ava could only see their heads. What were they up to? She opened the window and craned her neck, slightly unnerved when Bruno flung open the gate. "Don't do *that*," Ava said, more to herself, but when the innkeeper guided Molly further toward the front step, her voice got louder. "Seriously, *don't do that*!"

But, to Ava's horror, the innkeeper gave Molly a push between the shoulder blades. It looked gentle enough, but still: it was a push! And it forced Molly into a step – a step, out of the hotel!

"DON'T DO THAT!" Now Ava yelled, which made Bruno fling his head around. Spotting her, panic dilated his eyes, but instead of pulling Molly back inside – he slammed the gate shut, then hastened back toward the house.

"Holy shit." Ava bolted for the door, only to backtrack and put her shoes on. She could find only one, cursing as she whirled around the room, searching for its twin. She found it tucked away in a crevice of the armchair, the toe cap chewed off. "Goddammit, Captain!" Ava scolded the dog even though he wasn't there. She slipped into what was left of her shoe, shouldered her leather bag, and then she was out the door, running straight into Molly's room. She had to find her – had to save her somehow!

Fetching the porcelain turtle, Ava tossed it up in the air, caught it, and disappeared.

She landed on all fours, flicking Australian sand off her hands as she came back to standing. "What... the ...actual heck?" It was pitch-black. The beach had about tripled in size, a vast field of wet sand and tide pools shimmering beneath the moon as the ocean ebbed away under its pull.

"MOLLY!" Ava called out. As usual, she retrieved the stopwatch from her bag and pressed the start button. Twenty-four hours, counting down. What on earth had gotten into the innkeeper?

"MOLLY?" Ava called out into the darkness. "Molly? Where are you? Molly!"

How could Bruno just push an old and sick lady out like that? Discard her as if her sickness was an inconvenience? Had he no heart?

Ava would have given the matter additional thought, but then a more immediate one demanded her attention. A sound, creeping up from somewhere in the mangroves. A rustle, coming closer. Ava froze, her heart beating wildly in her chest. As the sound grew louder, she recognised it as the unmistakable rustle of something large moving through the underbrush. Her mind raced with the possibilities, but Molly's warning echoed in her mind like an ominous prophecy: *Saltwater crocodiles are most active at night.*

Ava stumbled backwards, her eyes scanning the dark beach for any signs of danger. She took a deep breath and began to move, every step feeling like a step closer to her doom. Her body was propelled by primal fear, and her mind was consumed with thoughts of what lurked in the darkness. As she approached the car park, at last, Ava's heart lifted with hope. Perhaps Molly was there, waiting for her in the safety of the car. But as she got closer, she saw that it was empty.

With shaking hands, Ava fumbled for the key hidden behind the back tyre. She unlocked the driver's side door and scrambled into the car, knocking over Molly's gas burner in the process.

She fished out her phone. It was still on London time, but a quick app check told her it was almost midnight in Queensland.

"*Fuck.*" Ava hit the steering wheel. How was she supposed to find Molly now? Heavens, what if the old lady had returned to the beach only to be taken by a croc herself? The thought was so absurd, so wild – a proper *Jurassic Park* scenario. But not impossible.

Ava shoved the gas burner and packet soups aside. She stepped on the clutch, put the key in the ignition and turned it. The fuel gauge was down to the last bar and flashing, but thankfully, the engine spat to life. Ava repositioned the car and switched on the headlights, shining down the path, the bright beams instantly attracting swarms of insects. She let down the window by half. Stuck her head out. "Molly?

Molly, it's me, Ava!" She honked twice, an almost comical sound of no use. She exhaled heavily, fogging up the window. Surely, Molly would know better than to get eaten by a 'salty' though, wouldn't she? After all, she'd lived here all her life.

The thought calmed Ava, if only a little.

When the mosquitoes besieged her, she switched off headlights and engine. She rolled up the window, then reached for the interior light switch. In the dim glow, her gaze wandered over Molly's hotchpotch belongings, hoping to find some kind of pointer.

She lingered on the picture taped to the gear lever, the one of Molly's daughter and grandkids.

Wait a minute, what had Molly said? *The hotel appeared for me the morning I left Annie's house.*

The realisation hit Ava like a ripe coconut: She had come to the wrong beach! This was not where Molly had stepped inside the Atlas.

"*Annie*," Ava exclaimed, wrenching the photo from the gear lever to examine it for clues. Annie was blonde, petite as her mother, and about Ava's age, with a toddler in her arms and a boy of maybe five years next to her.

What town did Molly say her daughter was from? Come on, Ava, remember!

She rummaged around the glove compartment next, flicking through a stack of mail. Unopened bills, late notices, and – thank the heavens – a yellow envelope covered in kids' doodles. Ava flipped it over.

"Mission Beach," she gasped when she found Annie's address inscribed on the back. "Mission fucking Beach!"

Ava took to the glove compartment again, retrieving a road atlas that looked like it dated back to the Australian penal colony era. As she flicked through the index of

Queensland towns – many of which sounded like places out of a children's book (Burpengary, Humpybong, Wonglepong, or Yorkey's Knob) – she did consider returning to the hotel for a quick walk through another doorway but decided against it, what with Bruno acting like a madman. She didn't want to confront him. Hell, she couldn't even *look* at him!

Ava flicked to the right page on the map. Mission Beach seemed close enough. A mere two hundred kilometres away, it was a small town just south of Cairns. Besides, what else could she do while she waited out the Australian night? Might as well cover the distance the old-fashioned way and drive.

She turned the key in the ignition, muttering words of comfort for both her and the car. Then they chuffed off, down the dark Australian back roads in search of poor old Molly.

It was just after two in the morning when the Mission Beach exit sign flashed in the headlights. Ava had found a one-horse fuel stop just when the car had beep-beep-beeped out a warning. Torrential rain had started bucketing down about halfway through her trip down the coast, turning the winding road into a full-on river, flanked by impenetrable rainforest.

Ava squinted, trying to see through the fogged-up windscreen, her nose practically touching the glass, her knuckles whitening under her firm grip on the steering wheel. She followed the main road to its centre, the old station wagon the only moving car in the whole town. She canvassed every bus stop and every shop front, assuming Molly would have taken shelter from the rain somewhere. Working her way through town at a snail's pace, she ended up at the oceanfront, where violent waves ate away the beach, and palm trees swayed in the storm, their crowns taking beatings from all sides.

Ava switched off the engine. Now the rain pounded like angry fists on the car roof, drowning out every other noise. She rubbed her eyes, contemplating what to do. It was highly unlikely Molly would have gone to see her daughter, what with Annie not remembering her. But maybe she knew of another place to hide out from the storm.

Ava yawned, last night's sleep deprivation catching up despite her resistance. Her head dipped off, the window feeling cold and damp against her temple.

She dozed off before she could decide there was nothing better to be done until this downpour ceased.

A PALM LEAF slammed onto the bonnet, and Ava jumped awake. The strong ocean gales had blown away the storm while she was out; now, golden morning light suffused the beach like an apology for last night's rampage.

Ava checked her stopwatch, relief washing over her. She had another eleven hours left until curfew. She unearthed a water bottle from the back of the car, quenching her thirst, then used a public restroom – both to do her business and check for Molly. A couple of beachgoers washed off sand and salt from their feet in one of the showers, but her friend wasn't there.

After subtracting another three hours off her time with a thorough search of the beach, still finding no trace of Molly, Ava backtracked, browsing through the laid-back seaside town, now strewn with people and puddles. When hunger got the better of her, she grabbed a coffee and an avo on toast at a coffee shop, asking the barista about Molly despite her better judgement. Even if someone had seen her friend, no one would remember anyway. She spent an additional two and a half hours at the ambulance station, watching the comings and goings to no avail. But as the day drew to a close and curfew loomed closer, Ava felt desperation creeping in. She was ready to return to the Atlas, face Bruno, and get the others to help. One more stop, just to be sure, then she'd be out of here.

Ava pulled up at Annie's address with just under five hours left on the clock. A traditional 'Queenslander', it was a white timber house on stilts with a veranda and a rusty iron roof. It looked a bit run-down and could have used a paint job, but it was still a home, cosy and warm. After parking the car in the driveway, Ava took the stairs up to the veranda, littered with children's toys. She knocked on the fly screen.

"Hello?" she called up at the roof gutter. "Anybody home?" She pulled back the screen, walked down the veranda and peeked inside the windows like a thief.

The high-pitched squeak of car brakes alerted her to someone's arrival. Doors opened, then slammed shut. A kid yelled, "Whose car is this, mummy?"

For a moment, Ava thought about hiding in the garden playhouse until everyone had gone inside, but then she remembered that she would not be remembered, so whatever awkwardness might arise wouldn't last long.

She rounded the house corner, ready to apologise for her trespassing, when—

"Molly!" The word erupted from her mouth. There, scrambling from the passenger's seat of what must have been Annie's car, was her Atlas friend, looking no less shocked to find Ava on her daughter's porch.

"Ava! What are you doing here?"

Ava's relief doubled when Molly still remembered her – something she had not been sure about.

"You know this woman, Mum?" Annie cocked a brow as she freed a little girl from the kiddy seat. The boy had run off to the garden, straight inside the playhouse. Good thing Ava hadn't gone in there.

"Yes, this... this is a friend of mine." Molly cleared her throat. "From Port."

"I thought you might want your car back," Ava said. She gestured at the old station wagon like a robot low on batteries. Her eyes, however, kept wandering between Molly and her daughter, shock boiling up inside of her like milk left on the stove. *Mum*, Annie had said...

"How very kind of you, my dear," Molly replied, keeping up with appearances.

"Sorry, Mum, will you be all right out here for a moment?" Annie said, worry flaring in her voice. "I'll be with you in a minute; I just need to get Mia inside. Someone desperately needs a diaper change." She gave her daughter a smooch on the cheek.

"I will be just fine, love. Ava and I have a lot to talk about."

"I'm sure you do," Annie said, her gaze wandering over Ava's pyjama pants down to her dog-chewed shoe.

As soon as the front door slammed shut behind Annie, Ava blustered down the stairs. "She remembers you?" she hissed. "Your daughter remembers you?"

"She does," Molly sighed. She grabbed some brochures from the mailbox, spread them out on the wet steps, then took a seat.

"How?" Ava blurted out.

"Shhhhhh," Molly cautioned.

"How is that possible?" Ava switched to a whisper. She sat down as well, not caring if her pants got wet.

"I don't know," said Molly. "She just does."

"So, Bruno lied. *Again*."

"I'm afraid he might have."

Ava's head spun like a tumble dryer. Too much. It was all too much.

"What did Bruno tell you? This morning, when he ushered you out of the hotel?"

"He didn't tell me anything," Molly shrugged. "But I was doing much worse when I woke up, so I wanted him to take me to hospital. He insisted on getting me up and taking me to the gardens to get some fresh air, and before I knew it, I was out the gate. From the beach, I went straight to the ambulance station. Mind you, I didn't yet know people would remember me. But then a nurse walked up to me and said, 'You're Annie's mum, aren't you?' And that's when I knew. She's a friend of Annie's, you see? She still remembered me from Mia's last birthday party."

"So, he knew. Bruno knew if you went out the garden gate, it would give you back your old life."

"He must have. There's no way he would have done anything to harm me. Bruno is a good man."

Ava had her doubts about that, but for the time being more pressing matters took centre stage. There was a pause as thought after thought went off in her mind like fireworks. "So that would mean that I..."

"You can go home, too." Molly nodded.

Ava covered her mouth, shaking despite herself.

"Who's this, Mum?" Annie had reappeared on the veranda, drying her hands on a kitchen towel as she started from scratch with Ava.

"Annie, this is my friend Ava." Molly placed a hand on Ava's shoulder. "She came down from Port to bring the car."

"Oh, that is so nice of you, Ava," Annie said and pushed open the fly screen. "I don't think you should sit on the wet stairs, though, Mum," Annie cautioned. "Why don't you both come in for some iced tea?"

"We'll be right in, darling," Molly said over her shoulder. She took to the handrail and tried to stand. "You must excuse Annie's concern," she said to Ava under her breath. "You see, we've just come back from the doctor for some more tests. Turns out it's not just the anaemia anymore. He said I might not have too long now." She breathed out heavily, her shoulders slumping down with gravity.

"I'm so sorry, Molly." Ava stood, too, holding her friend by the hands.

"It's all right, dear. I guess I've known for a while that something wasn't right. I just didn't want to alarm you lot because – well – we all thought there was nothing to be done, didn't we? The one thing the Atlas is not prepped for is a medical emergency."

"I can't believe Bruno would expose you to such danger," Ava gritted through her teeth.

"What makes you think he knew the truth? Maybe he's been lied to as well."

Ava doubted that very much, but there was no point getting into it now. "So, what will you do?" she asked Molly and helped her up the stairs.

"I will stay here, with Annie. Now that she knows the truth, she will not leave me out of her sight."

"A daughter's prerogative." Ava kissed Molly on the temple.

"Mum? What are you still doing out there?" Annie's voice came from inside the house.

"Coming, honey!" she called, then turned to Ava. "You should get back to the hotel now, dear. Go tell the others." Molly nodded in an indistinct direction. "But do come back and see me before you head home. All of you, you promise? I didn't get a chance to say goodbye to anyone. Oh, and would you please bring my Robert's ashes, too?"

"Of course, Molly. Anything you want," Ava promised.

"That is good. And don't be too hard on Bruno," Molly said. "I'm sure he meant well, if only you'll let him explain."

Ava was about to say all kinds of rude things about the innkeeper, but she bit her tongue. There was no more point in upsetting Molly. She was safe. She was home.

"Well?" Molly nudged her. "What are you waiting for? Give that turtle a toss and get out of here."

"I will," Ava said just when it began to drizzle. "But you better go inside now before Annie sends a search troop."

They hugged each other, saying their goodbyes, and then Molly disappeared inside. Ava walked down the stairs and toward the end of the driveway, stroking the porcelain turtle in her hand, an overwhelming sense of unease spreading through her as she replayed Molly's words.

You can go home, too.

It was the best news in the world, and yet the scariest: Her old life, and the mammoth task of giving it direction, was officially back on the table. It felt like being born all over again, only this time, she'd have a choice in the matter. She would have to, actively and wholeheartedly, decide to step back into that arena and pick her battle.

By no stretch of the imagination did she feel ready to do that.

And so, as soon as she had rounded the corner, Ava Marley took off running, just when the timer passed the four-hour mark.

17

QUICKSAND

"What happens when that hits zero? You turn into a pumpkin or something?" asked a guy with dreads and a Jesus beard, plopping down next to Ava by the bonfire, curious about the stopwatch she was staring at.

"Something like that," she replied, offering a brief smile. She had one hour and twenty-four minutes left.

Earlier, as Ava had hastened down the Mission Beach streets like a madwoman, a beat-up old van had screeched to a halt beside her, and a group of backpackers hailing from all corners of the world had invited her to join their beach party. Ava had agreed without giving it a second thought.

Now the sun sank below the horizon, and a warm glow enveloped the shoreline. Laughter and animated conversations melded with the rhythmic strumming of guitars and the soft lapping of waves. Silhouetted figures swayed around the flickering bonfire, their bare feet stirring up the sand, their safety from the 'salties' ensured by a make-do fence.

The guy beside Ava exhaled a puff of smoke and offered

her his joint. "Just don't lose a shoe, Cinderella." He winked, then rose to join the dance.

Ava took a few puffs, gazing into the dancing flames as she pondered why she was still lingering in Australia. After all, there was no question she would go back to the Atlas before her time ran out. Of course, she would. She had no intention of spending the rest of her life like a homeless person. She was not insane.

But to confront Helene, Yash, and Joao with the truth would mean she had to face it herself, and if the others checked out of the hotel as a result, she would feel pressured to do the same. She had scolded them for their readiness to throw in the towel, but after Costa Rica, she had experienced that same sense of relief, and the convenient weightlessness that came with being forgotten. There would be no going back as soon as Ava tossed the turtle in the air – for none of them. There would be no more running.

The haze took effect, and Ava rose to her feet. She slipped the stopwatch into her bag and dropped it in the sand. And then she, too, began to dance.

Naturally, everyone at the party had long forgotten who she was, but that didn't matter anymore. They were all strangers here. They were all just like her, seeking to escape and putting the future on hold. Life would never be this uncomplicated again, this sweet, and they all knew it. One day soon, they'd all return home, take up jobs and mortgages, raise families and pay taxes for the rest of their lives, forever yearning to go back to this moment – dancing beneath the stars on a tropical beach.

But as Ava twirled, hands raised to the sky, a realisation struck her: she didn't have to follow that path. Not yet, anyway. Even if Helene, Yash, and Joao chose to do so after learning the truth – that didn't mean *she* had to. They were not the boss of her, and who knew? With all their own troubles, they just might not want to, either.

True, returning to the Atlas was the only sane next step. But leaving it for good did not have to be the one after that.

It was this thought that finally propelled her to take action. It was time to expose Bruno's lies. It was time to get back. Stumbling toward the bonfire, Ava reached inside her bag, retrieving the souvenir.

"Good night, you mere mortals!" she called out to the dancing crowd on a whim. Only the grand exit she had envisioned never materialised. Because as Ava unbagged the tiny sea turtle, she found it broken in two halves.

Ava stared at the pieces in her hand, raw panic rushing to her head, sobering her up like a caffeine overdose. The porcelain turtle was a precarious thing to turn into a door in the first place. However, it would have been Ava alone who'd dealt the fatal blow when she dropped her bag so carelessly to go dance. Now, she could see the jagged edge of a rock protruding from the sand.

In a fight-or-flight response, she placed half a turtle in each hand and flipped them into the air. When she caught them, she stayed right where she was. She tossed them up again, this time with both pieces in one hand, a clump of panic expanding in her chest. She caught them but, again, she hadn't moved an inch.

The severity of the situation crept in with some delay. At first, the feeling equalled that scare when you locked yourself out of the house on the way to the dustbins: It sucked, but you had options. Wait for your flatmate to come home. Ask a neighbour for some tools. Call a locksmith. At the worst, you were looking at a few uncomfortable hours on the staircase or losing a bit of cash. It would sting, but you'd learn from the experience.

This was not like that.

And as Ava burnt through her options, she realised it, too. From there, the panic became like quicksand – the more she fought it, the quicker she drowned in it.

"Anybody got some super glue?" Ava shouted at the crowd.

"Why, you wanna sniff some?" the guy with dreads shouted back, and everyone broke out in laughter.

Ava pulled her hair tie, desperately wrapping it around the two porcelain pieces, flipping them up.

She stayed right where she was.

She pulled out the stopwatch, her hands trembling. Twenty-two minutes left.

As the shock grew, her mind froze over like a computer with too little RAM. All that was missing was the spinning rainbow wheel.

She stumbled away from the bonfire in a daze. Behind a palm, she doubled over and then vomited. She wiped her mouth, staring at the timer. Twenty-one minutes and nine seconds.

She broke into a run, away from the beach and down a darkened path toward the town lights.

Reaching Annie's house with twelve minutes left on the clock, Ava came up the stairs, spotting Molly through the kitchen window doing the dishes.

"Ava?" The old lady gaped when she saw her. She stepped out of the kitchen and met Ava on the porch.

"Annie is taking the kids to bed," she hissed. "What are you doing back?"

"I… I never left."

"What? *Why?*"

Wordlessly, Ava handed her the turtle halves like a kid would a broken toy to an adult.

"Goodness, gracious..." Molly gasped. "Toss them up anyway, maybe it would still—"

"I have," Ava replied, shaking her head.

"How much time do you have left?" Molly's voice came from somewhere out of space.

Ava showed her the stopwatch, and then panic spread over Molly's face like a rash. "Here, try this one," she said, slipping her Jesus necklace over her head. Ava cast it up with the despair of someone who'd just been charged with a life sentence. She stayed right where she was.

Molly rushed inside and came back with a tube of super glue, just as the timer passed the ten-minute mark. But only one look at the white crack down the turtle's shell, smeared with dried-up glue, and Ava knew it wouldn't work.

She had never hated being right so much.

Molly didn't even pretend there was much hope left. "Ava, listen to me now," she said, her voice heavy like an anchor she wanted Ava to grab. "I want you to know I got you, do you understand? We need to stick together now, you and I. You will stay here, and I will look after you."

"Forever," Ava scoffed.

"For as long as I'm still around, at least," Molly muttered.

"But don't you think you will forget me, too? When the time's up?"

"I'm sure that won't happen. After all, I still remembered you even though I left the hotel, didn't I?"

"I guess. But, Molly, I can't let you do that."

"Yes, you can. And you will. It is my fault this happened to you. Had it not been for my being sick..."

"Molly, don't—"

"No. It's the truth. Had it not been for my being sick – and my making such a stupid, fragile doorway – then this would never have happened to you. Please, Ava. You must let me take care of you now. I couldn't live with myself if you didn't."

Ava turned away. "Okay," she whimpered, fighting back a swell of tears when Molly placed a hand on hers.

"That's a good girl."

"What on earth are you doing out here, Mum?" Annie stuck her head out the front door. "Oh, hello? Who's this?"

"Honey, this is my friend Ava from Port," Molly replied on autopilot. "Let me just deal with her quickly," she whispered to Ava. "You go wait in the car."

Ava made her way to the driveway in a daze. She opened the car door and slumped into the driver's seat with seven minutes left. But even if Molly still remembered her once those were up – and that was a big if – there was no way Ava would impose on an ailing woman and her already struggling family. There was no way she would impose on *anyone* like that. No, this was her problem now. Hers, and hers alone. Molly sure as hell had enough on her plate.

Watching her and Annie through the kitchen window, Ava reached for a pen and one of the old letters in the glove compartment. She scribbled a note on it and then peeled the family photo off the gear lever. She also fetched a folder of important-looking documents, a quick scan of which revealed things like birth certificates and legal papers. When she got out of the car, Annie craned her neck behind the kitchen window, no doubt asking who that woman in pyjamas was. Ava moved quickly, placed the letter, the photo and the folder under a toy truck on the bottom stair, and then hastened back to the car.

Best if she left now, while there was still time on the clock. She didn't want to wait and see if Molly would remember her. She didn't want to know. Because knowing might make her weak, one day. Might make her come back here and impose on the poor, old woman after all, when she'd splintered under the pressure of a life forgotten.

Ava turned the key in the ignition, and with less than five minutes left on the stopwatch, she drove off.

Molly would have heard the engine starting. Would have hurried to the front door as fast as her weak bones allowed and just about seen the headlights disappear. And, clambering down the stairs, she would have found the note:

It was not your fault.
I'm sorry about the car.
– A.

Ava accelerated into the darkness, the stopwatch resting on the passenger seat, its relentless ticking chipping away at her hope. As the final minute approached, she pulled over to the roadside.

Fifty-eight seconds.

Ava cradled the stopwatch, and a pang of regret surged through her. If only she had heeded Molly's advice and returned to the hotel when her friend had told her to.

Forty-five.

But she had toyed with danger, and now she had to pay the price.

Thirty-two.

Where would she even go from here? What would she do? Carve out a miserable existence living in Molly's car for the rest of her life? In a fit of rage, Ava hurled the stopwatch.

Nineteen.

Eighteen.

No, she refused to accept such a fate. She still had one last move to make, one slim chance to take. It was a gamble at best, but what did she have left to lose?

Ten seconds.

Nine.

Eight.

Now a strange serenity washed over her, a sense of surrender born from reaching the end of her tether.

Three.

Two.

One.

The timer chimed, and Ava revved the engine as though gearing up for a high-stakes race. Zanzibar. She would make her way back to Zanzibar. The island was the only fixed point left on her horizon. It was there that the Atlas had first appeared for her. It might appear again. Yes, she would fight her way back to where it all began.

Come whatever the hell may.

18

DAWN

Three days and nine gruelling hours later, Ava dismounted a Zanzibari taxi as if it were a warhorse. She was absolutely knackered. Every single one of the odd 15,000 kilometres between Mission and Pomboo Beach had left its mark on her; every hurdle she had taken to get back here had pushed her further towards her breaking point.

After leaving Annie's place, she spent a night at a backpacker's in Cairns, from where she booked her online ticket to Zanzibar via Dubai. She also posted a letter to Annie, informing her of the car's location and did some quick shopping, swapping her pyjama pants and chewed-off shoes for more decent attire, simple jeans and a sweater, plus some new sneakers.

That was the easy part. Within the anonymous web of technology, the curse of being forgotten was barely noticeable. In fact, hadn't she spent the last five years practically living like this anyway? Having dinner delivered to her doorstep with a simple tap of the finger? Paying bills through automated direct debits? Communicating on social media rather than face to face? Life had long become a conglomeration of pixels rather than a living, breathing, interactive experience.

But even in this day and age, the internet could only get her so far. The real world still held plenty of bottlenecks, where eye-to-eye contact was not only a necessity but a gatekeeper. An airport, for example, was the last place you wanted to wriggle through if no one remembered your face. Unfortunately, Ava had no other choice.

The trouble started with the simple act of queuing at security. Passengers behind her kept forgetting she was there, then argued that she'd been pushing in front of them and should go to the back of the line like everyone else. It continued when one of the security guards insisted (twice) she'd been sneaking past the metal detector and needed to go again. It culminated at Immigration, where she had to explain how she'd gotten into Australia in the first place. When her answers fell short, the officer in question was set on arresting her, but just when he stepped outside to do the deed, he'd forgotten Ava, and she'd grabbed her passport and snuck away.

However, things didn't exactly get easier from there. After such a rocky start, she'd hoped the rest of the journey would be a bit more of a breeze, but that hope shattered faster than an airplane tray hitting turbulence. What followed was a full-on strip search at Dubai airport after she'd refused to go through the metal detector again (it had been the fifth time, and she had been afraid to miss her connection), continuous fights for her airplane seat with her neighbour (who kept insisting it wasn't hers every time he dozed off or went to the toilet), and yet another Immigration disaster, resulting in the temporary loss of her passport in Zanzibar – the entire trip had turned out to be not a breeze at all, but a fully formed cyclone.

If her entire future wasn't hanging in the balance, she would have stopped off at the Kasa B & B for a night. But she'd figured if the Atlas was still there, she could sleep all she wanted in her old, beloved room five.

Now, the afterglow of another day faded into night, and the corrugated metal roofs of Pomboo Village loomed before her, reflecting pearly light like the inside of an oyster shell. Goats and cows trotted down the road. The occasional hen dust-bathed its feathers on the wayside. A couple of women wearing colourful, modern fashions waited at the bus stop for the last dala-dala back to Stone Town, their big earrings and dyed blonde hair a bold contrast to the burkas prevailing in most corners of the island.

Ava made her way down the sandy paths of Pomboo village, laced with coral rock houses and banana trees, following the sound of waves lapping against the shore. Local men had gathered around a boom box at what looked like the only bar in town, drinking beer and cocking eyebrows as she shuffled past. Kids followed her around. A boy took her hand, searching her pockets for any sweets with the other. But – disappointed by the void he found – he quickly lost interest and scattered.

Ava pushed on, uncomfortable with the unwanted attention. Passing the tree line, her heartbeat quickened. Any moment now, the yellow gate would appear. Any moment now, it would pop up. It just... it *had* to. It...

It didn't.

It really wasn't there.

Ava stumbled down the shoreline, still hoping, still searching. Searching. Searching. But finding nothing. Nothing, except coral rock, and sand, and palms. She dropped her bag, heavy as her heart. Walked a few more steps. Cast a few more glances. But there was no yellow gate. No sign mounted on a paddle. Just nothing.

The exact situation had played out inside her head at least a thousand times, a nightmare on repeat, startling her from what little sleep she'd found along the way. But now that it had happened, now that all hope had gone, it felt different. *She* felt different. Calm, no – empty, like a washed-out shell. Stranded. Beaten. Blank.

Ava sank to the ground, her gaze lost somewhere out at sea where the horizon melted away in mellow twilight tones, her fingers grasping the sand, finding even more nothing to hold onto. Mosquitoes nipped at her skin, all clammy from the trip. She allowed it. She let it happen. And she would have stayed here, motionless, waiting for the tide to wash over her, had it not been for the stranger approaching her. The woman, picking up Ava's bag, then slumping down beside her like a long-lost friend.

"Mango?"

The stranger offered a slice of the fruit on a pocketknife.

Ava jumped, bewildered by the intrusion into her comfort zone, not to mention the knife two inches from her face. She didn't move off, however. There was something familiar about this woman. She must have been in her forties. Her hair cut short, she wore a washed-out, buttoned shirt and military pants with deep pockets. Her complexion was dark as heartwood, and her sharp eyes seemed to know more than she let on.

"So, tell me," the woman said. She ate the piece of mango herself, straight off the knife. "What brings you back to the island on this fine evening, Ava Marley?"

"How do you... *Did you go through my stuff?*" Ava grabbed her bag. She unzipped it and searched for missing items.

"Of course not. And I'm insulted you should even think

that." The woman acted appalled. Her voice bore a strikingly American accent, with a subtle hint of Zanzibari flavour lingering in the finish. "I'm dying to know, though," she said, tapping her knife in the air as she chewed. "Are you here because you left through the garden gate, or did you miss curfew?"

Ava froze mid-movement like a cat spotting another pair of eyes in a dark alley. "What did you just say?"

The woman looked at her as if waiting for the other shoe to drop.

Ava, however, needed a moment to grasp the news, now buzzing between them like mosquitoes. Next to her sat a woman who knew of the Atlas... A woman whom, apparently, she'd met before but had since forgotten about... So this had to be another maroon, another guest who'd missed curfew!

Ava knew of only one person who fit that bill. An elusive guest who, according to the innkeeper, had swept through the hotel like a ghost. A woman whom Bruno mentioned had gone missing...

"You're il fantasma, aren't you?" Ava considered the stranger. "You're Dawn."

"You know my name." Dawn gave an impressed kind of half-nod. She had a serenity about her as if she'd been through hell, and now no small fire could burn her anymore.

"Bruno told me about you. You know, the innkeeper?"

"Is that what he goes by these days?"

Ava wasn't sure if the comment referred to the name or the job title, but at this point, it wouldn't even shock her to learn Bruno had lied about either.

Dawn sliced off another piece of mango. "Last time I saw Bruno di Mare, he was just another lost soul, desperate to run from life like all the rest of us," she said, offering Ava the fruit again, who took it this time around.

"And when was that?" Ava asked, then took a bite.

"Three months and five days ago," Dawn sighed. "Right before he evicted me."

"He *what*?" Ava almost choked on her mango.

"He tampered with my travel souvenir, and I missed curfew because of it."

"What do you mean he *tampered* with it?"

Dawn turned toward Ava, framing her words with mango and knife. "I used the same doorway every morning after breakfast," she said as if sharing a conspiracy theory. "A seashell that took me to my aunt's house here on this beach. She's the only blood relative I have left, and she needs caring."

Ava nodded impatiently.

"Anyway, I stored the shell in one of the kitchen drawers at the hotel, where I kept all the doorways I'd made. Only when I tossed this one up that morning, it didn't take me to my aunt's house."

"Where did it take you?"

"Dropped me right there, out in the Indian Ocean." With her knife, Dawn tapped toward the horizon.

"No!"

"I'm telling you!" Dawn straightened her back, crazy-eyed. "I nearly drowned out there!"

"But couldn't you have tossed up the shell from the water?" Ava remembered Bruno telling her about that one time he himself had landed somewhere in the middle of the ocean, trying out the south-pointing spoon.

"I cannot swim!" Dawn erupted. "Went under quicker than a rock! Ever try casting up a seashell when you're completely submerged in water?" She glared at Ava. "Yeah,

works great – *not*. Damn thing trundled straight to the bottom of the ocean. I would have *died* that day, had it not been for a fisherman sailing past and fishing me out!"

Ava gave Dawn a moment to calm her nerves. "So, you're saying Bruno replaced your shell with another?"

"I'm sure of it."

"How do you know it was him and not another guest?" Ava asked although she thought it was precisely the kind of thing Bruno would do.

"There were no other guests at the time except him and me." Dawn shrugged. "But" – she ducked her head – "he mightn't have acted entirely unprovoked."

Ava lifted a brow. "Go on."

"We had this silly rivalry, him and I – *he* started it though, just want to make that clear. Out of the blue, too, I might add. At first, him and I got along famously. He introduced me to all kinds of side hustles all around the world to help me save up money for my own business one day. But then, from one day to the next, I became this... this *thorn* in his side. Never understood why, but he just started trying to get me to leave. Anyway, it started innocently enough. He hid my Harvard keychain right before an important class he knew I was dying to attend, so I sawed his favourite nutcracker in half... That kind of thing. It was my idea to start replacing the souvenirs with duplicates. I suppose that's when the whole thing spiralled out of control. Until I nearly drowned out there, and now I'm stuck right where I started."

"You think he meant to do you harm?" Ava asked, careful like a mouse in a lion's den. She realised then how much the answer mattered. The innkeeper was certainly deceitful, but was he vicious? Was he *cruel*?

"Do I think he wanted me to drown, you mean?" Dawn

cocked a brow. "No. I don't." She tossed the mango pip, then cleaned the knife on her pants. "Do I think he allowed for the possibility I might lose the shell in the water and miss curfew? *Hell, yes.*"

The tide washed in, and Dawn stood, backing up toward the palm trees.

Ava brushed the sand off her hands, grabbed her bag, and followed. "So, you're from here, then?" she asked.

"Born and bred right in that village." Dawn nodded at the rooftops of Pomboo. "Never quite fit in, though."

"How come?"

Dawn bent over to pick up a coconut. She shook it but tossed it when she didn't seem to like the sound it made. "Guess people found me weird," she said with a shrug. "The village's odd bird. Head always in the clouds, dreams too big to fit under these palms. Refused to marry for the longest time. Didn't want any children. Just stuck my nose into every book I could find."

"Is that why the hotel appeared for you? Because you felt like you didn't fit in?" Ava helped Dawn pick up coconuts but had no idea what a ripe one might sound like.

"I suppose." Dawn seemed to have found a coconut she liked. She tossed it up like a volleyball, caught it, and then walked toward the trees. "As long as I remember, I've wanted to get off this island. Go overseas. Get a university degree and start a new life somewhere far away. And I always had faith that it would happen one day, you know? If only I saved money, applied for scholarships, kept on believing in my dream. But by the time I turned thirty-five, I still hadn't moved any more than these trees had. That's when I realised it might never happen."

Night had now entirely fallen, and Ava kept hitting her toes on coconuts and coral as she followed Dawn, who steered them away from the village. Eventually, they reached a ramshackle hut tucked away against the jungle like a children's fort. "Welcome to my humble abode," she said, spreading her arms. She sat in front of the make-do shelter, built from coral rock and debris.

Ava sat down too. "What did you do when you realised your dreams might not come true?"

Dawn dropped the coconut in the sand and reached for some kindling from a neatly stacked pile. "Nothing, at first," she said, laying a campfire. "But giving up is rarely marked by a special occasion, isn't it? Succeeding is. You know, when you get that *one* job, marry that *one* partner, or sign that *one* book deal... But giving up?" Dawn drew down the corners of her mouth. "Giving up happens gradually, kinda like gaining weight. You don't notice it, and no one tells you, either. Until one day you try on an old pair of jeans and realise they don't fit you anymore."

Ava chuckled.

"As for me," Dawn continued, "the more time passed, the more sand blew over my dreams until I couldn't even see them anymore. Eventually, I took up a job in a holiday resort and agreed to marry a man who thought he could tame me." She grabbed a palm-sized, pre-made ball of dried palm leaves, which she set afire with a match, then stuffed it underneath the kindling and blew on it. At first, only smoke rose up the side of her face, but then a crackle announced the flame, which soon began to lick the dry sticks. Dawn leaned back, feeding the fire with bigger pieces of wood. "Three miserable months into my marriage, I come out here one morning, and there it is, the yellow gate. Now, I grew up on this beach. I knew every grain of sand. So, you can imagine my surprise when it suddenly popped up in front of me."

"When was that?"

"Three years ago."

"You've been there for *three* years?"

Dawn put a big log on the flames, now dancing fiercely in the ocean breeze. "And I didn't waste a single day of it," she said. "Attended seminars and lectures at the most prestigious universities across the globe. Cambridge, Harvard, Yale, Brown – you name it. Over the years, I've studied Sustainable Economics, Environmental Science, Politics, Agriculture and Crop Science... I could never sit the exams, of course, but I kept all my notes at the hotel, and all my savings, too. Stacked them in my textbooks."

Dawn placed the coconut between the soles of her feet, then began boring a hole in the shell with the tip of her knife. "So, you can understand how much it sucked when Bruno kicked me out," she said.

"I found them!" Ava said. "Well, Bruno did. They were still in room five when I arrived."

"He had better not have destroyed them." Dawn pointed her finger in warning. "They are my most valuable possession. I want them back."

"He didn't. The books are still in my... in room five, I mean. And your notes are stacked in the cabinet in the upper hall."

"You better be right about that... *There* we go." Dawn had put a hole in the coconut's shell. She lifted the fruit above her head, milky water trickling into her mouth. When she was done, she handed Ava the fruit.

"I cannot imagine why he would do something like that. Thank you," Ava said, taking the fruit and copying what Dawn had done. But she spilt most of the coconut water, thus handing it back rather quickly.

"I don't know, either." Dawn finished off the water, then

hacked the coconut in half. She broke the white meat apart with the tip of her knife, a well-practised routine. "But he was busy himself, you see. Always scheming, working on some secret plan... I must have been interfering; that's what I've come to believe. Only in what way, I couldn't tell you. As far as I'm aware, I only ever minded my own business." She handed Ava one half of the coconut, then began scraping out the meat of her own half with her fingers. The two women went silent for a moment, munching away.

"What are the chances, though, right?" Ava paused when the thought struck her. "The yellow gate appeared for both of us in the same location?" She looked through the flames at Dawn, and Dawn stared right back, her tongue taking a long time to remove a piece of coconut from between her teeth before she answered.

"Listen," she said and put the fruit down. "There's something you need to know."

"I'm all ears." Ava straightened her back.

"It... it didn't exactly happen by chance, at least not for you. I kind of... lured you here under false pretences, hoping the hotel would appear for you, and it did." Dawn held Ava's gaze, filling the gaps Ava had long attributed to a random case of memory loss caused by a spiked drink, or a hit on the head, maybe.

"You see, I'd been trying to get people to find the hotel for months, but it never appeared for any of them. You seemed pretty desperate to get away from something. I thought there was a good chance the hotel might appear for you. The plan was to slip in right behind you. Only that didn't work – *obviously*." She gestured at her surroundings, indicating that she was still here, not there.

Ava was preoccupied with piecing together the events, retracing the morning when she had woken up on this beach, unable to recall how she had ended up there, or how an entire *day* had gone missing from her mind. Suddenly, it all made perfect sense.

"So, what happened, exactly?" she asked. "Did you kidnap me at my hotel in Stone Town?"

"Actually, we met right when you left the airport. You just don't remember. I sold you that kikoi around your neck. Almost had you then but lost you in a crowd. I stayed on your heels the entire day, studying you, getting to know you. I even saved you from a sleazy tour guide who was hitting on you. Told you my name was Sunny. But then I stuffed up our conversation, and you ran off."

"Seems like an awful lot of trouble with nothing much to go on. I mean, there was no way of knowing if the gate would show up for me."

"You can say that out loud, sister." Dawn tossed the empty coconut shell into the fire. "But, you see, none of the islanders I'd tried had proven successful. I began to assume that maybe the spots were limited by country or, I don't know… *something*. That's why I began targeting tourists."

"Couldn't have been easy, getting me all the way from Stone Town to this beach," Ava noted with a dash of acknowledgement. She knew of the struggles all too well by now.

"It was an absolute bitch," said Dawn, poking a stick in the fire. "I lost you seven times along the way. And you know what that means: I had to start from scratch after every single one. Took me an entire day to get you here. But at least I'd found a cover story that broke the ice quickly and made you trust me."

"What did you tell me?"

"I told you I was a marine biologist, off to count sea turtle hatchlings on Mnemba Island. I didn't ask you to join me, though – that's where I'd gone wrong several times before. It had to be your idea."

"And how did you make me spend the night on the beach?"

"Told you to think of it as an adventure. You were dying to do it, actually."

"I was?"

"Absolutely. We stayed up all night talking. About your father's coffee business and the environment and what we both would do if we called the shots... Was great, actually. You learnt a lot from me." Dawn gave a cheeky wink.

"So, what would you do if you called the shots?"

"What, you don't remember?" Dawn acted appalled, and Ava played along, making a face.

"Well," Dawn said, "first off, I'd get a divorce." She winked. "And then I'd start my own business here in Zanzibar, something that connects me to my Tanzanian roots. I'd employ locals, empower Zanzibari women. Give back to the island that raised me, you know?"

"I thought you wanted nothing more than to get off this island."

"Used to." Dawn shrugged. "Until I was forgotten. Don't get me wrong: For the first month after Bruno kicked me out, I cursed the odds, of course. Why, I thought, why did I have to get stranded *here* – why couldn't it have been Oxford or New York City? Somewhere useful, somewhere with something to do! Eventually, I was forced to take a long, hard look at this place that gave birth to me. I finally had to confront the life I always wanted to swap for another. But I think it was only until I couldn't get back into the hotel behind you – when it really clicked with me that I'd be forgotten forever – that I learnt the one lesson I needed to learn."

"Which is what?"

"Life's a gift," Dawn said simply, raising her shoulders. "Every moment of it. As long as I can remember, I wanted to be someone else, *somewhere* else, or for something else to happen, and I've missed out on the whole thing. All those tiny moments that make a life – I never even noticed them. Now, all I have is moments. People forget me as soon as they leave the room, turn a corner, bat an eyelash. So, I try to make each conversation last. I've become a better listener. I ask questions. I try to help wherever I can. It's funny, I know these people better now than I ever did when they still remembered me. I care about them, and I want to use the time I have left to make their lives a little bit better, whether I'm remembered or not."

Ava nodded, and the two women fell silent for a while.

"Sometimes I think I asked for this to happen," Ava confessed. "That I somehow manifested this because I ran away from my own life."

"That's exactly the impression I got when I first met you – which is why I picked you, of course. You were a complete mess, you know?"

"Thanks, Dawn."

"Don't mention it. Anyway, that morning you found the hotel, I left you just before the sun came up, hiding in the bushes. Figured one needed to be alone for the gate to appear."

"And you actually saw the gate, did you?" Ava was curious to learn about the framework outcasts like them could operate within.

"I actually saw the gate," Dawn affirmed. "I also saw that bastard Bruno talking to you. Took all the willpower I possessed not to run up to him and punch him in the face."

"Why didn't you?"

"I had come too far with you to risk my anger getting in the way."

"But in the end, you couldn't come back in?"

"Nope. God knows I tried. I was right behind you, but you slammed the door in my face when you saw me."

"I'm so sorry, Dawn. That's awful," Ava said. "I don't remember this at all." Ava looked at Dawn through the flames, a sharp pang of guilt gnawing at her. She racked her brain to recall the incident, growing increasingly frustrated as she drew a blank.

"How could I just shut the door on you like that?" She met Dawn's eyes. "I should have pulled you in with me."

"You know what? It was a reflex. Would have been hella scary to see me coming at you out of nowhere. I probably would have done the same. And as for the pulling me in with you? I've been thinking about that a lot, and I don't think you could have. If it hadn't been for you slamming the door shut, I probably would have tripped over some coral and missed my chance like that. Simply put: I was never meant to make it back inside that morning."

"Do you think that's because there was only one empty bed left?"

Dawn rested her head on her hand. "Maybe. But in that particular case, probably more likely because the hotel didn't appear for *me* that morning – it appeared for you."

Ava picked up a stick and began poking around in the embers. The cicadas had long started to buzz, and weird howling noises came from the trees around them – bush babies, according to Dawn. She tossed some herbs on the fire, which seemed to keep the mosquitoes at bay, and Ava shared an aeroplane sandwich. Something was lurking in the shadows beyond the fire, a hard truth Dawn might have faced a while ago and Ava was still dreading. But they seemed to have silently agreed upon leaving that which could not be changed out there, for now, drowning in the cicada's buzz and the rush of ocean waves. Tomorrow would be soon enough to face it – all over again, or for the first time.

"So, do you think we were always meant to enter the hotel? That our whole lives led up to that moment when we saw the yellow gate?" Ava asked.

"I don't know. Maybe." Dawn shrugged. "In your case, most definitely. With all those daddy issues you got bubbling underneath the surface."

"I don't have daddy issues!"

"Oh, I'm sorry. What would you call it when a young woman runs off to a strange country, agreeing to sleep alfresco on the beach all by herself for nights on end, all so that she doesn't have to deal with the fact that her father offered her a job in his multi-billion-dollar empire?"

Ava furrowed a brow. "Alfresco?"

"What? It's Italian." Dawn smirked. She tossed Ava a blanket and lay down on her side, heralding bedtime by falling silent.

Ava felt a bit uneasy, out here in the wild. But apparently, she'd done this sort of thing before and loved it. So she arranged her bag like a pillow, lay down, and tried very hard to think of it as an adventure.

Looking up at the stars, she was about to doze off when she picked up the conversation once more.

"*One* night," she mumbled.

"What's that?"

"I only spent one night sleeping outside," Ava said. "And I wasn't alone. You were with me, just like you are now."

"Whatever, Marley." Dawn rolled over to the other side. "Just don't count on me to fight off the rats when they come to nibble at your toes. And I take my morning coffee with a spoonful of sugar."

Ava could discern the smile in Dawn's voice and thought she knew what might have caused it. It was the same thought that had lifted her own mood tonight:

At least neither of them was alone anymore.

19

THE SECOND COORDINATE

The waitress, slender and with red-dyed micro braids, brought over two cups of black coffee and two plates of jackfruit scramble and toast, the smell of which made Ava's mouth water.

She had insisted on taking Dawn out for breakfast, and Dawn had agreed under the one condition that she got to choose the restaurant. There were but two choices: The resort where she used to work – an over-the-top luxury palace with no soul – and a beach café with indigo-painted beams and a handful of tables under a bending thatch roof.

Ava would have chosen the latter anyway.

"You know," she said, pouring some sugar into Dawn's cup. "I've been thinking about what you said yesterday, about you interfering with Bruno's plans?"

"What about it?" Dawn buttered her toast.

"I know what he was up to."

Her mouth full, Dawn circulated her knife like a coil, gesturing at Ava to continue.

"I think he lied to the new guests – the ones who arrived after you were gone – about how it all works."

Dawn frowned. "What did he say?"

"You know the fifth house rule on the entry sign? 'Guests must never exit through the garden gate'? Well, *he* made it sound as if that meant you couldn't leave at all, else you were forgotten, *and* the Atlas was gone, too. Obviously, that petrified everyone. We all thought we were stuck there forever."

Dawn put the knife and fork down. "What on earth are you talking about?"

"What do you mean?"

"What is the Atlas? And what house rules?"

"Well, the... the hotel is called the Atlas and..." Ava stammered, reading Dawn's face. "It is not?"

Dawn shook her head.

"That. Bastard." Ava stared blankly. "Not even the hotel's *name* was real?"

Dawn raised her shoulders. "We just called it 'the hotel.'"

"He made it all up..." Ava whispered. "The whole thing." In her mind, she went back to that empty room at the museum in Naples, picturing how Bruno would have visited alone, brooding for hours in the shade of the hulking statue.

"What I don't understand is, *why*?" Dawn said, squinting like she was staring into the sun. "What was his goal? He wanted to keep you all as prisoners?"

Ava leaned forward. "You won't believe it when I tell you."

And while they finished their breakfast, she told Dawn about Bruno's elaborate, yet slightly unhinged, mission for humanity, about his theory of repentant titans and unsung heroes.

"So that's what he was preparing to do!" Dawn interlaced her fingers behind her head, a smile playing around the corners of her mouth. "Asante dada," she said as the waitress came to clear the plates. "He wanted to start a whole new way to live at the hotel, but he couldn't as long as I was around." She knocked a fingertip on the tabletop. "Because I knew the truth."

Ava considered her companion for a moment, a question priming on her tongue. "So, you think it's all bullshit, this whole idea of a higher purpose?" She tried to phrase it matter-of-factly but didn't quite succeed.

"Oh, the hotel has a higher purpose, all right." Dawn folded her arms. "It's just not what Bruno had you believe. The hotel exists for people like you and me to get a second chance at life, not *run* from it forever. You get to see the world without you, and you get a break until you're ready to start over. That's why you only get twenty-four hours in one location – so you cannot begin a whole new life without fixing up the old one first."

"How do you know all of this?" Ava finished her coffee and paid when the waitress brought the bill, ordering another cup to go.

Dawn answered only after they'd left the restaurant and strolled down the beach, shoes in hand, feet in the sand. "The first thing you should have come across upon entering is the guestbook. But I suspect Bruno had removed it by the time you arrived, judging from how little you know."

Ava shrugged, assuming Dawn was right.

"The guestbook explains the entire thing. Generations of guests have filled those pages, giving tips and assistance for new arrivals, sharing their favourite doorways and their stories of recovery. It's an inspiring piece of history. I do hope Bruno didn't just burn it or something."

"He didn't," Ava reassured her. She remembered a guestbook resting on Bruno's nightstand the night after Casablanca.

"Anyway, there are all kinds of other remnants from former guests all over the house. One guy made a whole video series about the place and what to be aware of. It's in Chinese, but there are translation manuals at reception. And then, there's the Book of Doors, a massive help when you first arrive."

"That's still around, but Bruno said he was the one who compiled it."

Dawn scoffed. "Now, that's just presumptuous. It would have taken decades to compile that list." She slowed down her steps when the rooftops of Pomboo appeared up ahead. The village children ran up to them as they'd done the day before, but at a stern warning from Dawn, they dispersed like a swarm of tadpoles spooked by a heron.

"I'm sorry your experience at the hotel was ruined. It's not supposed to be like that." Dawn sat in the shade of a stranded dhow, threading her fingers through the sand.

"It's all right," Ava replied and sipped her takeaway coffee. "I didn't know it was supposed to be different. Still got my money's worth, I guess."

Dawn huffed out half a laugh. There was a silence then, and it felt a little awkward. "Hey, you ever tried the doorway to that hidden corridor at the Edinburgh National Museum?"

Ava shook her head, and Dawn made a tsk sound. "That was my favourite," she said.

And then it had arrived, the moment they'd both been dreading since the night before, the truth they knew they couldn't shut out forever. This was it, the end of the lane. There was no going back, and there was nothing left to say. As of today, they were both stranded, both forgotten by the world. Whatever hope they might have held onto in the past had drifted out to sea.

Suddenly, their encounter had turned into something else, something that felt an awful lot like meeting up with an old high school friend you hadn't seen in years. The conversation flowed for as long as you refreshed each other's memories, gossiped over that one teacher you both hated, reminisced about times gone by. But once those topics had been covered, you quickly realised you had not much else in common anymore, except for a past now forever lost.

"So, what do we do now?" Ava asked. She came down on her haunches next to Dawn, filling her empty paper cup with sand.

"Now we each go our separate ways," Dawn sighed. "I don't suppose you want to live on Pomboo Beach for the rest of your life."

"I guess." Ava looked up, her gaze lost somewhere in the waves lapping against the shore. She didn't like the idea of parting with the one person in the world who'd remember her. She didn't like it one bit. "Except, I mean, did you ever stop to wonder..." She came back to standing, her eyes scanning aimlessly as a wild thought took shape.

"What?" Dawn rose as well.

But as soon as hope had kindled, Ava stifled it, chiding herself for even considering the thought. "Nothing," she said, pouring the sand out of her cup. "It was a silly idea. Forget I said anything."

"No, please. Tell me," Dawn insisted.

"It's... it's this thing Bruno mentioned," Ava said and scratched her neck. "I'd asked him once if the Atlas – the hotel – was actually standing somewhere permanent, here on earth."

"You think it's out there somewhere," Dawn said in a been-down-that-road kind of way.

"Don't you?"

"I guess." She picked up a rock, flat as a coin, and wiped it clean with her thumb. "But what of it? We can't travel to every beach in the world to look for it. It would take us the rest of our lives, and then some."

"See, that's just the thing." Ava took a step toward Dawn, a hint of excitement in her voice. "It wouldn't have to be *every* beach in the world. Bruno also said the original beach should be located somewhere in the Americas because of—"

"Because of the hotel's time zone."

"Yes, and the locations of the earliest doorways," Ava added.

"I know. I've heard this theory before. Still, that leaves an awful lot of coastlines in both North *and* South America to browse, not to mention thousands of tiny, little islands."

Ava exhaled her disappointment. "You're right. Of course, you're right." She walked toward the shore until the waves kissed her toes. "See?" She pointed her paper cup at Dawn. "Told you it was a silly idea."

"No, no. I thought about it, too. It's just not possible, that's all."

Dawn had come up next to Ava. Now both women stood barefoot in the water; one tossing stones, the other ideas.

Ava crumpled her cup, about to store it in her bag, when...

"Unless..." She mumbled, looking down at a coffee bean depicted on the now crumpled outside.

"What now?" Dawn pricked up her ears, and Ava huffed out a breath as a lightbulb went off inside her head.

“The Bean Belt…” she whispered, more to herself than to Dawn.

“The what belt?”

“*The Bean Belt!* Come, have a look at this.” Ava came down on her knees. She drew a circle in the sand with a rough outline of the continents inside.

“Let’s say this is the time zone the hotel is on, yeah?” she said, wedging the Americas in with two vertical lines. “Now, what if I told you we won’t need to go to *every* beach in this zone but that we could narrow the search even further?”

Dawn squatted, looking more sceptical than ever. *“How?”*

Ava’s eyes glinted with excitement. “By adding a second coordinate.” She sat back on her heels. “Hear me out: Every coffee enthusiast knows that coffee beans require very specific climates, climates that are found exclusively along the Bean Belt.” She drew another two horizontal lines close to the earth’s equator. “The hotel *must* be within this belt.”

“How can you possibly know that?”

Ava smiled triumphantly. “The flowers,” she said, the word sending goosebumps across her back. “The flowers in the hotel garden. They’re all tropical plants that require a similar climate to coffee beans.”

At last, Dawn reciprocated the excitement. “You’re right,” she whispered. “You’re absolutely right. I don’t know how I didn’t see it before.”

“Right?” Ava showed her open palm, her fingers splayed wide. “Now, with both our longitude and our latitude, the hotel should be within this perimeter.” She circled the intersection between the time zone and the Bean Belt. “Somewhere around the Caribbean.”

She sat back, folding her arms victoriously.

“It’s brilliant,” Dawn shrugged, impressed. “No, really. It makes a lot of sense.”

Ava exhaled sharply through her nostrils, still amazed that she'd thought of this herself.

"But..." Dawn objected.

"But, what? It's *genius*!"

"Well, even if this were true, that still leaves us with thousands upon thousands of beaches."

"We can probably narrow it down even further," Ava said. "For instance, it wouldn't be a busy, touristy beach, right? It would be remote. An off-the-beaten-track kind of place, like Pomboo."

Dawn shook her head. "That's not enough to go on. We need a more specific pointer. Something that would pinpoint it to a unique location, like a dialect that's only spoken in a particular region. You know what I mean? Think, Ava. Was there anything distinctive you noticed about the hotel's architecture, or did maybe a certain type of butterfly ever catch your eye?"

Ava looked over at Dawn. "Not a butterfly, but..."

"But, what?"

She shot up, struck by a memory. "I need internet!"

"What for?"

"I just remembered something. Something another guest showed me in a book once." Ava grabbed Dawn's arms, her voice quickening with excitement. "A flower... a... a white frog orchid!"

"Follow me." Dawn plodded up the beach and into the jungle, and Ava followed her, stumbling through the undergrowth, pushing aside creepers and vines hanging like curtains in their path. Coming out on the other end, a massive palace towered up ahead. They snuck toward it, crouching down below a window of what appeared to be a fancy restaurant.

"This is the resort I used to work at. Have a look on your

phone for the guest Wi-Fi."

Ava did as told. The connection was shaky at best, but at least it wasn't password-protected.

Slow like drops from a leaky valve, the search results trickled in. Ava clicked on the first link, waiting with gruelling anticipation as the page loaded.

"Jackpot," she gasped as soon as she'd read the first paragraph.

"You're *joking*!" Dawn burst out, grabbing Ava's hand, and Ava, with shaking vocal cords, began to read.

"Dendrophylax lindenii, more commonly known as Ghost Orchid or White Frog Orchid, due to the unique, frog-like shape of its flower, is an extremely rare orchid. Only a handful of people know the exact locations of these highly poached plants." Ava's voice loudened with excitement. "What is known, however, is the White Ghost is found almost exclusively in..." She stopped and looked up from her phone, smiling brightly at Dawn while the goosebumps ran rampage across her skin.

"In what? Found exclusively in what, goddammit?" Dawn shook her, then grabbed the phone and read herself. "Found almost exclusively in the humid and marshy vegetation of southern Florida, in the United States." She looked up, dumbfounded, and Ava's lips curled into a victorious smile.

"Dawn? We just narrowed down our search to a single location."

20

A MAD PLAN

"But how do you know the boy didn't plant this orchid in the garden himself? I mean, he could have just bought one, right?" Dawn's eyes wandered searchingly between Ava's. They sat in the back of a crowded dala-dala to Stone Town, surrounded by locals in vibrant attire and weary tourists clutching sun hats, their eyes wide with the novelty of the bustling journey.

Ava flipped out the phone again and read to Dawn. "Listen to this: Poachers usually end up disappointed. Replanting Ghost Orchids is thought to be impossible, as the flower's complex growing requirements cannot be simulated. The only way to observe these elusive specimens is as Mother Earth intended – in its natural habitat."

"So, you're saying..."

"I'm saying the orchid was not planted in the hotel garden, but the hotel would have been built *around* the orchid."

"And you're one hundred per cent sure this is what you saw in the garden?"

Ava put her head on one side. "Not in the garden, no,"

she confessed. "Joao only showed me a picture in a book. In the garden, he pointed out what I gather must be the roots. You see, it blooms during the warmer months, and sometimes not at all." Ava showed Dawn the paragraph on flowering seasons. She looked at Dawn, whose eyes were now stuck in some form of deadlock, staring into the jungle.

"So, what do you say, Dawn? I mean, this is worth a shot, right?"

"Sure," Dawn said, her voice suddenly changing. She clapped her kneecaps. "Just make sure you'll send me a postcard from Florida."

Ava knitted her brows. "I'm not going without you."

"Well, you'll have to. There's no way I can get a visa for the United States. Tanzania is not high on the international relations list, you know?"

That shook Ava up. "But you do have a passport, right?" she asked, concern flaring in her chest.

"*Of course,* I have a passport!"

"Then I'm sure we can figure something out," Ava said gently.

Dawn scoffed. "Easy for you to say, Kate Middleton." Dawn crossed her legs over and leaned back, looking at passing palm trees and coral rock houses.

Ava leaned in. "Let's get back to the city and do some proper research," she said. "I'm sure there will be a way."

~

THE OLD-WORLD CHARM of Stone Town welcomed them back with a warm embrace as Ava checked into the Kasa Bed and Breakfast. She had intended to cover the cost for Dawn as well, but the proud woman gently refused.

"I've got a spot of my own here in town," she insisted,

her tone blocking further inquiry. Ava, respecting her friend's independence, did not press on the issue.

Now, they found themselves perched atop the Kasa's rooftop bar, soaking in the hues of a Stone Town dawn. The city below was stirring awake, the early morning sun casting long shadows on the labyrinthine alleys, painting a picture of timeless beauty.

Ava, brimming with optimism, had already applied for her entry to the United States online. Her approval came back almost instantly, further fuelling her enthusiasm. Dawn, on the other hand, was denied even the possibility of an online application.

"Maybe we should try the consulate," Ava suggested, trying to keep the hope alive in her voice.

Dawn scoffed lightly, "Come one, Marley, you know how that's gonna go. I'll be forgotten before they even process my name."

Ava, perturbed, asked, "So, what do we do now?"

"Well, I could try to slip past the border officials, but if that doesn't work..." Dawn trailed off, a concerned look exchanged between the two women.

Finally, she sighed, "I guess you'll just have to go without me."

Ava mulled over the idea, but it didn't sit well with her. Dawn was her only tether to her past, the only one who remembered her. Besides, abandoning her would be like slamming the door in her face all over again.

"No, we're in this together," Ava stated firmly.

Dawn bristled at her persistence. "We hardly know each other! You can't risk your entire future for me."

But Ava was only half-listening, her attention focused on her phone. "What about the other locations for the white frog orchid anyway?" she mused aloud.

Dawn looked puzzled, "What other locations?"

Ava's fingers danced over her phone, "It says here that the orchid is found *almost* exclusively in Florida. But 'almost' implies there must be other places."

"Drop it, Ava," Dawn retorted, weary of the subject.

Ava, unswayed, exclaimed triumphantly, "Ha! There's one other location where the orchid occurs, and it's in Cuba, baby! How's your visa status for Cuba, Dawn?"

Dawn frowned. "This might surprise you, but I don't keep track of every country's visa requirements."

"I actually don't know myself," Ava murmured, already pulling up the Cuban Embassy's website. Her face lit up with a victorious grin. "Today's our lucky day, Dawn! Cuba issues thirty-day visas upon arrival for the both of us! Now you'll have to come!"

"As much as I'd love to go on a backpacking trip with you, I'm afraid I'll have to pass. 'Cause this outcast here has nothing but a pocketknife to her name and will sleep in an abandoned building tonight. I can't exactly afford a round-the-world trip right about now," Dawn said.

Ava leaned in, her voice hushed and sincere. "Don't even mention it."

Dawn's eyes flared with indignation. "Oh, but I am! I am mentioning it. I'm no charity case, Marley. I don't need your handouts. Breakfast is one thing, but this? This is way too much. I could never accept that."

Ava held Dawn by the shoulders. "Yes, you can." Her mind raced as she tried to calculate whether she even had enough savings to cover the cost of both of their tickets. After her travels to Zanzibar and Australia, the remaining inheritance from her mother was dangerously depleted. But better to spend the rest of her funds on a real chance for the both of them than watch them slowly seep into the sands of Zanzibar.

"You can't let something as silly as money stand in the way. This is an emergency."

Dawn pulled away, her voice bitter. "Only someone like you would ever call money silly."

Ava softened her tone, regretting her choice of words. "I'm sorry, but this is your *life* we're talking about," she said gently. "What if I thought of a way you could pay me back?"

Dawn frowned as if Ava had said something utterly stupid.

But now Ava's eyes shone with conviction. "Come on, Dawn. Let's find that damn hotel, and then you're going to start one hell of a business with that money Bruno helped you make. And it better turn a profit quickly, woman, cause you might be no charity case, but I am no fairy godmother, either," she joked, and Dawn couldn't help but chuckle a little.

"I mean it," Ava continued, "you better become the first Zanzibari business woman giving a TED Talk, if you know what I mean." She leaned in, touching Dawn by the shoulder. "Seriously though, I can't do it without you, Dawn. Just look at this as a loan, an investment."

Dawn exhaled, and the resistance left her body like a curse. *"Fine,"* she said, folding her arms. "But this *is* just a loan."

"Just a loan," Ava agreed. "I do have one condition, though."

"What now?"

"You are not going back to that abandoned building tonight." She stretched a hand out. "Deal?"

Dawn shook her head, a wry smile tugging at her lips. "I shouldn't have told you. It's not as bad as you think."

Ava held her gaze, unyielding.

Rolling her eyes, Dawn finally relented and shook Ava's hand. "All right, all right. It's a deal."

Dawn stroked the back of her head, looking equal parts excited and terrified. "This is a mad plan," she muttered. "Absolutely mad."

Ava leaned across the table, cradling Dawn's face in her hands.

"Just think of it as an adventure," she grinned.

~

BUT EVEN THOUGH they had settled on Cuba instead of Florida, Dawn's passport issues remained. The disparity in travel freedom between their passports was striking: Ava could travel visa-free to a staggering 107 countries, while Dawn was limited to just 38, most of which were in Africa. With Cuba luckily issuing travel permits upon arrival, that didn't matter for their final destination, but the problem was getting that far! Dawn wasn't even allowed to stop over at most airports without obtaining a transit visa, a process as cumbersome as getting a regular visa, involving embassy visits, proof of sufficient health insurance, and long waiting periods. This eliminated all major stopover options in the European Schengen zone, the United States, and Canada for their Caribbean journey from Tanzania.

Ava hesitated to share this information with Dawn, fearing she might back out again. In the end, she found only one feasible route considering Dawn's passport restrictions: they would take a ferry from Zanzibar to Dar es Salaam, fly to Istanbul (where both were allowed to transit as long as they didn't leave the airport), then catch a direct flight to

Caracas, Venezuela, another transit-friendly airport for Dawn. Finally, they would board a flight to Havana.

And so, as the morning of their departure arrived, with the first light of dawn casting a warm honey glow on Stone Town's port waters, Ava and Dawn boarded the mainland ferry, armed with something resembling a plan, but accompanied by a whirlwind of anxiety.

From this point on, there was only one direction to go: forward.

21

COWARD

The port of Havana was a kaleidoscope of colour and activity, where past and present collided in a symphony of sound and movement. The sun had just dipped below the horizon, casting a warm, golden hue over the city. Ava and Dawn watched from the deck of a monohull sailboat, the city's iconic skyline softened by the gathering dusk. The salty tang of the sea filled their nostrils, mixed with the distant aroma of fried plantains wafting from the shore. Around them, the harbour was a hive of activity, buzzing with fishermen hauling in the day's catch, and the distant murmur of laughter and music floating across the water.

Ava was still processing that they'd actually made it here; the journey had passed by in a stressful blur of flights, border controls, and navigating unfamiliar territory. Istanbul airport had been like an overwhelming whirlwind; Caracas tried their patience due to a major delay, and on both flights, an unwavering sense of hope had proven to be the glue that held it all together. By the time the two women had arrived in Cuba and actually got their passports stamped, exhaustion had overcome Ava's body like a heavy blanket. Still, she savoured the thrill of finally being here. They had persevered through exhaustion and uncertainty, all in pursuit of this moment. She was certain it would all be worth it in the end.

Ever since they had settled on Cuba instead of Florida, she was convinced the hotel had to be here. Her reasons weren't exactly scientific; it was more of a feeling she couldn't shake. She had entered a kind of flow state, finding ever more signs and signals along the way. Of the utmost help was a scientific paper on the habitat the white ghost orchid required. For this paper, botanists in Cuba had closely examined an area located in the far west of the island, on a rugged peninsula named Guanahacabibes.

Guanahacabibes, they said, boasted natural wonders and biodiversity. It was a long-forgotten Garden of Eden the Cuban government had only recently opened to tourism. What's more – and this had Ava practically geek out – the ocean waters beyond this peninsula were rumoured to be one of the possible sites of the sunken city of Atlantis. Now, Ava had never (ever) been one to believe in conspiracies of any sort, but recent events had, understandably, made her question all kinds of things deemed impossible in this world.

After all, Atlantis was said to be the lost city of the gods (or, if one believed a particularly dedicated YouTuber, a city built by extra-terrestrials – *aliens* – on a fleeting visit to Earth) – a city with far superior technology and a civilisation designed for the greatest possible benefit. And even if this was a bit 'out there' (like, literally), Guanahacabibes did lie only a stone's throw from the Mexican Yucatan peninsula, the former Mayan Empire, another ancient culture steeped in mystery. Lastly, the legendary home of Che Guevara was known to be trapped in this magical time warp, a place where one could still expect the unexpected.

Whatever one chose to believe, the western tip of Cuba was undeniably a piece of land imbued with rich but long-lost history, both culturally and naturally, and it certainly was way off the beaten track. Ava couldn't imagine a more fitting pocket of the world to hide a magical hotel in. She had set her sights on one particular beach in the north of the peninsula called Playa Las Olvidado – the Beach of the Forgotten, an almost poetic, if not to say auspicious, name for someone who was... well, *forgotten*.

Chartering the sailboat had been Dawn's brainchild. Despite her fear of swimming, she knew a surprising amount about sailing. Her father, a fisherman at Pomboo, had taught her.

Here on deck of the sailboat, which was named *Satori*, a sense of freedom washed over Ava. The feeling was a refreshing change from the constant limitations of their peculiar predicament. Being forgotten was a curse they both had learned to live with, but out here on the water, it mattered less. Here, they weren't dealing with receptionists who couldn't remember them, or trying to navigate public spaces where they left no lasting impression. Here, they could simply exist. The ocean didn't forget them, the wind didn't erase their presence, and the boat held their memories in its gentle rock. They would spend the night anchored in the port, planning to start the next day at the crack of dawn to tackle the three hundred odd nautical miles to Playa Las Olvidado.

"So, what will you do differently?" Dawn asked as Ava joined her in the cockpit. "If we really find it, I mean?"

Ava cleared her throat, contemplating how truthfully she should answer that one.

"I think I might stay a little longer," she said at last. "At the hotel, I mean."

"Really? Pfft, not me. The moment I get my study notes, I'll be out of that garden gate for good."

"But don't you want to confront Bruno?"

"I don't give a rat's ass about Bruno! I don't need to confront him, I don't need to forgive him. I just need to get as far away from him as possible." Dawn looked over at Ava. "Is that why you want to stay a little longer, though? Because you have unfinished business with him?"

"Yeah, that. And some other stuff."

Dawn frowned as if she could see straight through Ava. "How much longer are you planning on staying, exactly?"

"Like, indefinitely?" Ava said. She didn't know why she went for the whole truth. Dawn was sure not to like it.

"What utter horseshit is that?"

Not to like it one bit.

Ava rose, fetching her kikoi to cover her shoulders as the wind picked up. "Guess I'm just not in a hurry to get back home, that's all."

"I'm sorry, but that doesn't make *any* sense." Dawn blinked a few times as if to throw off fatigue. "The only reason we're trying to find the hotel is so that we can leave for good."

"You don't understand, it's —"

"You're damn right, I don't!"

"It's to do with something I found out, in this reality."

"Aha. At last, we're getting somewhere. What did you find out?"

"I found out that in this reality – the one where I don't exist – my parents never got divorced. They stayed together, happily ever after."

"So?"

"So, without me, they were better off, just like many other things."

"What things?"

"Just... *things*. Like, my flatmate, who has a great boyfriend in this reality."

"How do you know he's great?"

"They live together. So, he must be."

Dawn shook her head like a coiled spring. "Yeah, that's a great indicator of a happy relationship. What else?"

"I don't know" – Ava flung her hands in the air – "the business."

"Marley's Coffee?"

Ava shrugged affirmatively.

"What are you basing this on, exactly?"

"I've *seen* it, Dawn. With my own eyes. I've seen the world without me in it, and it's a much better place, trust me. Especially my parents were much better off without me."

"Ava, you listen to me now." Dawn stood and held Ava by the shoulders. "You cannot sacrifice your own future for the sake of your parents, one of whom isn't even alive anymore. That is madness."

Ava wrenched herself free as the tears began to pool.

"Besides," Dawn went on, following Ava as she clambered to the bow, "how can you possibly know not having you was the reason they stayed together? Or, or... how do you know this isn't all a dream?" She gestured wildly at the air around her. "How do you know there aren't a *million* other possible realities out there? You cannot know any of that."

Ava bit the inside of her lip, lost for words.

"But that's not even it, is it?" Dawn scrutinised her like a far-off shore through binoculars.

"What's not what?" Ava snapped.

"The truth." Dawn nodded. "Why you want to stay on at the hotel."

Ava brushed back a strand of hair. "Let's just forget I said anything," she said. But now she was trapped at the bow. Trapped, like krill in the baleen of a whale.

"You're scared." Dawn held onto the headsail's halyard, barring the way. "You're scared to make a choice. You just can't admit it, not even to yourself. And as long as you're at the hotel, you won't have to. As long as you're at the hotel, you're off the hook. You don't need to deal with the job offer – or anything else for that matter. You're a *coward*, Marley. You know exactly what you want to do, but you're terrified to actually go out there and do it."

Ava pushed past Dawn. "How would you know what I want?"

"Because you told me."

"Wow. It's so convenient, isn't it, Dawn? Keep bringing up a night I can't remember. How do I know what you're telling me is even the truth?"

Dawn crossed her arms over, her voice turning angry. "Are you honestly going to stand there and accuse me of lying? Are you honestly going to tell me you don't know what you want your life to be?"

Ava turned her head into the wind. She didn't reply.

"I like you, Ava," Dawn said. "You have a kind heart, and you care about the world. I know it's tough losing a parent, I've lost both of mine. And I can only imagine what it's like to face a legacy as daunting as the one your father wants you to step up to. But if you keep on hiding at that hotel, if you keep on running?" She came up next to Ava. "Then you're discarding a gift millions of people would literally kill for. You have a *choice*, Ava. And you're letting it go to waste. *Listen*," she demanded, the word sharp like coral. "You owe it to them – no, you know what? You owe it to *me* – to take that job or leave it. And if it's a 'No thank you', then so be it. But don't you hide at the hotel for the rest of your life, telling yourself the world is better off without you. Because *that* would be convenient."

Ava hovered on the cabin stairs, stiff like an oar. "Well, we might not find it anyway, so..." she gritted through her teeth but didn't know what came after 'so'.

When, at last, she blustered below deck, Dawn's words kept stirring her like the waves stirring the hull.

~

THE NEXT MORNING, the sun came up slowly, like a whale coming up for air. The sky was streaked with shades of pink and orange, and the sound of seagulls filled the air as the sailboat gently swayed on the calm waters of the port.

Shortly after Ava had gone to bed, Dawn had come down as well. At that point, Ava had still been too indignant to speak, but about halfway through the night, she was ready to admit how wrong she'd been. She squirmed on her berth for hours, waiting for the morning, the apology burning in her throat like a suppressed cough, the tension below deck penning up like soda in a bottle that'd been shaken. The *Satori* was way too small to hold a grudge, and Ava was distinctly aware that Dawn had been spot-on with everything she'd said.

The moment she heard her bunkmate clear her throat, Ava shot up. "You awake?" she said into the dimly lit cabin.

Dawn harrumphed into her pillow.

"I take that as a yes." Ava made for the kitchen with a single step, jumping into her apology against the simple sounds of morning: water pouring into the kettle, the click-

click-clicking of the stovetop's spark, followed by a short stream of gas and the whoosh of a flame.

"I wanted to say how sorry I am, Dawn. You were right. About everything. I *am* scared to go back. Terrified, actually. Because what if I choose wrong? What if I make a terrible mistake?"

"Then make a mistake."

Ava swivelled around and found Dawn sitting cross-legged on her berth.

"Chances are, you're gonna live, no matter how much you screw up." She shrugged. "And you'll probably come out stronger for it."

"You make it sound so easy." Ava tore open a bag of biscuits and handed it over. She fixed her gaze on Dawn, a question poised on her tongue. "What did I say, Dawn? When we talked about calling the shots? What did I say I would do?"

"You said you would do something that would have made your mother proud," Dawn said gently. She fished out a biscuit and began to crunch. "So, let's find that damn hotel, what do you say? It's about time you used it for what it is – a chance to fix your life, not run from it."

~

IT WAS late afternoon by the time the *Satori* entered the Gulf of Guanahacabibes. Hugging the coastline as close as they could, they began scanning with the binoculars. However, to reach Playa Las Olvidado, they would have to sail all the way to the other end, then circumnavigate a north-pointing headland. Las Olvidado should lie right on the other side, facing exactly west.

When, at last, they tacked to push past the headland, a

strange sense of emptiness overcame Ava, followed by a wave of panic when she remembered the last time she had felt this way: on Pomboo Beach, when the hotel hadn't been there, either.

"Here we go, this is it!" Dawn announced as she tightened the sails in the strong west wind hitting them now.

"Take the tiller, will you?" Ava asked and scrambled to the bow. Binoculars bouncing around her neck, she whispered continuously, "This is it, this is it… this *has* to be it."

She scanned the shore, quickly dizzying from the distorted vision. But she kept on going, kept on searching. A narrow stretch of sand flanked by coastal forest, Playa Las Olvidado was devoid of any people but ablaze with golden light, the setting sun shining directly at it. *Satori* passed a ramshackle gazebo and a building long fallen into ruin that had Ava's heart briefly stop. But it turned out to be only the abandoned dive centre she'd read about online.

A plain lighthouse marked the end of the beach, and when Ava saw it, her heart sank like the anchor Dawn had decided to drop.

"Nothing?" She came to the bow, taking the binoculars from Ava.

"Looks like it," Ava said, squinting as if the sun was blinding her.

"Let's go on land," Dawn suggested. "Check properly."

Ava jumped off as soon as they hit the shallows, pushing the boat onto the sand.

The beach was deserted except for a few scurrying crabs and a pair of seagulls fighting over a scrap of food. The sand was hot and gritty under her bare feet, and the humid air stuck to her skin. As they walked off in different directions, she couldn't shake the feeling that they were wasting their time. She had been so sure they would find the hotel here, but now she was losing hope. She slumped into the sand, her gaze fixed on the endless stretch of beach. The only sound was the waves lapping against the shore, a harsh reminder of their isolation. The palm trees swayed gently in the breeze, mocking her with their serene beauty as the disappointment began to sink in.

With a heavy heart, she pushed herself to her feet and trudged back towards the boat, feeling more lost than ever before.

22

FREE TO GO

A sudden scream jolted Ava back to reality. She looked up, heart racing, to see Dawn's figure darting through the thickets, her voice echoing in a high-pitched shriek that could only signal one thing – danger. Ava scrambled forward, fear gripping her chest. Had her friend encountered a wild animal or worse? As Dawn emerged onto the beach, her frantic gestures only added to Ava's concern. She picked herself up, worried her friend might have injured herself. Dawn had traipsed around barefoot as well, and these coral rocks cut deep. When her friend came running up the beach, she flailed her arms around, frenetically gesturing toward the tree line, now topped by the setting sun. Maybe she had actually seen a wild animal.

But the closer Dawn came, the more Ava realised her captain wasn't panicked – no, she was elated.

Cheering, Dawn skipped along the shore, and at last, Ava could hear what her friend was yelling: "I found it, Ava – I found it!"

"*What?*" Ava broke into a sprint, thinking her ears might

have tricked her. Dawn kept on shouting, but Ava couldn't hear anything now that she ran into the wind. At last, she caught up with Dawn, who repeated the words in all their simple beauty.

"I found it, Ava."

"Wha – *How*? WHERE?"

"Beyond those mangroves." Dawn pointed, catching her breath.

Ava grabbed Dawn's face with both hands. "Swear you're not messing with me!"

"I swear I'm not messing with you," Dawn said, tears flooding her eyes. "You were right. You were *right*!" A flabbergasted laugh escaped her, and her face brimmed with joy, and shock and utter, utter relief. And Ava knew it had to be the truth.

"Sh- show me," she gasped, turning Dawn around. They began to run up the beach, taking each other's hands. Their legs, shaking with excitement, kicked up plumes of sand. Dawn showed the way to a path cutting through the mangroves. They passed the first line of trees, and there it was: the dingy wall, once white, now covered with cracks and mould. The surrounding forest had practically swallowed it up; no wonder Ava didn't see it from the boat. Bruno's sign with the house rules wasn't there, but the path led straight to the round yellow gate, now gleaming in that last bit of light like the sun itself.

As they approached the gate, they slowed down to a walk, taking in the rundown surroundings. The air was thick with the smell of salt and dampness, and the only sound was the rustling of the leaves in the trees. Ava looked at Dawn, and they both knew they had made it.

She pressed down on the handle, and the gate opened with that old familiar squeak, sending shivers down her spine. But just when she was about to cross the doorstep, she hesitated, looking back at Dawn.

"You go first," Ava said with a faint smile.

Dawn stepped forward, reaching out a hand. "Together?"

"All right, together."

They took a step forward, but as they tried to cross the threshold, an invisible hand seemed to push them back. They tried again, but the same thing happened – it was as if the hotel was denying them entry. Ava reached out tentatively, but her hand met with an unseen barrier, tingling as if an electric shock had passed through it. She recoiled, rubbing her skin. Dawn stepped back and looked at her with a mixture of fear and confusion.

"Do you think it's full?" she asked, her voice tinged with worry.

Ava felt a chill run down her spine. "It shouldn't be. With Molly gone, there should be room for both of us," she replied, trying to stay optimistic.

Dawn furrowed her brow, concern evident in her eyes. "What if others have found it in the meantime?" she asked. "What if there's just one spot left? Or none?"

Ava thought for a moment before turning to Dawn. Gently, she placed a hand on her shoulder. "Try it without me."

"What? No. I can't do that."

"Yes, you can. You've been an outcast for much longer than me. It's your turn. Go ahead, I want you to."

"But what about you?"

Ava offered a reassuring smile. "I'll wait here until you've come out in Zanzibar."

Dawn paused, her eyes wandering between Ava's. She

couldn't hide her eagerness to get out on the other side. "I won't need long," she said at last.

"I know," Ava replied.

"Seriously, all I'm going to do is fetch my books and notes, and then I'm out of there," Dawn assured her, then she gestured at Ava's bag. "You still got that stopwatch Bruno gave you?"

Ava nodded, her hand instinctively reaching for it.

"Give me one hour, then try it again," said Dawn.

"Take two."

"All right." Dawn pulled Ava into a tight embrace. As they released each other, she pivoted and was just about to step over the threshold when she suddenly stopped. "Promise me that you'll leave the hotel, Ava," she said and turned around once more. "Promise me you'll find me on the other side. I'll be waiting for you back at Pomboo."

Ava looked into Dawn's eyes, her expression resolute. "I promise. Now go – *go*."

Dawn gave her a determined nod, eyes glistening with unshed tears. As Dawn crossed the threshold back into the hotel, a surge of relief washed over Ava. It had worked. The gate had finally opened for her friend, allowing her back in.

Ava started the stopwatch. She lowered herself onto the doorstep, gazing at the sun dipping behind the trees, and her heart swelled with gratitude, knowing Dawn could finally go home.

With each passing minute, the sun dipped lower, its rays growing softer and more subdued. The world seemed to hold its breath, anticipating the final moments of daylight. And then, with a gentle farewell, it slipped below the horizon, painting the sky in fiery hues before giving way to a deepening blue. As darkness settled over the beach, a blanket of stars emerged, twinkling and winking above. Soon, the night came alive with the chorus of crickets and the distant melodies of nocturnal creatures. Ava sat in awe, and for the first time in a long time, felt a profound sense of peace and wonder. It was a moment to cherish, a moment not to be missed. She couldn't help but feel grateful for the privilege of being here, of being alive. And she could not wait. To step back inside the hotel. To find her answers. To make a life for herself, and make the most of it. As the stopwatch finally chimed zero, her legs twitched, and her heart raced, and she felt the urge to run – not away from life, but, at last, toward it.

With gentle strokes, she smoothed and levelled the sand at her feet, creating a blank canvas. Smiling, she etched a sentence into the soft grains with her fingertip: AVA MARLEY WAS HERE.

She stood, brushing the sand off her hand, then rested it on the doorknob. The moment seemed suspended in time, as if the air held its breath, mirroring the anticipation coursing through her veins. The simple act of crossing the threshold felt momentous, as if it marked the beginning of a new chapter. As she took that first step forward, a surge of emotions flooded her. Excitement and curiosity intermingled with a hint of nervousness, forming a palpable energy. She lifted her other foot, gently placing it onto the gravel path. As her weight shifted onto that foot, an unexpected force tugged at her arm, momentarily startling her. It felt as if she had tossed another souvenir into the air and travelled through one of the doorways. A flicker of panic tinged her thoughts, the fear that the hotel had once again cast her out. But as her eyes focused, her heart skipped a beat in recognition. It wasn't the hotel's rejection she faced, but the warm embrace of a familiar presence.

"Thank God, you're back!" Helene's voice rang out, brimming with relief and joy as she enveloped Ava in a tight embrace.

Behind her, Yash stood on the path, next to a man with Asian features Ava had never seen before. "We just ran into your friend," Yash said. "She told us you were coming. I am so glad you're safe, Ava."

"So, Dawn made it out okay?" Ava asked as she hugged him.

"She left a couple of minutes ago," affirmed Helene. "Quite the character she is. Told me, if you don't leave here by the end of the week, I have her permission to personally kick you out."

"That sounds like her, all right." Ava chuckled. "And I'm assuming you're the new tenant of room five?" She turned to the man next to Yash, offering her hand.

"Four, actually," he replied and shook her hand. "I took up Molly's room. It is nice to meet you, Ava. Dal is my name, from North Korea." Standing tall, but not imposingly so, Dal exuded a calmness and resilience that seemed to radiate from his core. A well-worn tweed jacket draped his lean frame, and his hair, greying, was cropped close to his head.

"Ava!" Joao's voice came up from behind Yash. He pushed past the photographer and flung his arms around her. "We were looking all over the world for you!" he burst out. "How did you manage to get back? Dawn mentioned I had something to do with it, but she didn't want to say!"

Ava beamed at Joao. "It was your orchid," she said. "Your white frog orchid."

"No way!" Joao's smile widened even further. "Come, come, have a look!" He pulled her arm, leading her to the spot in the garden where, a few days ago, nothing but tangled roots had sprouted from a mouldy trunk. Now, the ghost orchid was slowly coming into bloom, gleaming white like snow against the dark greens and spreading its distinct frog legs.

"She is very early this year. Maybe she wanted to welcome you back as well." Joao squeezed her hand.

"She is absolutely gorgeous," Ava said, smiling. "But guys, I need to tell you something." Her tone turned serious as her gaze fixed on Helene. "Something about Bruno."

"They already know."

The innkeeper's voice emanated from the gardens, and Ava pivoted swiftly. She spotted him sitting on the veranda steps, looking as miserable as a plant, neglected and wilted in its pot.

"Hello, Ava." He inclined his head at her, but the eye contact made his lips tremble, and before he could control it, tears pooled in his eyes and streamed down his face.

Fury surged through Ava's chest. "How dare you cry right now," she snarled, her voice quivering.

The innkeeper sobbed, his face a grimace of shame. "I am so sorry, Ava," he whimpered. "I wanted to come clean as soon as I found out Molly was ill. I... I was definitely going to after she collapsed. Lo giuro. I swear. When both you and she disappeared, I told everyone straight away. I do not expect you to ever forgive me," Bruno mumbled. "I don't deserve it. But I do need you to know how incredibly sorry I am, for all of it."

Ava inhaled sharply, ready to let off the steam that had accumulated for days, but Helene was quicker.

"Oh, how noble of you, Signor di Mare!" she mocked him, sweeping a dramatic curtsy. "And what a repentant sinner you are! I can't believe I've been duped by yet another swindler like you!"

"Come on, Helene. Leave him be," Yash insisted. "This isn't helping anybody."

"It's helping *me*, to be honest," Helene replied.

"What about Dawn, Bruno?" Ava forced out, her words biting the air.

The innkeeper gave a nod. He removed his glasses, dragging his sleeve across his face in a weary gesture. Once he replaced them, his eyes found Ava again, their expression twisted as though her very presence inflicted a deep, raw hurt. "I just meant to scare her, I swear," he confessed in a whisper. "I didn't want her to break curfew. And certainly not... not..." His voice faltered, cracking under the weight of his words. "I thought about going to Pomboo, to search for her. I wrestled with that thought countless times. But the fear of what I might discover... The fear that she could have... have drowned. I'm so deeply sorry. I wanted to apologise to her directly, but she wouldn't even give me a glance."

"And can you blame her?" Ava challenged, not really seeking a reply. A silence hung in the air as Bruno fumbled for a handkerchief and blew his nose.

"Tell me why you came to talk to me at the garden gate," Ava prodded, her tone firm. "The truth this time."

Bruno sighed. "The truth is, I recognised Pomboo Beach when I first saw you outside the gate. That is why I came to talk to you. It was not to help you or to ease you into our ways. I feared it might not have been a coincidence – two people finding the hotel at the same location. I was terrified Dawn might come back inside instead of you. You must understand, at that point, I had enmeshed myself in so many lies, I ... I couldn't risk being found out. I came and talked to you only to head off Dawn if I had to."

Ava sucked in air through her mouth, about to explode, when Bruno jumped right back into the silence. "*But* everyone knows the truth now," he assured her. "No more secrets." He turned to face the others. "Ava is back, safe and sound. So, there is no more reason for any of you to stay. You are all free to go." He gestured at the garden gate, his words hanging in the air, but then a collective hesitation settled among his guests.

"Well, we don't have to leave right this second," Yash interjected, his words laced with reluctance.

"Yeah, there's no rush," Helene swiftly chimed in. "Let's just go back inside for now," she proposed, wrapping an arm around Joao. "What do you say, buddy, hm? Shall we make some dinner?"

"I could smash a mountain of pancakes right about now," the boy said and started walking up the path. "You have pancakes in North Korea?" he asked Dal, who had quietly joined his stride.

"You coming, Ava?" Yash called out.

"In a minute," she replied, gears turning in her mind as she felt the need to be alone with Bruno. She allowed herself to fall behind, and the innkeeper did the same. It was as if he had chained himself to her, forbidden to move unless she did. Hands shoved in her pockets, Ava considered the flower heads, drawing slow but shaky breaths as she thought about what to say. Ever since she'd met him, Bruno had balanced on that knife's edge between shadow and light, never quite crossing over to either side, determined to pursue his course, yet trying not to hurt anyone in his wake. But what he didn't seem to realise – at least never until it was too late – was that he *did* hurt those around him. Molly had stayed for months at the hotel, thinking she was trapped there and with a severe health condition that had probably only worsened throughout. Then there was Dawn, whom – granted – he probably hadn't wanted to drown in the Indian Ocean but whom he had condemned to a life forgotten, nonetheless. As for his wife, Martina, Ava would never presume to know what went on inside their marriage, let alone inside Martina's mind. She would never make a conjecture about who was at fault. But there was no denying that Bruno was riven by regret when it came to Martina. Clearly, he would do things differently if he could turn back time. Ava couldn't help but wonder – being the eternal movie buff he was – did the innkeeper regard himself the hero of his own story, or the villain?

"You know what, Bruno?" she said when the thought struck her, "It's a good thing you don't like happy endings. Because you sure as hell aren't headed for one."

"Ava, per favore," Bruno said. He reached out a hand, but Ava jerked away from him like a startled deer. She climbed the stairs and went inside, determined not to waste one more second on the innkeeper who never was one in the first place.

Bruno stayed behind in the garden. Motionless, like a statue in a museum.

23

EXIT THROUGH THE GARDEN GATE

Ava sat at the kitchen table, surrounded by friends, eating chunky slices of watermelon. Cicadas buzzed outside the window. Distant thunder heralded a storm. The hotel's famous guestbook at long last before her, she flicked through its pages while Helene, Yash, and Joao filled her in on what had transpired at the hotel since she'd missed curfew. Dal leaned against the kitchen counter, quietly listening, his eyes, dark and alert, twinkling with hidden wisdom behind a pair of sleek, metallic-rimmed glasses.

"I was angry when Bruno came clean, of course. Furious, if you must know," Helene exclaimed while she made a heart on the tabletop with the melon pips. "I still am – unlike these two." She jerked her head toward Joao and Yash.

"He made a mistake, and he came clean." Yash shrugged. "And honestly, I was the first to buy into the idea. You were a close second, Hel. We wouldn't have stayed here any less time had he told us the truth, and you know it. We wouldn't have done anything differently."

Joao agreed with a wholehearted nod.

"What do you make of all this, Dal? This must all sound very confusing." Ava looked at Dal, who took a seat at the table.

He raised his brows, which made his forehead wrinkle like that of an elephant's. "Well, it seems, I have joined for dessert while all of you are already several courses deep in the menu. But I am, of course, very grateful to be here."

"And you are aware of how it works, are you?"

Dal nodded slowly. "I have been told this place provides a refuge for those seeking an escape, yes. And I can see why it might have showed up for me."

"Wait till you hear about this guy, Ava!" Joao interrupted. "Dal here is like a famous historian, right? He was all about telling the real stories of the people in North Korea – the ones the government wanted to hide. He's like a superhero, but instead of fighting bad guys with lasers or something, he battles with words."

"I don't know about superhero, Joao..." Dal interrupted, scratching the back of his head.

"I'm sorry, you're right." Joao nodded, his eyes scanning the table. "You're more like... like an avenger, that's it! Listen to this, Ava: Dal found these secret documents from way back in the fifties that proved the government was telling lies, and he started sneaking those into his books, so people could know what was really going on. But the government, they didn't like that one bit. They called him a traitor and locked him up!"

"All right, all right," Yash said and patted Joao's back. "Why don't you let the man tell his own story?"

"I think the boy summed it up sufficiently," Dal mused. "Long story short: the government confiscated my passport and kept me a prisoner in my own country for the last decade. I managed to escape with the help of some acquaintances from Japan a few months ago, but now I can never return to my home country, or so I thought."

"I'm so sorry, Dal. That's terrible," Ava said.

"Well," he replied, a mischievous smile playing around his mouth. "We shall see. My being here might just prove to be a more effective service to my country." He gazed up at the kitchen clock. "Now, if you will excuse me, I have a state banquet to disrupt." He winked and retrieved a salad fork from his pocket, which he twirled between his fingers, tossed into the air, and then disappeared.

"Absolute legend," Yash said, his expression filled with admiration. "He's friends with the Dalai Lama, did you know? And he's won the Anne Frank Award."

"You cannot *win* the Anne Frank Award, Yash," said Helene. "It's given to you if you show extraordinary courage."

"Potato, potahto."

Ava watched them bickering, a question poised at the tip of her tongue.

"So, why are you still here, guys? Why haven't you left yet?"

Helene raked her fingers through her hair. "Well, we couldn't just leave and forget about you! Once we went to find Molly, and she told us what happened, we made a pact that we would not leave until we found you."

Ava's face lit up at the mention of Molly. "So, she remembers me?"

"Yeah, she does." Yash grinned. "She remembers all of us. Her daughter doesn't. Which is quite the shame," he said.

Helene tsk-ed. "Someone has a crush on Annie..."

"Anyway," Joao cut in, "we also went to Pomboo Beach, but you must have left already. So, we began to talk with the

border people in Australia and Tanzania. We were scared they might have sacked you at immigration and then forgotten about you. That's what we thought had happened, anyway. But we kept on searching no matter what."

"Thank you, guys," Ava said, hugging the guestbook. "I can't believe you did all that."

"Mais, bien sure. We are friends, after all. Aren't we, buddy?" Helene hugged Joao, who had suddenly fallen silent. "What's the matter, mon ami? Spit it out."

"It's just that Ava has a point..." Joao stammered. "Now that she is back, must we all go home, or what?"

"I wouldn't say that. We can stay here, non? No one needs to leave if we don't want to?" She looked at Ava as if she knew the answer already.

"Guys," Ava began softly, "let me tell you what Dawn told me: the hotel manifested for us for a reason. But it's not to provide us an escape from our lives indefinitely. It's to give us a chance to mend what's broken in them. If Bruno hadn't interfered, our approach would have been different from the start. Just look at this if you don't believe me."

She set the guestbook down on the table and started leafing through its pages. "These entries are from previous guests, all narrating their journey of transformation, how they lent each other a hand, and then took a fresh start from a stronger position. Here, listen to this one, for example. By Anthony Simmons: I arrived at the hotel, feeling lost and suffocated by a life that no longer fit. But the magic of this place took me to the heart of the Amazon rainforest, where I learned from the indigenous tribes about their connection with nature. Living simply, I found a peace I had never known, and I realised that I was not lost but misplaced. When I leave the hotel, I would like to start a sustainable farm, using the knowledge I gained from the tribes. And then I won't be forgotten but rather remembered for my contributions to sustainable living." She pushed the guestbook over to Helene. "Come on, you read us another one."

Helene flicked through the pages, picking a story that resonated with her. "By Aiko Tanaka: I was a single mother, struggling to make ends meet," she read aloud, her voice mellow. "The hotel gave me an opportunity I never dared to hope for. While I was a forgotten guest, my kids were cared for by an incredible foster family, and, knowing they were well looked after, I was able to follow my dream of going to France, where I studied the works of all the master chefs. The world may have forgotten me during my time in the hotel, but I used it to transform myself. Now, I am all set to open my own restaurant, and I cannot wait to return to my children. The hotel didn't just change my life; it gave my family a whole new start."

Helene looked up, tears welling in her eyes. She handed the book to Yash, who began turning pages as well. "By Tobias Lindberg: I was trapped in a cycle of addiction," he read aloud, "feeling like a ghost in my own life. Thanks to the hotel, I discovered a small fishing village in Japan that I kept returning to. There, I learned the art of patience and mindfulness from the local fishermen. In the quiet rhythm of the sea, I found sobriety, and when the world had forgotten me, the other hotel guests remembered, providing me with endless support and love. When I leave this place today, I will use my second chance to start a community support group for those battling addiction. Instead of being a ghost, I am planning to become a guide for others on their journey to recovery." Yash finished reading. "That's pretty empowering stuff, actually," he said, just when Joao silently slipped out the door.

"He is scared," Helene murmured as soon as the door had shut behind him. "He doesn't want to go back home."

"Yeah, but *he* sure as hell shouldn't stay here," Yash said as he reached for the last piece of watermelon. "He's *fifteen*. He's got his whole life ahead of him!"

"So, how can we help him?" Ava asked, her tone resolute. "Let's make use of this place – *properly*. What would it take, hm? What would it take for each of us to feel good and confident about stepping through that gate?"

"Well," Helene began, leaning back in her chair, her gaze distant yet determined. "For me, it would mean bringing Andre to justice. Exposing his deceit, his scams, everything. He's hurt too many people. I couldn't stand by and let him continue. I would want to ensure he pays for what he's done."

Nods of agreement came from Ava and Yash. Ava then spoke up, her voice firm with resolve. "I want to stop running. No more drifting, no more aimless wandering. When I leave here, I want to have a concrete plan for my life, a direction. I want to know what I'm doing and where I'm going."

"What about your family business, Marley's? I thought you had a job lined up there," Yash said.

Ava nodded. "There is an opportunity to join the company, yes," she admitted. "It runs out on April twenty-fifth."

"Well, that's it, then," Helene said, placing a hand in the middle of the table. "That is our deadline. Before April twenty-fifth, we will all get our shit together. Deal?"

"Deal," Ava said, laying her hand on top of Helene's.

The room fell silent as they turned to look at Yash. He shifted uncomfortably under their gaze. "Honestly, girls," he began, "I don't know what I want, let alone what it would take to make me feel good about leaving. I thought coming here would answer some of my questions, but I feel like I'm now further away than ever from finding any answers."

"You might be closer than you think," Ava said encouragingly. "If this place has taught me one thing, it's that everything will fall into place exactly when and how it's meant to. How about a leap of faith, what do you say?" With a wink, she nodded towards the centre of the table.

Yash let out a drawn-out sigh, his eyebrows lifting as he rubbed the back of his neck. "Yeah, all right. Let's do it." And with that, his hand joined the others on the table.

And so, over the coming days, and beneath the enchanting roof of the hotel, Ava, Helene, and Yash each embarked on the journey of shaping their individual paths.

Submerged in a sea of paper trails, Helene began to unearth the machinations of her swindler husband. She discovered off-shore accounts filled with ill-gotten gains, shell companies created for the sole purpose of hiding assets, and a network of complicit associates who enabled his deceit. She found invoices for high-ticket items purchased in cash – sports cars, luxury watches, expensive artwork – none of which she'd ever seen. She pieced together the puzzle of his frequent, unexplained absences, linking them to secret meetings with co-conspirators in dimly lit bars and discreet hotel lobbies. In a safety deposit box at a bank she'd never heard of, she found passports in Andre's name but with different aliases, and she uncovered a trail of victims, innocent people who had lost their life savings to Andre's elaborate investment scams just like her.

Each revelation was like a stab in the heart, but it only fuelled her determination. She meticulously documented every shred of evidence, every connection, every lie. Her resolve hardened with every deceitful transaction and clandestine meeting she uncovered. Helene was determined to bring Andre's fraudulent empire crashing down and ensure he faced justice for his crimes.

Yash worked tirelessly alongside her, helping her sift through the endless paper trails and digital footprints. With his keen eye, he pointed out discrepancies and patterns that Helene may have missed. Ava provided a comforting presence, often just sitting with Helene as she navigated this painful journey, offering a listening ear and comforting words when needed.

And as Helene unravelled Andre's deceitful web, she seemed to grow stronger from it. The ordeal, shameful as it was, slowly transformed her, and it ignited within her a desire to use her newfound strength to help others who might find themselves in a similar situation. She decided to turn her pain into power, to voice her story and inspire other women to stand against deceit and manipulation. As soon as she left the hotel, she was planning to break her silence and expose her husband's true nature to the world. She even began outlining a novel with a character strikingly similar to Andre as the villain.

Meanwhile, Yash found himself charting a course through completely unexplored territories when he accompanied Ava to Mission Beach one day, delivering Robert's ashes to Molly as she had requested.

Their knock on the door was answered by Annie, and Ava immediately noticed Yash's fascination, his gaze softening as he took in the young woman standing before them.

After Ava had introduced herself as the usual "old friend from Port", Annie led them into the living room where Molly sat, her frail form dwarfed by the plush armchair. Recognition and relief washed over Molly's face when she saw Ava. Her frail hand reached out, gripping Ava's with a strength that belied her illness. "My dear Ava," she whispered, her voice thick with emotion. "I thought I'd never see you again."

As they shared their reunion, Yash was drawn to the garden, where Annie was tending to her two children. Ava watched from the corner of her eye as Yash, usually the reserved, cool type, engaged with the children, his laughter echoing in the warm afternoon air, his eyes always finding their way back to Annie.

Molly had noticed it as well. "That one," she said, her voice a mere rasp, pointing at Yash, "he's got a good heart. He just doesn't know it yet."

And that was how Yash found direction in the most unexpected of places. From that day on, he returned to Mission Beach every day, armed with a smile, determined to bring a ray of sunshine into Annie's life. Even if it meant reintroducing himself each time, his heart seemed to refuse to waver. He spent his time assisting Molly in her fight against her illness, and getting to know Annie and her children, creating new memories for them every day.

Ava couldn't have been more delighted for him. The two of them had never quite clicked, and besides, she had her own endeavours keeping her occupied. She had embarked on a global quest to uncover her true passion – the wonderful world of coffee. She traversed the bustling plantations of Colombia, tasted the rich, bold flavours of Ethiopian brews, and studied the intricate art of latte designs in the trendy cafés of Melbourne. Each destination was a new chapter in her exploration of the coffee world, a journey that was slowly moulding her future.

However, the visit that provided the most inspiration was to the port of Trapani in Sicily, where she had a tour of Aldilà, the sail-shipped coffee company that Bruno had spoken of at Madre Tierra. Aldilà was not just a business, but a beacon of sustainable entrepreneurship. The company was unique in its practice of shipping coffee from Honduras in an entirely carbon-neutral manner, utilising only the power of the wind. Once the coffee reached Italy, it was sold from their quaint harbour café in Trapani, a charming place that buzzed with life and the rich aroma of coffee.

Ava saw so much room for potential growth and innovation with a business such as this one. She noticed gaps in their marketing strategy, the lack of an online presence, and the possibility of expanding their reach beyond the confines of Trapani's harbour. She felt a surge of excitement at the thought of doing something like this, of applying her knowledge and passion to help this sprouting arm of the industry grow and reach its full potential. It was a cause she could believe in, and she could really see herself diving headfirst into this adventure.

And while they were all busy forging their own path, she and Helene and Yash all pooled their efforts to safeguard Joao. Guided by Helene's recently acquired legal expertise, they assembled a substantial body of evidence against Joao's abusive father. This included documented instances of physical abuse, captured in photographs and videos from Joao's smartphone. They discovered medical documentation that detailed Joao's repeated injuries, which didn't align with the father's justifications, particularly the most recent incident where he had hurled a bottle at Joao, causing the scar on his eyebrow. Yash had managed to secure photos of this wound with Ava's disposable camera during the first movie night, which should further strengthen their case.

Beneath Dal's insightful leadership, the crew also sprang into action to assist his North Korean compatriots. He taught them how to operate a shortwave radio to transmit messages of hope and factual news into North Korea, countering the regime's propaganda. They also assembled care packages filled with essential items such as food, medical supplies, and books that Dal had written, revealing the true history of North Korea. Using the hotel's magic, they transported these packages to safe drop-off points within North Korea, places that Dal knew would reach those in need without arousing the suspicion of the authorities.

Each action, each plan was executed with careful precision and unwavering determination, a testament to the impact one could make when guided by a purpose as profound as Dal's.

Spending time with him, the hotel shed another layer for Ava. When she thought about what he and his compatriots must have gone through, she felt guilty – if not ashamed – that the hotel had appeared for her at all. There were only five rooms... *five*. And she had taken up one of them, had occupied a spot someone else would deserve – would need – much more. War refugees. Victims of domestic abuse. Political dissidents seeking asylum. The list was endless.

Yes, it was high time to free up space.

As a team, they had accomplished what they set out to do: They had turned the entire hotel into a beacon of hope, not just for themselves, but for those they were able to reach out to.

Only one person had remained conspicuously absent. It seemed as if Bruno had vanished into thin air, and Ava couldn't help but wonder several times that week if he had indeed slipped through the garden gate, departing as silently as a whisper.

"You really think this is going to work?" Joao asked as Ava guided him past the hedges and toward the garden gate.

"It's going to work," she assured him. "Trust me."

"But what if it doesn't?"

Around the last bend, Helene came into view, lined up with the rest of the hotel guests. "It will work," she said, reaching out a hand.

It was the evening of April the twenty-fourth, and Joao was the first to leave.

"I can't do it. Please don't make me, Helene." Joao pulled back, clasping Helene's hand. "Please let me stay here."

Ava took a step closer to Joao, placing a gentle hand on his arm. "Joao," she began, her voice soft yet firm. "We understand your fear, really we do. But you're not going back to your father. We've made sure of that."

"And remember," Helene added, squeezing his hand reassuringly, "you're going back with evidence, with proof. It's not your word against his anymore. You won't be alone in this fight."

"But why can't I just stay here until I'm older? Why do I have to go back at all?" Joao's voice quivered with apprehension.

Yash stepped forward, his usually playful eyes reflecting a deep seriousness. "Joao, mate, these years of your life... they're important. They're about more than just getting older. They're about growing, learning, and discovering who you are. You don't want to miss them, trust me."

Ava nodded in agreement. "You shouldn't have to skip them."

Helene touched his chin. "Hey, you know what? It's going to be all right. You're going to be all right. All you have to do is walk through that gate right when I toss up my souvenir. Then you'll meet me on the other side, and I'll do all the talking, okay? And if they don't agree to help you by the time I'm done with them, I swear I will not leave you hanging. I will put you up in a hotel for a few days, and then I will return to Florida and take you away from there myself."

Joao swallowed. "And if they *do* help me? What then? Will I never see you again?"

"Tell you what," Helene replied and drew a pen from her pocket. "This is my landline number in France." She scribbled the digits on his arm. "You call me in two days, all right?"

"And you promise you'll pick up?" Joao stared at her with all the seriousness of a fifteen-year-old.

"I swear. Now, go – *go*!"

At last, Joao made it toward the gate. The others had said their goodbyes already to make his departure as quick and easy as possible. Now they simply touched him on the shoulder, wished him luck, and promised him one hell of a great life once he'd come out on the deep end. But as Dal opened the gate, Joao turned to Helene once again.

"You'll be there, right?"

Helene held up the travel souvenir, a key chain that read WELCOME TO MIAMI. "Right behind you," she promised.

The moment Joao was out the door, Helene tossed the souvenir up in the air. "Wish us luck, guys," she said before she caught it and was gone.

A few hours later, Helene stormed inside the living room, where the others had anxiously awaited her return around the fireplace.

"Well, it worked," she announced with a glowing face, and she was met with a round of ecstatic cheering and applause. "He still has a way to go, of course, but they took to his story like fish to the bait! They absolutely loved him and promised he would never have to return to his father's place." She sank into an armchair, only to shoot right back up. "Actually, I better get going as well. Have a promise to keep, after all."

"I guess I'll go too, then," Yash said. "Can't picture this place without you, Hel."

"Aww, that's so sweet." Helene moved forward to give him a hug. "And what about you, Ava?"

"Yeah. Guess I'm ready."

There was a pause as their eyes flicked towards Dal, a silent question hanging in the air. Dal met their gaze with a resigned smile. "I'll be staying," he admitted, his voice soft yet steady. "I have more work to do here."

Of course, they had anticipated this. Dal's passport had been seized, making his homeland a forbidden territory.

"Besides," Dal continued, rising to his feet. "I fear that the victories I've managed to carve out from here – all the good we've done together, friends – might dissolve if I re-enter the world to be remembered. I might just have always been meant to stay for good."

Ava reached for his hand, pressing it in admiration. There was a certain poignant irony to Dal's decision to stay. It was the ultimate sacrifice – to continue working tirelessly for the betterment of his country and his people while remaining an unsung hero himself. His efforts would ripple out into the world, yet his name would remain unspoken, his face unseen.

"Man, you're such a legend," Yash said, giving Dal a heartfelt hug.

The group congregated a short while later under the twinkling blanket of stars that draped the garden. Helene was unable to hold back her tears, and even Yash wiped his eyes discreetly. Only Captain, the dog, bustled around their feet as if oblivious to the impending goodbyes.

"This is not forever, though, right?" he asked Dal, a hopeful glint in his eyes. "You'll come visit – just like I did with Molly, yeah?"

"Maybe more than you like," Dal retorted with a wink, the corner of his mouth twitching into a playful smirk.

As Ava was about to turn around, her heart set on her departure, a sudden bark echoed through the silent garden as Captain darted back toward the building. Ava's gaze followed the dog and landed on a shadowy figure inside the hotel. It was Bruno, standing by the bay window, his silhouette outlined by the dim indoor lights.

As the others shouldered their belongings, Ava froze and fell behind.

"You know what, guys?" she said, shoving her hands in her pockets. "I… I think I need to stay a little longer, after all."

Helene turned towards her, a frown of concern creasing her forehead. "But you promised Dawn you'd leave."

"I will, Helene," Ava reassured her, her gaze flickering back to the distant figure of Bruno. "I'll leave tonight. There's just… one more loose end I need to tie up."

Her words seemed to pacify Helene, who nodded hesitantly. The two women exchanged a warm embrace before one stepped away, preparing to depart, while the other sat down her backpack, navigating the undercurrent that guided her decision.

And then Helene took the first step out, tucking her arm into Yash's. "So, where will you be going from here, anyway?" she asked.

"Well, I'll come out in the Maldives, and from there, it's only a short flight over to Australia, you know?"

That was the last Ava heard before Dal closed the gate behind them, then quickly tossed a souvenir and disappeared himself. Ava left her pack behind in the garden and walked back up to the hotel.

A full moon had emerged above the roof, illuminating every corner, revealing every last secret.

24

TO BE REMEMBERED

"I thought everyone had left," Bruno remarked, a hint of surprise lacing his words. Ava had found him in his favourite spot, standing by the bay window in the living room, gently stroking Captain's ear.

"Not quite yet." She advanced towards him, the guestbook tucked securely under her arm. The room was engulfed in an eerie silence, a stark departure from the usual lively symphony that inhabited the space. Noting the lack of music, Ava gravitated towards the record player. She selected an album, and the voice of Billie Holiday gradually filled the room with a deep sense of melancholy.

"So, you want to talk this out?" Ava asked.

The innkeeper swallowed. "I would like that very much."

"I thought maybe you would also like to write a little something about us," she said, handing Bruno the guestbook as she settled on the bench.

Bruno scratched his chest. "You think I would do us justice?"

"You'd certainly be the one to try the hardest."

The innkeeper was about to sit down when she stopped

him. "What? No beverages? Where are your manners, innkeeper?"

"I could fetch something quick if you'd like?"

Ava gave an affirmative nod, prompting Bruno to head to the kitchen. He returned shortly, a tray bearing a teapot and two cups clinking gently against each other in his hands. Seating himself, he poured them each a cup of tea.

Ava studied him, her gaze unwavering as he handed her a cup. Finally, she broke the silence.

"Why'd you do it, Bruno?" she asked. "The Atlas, the lies… all of it. Why'd you do it?"

Bruno inhaled deeply, as if the air contained the whole truth he was about to spill.

"Because when I first arrived, I was so relieved to be here. So grateful to get a break. I'd been struggling for years. I was done struggling. Coming here was like the answer to a prayer I never thought anyone would hear. But what killed me was the *choice* – that nagging question of whether I should go back one day. You can't imagine how much I would have loved for that choice not to be mine. And then, as chance would have it, most of the other guests left in a very short period, and the hotel didn't fill up again – all empty except two. That's when I came up with the plan. At first, I didn't think I would ever go through with it. It was just a crazy idea I entertained, alone in my chamber. But then, one after the other, new guests arrived – *my* guests. First Helene, then Yash… And that's when I pulled the trigger."

Bruno paused for a moment, stroking the edge of his cup. "I truly believed Helene and Yash would be better off if I told them there was no going back, if they didn't have to face that choice. And after the first shock subsided, it seemed to work. They both seemed so relieved, so ready to leave it all behind. I thought I'd done the right thing. But when Molly showed up and I realised how sick she was... and then Joao... *fifteen* years old..." Bruno put his cup down with a shake of the head. "I knew I couldn't go on forever. Of course, I knew. But I was so deep in the lie at that point, I couldn't dig myself out anymore. I didn't know how. I had good intentions, please believe me when I say I truly wanted what's best for all of you. But I was wrong. I was very, very wrong."

Ava sipped on her tea. "I think I get it now, though. This place..." She gazed around the room, alive with the wealth of places it harboured. "It really puts a spell on you, doesn't it?"

"In der Tat," Bruno said and looked around as well. "It does indeed."

"One more thing." Ava leaned in as if about to whisper.

"Anything." Bruno leaned in, too.

"What about the money?"

"The... oh, the money! In the box!" Bruno sucked in air through his teeth as though slurping hot espresso. "Yeah, I'm afraid the hotel does not supply guests with money."

"I *knew* it!" Ava clapped her hands. "It was you, wasn't it?"

"It was me."

"Where'd you get it?"

"All kinds of side hustles paid in cash... selling my sourdough at farmer's markets, teaching German if I could find a student, participating in medical studies. Fruit-picking, working as an extra on film sets – you name it."

Ava shook her head. "I knew it."

"You sure did." Bruno gazed at her for some time then, as if he considered saying something else but didn't know if he should. "You know," he said at last, "while all of you started fixing your own lives, I started a little something as well. I joined the program. The meetings are anonymous – as we all know – so it's one of the few pastimes I could pick up without difficulty." He attempted a smile, but it faltered quickly.

"Bruno, that's fantastic," Ava said and touched his hand. "Good for you."

"Well, I don't know about fantastic. But it might just be a start."

"Don't you need a sponsor for that to work, though? I could stay a while longer if you'd like. You know, seeing as no one at those meetings remembers you?"

Bruno shook his head. "Sponsors must have gone through the twelve steps themselves."

"Well, I could still stay and hold you accountable. Can't be easy, doing it all on your own."

"Dal offered to help with that. He has been a great friend to me, actually."

"Ah, of course. That makes sense," Ava said, lifting her cup, which was long empty.

Bruno took it from her. He placed it on the tray, then offered his hand as if asking her to dance. "Peaberry?" he said with a half bow. "It is time. Go home. Live your life. You are not Dega. You are Papillon. You were always Papillon."

~

For the last time that day, Ava headed for the front gate, passing Captain, who had dozed off on the veranda, walking down the stairs, past the old fig tree and the bubbling fountain. About halfway down the gravel path, Captain came scuttling, and Ava gave him one last cuddle. She would miss the old fluff ball.

"Be safe out there." Bruno pulled open the gate, holding

back Captain on his collar, the dog going mad with the wealth of smells blowing in from all corners of the world.

Before she stepped over the threshold, Ava stopped and turned toward him once more.

"You're wrong, you know?" she said. "About that ending of *Papillon*."

"Oh?" The innkeeper pushed up his glasses.

"Yeah. I think, if only Dega chose to see it, he would find there is plenty of hope left for him, out there in the real world." She inclined her head at the gate.

Bruno moved toward her then, a single step, but he stopped himself, confined by a wall only he could see. "You really think so?" he asked, his voice thin as a thread.

"I do."

"But do you think he would make the jump? He's not as strong as Papi, you know?"

Ava squinted away a tear. "I think he deserves to be remembered," she whispered.

"Despite everything?"

"Despite everything."

She considered him for some time then, as if her eyes could will him to move, to come with her, if only she looked long enough.

But Bruno wouldn't move. And so, with one last smile at her innkeeper, Ava Marley crossed the threshold alone.

Wondering if one day he might follow.

25

A VISIT LONG OVERDUE

Ava sauntered down the old familiar Shepherd's Bush streets as if she were in Paris. A bit of sunshine had transformed London into a whole new city, with families gathering for a picnic in the park, music resounding from wide open windows, and commuters even cracking the occasional smile. She'd arrived at Heathrow a couple of hours prior, growing restless with every tube stop trundling past. She'd gotten out at Wood Lane, walking the last bit despite her heavy pack.

As she rounded the final corner, she spotted someone about to leave her house – someone hooking up the door. Ready to break into a rant, Ava just about caught herself when she realised: it was Mel!

Ava approached, her heart flipping in her chest. This would be the ultimate test to see if everything truly was back to normal. But the moment Mel spotted her on the sidewalk, her expression left no room for doubt. She didn't exactly look happy to see Ava. Rather, she was her usual, flaming self.

"What the bloody hell took you so long?" Mel blurted

out. She wore her chef uniform, her blonde curls tamed with a crimson hair tie.

"Nice to see you, too, Mel."

"Yeah, yeah – *he's been up there for hours*!" Mel hissed, pointing up the staircase.

"Who?"

"Who do you think? Your dictator of a father."

"Ethan?"

Mel shot her a wide-eyed look as if to say, 'Who else, stupid?'

"What does he want?" Ava looked up at the house wall as if Ethan could be sitting there, perched on a windowsill.

"Fuck knows." Mel got out some lip balm and applied it. "I didn't talk to him. Hey, how was Bali, by the way?"

"Zanzibar."

"Same thing. So, how was it? Met any cute surfer boys?" Mel pursed her now pink lips suggestively.

"Not much of a swell on Zanzi... You know what? It was great. I'll talk to you later."

Ava was about to go in when another thing occurred to her. "Hey, are you the one always hooking up the door?"

"Yeah."

"Why would you do that?"

"Lost my house key the first week we moved in." Mel shrugged.

Ava scratched her eyebrow. "Unbelievable..." she sighed.

"What?"

"Nothing. Just glad to be home, that's all."

Mel planted a snog on Ava's cheek. "Me, too. All right, I got to run!" And run she did. "Catch you later! And then I want to hear all about Sri Lanka!"

"Zanzibar!" Ava yelled, but Mel had already disappeared around the corner.

Ava took to the stairs. Climbing up to the fifth floor, she rehearsed a possible conversation with Ethan, no doubt in her mind what the visit was regarding, however unusual it might have been.

Outside the flat, Ava caught her breath before unlocking the door, her key turning as smooth as oil again, the name tag on the doorbell back to the old, handwritten HOLBORN + MARLEY.

"Hello there," Ethan's voice came from the kitchen.

"Oh, hi," Ava said and tried to sound surprised. She dropped her pack, then walked down the hall.

Ethan sat on the bench in the corner, a drink before him which Ava recognised as one of Mel's Mean Micheladas.

"I see you have been well looked after." Ava nodded at the drink.

Ethan cleared his throat. "Yes. Your flatmate insisted. I didn't touch it, however. A bit early for cocktail hour."

"Wise choice," Ava said. She took a seat across from her father. "To what do I owe the pleasure?"

"Well, your message said you would be returning today, and I came by to... well, to apologise." He paused, the word sitting between them like a strange thing neither knew exactly how to handle. "Ava, I should never have gone to the deli that morning. I should never have pressured you like that. I mean well, you know. I just want what's best for you. But I guess, sometimes I don't know myself what that even looks like."

Ava trailed the table edge with a finger.

"Thank you, for coming here," she said. "And for saying that. In your defence, I didn't know myself for the longest time, so I guess, as parent, there was reason to be worried."

"Be that as it may," Ethan said, scratching his clean-shaven chin. "I couldn't help but notice you have returned in time."

"I know. I owe you a decision." Ava gave a small nod. After a brief pause, she fixed her gaze on him, fighting the old unease that used to come with confronting her father. "I am not going to take the job. I came back on time because I wanted to tell you in person. And I wanted to say thank you for the opportunity. But I'm afraid it is a 'no thank you.' I cannot come work for you. I need to do my own thing, leave my own mark."

Ethan's expression remained composed, hiding any disappointment he might have felt.

"And what are you going to do instead?" he asked, folding his arms.

"I'm going to apply for a job. In Italy, actually."

"Is that where you were these past few weeks? Laura was sure you'd run off to Marrakesh or someplace."

Ava chuckled. "Italy was one of my stops, yes. Among other places."

"Well, as long as you have a plan."

The words hung in the air, forming a blanket of silence that stretched between them. The tick-tock of the kitchen clock suddenly seemed too loud, filling the room with its monotonous rhythm. Ava shifted her gaze to the table, tracing the wood grains with her fingers while Ethan stared at the untouched michelada.

"Right, time to get back to the grind," Ethan said, patting his knees before he rose from his seat. He moved towards the kitchen door when Ava's voice stopped him in his tracks.

"Dad?" she called out, and he turned back toward her. "Why not take a seat again? Stick around for a bit longer. Maybe give that drink a try, after all."

26

NOT THE END

Ava sat with two cups of espresso, still too hot to drink. Lunchtime had passed at long last, and the Romans slowly came back to life after the August sun had temporarily shut down their city for the midday riposo.

"Sospeso?" The waiter had asked when taking her order of two cups. But Ava had shaken her head. She was meeting a friend.

The phone buzzed, announcing a voice message. She picked it up, covering one ear with a finger to drown out the traffic noise.

"You little mischievous beast," Dawn's voice blared from the speaker. "I have a bone to pick with you. Did you enter my name for the TED Speaker Conference? 'Cause they sent me an email, asking if I'd be interested in flying to New York and giving a talk. What the hell, Marley? You better call me back."

Ava's cheeks dimpled as she typed a reply to Dawn, promising to call tonight.

After she left the Atlas, Dawn had wasted no time launching her own start-up – a coffee roastery in Stone

Town with an all-female staff – and by the time she had opened doors, Ava had convinced Aldilà to forge a partnership.

She had started working for them the same year she had left the hotel. Now she split her time between Italy and Costa Rica, to which she had at long last returned, sailing between the two countries just like the coffee beans. Naturally, she had also established business relationships between Madre Tierra and Aldilà.

Today's visit to Rome arose from an expansion of the company Ava felt incredibly passionate about. With her involvement, the sail-shipped coffee from Sicily hadn't changed one bit, but it had grown exponentially since. Beyond the flagship café in Trapani, Aldilà coffee beans were now delivered all across the country, and soon the whole of Europe. Two more cafés had opened, in Naples and Rome, and another one was set to open in Milan before the end of the year. Ava would never have repeated her father's mistake of forcing a Marley's philosophy on the Italians. Aldilà remained entirely rooted in Italian tradition, and the people had taken to it like ground coffee to hot water.

"Is this one for me?"

Ava jumped when she heard the voice right next to her ear. "You need to stop doing that, seriously," she scolded Dal, who had popped up beside her. His hair had turned all white with time, and he had taken to walking with a cane, but he had kept busy nonetheless, advocating for human rights in North Korea and beyond, and creating doorways to wherever the former Atlas crew had flocked. He'd been to Aldilà's café opening in Rome last year and had asked Ava to meet him here today whilst on her business trip.

"I'm sorry, truly," he said and took a seat. "I didn't mean to scare you... at least not a lot."

"How is everybody?" Ava asked, pushing one of the cups toward him.

"Everybody is really good. Helene has finished her second book; Joao is busy getting his driver's license. Wants to go on a Euro-trip this fall – to France, of course." Dal winked. "His foster parents are not convinced. And I was just with Yash and Annie. His Australian residency has finally come through, and the baby is two months old now. They named her Molly. Look, I've got photos." Dal retrieved a phone from his pocket, showing Ava the most recent snapshots.

As Ava flicked through them, she couldn't help but chuckle at the sight of 'domestic Yash.' He had changed the most out of all of them. Molly had sadly passed away, eight months after leaving the Atlas. But by that time, Yash and Annie had fallen in love, and Molly had given them her blessing. For Yash, it had been the remedy he didn't know he needed. Becoming first a stepdad to Annie's kids, and now a father of one of his own, had at long last calmed him down.

"You're totally spoiling those kids, you know?" Ava said and handed the phone back to Dal.

"Good thing they won't remember me then." He grinned and sipped on his espresso.

He had become like a grandpa to the whole crew, keeping in touch, sending birthday gifts, paying visits whenever anyone had the time.

So, in the end, the innkeeper had been right about one thing: The hotel somehow did pair the right people at the right time. As lost as every single one of them had been before, the hotel had acted like a confluence, steering them toward one another like tributaries into a river.

"And what's going on at the hotel? You guys busy?" Ava asked. She paid for their coffee, and they began to walk down a cobbled alley, overgrown with creepers and narrowed by protruding balconies.

"Always busy," Dal said, shoving one hand in his pocket while the other one wielded his cane. "Turns out, putting up tents in the garden did the trick: We can now accommodate not five but twelve guests in total, and the turnover has become much quicker, too, thanks to the measures Bruno and I put in place. People are really getting the support they need."

"How is he, Dal?" Ava asked. "How's Bruno?"

Unlike Dal, the innkeeper had never visited anyone over the years.

"Well, I'm glad you asked," Dal said. He placed a hand on her shoulder, steering her out of the backstreet maze and across a busy piazza. He stopped in front of what appeared to be a historic gate, lined with pompous marble statues and ancient trees. "Bruno left the hotel," he said. "A couple of months ago."

"*What?*" Ava gaped at Dal, eyes squinting against the sun. "Why didn't you say anything?"

"He asked me not to." Dal shrugged.

"But where did he go?"

"Well..." Dal shifted his gaze away from Ava and past the giant gate. "Let's just say there is a reason I wanted to meet up with you while you're in Rome."

Ava jerked her head back. She hadn't paid any attention to where exactly Dal had taken her, realising only now that they were standing at the entrance of a public park.

"Go ahead," Dal said, smiling.

Ava looked back at him suspiciously as she made for the park, which, at last, she recognised. Dal had taken her to the gardens of Villa Borghese.

Crossing meadows where flocks of tourists napped in the shade of ancient oaks, Ava upped the tempo with another look back at Dal, whose nod implied he would follow at his own pace.

Rushing through the gardens, it didn't take her long to find the cafeteria selling fridge magnets shaped like ice cream cones. She passed a line of cypress trees, nervously scratching the top of her hand as she knew she was getting close. Rounding the corner, she stopped mid-stride when Bruno and Matteo's old darling bench came into view, but her heart sank when she found it empty.

She scanned the other benches but couldn't spot a familiar face, so she decided to wait for Dal. That's when she heard the dog barking. Instinctively, she turned around. Captain, the old fluff ball, shot around a bend, coming straight for her.

"Hey, buddy. How're you doing?" Ava came down to her knees, showering the dog with cuddles. "I've missed you. Where's your owner, hm?"

"Hello, Ava."

She looked up when she heard the familiar voice, and there he was. Bruno di Mare had collected a few more wrinkles around the eyes, his stubble was all grey now, and he looked at her through a new pair of rimless glasses.

"You look well," he said.

"So do you," Ava replied and stood.

Bruno scratched his temple as if unsure whether to believe that.

"Are you here to meet..." Ava gestured at the bench.

"No. No, I'm not here to meet Matteo. He..." Bruno

cleared his throat, but it made his voice thinner, not stronger. "He doesn't come here anymore."

"What happened?"

"I was too late." Bruno looked at his feet, shoving his hands in his pockets. "I left the hotel, a couple of months ago. Per sempre. For good. I wanted to be with him. But he had passed in the meantime. Lung cancer." Bruno swallowed, briefly touching his nose. "Guess I really wasn't headed for that Hollywood ending, was I?"

"I'm so sorry, Bruno," Ava said and touched his arm. "I should never have said that."

"Va bene," Bruno said as tears pooled in his eyes. "It's all right. He... he was with his family in the end. He'd always wanted to go back to Napoli, so..."

But Bruno failed to find the words. Captain was by his side the moment the sadness crept in, begging for a stick to be thrown.

"So, how are you getting on now?" Ava fell into step beside Bruno, who had thrown the stick and then begun to walk.

"I don't quite know, to be honest," he sighed, dragging his feet. "Day by day, I suppose. Got my old job back at the Institut. Still come here every day, to remember. This one keeps me busy, of course. Ehi, Capitano?" He petted Captain when the dog returned with the stick. "Oh, and I sponsor this kid at my AA meetings now. Other than that, I guess I just keep on... keeping on."

"It's not the end, then," Ava said and felt the need to tuck her arm into his. "We still have some time to get it right."

And Bruno smiled a little at that.

At the cafeteria, Dal caught up with them.

"Ciao, my friend," Bruno said and took Dal's hand with both of his. "You look a bit breathless. Stai bene, old man?"

"Look who's talking," replied Dal. He held Bruno by the shoulders and looked him up and down. "You haven't exactly aged like a fine wine yourself." They chortled, hugging.

"Now, how about a caffè?" Bruno rubbed his hands together.

"If I drink any more coffee, I won't need a souvenir to return to the hotel," Dal waved him off. "I'll shoot back to Cuba like a rocket!"

"Something a little more grounding, then." Bruno guided them toward a table. A waitress approached and kissed him on both cheeks. "Ciao, Giulia, come stai? I would like you to meet two very dear friends of mine. These are Ava and Dal."

"Che bello!" the waitress exclaimed, shaking their hands with passion. "I'd begun to think this one didn't have any friends! Always comes here alone! Tell me, how did you meet?"

"Yes, how did we meet, gentlemen?" Ava asked, chuckling.

Bruno tapped his lips. "Didn't we stay at the same hotel once?"

And then they laughed and sat and chatted like old friends while the afternoon sun capped the cypress trees, and Captain dozed off at their feet.

Thank you for reading The Anywhere Hotel. If you enjoyed the story, please consider **leaving a review.** It can make a real difference in helping my book reach new readers.

And guess what? You don't have to check out of the hotel just yet!

... Ever wondered how the old fluff ball Captain ended up at the hotel? Download his novella for free and find out! The story is a Gisele Stein Reading Group exclusive and features the beloved hotel dog, PLUS get two additional bonus gifts free:

ACKNOWLEDGMENTS

I'd like to express my gratitude to a group of people who've been instrumental in the creation of this novel: My dad, who despite the roughness of my early stories, always remained an eager reader and fan of my work, and whose keen eye helped to shape the story you have just finished reading. Sophia Swithern, a gifted storyteller whose talent inspires me to become a better writer. Her critiques were a beacon in the rough seas of manuscript drafts, never allowing me to take 'the easy way out'. My sister, for her constant support and advocacy of my work, and my mum, for her enduring belief in my abilities. I owe a special thanks to Kristen Tate, my editor. A mentor in the truest sense, her knack for identifying what a story lacks and her feedback on my manuscript restored my confidence at a time when I thought I'd lost it for good. And finally, to Frank, who is there every step of the way, never allowing me to quit and always believing in me.

ABOUT THE AUTHOR

Gisele Stein writes travel fiction with a sprinkling of magic and places that feel like characters. A former tv-producer from Berlin, she navigated an unusual career change after a restless decade of backpacking-trips and tv-jobs: She trained as a safari guide in South Africa, eager to fulfil her desire to reconnect with Mother Nature and get out of her comfort zone. During her Africa-stint, she met her now husband, an Aussie who whisked her away to Australia's Southwest, a charming pocket of the world she is grateful to call home today. An ocean-lover, Gisele tries to spend as much time as possible by the sea and hopes to befriend an octopus one day.

For updates, giveaways, and latest releases you can sign up to join her reader's group here:

www.giselestein.com/free

Printed in Poland
by Amazon Fulfillment
Poland Sp. z o.o., Wrocław

25494307R10188